OPTIONS

Rosemarie A. D'Amico

iUniverse, Inc.
New York   Bloomington

iUniverse books may be ordered through booksellers or by contacting:

iUniverse
1663 Liberty Drive
Bloomington, IN 47403
www.iuniverse.com
1-800-Authors (1-800-288-4677)

Because of the dynamic nature of the Internet, any Web addresses or links
contained in this book may have changed since publication and may no longer be
valid. The views expressed in this work are solely those of the author and do not
necessarily reflect the views of the publisher, and the publisher hereby disclaims
any responsibility for them.

ISBN: 978-1-4502-6377-1 (sc)
ISBN: 978-1-4502-6379-5 (hc)
ISBN: 978-1-4502-6378-8 (ebook)

Printed in the United States of America

Visit the author's website at www.rosemarie-damico.com

iUniverse rev. date: 11/18/2010

A FEW WORDS, FIRST

Someone once dared me to write this book. So I did. And, what happened next, happens to most authors. I couldn't get it published. I couldn't get an agent. So, I put the book away for thirteen years. Then one day in December 2008 I read an article in the National Post about self-publishing and a company called *Smashwords* (and *Smashwords* led me to *First Choice Books* the first printer of this book and now *iUniverse*, my current publisher). And that article got me thinking about resurrecting *Options*. Now, I'm anxiously awaiting to find out how soon I can say, "And the rest was history".

My mom and dad would be so proud of this published version.

Thanks to Dan Gathof for daring me thirteen years ago. Kudos to Deborah Cathcart and Roxanne D'Amico who helped me with proofreading and Sheila Purcell for her eagle eye. Thank you Kate D'Amico, for you know what! And a very special thanks to my son Jordan, who photographed and designed the cover.

I hope you have as much fun reading this story as I did writing it.

Ottawa, Ontario
April 2009
Second Edition September 2009
Third Edition October 2010

For my husband, Darryl. My hero, my best friend, the love of my life. This one's for you Sifu.

CHAPTER
one

The paramedics arrived at the reception about twenty minutes after I did. Evelyn had stopped breathing at this point, and I was sure I was going to throw up.

I had been working late in my office when the party noises from the boardroom down the hall had finally broken my concentration and started to bother me.

The company I worked for, TechniGroup Consulting Inc., or TGC for short, was holding a cocktail party for the latest company it had bought out, Marshton Systems. Marshton was the eighteenth company acquired by TGC in the last twenty-two months and each time an acquisition closed, we held a reception in the main boardroom a few days after the official closing. The acquired employees and select groups of TGC employees would rub shoulders, share war stories and embellish their work experience.

Each of these little get-togethers was a command performance if you received an invitation, but I tried at all costs to avoid them. I worked in the legal department at TGC where most of the legal work was done on the acquisitions, so by the time the party rolled around I had usually had my fill of the owners and executives of the acquired companies.

When the party sounds finally seeped through my closed office door, I reluctantly turned off my computer, made a weak attempt at tidying up the chaos on my desk and headed down the hall.

The boardroom was packed with about sixty people. The bullshit was flying and the smell of cigar smoke and scotch permeated the air. Office buildings in Toronto had been smoke-free for a few years but that didn't deter some of our folks from lighting up. Municipal by-laws didn't apply at TGC after hours. I eased in the door and surveyed the crowd before I tried to make my way through the crowd to the bartender on the far side of the room.

"Kate," I heard in my ear. It sounded like a whisper but could have been a bellow because of the noise level. I turned around and looked at Evelyn, whose cheeks were so red, she looked like she had a sunburn.

"Ev, what's wrong?" I asked. I had to raise my voice to be heard over the noise.

"I'm fine, it's just hot in here," she said. She waved her hand back and forth in front of her face and changed the subject. "Another good turnout. Amazing isn't it, how everyone shows up when there's free food and booze." We laughed.

"I need a soda water. Wait for me here and I'll be right back."

"Evelyn," someone to my left called out.

I turned around and watched Tom James dragging an unbelievably handsome man with him. The perfect specimen he was towing behind him was Philip Winston, the Third, Vice-President of Operations of Marshton Systems Corp., the company we had just acquired. Philip "don't call me Phil" Winston and I had spent a considerable amount of time together over the last couple of weeks and I was less than enamoured with him. I started to push my way through the crowd towards the bar. Ev grabbed the back of my jacket and said, "Don't leave me Kate."

I turned around to her, smiled and said, "They're all yours, Ev."

I felt a wee bit sorry for Evelyn, having to put up with those two peas in a pod. Tom James, Thomas O. James on his business cards, was our resident Vice-President of Human Resources. If his life depended on it, he couldn't make a decision without forming a committee and I had nicknamed him our "Tower of Jell-O" to go with his initials. Tom was my leading candidate to be the poster boy for the Peter Principle.

Philip Winston on the other hand had impressed the powers-that-be in our organization. I was still reserving judgment but was certain no one would ask my opinion. Philip clearly wanted a job with our company so he was still on his best behaviour.

Physically Tom and Philip were very similar. Both were tall, dark and handsome, and they both obviously worked-out. I knew Tom didn't work out for the pleasure of it or because it was good for his health; Tom worked out because it made him look good. Philip on the other hand was rumoured to have had played college football in the U.S. and that could account for his good physique.

Personally, I found it hard to believe that Philip would expose himself to something as physical as football because it might have marred his perfect image. Two peas in a pod. Nice suits, nice hair, great skin, great smell. Big deal. Where was the substance? I sighed as I thought about the possibilities of a guy with the looks and physique of Philip or Tom and the personality of, who? I'd have to keep looking.

I veered to the left to avoid a group of beancounters who were patting themselves on the back for closing the deal. Right, I thought. Those idiots couldn't close a door without direction.

I lifted my hand to wave to the Chairman's secretary across the room. Chris Oakes, the Chairman of the Board was flicking cigar ashes on the boardroom rug and I thought we'd be lucky if he didn't set the place on fire. As I watched in amazement, he casually put the lit cigar on the boardroom table, as if it was a large ashtray, and turned around to grin at one of the Board members. Idiot.

Christopher Oakes had very large front teeth and when he smiled, which was rarely, he reminded me of a beaver. There was something dark on one of his front teeth and I wondered if it was a leftover from breakfast or lunch. My stomach turned slightly at the thought. Being anywhere near the man usually made me nauseous because if his last meal wasn't stuck between his teeth, it was stuck to his face. Or his ear. Or his neck. It went without saying that a goodly portion of his meals became accessories to his wardrobe. Breakfast on his tie, lunch on his breast pocket.

Sometimes it wasn't food on his face or neck. It was toothpaste or shaving cream. I remember as a child watching my father shave and the very last step he took was to wash his face to get the shaving cream off. Dad would fill his hands with water and rub the water all over his face and neck. He did this a couple of times. On the off-chance there were traces of shaving cream left, Dad would get them when he towelled his face dry. This display of male ablutions has stayed with me all these years and I've been tempted many times to ask Chris if he'd like a live demonstration in the art of cleaning one's face after shaving. The man had obviously never had a lesson.

Chris comes to the office every day with more than just traces of shaving cream on his face. Globules hang from his earlobes. Patches remain under his nose. Worse than the shaving cream though is the toothpaste which sits on top of the shaving cream. Chris either does not wash his face or he does everything in reverse order. The man was a slob of the first order. I've tried to describe this to people but no one believes me. Ask anyone at our office.

I finally made my way to the bar and shouldered my way through.

"Hey Mark," I said.

"Kate." He smiled. "Soda water with lime, right?"

I smiled back. Mark worked in the mailroom and was one of the few employees entitled to collect overtime pay. He volunteered to tend bar for these occasions because he could always use the extra money. And the tequila shots he snuck on the side were just an added bonus.

I tried my John Wayne imitation and leaned on the bar. It was hard to lean your elbow on anything and look casual about it standing up when you're only five feet tall. Actually, four feet, eleven inches but I tell everyone five feet. My mother used to tell me my grandmother was a legal midget at four foot ten, so I wasn't going to push it.

I was reaching inside my jacket to tuck my blouse back in when I heard a commotion on the other side of the room. I craned my neck and stood on tiptoes to see what was going on. The conversation level in the room had completely changed and I could now hear panicked voices.

I turned to Mark. "They've probably just realized they bought a dud of a company and Oakes is trying to sell it back to them," I said with a laugh.

Mark cracked up. His laughter was suddenly the only sound in the room and several people turned around and glared. I heard something about an ambulance on its way. Oh god, I thought. As much as I disliked most of our executives, I prayed it wasn't one of them. We couldn't afford any more valleys in the stock price. Illness in a senior executive was one of the things that would make the newspapers, and any publicity, good or bad, was something this company didn't need. Recently, any news, good or bad or indifferent about TechniGroup had put the stock into a nose-dive.

I pushed my way through the crowd to see what was going on and ended up having to hip-check a couple of people on the way. People stood around dumb and mute, probably thinking about forming a committee to figure out what to do.

I reached the front of the room and saw Vanessa Wright, the Chairman's secretary on her knees beside a body. Jay Harmon stepped in front of her and put his hands on my shoulders to stop me.

"Stay there, Kate," he said softly.

"Who is it?" I choked out.

"Just stay there Kate. It's going to be okay."

"Jay, what the fuck is going on? Who is it? What happened?"

"Kate, it's Evelyn. She started to choke and we can't revive her. Someone's calling an ambulance and they should be here soon. Just stay calm."

"Nuts," I yelled. "Who gave her nuts?"

"Omigod," said Jay. He turned around and grabbed the nearest person and ordered them to run to Evelyn's office and get her EpiPen.

Everyone in the office knew Evelyn had a severe allergy to nuts and for that reason all food brought into the office was nut-free. The caterers had specific orders. They weren't even allowed to cook with peanut oil. I looked at the credenza on the other side of the boardroom. It was piled with food. I started to feel sick to my stomach.

I knelt down beside Vanessa. "Vee, how is she?" I asked.

Vanessa had a panicked look on her face. "I don't know. She won't talk to me. Look at her face. I can't get her to respond to me," Vanessa whispered.

I turned around to find Jay in the crowd. He was right behind me. "Jay," I said. "Take Vee. Get everyone out of here so the paramedics can get through. Get Mark to go out to reception and unlock the main doors so they can come right through. And get everyone else out of here and give Ev some air."

I looked past Jay at the crowd standing around like a bunch of village idiots. My hand caressed Ev's forehead and I started to talk softly to her. "Come on Ev. Talk to me. It's going to be all right. Things are going to be okay."

I looked around in desperation for the employee who was sent to Ev's office for the EpiPen. He hadn't returned so I eyed the person nearest me.

"Come on people, don't just stand there. Go help find her EpiPen. Come on. Come on," I barked out like a drill sergeant. Three people ran out of the room. Two of them were members of the board of directors. Shit, I thought, those two couldn't find their way out of a paper bag.

Time was quickly running out and I knew that every second counted here. Ev had told me (and almost everyone in the office knew this) that speed was of the essence if she ever had one of these attacks. I know it had happened once before but Ev had known what was going on at the time and had quickly injected herself.

The employee who had gone looking for her EpiPen ran back into the boardroom looking totally panicked.

"Here." He shoved the EpiPen kit at me. It was a long, tubular container with a yellow cap. I flipped open the lid, turned it upside down and the syringe containing the epinephrine slid out onto the floor and I quickly picked it up. There was something wrong with the syringe. Evelyn had showed most of us how to use the EpiPen, just in case we ever found ourselves in the God-forbid situation that we living right now. I held the syringe in my hand and stared at it.

"Inject her, Kate," Jay urged me.

And then I realized what was wrong. There was no blue safety release button on the top. Ev had drilled us and I remember distinctly her telling us, "yellow, blue, orange, click". Yellow cap on the outer tube, blue safety cap on the syringe, orange tip covering the needle which dispenses the magic, and click, the magic is dispensed. There was no blue safety cap. What did it mean? My brain was racing.

Fuck it, I thought. Maybe I was mistaken. I leaned over Ev and jammed the Epipen into her left thigh. I waited for the click. Nothing. I pushed it harder. Again, nothing.

I looked at Evelyn and she didn't appear to be breathing. I put my ear to her lips. I'd seen that on TV. Just exactly what that was supposed to do, I didn't know but I had to do something. Jay quickly kneeled down on her other side and started giving her CPR.

Mark came running in the room and announced that the paramedics had arrived. They pushed their way through the door, one pulling a gurney and the other pushing.

"Okay everyone. Back up," the first one said.

The second one, a young woman about twenty-five got down beside Jay and said, "I'll take over. Tell us what happened." She started CPR on Ev.

Jay looked at me. For the first time in a long while, I was at a loss for words. Jay turned to the paramedic and said, "She collapsed. She wouldn't respond and she stopped breathing a minute ago. I started CPR. We think it might be something she ate. We know she has an allergy to nuts."

"Here." I held the Epipen towards the medic. "I don't know if it worked. There was no blue cap."

The other paramedic was the largest male specimen I had every laid eyes on next to William Perry, The Refrigerator. His name tag said MARION O'LEARY. I bet the guys back at the stationhouse didn't tease him about his name. Marion ignored my outstretched hand and the Epipen. He was checking Ev's vital signs and started barking out questions. "Age?"

"Sixty-five," I responded.

"Any other known medical problems?"

"No," I whispered. I looked at Ev and thought I was going to throw up.

Jay stood up and stepped over Ev's legs. He took me by the arm and steered me through the boardroom door out into the hallway. I leaned back against the wall and dug in my jacket pocket for a cigarette. My hands shook as I lit up and blew the smoke in Jay's face. He was in my personal space and he deserved it. He gave a disgusted cough and backed-up. Under normal circumstances he would have started in on me about my smoking.

"Kate, someone has to call Danny," Jay said.

"I know," I sighed. Danny is Evelyn's son and the apple of her eye. He's forty-four years old and still lived with mama at home. I think he's a wuss.

Evelyn Morris is the longest standing employee at TechniGroup having started with the company as a receptionist seventeen years ago. She'd worked her way up through the ranks and was now in charge of the administration of the employee stock purchase plan, bonuses, executive incentives, and the one thing more powerful than sex in our company, stock options. It's an inside joke at our company that if you're married to a guy at TechniGroup who can't get it up, just start talking about his stock options and the guy could take on Hugh Hefner's harem.

Ev had been in many different positions after spending nearly ten years as the receptionist and most of her jobs had been within the finance department. Before stock options and the employee stock purchase plan, she had supervised the payroll department. Everyone thought her transfer to the new job was a step down but it suited Ev just fine. Theoretically she should be retiring soon, but our company has no mandatory retirement age.

I heard some activity inside the boardroom and eased over to the door. I didn't want to look.

The paramedics had finished strapping Ev on the gurney and were wheeling her out. The building security guard who had escorted them up from the lobby was leading the way and acting like the lead leprechaun at a St. Patrick's Day parade. He elbowed me aside. Officious bastard, I thought.

"Is she okay?" I asked. No one answered me. "Hey!" I grabbed the female paramedic's arm as she went past. She shook me off.

"Look," she said. "We're taking her to Toronto General. The doctors can fill you in."

We were racing down the hall. The security guard opened the glass doors at the reception and stepped back to let us through. The elevator was waiting and I tried to push on after the gurney.

"Sorry miss," Marion the Refrigerator said. He pushed the ground floor button and the doors closed.

I stood there shaking. Buck up, I told myself, Evelyn will be fine.

"Kate."

I turned around and there was my shadow. "Jay. I've got to call Danny. Will you come to the hospital with me after I talk to him?" I started back down the hall to my office to make the call.

"Sure," Jay called after me. "I'll meet you down in the lobby beside the elevators to the parking garage in five minutes. I'll just get my jacket."

I had no success in trying to reach Danny. The phone just kept ringing off the hook. After three or four tries, I hung up in frustration and headed for the elevator. I went out the back door to avoid the crowd in the boardroom and impatiently pushed the elevator button. I said a silent prayer for Ev in the elevator.

Jay wasn't downstairs when I got off the elevator. I looked at my watch and saw that it was almost eight-twenty. Come on Jay, I thought impatiently. I hung around for another five or six minutes and was about to leave without him when the elevator doors opened and he rushed off.

"Jesus Jay. Where the hell have you been? Ev could be dying."

I realized as soon as I said it, I shouldn't have opened my mouth. I felt like I had just jinxed the pitcher.

CHAPTER
two

I was outside the hospital having what seemed like my fifteenth cigarette in two hours when Jay came out to find me.

I had been thinking about Ev and praying that she was going to be alright. Ev and I went back a long way. I remembered my first day on the job at TechniGroup and how Ev had helped me out of one of my most embarrassing moments. I had been working as a temp secretary and got a call from the agency that they needed someone at TechniGroup. I started on the 2nd of January and it was one of those days in Toronto that feels like spring but you know it can't last. The snow that had been dumped in record amounts in December was turning to slush because of the mild temperatures. I had taken the streetcar to work, and when I got off at my stop, my feet went out from under me on the second step, and I landed on my ass in the slush on the side of the road. I wasn't hurt but my clothes were soaked through. The black slacks I was wearing started turning white from the salt on the roads. I arrived at the office and explained how embarrassed I was to Evelyn, who was the receptionist at the time.

She led me into the kitchen off the reception area and started applying dry-cleaning fluid to the back of my pants. While they were on. I was bent over the counter and Ev was wiping away at the back of my slacks when the former owner of the company walked in. Personally, I saw the humour in the situation and Ev certainly did. He quickly got his coffee and made a fast retreat. Ev and I laughed so hard I thought we were going to pee our pants.

We became fast friends on that first day and she became like a second mother to me. I have been with the company now almost seven years, certainly longer than all of the current executives.

Five years ago, the original founder of the company died. As founder of the company he had maintained a majority interest in the company and the rest of the shares were held by the public.

9

His majority shares were pledged as security for most the debt of the company, so when he died the consortium of banks that had loaned him the money called in their loans. They ended up owning the majority share of a $600 million, publicly-traded high tech consulting firm that they knew nothing about. One would think they'd know something about high tech consulting if they lent the company that much money, but bankers are just as stupid as the rest of us.

The bankers' first order of business as majority shareholder was to hire a new Chairman and Chief Executive Officer. In their infinite wisdom, they went to the Board of Directors of our company, who formed a search committee to find a new chief executive officer. It took them four months but the committee found us a CEO. CEO, Christopher Earl Oakes. The guy wears monogrammed shirts with his initials CEO on the pocket. His lifelong dream was to be a chief executive officer so he could live up to his initials. What great heights we aspire to.

Chris had been an executive vice-president of the company that was our major competitor and he was the perfect example of why one should always check references before hiring someone. My sources told me that the senior management of the company that we hired Chris from had "remoted" Chris. Not promoted. Not demoted. Remoted. They had put him aside and were doing their best to ignore him and we saved the day when we recruited him. Chris was an executive vice-president in charge of nothing at the time we hired him. He had no staff reporting to him, no clients, no budget. Word on the street was that Oakes' former employers had the biggest going away party in the history of their company when Chris left. And Chris wasn't invited.

Our Board members who were given the responsibility of finding a new chief executive officer actually believed they were stealing a star performer, just because he worked for the competition.

His one crowning glory in the four years he has been our peerless leader was to increase the share price to a high of $16 from $6 when he joined the company. That price was very short-lived though, and the shares are now trading at about $11. The company's current bottom line certainly didn't justify the price of the shares, but many shareholders out there are betting on Chris Oakes turning the company around.

Chris' first order of business when he joined was to fire all of the top management of the company and hire his hand-picked replacements. Our executive payroll tripled. So far, the shareholders haven't lynched him. I think shareholders are just as stupid as bankers.

My wandering thoughts were interrupted.

"Kate," I heard Jay say behind me. I turned around and knew by the look on his face that the news wasn't good. He took a step towards me and said softly, "She's gone."

I turned around and threw-up in the stone column ashtray that progressive organizations place outside their places of business for us social pariahs, smokers. Normally, it could hold a cup of sand and ten butts. It wasn't a pretty sight.

Jay placed his arm around my shoulders as I was heaving into the ashtray.

"Fuck off. Leave me alone," I spluttered.

He backed off. Jay knows what's good for him. I fumbled in my purse for a Kleenex and found one that had been used about three times. Not very effective for wiping off the chin in the circumstances, but it did the trick. I took a few deep breaths, in through the nose, out through the mouth. Or was it the other way around?

I turned back and looked at Jay. He was standing on the other side of the entranceway. When he left me alone, he really left me alone.

I felt like someone had knocked the wind out of me. I wanted to scream. No one close to me had ever died. I headed towards the parking lot at a fast clip and Jay came running behind me.

"Hey."

I kept going, digging in my coat pockets for my car keys.

"Hey. Monahan. Kate. Jesus Christ, Kate, wait up."

I stopped.

I knew I was going to start to cry and that wasn't allowed in front of other people. The only time I cried was when the heroine of one my favourite novels lost her true love in a ship wreck.

I sniffed a few times to try and clear the lump in my throat and knew it wasn't going to work. The tears started streaming down my face and I tried to cry quietly. Like when you're at a movie with a girlfriend and you don't want to let on you're crying and you're wiping your eyes with salted fingers from the popcorn. You do it quietly. Your girlfriend's probably crying as much as you, but women of the new millennium have to be tough.

Jay caught up to me but I ignored him as I continued on to the car. I fumbled with the lock. It was stuck again. Cheap piece of shit. I kicked the car door.

Jay took the keys from my hand and opened the door.

"You drive," I sniffed and headed around the car to the passenger side. When I reached the back of the car it hit me like I had been slammed into the boards by Bobby Orr. Evelyn was dead. I started gasping for air, sobbing. I held on to the back of the car and cried. Fuck the new millennium, I thought.

Jay stepped to the back of the car and took me by the shoulders. He knew he was invading my personal space but he was a brave sort. He leaned over and put his arms around me and hugged me tight.

Jay patted my back, patted my hair, patted my shoulder. He just didn't know what to do. Under normal circumstances he's the Rock of Gibraltar to most women, but in all the years Jay had known me, he had never seen me cry. When I finally dried up, I asked him if he had a tissue. He dug a clean one out of his pocket and held it up. I blew my nose and hiccupped a few times.

Jay tried to ease himself in the driver's seat and got stuck with his rear in the seat and only one leg in. I had to lean over and reach the lever under the driver's seat to push it back. I'm so short they tease me at the garage that they're going to have to put blocks on the pedals so my feet can reach. Jay finally got the seat pushed back far enough so he could fit in and disgustedly reached behind his back and tossed the two pillows I use for extra height into the back seat.

"Isn't there a height restriction for getting a driver's license?" he teased. I smiled weakly.

"Where to?" he asked as he started the engine.

"Ev's place. I want to see if Danny's home yet. He hasn't answered the phone and I've left about ten messages. Someone has to let the family know. I told the doctors that I'd look after contacting her kids."

Jay put the car into gear and headed out of the parking lot. It had been a long day, a long week, Jesus Christ, it had been a long month. I knew it was going to be a long night.

CHAPTER
three

There was no answer at the door at Evelyn and Danny's place. I was surprised. It was almost twelve-thirty and you'd think the video arcades would be closed. Aren't they normally populated by twelve year old boys who should all be home in bed by now? Danny wasn't a drinker and he didn't have a girlfriend so I was surprised by his absence. I had no idea where his twin brother Jonathan or his sister Elaine lived. I had only met the brother and sister a few times at family get-togethers and birthday parties for Ev and didn't feel comfortable telling them the bad news. I didn't feel comfortable telling Danny either, but at least he was a known entity.

Danny was a mommy's boy. His identical twin Jonathan was the exact opposite. Jonathan had been married three times, no children. Thank God, Ev used to say. Their older sister Elaine was married and had one child, Sarah. Pictures of Sarah and Danny were plastered all over Ev's office.

Evelyn's husband died in 1955 in Korea leaving her with a three year old and two babies. It had been a struggle financially for Ev, but she never complained. Jonathan took his first bride when he was nineteen and was fast on his way to becoming a male Zsa Zsa Gabor. Elaine was a homemaker whose husband sold something, I couldn't remember. They were the steady ones. Danny on the other hand had never held a job for more than a year, was one credit short of about eight different university degrees, and was totally inept when it came to women, other than his mama. Danny would regularly show up at the office with a homemade lunch for his mother and sit beside her and watch her eat it. He called her about six times a day, and every hour on the hour if she worked late. On nights when Ev was late at the office, she had to call him when she was leaving and he'd meet her at the subway stop. Ev used to throw her hands in the air and ask for medical proof that the umbilical cord had been cut when Danny was born. Danny was very protective of his mama and her death was going to devastate him.

"I hope she has more life insurance than the company provided," I said to Jay. "Danny's going to find it tough enough coping without his mama. When he has to find steady work, that should just about do him in."

"Give the kid a break," Jay said.

"Kid?" I snorted. "Jay, he's almost old enough to be your father. He's no kid. He's forty-four years old."

Jay shut up. He was twenty-eight years old but tried to act forty-eight.

We were sitting in the car outside Ev's house. The streetlights cast shadows on the cars parked on the street. Other than the parked cars and Jay and I, the street was deserted. The car was facing in the direction of the Davisville subway station so we could see Danny when he walked down the street. I lit another cigarette and before Jay could snort at me, I rolled the window down.

"Nuts. Fucking nuts. Why would Ev be so stupid to eat something with nuts in it?" I asked out loud.

"Kate, do you think she would knowingly eat something with nuts in it?"

"I was talking to myself," I snapped back.

I turned in the seat and looked at Jay. He was looking straight ahead and was running his hand through his hair. It was standing straight up. He did this repeatedly.

"You're brushing. Stop it," I ordered.

Jay mumbled something.

"Pardon?" I asked.

He turned to me and grinned. "I said leave me alone, Kate. I haven't said a word all night about the two packs of cigarettes you've smoked. Stop nagging me about brushing my hair with my hand."

It was about the only nervous habit he had. But he did have a point. Brushing his hair with his hand wasn't going to give him emphysema and his teeth weren't going to turn that lovely shade of gold that smokers get for no extra charge.

We sat quietly for a few minutes. "I'm going to have the caterers fired. That's the last fucking time they get our business. Someone must have screwed-up and cooked something with peanut oil."

"You can't blame the caterers when they didn't provide the food," Jay said.

"Whaddya mean, they didn't cater? We always get them to cater."

I closed my eyes and tried to picture the credenza in the boardroom. I could recite from memory the items that should have been laid out, because we always get the same food, every time. But when I closed my eyes to conjure up a picture of the food at today's reception, something was out of whack. I could see mismatched Tupperware containers, paper plates, odd and unmatched cut glass and crystal bowls, pottery platters, and very different looking food. I shook my head. The food today had been yummy stuff like brownies, potato salad, cold cuts, celery with Cheez Whiz, devilled eggs. But where were the chicken livers with bacon, mini quiches, smoked oysters?

"Who catered the food today?" I asked Jay.

"Don't you ever read your e-mail? It was a potluck. All the employees attending the reception were told to bring something homemade. Orders from the CEO. He wanted a more 'homey' style reception. Even he brought something. We all joked it was probably some of Baby's dog food." Baby was Chris Oakes' dog. "Vanessa reminded everyone in the e-mail about Ev's allergy and we were told to avoid nuts and peanut oil."

I vaguely remembered the e-mail and was flabbergasted. Potluck? Just who the hell did Chris Oakes think he was fooling?

CHAPTER
four

Telling Danny was the hardest thing I've ever had to do. He blubbered like a baby. He was late getting home because he had gone to a double feature at one of the old movie houses downtown. Jay stayed with him for the night and I went home.

By the time I got to my place it was close to three a.m. and I realized that no-one at the office had officially been informed of Evelyn's death. It was too late to call anyone, but not too late for voice mail. E-mail was the communication tool of choice for all of our executives, except our CEO, who only ever used voice mail. The executives each had their new-fangled Blackberry's and were glued to them all day. They preferred e-mail rather than talking face-to-face.

Our CEO, Chris Oakes, didn't know how to use a computer, let alone e-mail, and there was no hope we could bring him into the new millennium and get him to use a Blackberry. He was stuck in the early nineties, in love with his voice mail. He didn't use the system just to get messages, he would create his voice messages and send them to someone on our system. He did this all day long. Never once did he think of using the phone to call someone and talk to them live; he and the other executives were the same, never talking to people, just using electronic means to send messages - that way they could be tough guys without ever having to look someone in the eye. Our Chief Executive Officer sits in his office, creates a voice mail message, sends it to Vanessa his secretary, and then sends her another urgent message telling her to check her voice mail. They were all a bunch of gutless wonders.

So needless to say, even though we had e-mail, and most of the executives had their Blackberry's, we were all masters of voice mail because that was the communication tool of choice for Chris Oakes. So I dialled-in to the office voice mail system and logged on to my personal mailbox. The nasal computer voice told me, "You have ELEVEN new voice messages". Emphasis on the ELEVEN. If it were ten, there wouldn't be any emphasis. For some reason, the computer voice thinks ELEVEN is a lot of messages. On a good day, Chris Oakes fires off ELEVEN messages in eight seconds. That includes time to dial all the appropriate numbers, clear his throat three or four times on the message, yell some obscenities, threaten to fire you, and hang up. Sometimes, Chris Oakes has been known to send ELEVEN messages to ELEVEN different people, and all of them consist of the same message. "Uh... Uh... Uh..." Wow. Can we quote you on that Mr. Oakes?

I decided to skip the ELEVEN messages and listen to them in the morning. I created one voice message to Chris Oakes, Vanessa Wright, Tom James and Harold Didrickson. I let everyone know what had happened. "This is a voice message for Chris, Vee, Tom and Harold. Just to let you know that Ev died tonight. She never recovered consciousness. I'll see you in the morning." Short and sweet. To the point. Jesus, I hate voice mail. But it's great for us gutless wonders.

I had dropped my coat on the floor in the front hall as I was talking on the phone. Correction: sending a voice mail. I keep my phone in the front hall and refuse to have more than one in my apartment. I talk on the phone so much at the office that I usually ignore my phone at home when it rings. I don't have an answering machine, call waiting, call display, three party calling, or any of those fancy features at home. Some things are sacred.

I flipped off the hall light and picked up my coat but was too lazy to fight the closet door so I dropped it back on the floor. I stumbled down the hall, blew a kiss to my most recent, and hopefully still alive, goldfish - Snapper the Fourth. I had only had him a couple of weeks and made a mental note to check on him in the morning.

I loved pets but the building super wouldn't let me keep any in the apartment so I snubbed my nose at him and bought a goldfish. That was three years ago. I was on my sixteenth goldfish and I've had to change pet stores. They thought I was doing weird scientific experiments on them, I had bought so many. I am determined to discover the secret of keeping a goldfish alive for more than forty-eight hours, but it's proven to be a daunting task. I have just as much luck with plants.

I filled the coffee maker and set the timer on it to brew at seven-thirty.   I was going to treat myself and not go in to the office until eight in the morning.   It'd been a long night.

I stripped off my jacket, blouse and skirt and left them where they fell.   My bra, underwear and pantyhose got tossed in a corner. I got out a clean pair of white gym socks, put them on and got in to bed.

I groaned as I sank into the bed and let the goose-down duvet settle over me.   My eyes felt like they were full of sand from all the crying I had done earlier.

I woke up drenched in sweat and my mouth was so dry my tongue was stuck to the roof of my mouth.   I had been dreaming I was lost in the middle of the desert, looking for Evelyn and calling out her name every couple of steps.   My voice was failing me when I woke up.

The clock radio beside the bed read four fifty-five so I got up and pulled on my sweats and one of my dad's old army sweaters that reached below my knees.   I by-passed the automatic timer on the coffeemaker and chained-smoked two cigarettes while the coffee dripped through.   My father would call this a 'whore's breakfast'.

I poured myself a coffee and wandered into my living room, and stood at the French doors which led on to my two square foot balcony overlooking the street.   Things were pretty quiet at this time of the morning.   I reached under the lampshade of the vintage tiffany lamp on my desk and pulled the chain and the light softly lit the top of the desk and the surrounding floor.   I sat at my desk and rummaged around through the drawers to find the pictures taken last summer when Ev and I rented a cottage.

What a time we had.   We laughed all day and cried a little every evening.   We'd put on our bathing suits and go down to the lake and tease each other about looking like beached whales.   I'm about ten pounds overweight and being the lady I am, I never asked Ev her weight, but I'd guess she was at least fifty pounds too heavy. We'd barbecue every night, hot dogs or burgers for me, and skinless breast of chicken for Ev.   At least she tried to lose weight.   After the dishes had been done, we'd fire up a couple of Coleman lamps and sit out on the screened-in porch and listen to the mosquitoes slam up against the screens.   With our feet up and a fresh pot of coffee, we'd both eagerly dive into the latest Harlequin romance we were reading.

I discovered Ev was a closet romance reader just like me one day when I got a call to take over the reception while Ev ran an errand for the Chairman. The phones were quiet and I was rummaging around for something to read when I eyed a novel tucked-in beside the telephone console. The book was covered with a handmade, crocheted jacket which completely hid the cover. I opened it to the first page and starting reading. "Her green eyes sparkled and the sun shone on her auburn hair." I sighed and settled down for a good read. Romance stories have always been one of my passions and one of my most guarded secrets. I made Ev promise she'd never tell anyone I read Harlequin romances. She laughed. "So the tough broad really does have a tender streak in her." By the end of each evening at the cottage one of us would be snivelling over the heroine's loss of her true love.

We had talked about renting a cottage for years and only got around to doing it once. We had promised each other last year on the drive back to the city, "same place next summer". My eyes filled with tears as I remembered.

I couldn't find the pictures and was only succeeding in making the desk a bigger mess than what it was when I started. Every drawer was jammed-packed with god knows what. My desk at work was just as disastrous but there at least I have a secretary who does all the filing and tries to keep it in order.

I was bilious now from all the coffee and cigarettes, and butted another one in the overflowing ashtray. I stood and lifted one arm over my head, slowly, and repeated the move with the other arm. My aerobic workout for the day. Sunlight was filtering through the windows but it was only six-thirty. So much for the late start I had promised myself. I headed for the bathroom and turned on the shower.

CHAPTER
five

I shoved my parking pass into the card reader in the underground parking garage at the office and made a quick right turn. At this time of the day the parking lot was virtually empty so I had my pick of the unreserved spots. My parking pass was the one and only perk associated with my job and I treasured it dearly. At our company only professionals were entitled to parking passes, and the fact that Kate Monahan, lowly support person had one, really pissed off the masses. It wasn't something I went around bragging about but one of the airheads in office management who had to give me the pass let everyone know.

When Harold Didrickson joined the company four years ago as General Counsel, he approached me to work with him and help him set up a new legal department. Until then I had been biding my time working for Shirley Benton as her legal secretary. Shirley was the only lawyer on staff at the company at that time and the legal department had consisted of the two of us.

I agreed to work directly with Harold, which set off a nasty chain of in-house political cat fighting. Shirley thought she was entitled to the job of General Counsel and to this day still speaks to Didrickson through clenched teeth. She also fought tooth and nail to keep me as her secretary. Shirley is one of the best at what she does - contract and computer law, and dealing with all the tech weenies. But she had no experience with public company law so when Chris Oakes was setting up his empire he brought in Didrickson. Didrickson had performed some legal work for the company in his private practice. In four years the legal department has grown to four lawyers, three paralegals and two secretaries. Didrickson hired the other two lawyers and I hand-picked and groomed the paralegals and secretaries.

Didrickson didn't budge much when I asked for a salary increase to take on the new job but he did agree to give me a parking pass. At the time, I thought it was a big deal. With the hours I had put in over the last four years, it was a good goddamn thing I had the parking pass because many nights by the time I left the office the streetcars and subway had stopped running.

TGC had accomplished a lot over four years. We had successfully closed the acquisition of eighteen companies in twenty-two months, we had raised hundreds of millions of dollars in equity on the public market, we successfully launched a multi-million dollar debt issue, and we had survived five internal corporate reorganizations. Harold Didrickson got great joy every time one of the deals would close. Each time a new transaction was proposed he would lock himself in his office and work out how he could make it as complicated as possible. By making the transactions complicated, Didrickson had everyone by the short and curlies because he was the only one who truly understood the whole deal. He would then drive the whole transaction from his desk by directing the outside law firms. He would expect everyone to grasp and understand his ideas immediately. When anyone had to ask for clarification on a certain aspect of the transaction, the dark side of his personality would shine. He had a terrible reputation on the street for being a mean son-of-a-bitch. Personally, I had no trouble with him. I put it all down to his short-man attitude.

I think the reason Didrickson was so keen to hire me was because he could tower over me. At four foot eleven, officially five feet, my nine year old cousin towered over me. He also towered over Didrickson who was only five foot four.

Didrickson was fair with me. He taught me as much as I wanted to know, and, over the past four years, I had gained incredible knowledge about the workings of a public company. He set high standards for himself and expected the same of his co-workers. I'm the lead paralegal in the department specializing in corporate securities work and I now know my way around the record books of companies. He taught me how to organize the logistics of closing an $85 million bank loan. I can do public offerings in my sleep. Didrickson has never had a legitimate complaint about my work.

I grabbed a prime parking spot on the first level and got out of the car. I ground out my cigarette under the toe of my shoe and slammed the car door, making sure I didn't lock it. One of these days I'm going to strike it rich and I'll be able to afford a car with locks that work.

I stepped off the elevator from the parking garage and turned right to sign-in at the security desk. It was seven-twenty and everyone was required to sign into the building before seven-thirty. I made nice with the security guard whose body odour knocked me back a few feet. It's hard talking and breathing through your mouth at the same time but regardless of his repulsive smell, I gave him a smile. I make it a point to be friendly with the guys on their way up. He didn't check my signature against the company master log because he sees me here most mornings.

"Which floor Kate? Twelve or thirteen?" he asked.

"Twelve," I replied. He pushed a button on his console and released the elevator to the 12th floor.

"Later," I said with a wave. I scrambled out of there and headed for the main elevator bank on the left-hand side of the lobby, breathing deeply. God, somebody has to talk to that man about his choice of aftershave, I thought.

TGC had two floors in the building, 12 and 13. The corporate offices were on the 13th floor but most mornings I headed to the 12th to pick-up a coffee in the main kitchen. The two floors were connected by an internal staircase through the reception areas so I would get my daily dose of exercise by walking up the staircase, usually only once. Every other time I had to go down to the 12th floor, I'd take the elevator. No use taxing this great body.

I got on the elevator and the button for twelve was already lit. Before and after business hours the security guards control the elevators for security purposes. As the elevator was going up I thought about pushing all the buttons for the other floors to see if they would light up. It's a game I play to see if I can catch the security guard. I'm quite juvenile when no one is looking, but my heart wasn't in it this morning.

I got off at twelve and turned right to the back doors. The entrance to the main reception was straight ahead off the elevators but the doors were still locked and the reception area was dark. Access to the premises was gained by flashing my security card in front of a black box on the wall beside the door. After making coffee in the main kitchen I threaded my way down the hall to the reception area to go up to the 13th floor. I huffed my way up the circular staircase and congratulated myself on only spilling a wee bit of coffee. Everything was dark but I could have been blind, I knew my way around this place so well.

When I reached my office the first thing I did was punch a series of numbers into the phone to turn on the overhead lights in our quadrant of the building. I hung my coat on the back of the door and settled into my chair. I lit my first illegal cigarette of the day and opened my bottom drawer to reveal my ashtray stash. Smoking is not allowed in the building, and I was sick and tired of having to go outside every time I needed a cigarette. Building management overlooked the no smoking policy when we had receptions in the boardroom but their goodwill was being sorely tried because the other tenants were complaining about the smoke which wafted through the building's air circulation system.

Everyone knew I smoked in my office, but I kept the door closed. No one had the balls to tell me to stop and besides, my ace in the hole was Chris Oakes, who openly smoked foul cigars in his office every day.

I reached over and switched on my computer to give it time to fire-up while I checked my voice mail messages. The red light on my phone was flashing, indicating messages waiting but I already knew I had at least ELEVEN new messages waiting. I grabbed my notebook and a pen, and logged-on to the voice mail system. The computer-generated voice intoned, "You have THIRTEEN new messages."

Two new messages had been received since three in the morning. Do these people never sleep?

The first three messages were hang-ups. Those type of messages I love. The computer voice told me the fourth message was from an internal number and was received on Thursday (the day before) at five-thirty p.m. I hit the number on my phone to listen to the message. It was Ev.

"Kate, it's Ev. Can't wait to have a drink with you at the reception. Later."

I slammed down the phone. It was eerie hearing her voice. My breath was coming in short gasps. Holy shit, I thought. Like talking to the dead. I turned around to log-in to my computer because whenever I'm stressed I tend to do mundane things. Things that don't require thinking. The computer was flashing a message: "System error. Contact system administrator."

"Fuck." I slapped the monitor. "Piece of crap."

This was typical. We have the technology. Right. A high tech company whose internal computer systems were so shitty it was embarrassing. Like the shoemaker's children who went barefoot. Our system would be down at least once a week, and it was especially frustrating first thing in the morning because the system administrator, an overpaid computer junkie, typically didn't arrive in the office until nine most days. He was normally so spaced out, probably from surfing the net all night, that it would take him a couple of hours to bring the system back on-line.

I pulled out our internal phone directory and found his home number. His phone rang at least a dozen times before he answered.

"Yeah," a voice mumbled.

"Ray, it's Kate. Get your ass out of bed and get this system up. Today is not a good day and I haven't kicked anyone's ass all week. You could be my candidate of choice."

There was no response. The asshole had probably fallen back to sleep.

"RAY," I bellowed into the phone.

"Yeah," he mumbled again.

I sweetly and quietly said, because my mother always told me you attract more flies with honey, "Ray, get your lazy ass out of bed." I haven't figured out yet why I need to attract flies.

He responded immediately. He recognized my sweet and quiet voice and exactly what it meant. "I'll log-on the system from home and see what's the problem."

"Are your feet on the floor?" I demanded.

"I'm standing up. Good-bye." He hung up on me. I made a mental note to take him off my Christmas card list.

I hung up my phone and stared at it. The red light was still flashing letting me know that I still had several "unread voice messages". I lit another cigarette and continued to stare at my phone. I finally logged back on my voice mail system and scrolled through my messages until I got to Ev's. The sound of her voice made my heart feel like stone. I was careful not to delete the message and hung up again.

I grabbed my coffee cup and headed for the kitchenette down the hall for another cup of coffee.

CHAPTER
six

The smell hit me as soon as I opened the door to the kitchenette. The room smelled like old garlic. Fresh cooking garlic smells great and garlic tastes great when you're eating it. But the next day, look out. I'm sure this is what Mrs. Skunk smells when she wakes up in the morning and Mr. Skunk breathes hello.

I looked around the kitchenette. The counters and table were piled with odd Tupperware bowls and platters heaped with non-perishable food. Everything was covered tightly in plastic wrap. The smell must be coming from the garbage, I thought. I put on a pot of coffee to brew and opened the fridge for a container of cream. I had to reach past several bowls of salads and platters of meat, also wrapped in plastic. Someone had done a good clean up job last night after the reception.

The kitchenette was off the main boardroom and this was the room where the caterers worked. Normally, they take all leftovers with them and there is never any evidence left the next day. Last night's left-overs would disappear fast when the staff realized there was something for free to be had in the fridge. I eyed the baked goods laid out on the counter and lifted the plastic off one plate heaped with brownies and ate two while I waited for the coffee to brew.

As I walked down the hall to my office I noticed signs of the place coming to life. I heard a voice in Didrickson's office and I could hear the normal bitching coming from behind the partitions where the paralegals and secretaries sat in an open area. They were having trouble deciding who was going to call Ray about the system being down. Jesus, what a bunch of lame ducks, I thought.

"Don't worry," I called over the partition. "Ray's on the case. I've already talked to him."

The chatter stopped.

"Kate, how's Ev?" one of the voices asked.

I slowed down before entering my office and turned around. Four half faces peered at me over the partitions.

"She died last night," I said abruptly. Jackie gasped and immediately started to cry. I turned on my heel and closed my office door behind me.

I sat down at my desk and put my head in my hands. Gee Kate, how to handle the staff. How to give them the news gently. One of your better skills. Diplomacy at its best. More like gunboat diplomacy. I dialled Jay's number and after three rings his phone kicked over to voice mail. "Call me as soon as you get in," was the message I left.

The first time I laid eyes on Jay Harmon I thought he was the most beautiful thing I had ever seen. I had just turned six years old and was desperate for a baby brother or sister. My mother would look at me like I was from another planet when I would ask her why we didn't expand the family. My brother and I were the only children and as far as my mother was concerned, two were plenty.

Cheryl Harmon was my best friend and she had three of the best sisters a person could want. Cheryl said that was my opinion. As far as she was concerned, if they all left her alone and took a flying leap (her words), then they'd be the best sisters a person could want. Jay was the fifth child and only boy.

I first saw him when he was three weeks old. Their father left two weeks later and I don't think anyone has heard from him since. He could be dead for all they know. His mother carried on, working two or three jobs, depending on the season. They were very close and I guess in those years they learned the meaning of teamwork. My brother and I had to do chores at home but nothing compared to what Cheryl and her sisters were expected to do. That sort of upbringing builds character, I suppose.

Jay was everybody's baby. His sisters took turns mothering him and often times there were fights over who got to play with him. Lucky for his sisters he was a very placid child. Jay got along with everyone.

By the time Jay started kindergarten he could read, print, write, add and subtract. For the first three years of his life his sisters played house with him but when they got bored with that they started playing school. He was their pupil and he soaked it all up. When he graduated high school he was offered a scholarship to the University of Toronto. He completed his degree in business and applied for a scholarship at the Richard Ivey School of Business at the University of Western Ontario to do his MBA. When he graduated from Western he came to work at our company.

Jay was recruited on campus to join our firm in the management trainee program. The MBA recruits would spend equal time over five years in the finance, human resources, research and development, sales, and delivery and support departments. To MBA graduates our company was an attractive place to start a career and it had all the magic ingredients: high tech, public company, management training program, full benefits, stock options, *and* a starting salary of $75,000. Jay's first rotation was working for Tom James in the human resources department where he mastered the tasks and our computer systems by the second day and was completely bored by the end of the first week. I talked to him about slowing down a little, soaking up the surroundings and learning by listening. He wanted to be the chief operating officer of the company. I told him he had to be there at least three months before he could apply for that job. He thought I was serious. I've been working on his sense of humour ever since.

Jay finished his second rotation in Sales and nine months ago he joined the Finance Department to work with Richard Cox, who was wearing two hats as our chief operating officer and chief financial officer. Lately, Jay felt he was doing some useful work. Cox had him working as part of the team on acquisitions and company financings. He also worked almost exclusively with Cox on stock options and materials presented to the board of directors.

My phone rang for the first time that morning. I glanced at my watch. It was eight-thirty. Everyone must be avoiding me.

"Kathleen Monahan," I answered.

"Kate, it's Jay. How're you doing?" His voice was soft and his concerned tone almost starting me crying again.

"I'm okay. We'll do fine. How'd it go last night? How's Danny?" I hurried to change the subject.

"He's coping. His brother and sister are there with him. I told them to call me if they needed anything."

"I had a message from Ev on my system when I checked my messages this morning."

"God, that's so weird," he said. "What did she want?"

"Nothing. Just said she was looking forward to having a drink with me at the party last night. Jay, I miss her so much already."

"I know. Everyone around here is going to miss her. I wish she were here right now. Rick Cox has been yelling for an option summary this morning. Have you got any idea when the system's supposed to be back up? If Evelyn were here I could get a printed copy but I couldn't find one in her desk."

"Who cares about stock options and Rick Cox? He'll probably forget in an hour that he asked you for it. I can see everyone's going to have a decent mourning period for Evelyn."

Jay chuckled. I didn't think it was funny. But he was probably laughing at me, not my comment.

"Who put the bug up Rick's ass about options?" I asked.

"I think Oakes is on his case. Maybe they're going to approve some more grants of options at the board meeting."

Stock options for the executives are the driving force behind recruiting at our company. Options are an incentive, like a future bonus, given to executives when they're hired. The reward for the executive is when the stock price goes up and they cash in. There's no mystique to options as far as I was concerned, but it was amazing the number of executives who never understood the value of what they had.

Many executives have come into my office and I've had to give them my basic primer on options. Stock options are simply the option for the executive to buy shares in the company. There were always three significant factors I would go over: the number of options granted, the exercise price of the options, and when the options were available for exercise.

The number of options granted varied, depending on the executive, and this was one factor that every executive clearly understood. They knew how many options they had but in most cases, that was the extent of their knowledge and understanding.

The exercise price was the price at which the executive could buy the shares from the company. This price was the closing price of the company's shares on the stock market on the day the options were granted to them.

In our company, options were usually available for purchase, or exercisable, one year after they were granted.

So, simply stated, if an executive was granted 1,000 options at an exercise price of $10.00, it meant that when the shares were exercisable, he could purchase from the company, 1,000 shares at $10.00 per share. If he elected to exercise (or purchase) those options (shares), he paid the company $10,000 and the company would arrange for the executive to be the registered owner of the shares. He could then turn around and sell those shares on the stock market. If the shares were trading at $15.00, he would make $5.00 a share, or a $5,000 profit. Definitely not rocket science.

Usually, top executives were granted 100,000 options when they were hired and depending on their performance, more options were granted each year. Several of our top executives were holding over 500,000 options. Most of them had exercise prices between $8.00 and $10.00. The shares were trading at $11.00, so there wasn't a lot of money to be made right now.

There was a time about three years ago when the shares had reached $16.00 on speculation that we were being taken over but because of insider trading rules none of the executives could 'cash' in. Harold Didrickson had informed everyone that there were 'windows', or time periods, when it was legal to exercise their options. At the time the shares skyrocketed to $16.00, our audited quarterly financial statements were in the process of being finalized. Our executives knew about the financial results and the public didn't, so that was considered a closed 'window' because they were in possession of inside information, and therefore, it was illegal to trade in the company's shares.

Options are an incentive to the executives to make sure the company grows and makes a profit. The executives understand the word incentive, but profit is a word we're still looking for in the company dictionary.

Grants of stock options have to be approved by the board of directors and once that was done, the lists of exercise prices and numbers of options granted are given to Ev to enter into the company's main computer system. After the information is entered, Ev would be able to tell the value at any given time of an executive's total stock option package.

Jay would also use the same system to generate reports for Rick Cox on how many options were outstanding and how many options were still available to issue. Legally, the number of options granted cannot exceed more than 10% of the company's issued and outstanding shares. TechniGroup's number of shares issued and outstanding was a constantly rising number because each time we acquired another company we would give the owners shares in our company, rather than cash. So with the number of shares constantly rising, the 10% limit was always going up.

"I'm leaving on time today," Jay said, "and if the system's not back up to get that report, Rick's going to have to get it himself."

"Yeah, right. Rick wouldn't know where the on/off button was on his computer. The guy's a techno-phobe. And you can quit your whining, you'll work until the cows come home. When was the last time you left the office on time?"

"I know, I know. Besides, Rick wouldn't know how to get into the stock option system even if he figured out how to turn on the machine."

There were three people who could access the stock option system: Rick Cox, Jay and Evelyn. Rick didn't know how to use the system and with Evelyn gone, that left Jay to do all the work.

"Well, *I'm* leaving on time today. Call me later if you need any help finding things in Ev's office." I hung up.

CHAPTER
seven

I got up and walked around my desk and stood in front of the closed door. Time to face the troops. Jackie and Sandra, the two legal secretaries and Jessica and Ken, the two paralegals deserved better from me this morning. As much as I was grieving for Ev, I'm sure they were just as shocked and saddened about her death. They had all worked closely with Ev over the years and would miss her dreadfully. The way I had broken the news to them wasn't fair. I'm always telling people to suck it in and buck-up so I gave myself a mental thrashing and opened the door. I walked around the partitions into the open-concept area where the four of them had their desks. They must have heard me open my door because all four had their heads down and looked like they were diligently working.

"Hey guys." Four faces looked up at me. Jackie still had tears in her eyes and Ken looked like he was going to break down.

"I'm sorry for snapping everyone's head off. You know I'm not good at that stuff. We're all gonna miss Ev." I paused and swallowed. "Thanks," I ended off. Big speech for me. Ranting and raving is more my style. I felt awful and shrugged my shoulders. Jackie smiled at me and I knew it was okay.

I turned around and went and stuck my head in Didrickson's office. He was sitting behind his massive, antique partner's desk with the phone stuck to his ear. He was taking notes on a legal pad and punching numbers into the phone. Obviously still checking his voice mail messages. I cleared my throat. He looked up and I motioned for him to call me when he was finished. He waved me in and I wandered over to the window to check out the view. Didrickson had one of the prime corner offices in the executive suite and the back wall of his office was all windows. I placed my forehead up against the window and stared down at the street. The cold glass felt good on my face.

I heard Didrickson hang up the phone and I turned around. He finished writing something and looked up at me. He said nothing.

"I'm fine, and you?" I said.

The man was either the coldest person I'd ever met or incredibly shy. After four years I was still trying to figure him out. On a personal level, he didn't speak unless spoken to, especially to people 'below' him. He never initiated personal conversations and showed little interest in anything except work.

"Sorry," he smiled slightly, but quickly put on his serious face. "I got your message about Ev. God, this is terrible. Who's going to look after her work?"

Fucking typical, I thought disgustedly. "Don't worry Harold. I'm sure we'll cope. Technically, she died before midnight, so should I tell payroll not to pay her for yesterday?" I deadpanned.

"Take it easy Kate. It's just that this is a bad time with the board meeting only a week away. There's a lot of work to be done." The man had such a heart.

"I'm sorry you're so shook up about Ev's death, Harold." I waited. I wanted to see if he understood my tone because sometimes I felt like I had to hit him with a brick - to him everything was so black and white. When he didn't respond I decided not to waste my breath on the issue. I changed the subject.

"What do you want me to start on for the board meeting?" I asked.

As Corporate Secretary of the company, Didrickson had responsibility for preparing all material to be sent out to the board members in advance of meetings. This was to allow the board members time to look over the material before they were asked to approve it. Usually the two week period before a board meeting was a mad rush trying to get all the papers together and nine times out of ten we ended up giving the material to the directors at the meeting because we never got our shit together in time. Didrickson took this very personally because when he joined the company he vowed that he would get the process in shape and the directors would always have plenty of time to look over the materials they were being asked to approve. It became an obsession with Didrickson and I think the other departments in the company deliberately sabotaged his efforts just to see him squirm. The worst culprits were the beancounters in the finance department who couldn't organize a senior citizen's game of shuffleboard.

On a quarterly basis the most important documents the directors needed to approve were the financial statements. And the financial statements were never done on time.

Now, call me kooky, but when you know, on a perpetual calendar until the year 2030, when every financial quarter ends, why is it so hard to plan to have something done *on time*? That's why Didrickson was sure the other departments were conspiring against him, just to make him look bad. He took it very personally. Sometimes rightfully so, because Harold became the scapegoat every time one of the directors would wake up from his seasonal slumber and realize what he was being asked to approve.

"Draft an agenda and remind me what sub-committee meetings we're having. You'll have to do agendas for each of the committees as well. Get the file from last year's third quarter meeting and bring it in. How are the arrangements for the dinner coming?"

"I'll check with Vanessa. She's doing all the meals and looking after the out of town directors. I'll get some drafts done up for you."

I left his office and went to the kitchenette. I like to embarrass Didrickson by bringing him coffee. He's never once asked for one and for that reason, I serve him regularly. When I'm really pissed off at him, I'll wait until he has someone in his office and I'll poke my head in and ask him if he wants a coffee. It makes him blush every time. Didrickson is so by-the-book, he would never dream of asking the support staff to do anything personal for him. I grabbed the third quarter board meeting file from last year on my way back to his office. I tossed the file in front of him and very gently placed the coffee on a coaster on the leather-top desk. He looked up at me and turned a nice shade of pink. Gotcha, I thought.

I wandered down the hall to Vanessa's office to talk about the board meeting. She was on the phone, as usual, and I stood in her doorway waiting for her to finish. As usual, Vee was impeccably dressed. Today she had on a classic, navy blue suit with a crisp white blouse. Her hair was perfectly done and it fell to her shoulders in soft waves. We were both cursed with gray hairs but Vanessa had the good grace to colour hers to cover it up. Her make-up was subtle and I caught a slight smell of her perfume. Perfect. She was beautiful but certainly had no pretensions. She went to the gym a couple of times each week and it showed. Vee looked up at me and made a face and I knew she was talking to Oakes.

"Chris, I can't hear you. Chris... Chris... are you there?" she said into the phone in a loud voice. And then she hung up the phone and started to chuckle.

"Quick," she said, grabbing her purse from under her desk. "Let's get out of here for coffee." She scrambled out from behind her desk and pushed past me in the doorway and started down the hallway. I trotted to keep up. Vee is the fastest walker I know and I'm always running behind her. How she can walk so fast in her three inch heels is something that defies physics.

"If he calls, I'm in the bathroom," she said to the receptionist as we headed for the elevators. She punched the button. "He was on his cell phone in the limo and I got fed up listening to him so I told him I couldn't hear him. He'll be on the phone now chewing out the phone company." We laughed. At least she maintains her sense of humour. Frankly, I think the woman is a saint. She puts up with an incredible amount of shit from Oakes.

Vee's desk had been next to mine when she started with the company about six years ago. I was working as Shirley Benton's secretary and Vee had been hired to work as a project secretary in the research and development department. She had kicked her husband out and needed to support her eight year old daughter. Her skills were a little rusty but she quickly picked up the office procedures. She had been Oakes' secretary now for two years. I knew she took the job with Oakes because she needed the money and it paid well. Her ex missed more support payments than he made and she couldn't depend on him.

We grabbed our coffees at the counter in the lobby cafe and sat down at a table in the enclosed room designated for smokers. We didn't speak until we had both had a couple of drags from our cigarettes. Our favourite coffee shop was soon going to be smoke-free when the city introduced the latest by-law which would ban smoking in all public places.

"God Kate, I didn't sleep last night. All I could see was Ev's face. I can't believe she's dead. I checked my voice mail about five o'clock and got your message. What happened? Was it a reaction to nuts?"

"The doctors wouldn't say. The resident in emergency said it looked like a reaction but wouldn't say one way or the other. He wanted to talk to the immediate family and I couldn't get in touch with Danny until later. I never went back in to talk to them after she died."

"How did Danny take it? How is he?" she asked.

I shrugged. "OK, I guess. I'll have to call him later and see if he needs help with anything for the funeral." I changed the subject. "What's up? What's going on? Where's CEO today?"

Vee and I referred to Chris Oakes by his initials.

"He's off on another secret mission. Totally hush-hush. If anyone asks, he's in the New York office meeting clients."

"Yeah, right. Now where is he really?"

"He's meeting with Jack Vincent."

"Well isn't that interesting," I said slowly. "We haven't heard of Jack for about three years. What's going on Vanessa? Come on. What's the dirt?"

Jack Vincent was a principal of one of the largest underwriting firms in Toronto and his firm had been the lead underwriters on a deal the company had tried to do that went sour. Sour and rotten. The consortium of banks that held the majority of the shares of our company when the original founder died five years ago had hired Jack's firm to find a buyer for their shares. Because we're a public company, this was of course highly confidential information, but before long, word leaked on the street and our shares started to inch up. There was speculation on the street that we were going to be bought up by IBM. That was one day. The next day the rumours had us being bought up by AT&T, and the next day it was another rumour. And the share price kept going up.

All of these rumours were way off base. In fact, the big fish on the hook was a German manufacturer that was looking to get into the North American market. The representatives of the banking consortium along with our executive team had been holed-up in a hotel in New York City for a week when the deal was almost ready to close. The owner of the German firm, Jozef Glass was leading his team of executives and his guns for hire, a Wall Street law firm. The negotiations were completed and the lawyers were finalizing their mountains of paper when the deal was suddenly called off. The Germans left town that day and our guys all returned home.

I heard later that Chris Oakes was the reason the Germans pulled out. Jozef Glass was a typical German and expected everything to be orderly and done his way. He must have thought he was awake in the middle of a nightmare when he finally called off the deal. Chris Oakes had done his smooth sales job about the company to Glass and the German bought it, hook, line and sinker. But as we got closer to the closing date, and everyone was practically living together, working around the clock, Glass got a taste of the real Chris Oakes. Manic depressive and psychotic behaviour became the norm. Chris would agree to something, in front of witnesses and then change his mind minutes later, denying total knowledge of his previous agreement. Bizarre behaviour that we were all used to but it finally got to Glass. After a particularly gruelling, eighteen-hour negotiation session, Jozef Glass telephoned Oakes at two in the morning and told him the deal was off. Of course, Oakes told all of us that he called off the deal, but we knew better. I guess it wasn't meant to be a marriage made in heaven. Our shares dropped from $16.00 to $8.00 overnight. The rumours on the street were right on the money that time.

Jack Vincent became *persona non grata* at TGC. The banks were desperate by then to dump their shares so they sold their shares to the public. This was accomplished in two public offerings in the space of twelve months. They got their money and we got some more shareholders. Right now we have one shareholder who holds six percent of the stock and the rest is disbursed among thousands of other shareholders.

If Jack Vincent was back in the picture after three years something must be up. If we were doing another public offering by selling treasury shares to the public to raise more money, I'd know about it. The board would have made the decision and we would have rammed the paperwork through and got the issue sold. We had done that several times in the past couple of years. And each time, we used a different underwriting firm than the one Jack worked for.

"You think they've hired Jack to find a buyer again?" I asked Vee.

"I hope so. And if they find a buyer, I hope they fire Chris' ass," Vee said disgustedly.

CHAPTER
eight

I had a terrible time getting motivated for the rest of the morning. I couldn't concentrate on my work and every time I started something, my mind would wander and I'd start thinking about Ev. I could hardly breathe in my office from all the cigarette smoke and my stomach was growling for some sustenance so I put on my jacket to head out in search of some lunch. I left my office door open to clear the air while I was out.

I dined out at one of Toronto's finer establishments and treated myself to one of life's delicacies. A Big Mac. With large fries and a Coke. Diet, of course, because one has to watch the waistline.

On my walk back to the office I swung my arms a little higher than normal and considered that my afternoon exercise.

I wasn't surprised to find that my office door was closed. People are so stuck up these days about second-hand smoke.

Jay was waiting inside my office. He didn't give me time to sit down before he asked, "Kate, do you have a copy of the list of options granted and approved at the last board meeting?"

"Yeah. But you should have a copy. Rick's group produced it and the final copy you gave us was the one put in front of the board for approval."

I dug in the filing cabinet for the material from the last board meeting. I heaved it out on to my desk and started thumbing through it. It was about four inches thick and nothing was in order. Every draft of every document was in the file, along with Didrickson's notes and piles of other crap. I'm not known for my filing abilities.

I finally found the copy that Jay was looking for. "Here," I passed it to him. I shoved all the papers back in the folder and piled it on the side of my desk. I sat down and lit a cigarette. Jay was comparing the list I gave him to another piece of paper he had in his hand and I leaned forward to nonchalantly look at the other piece of paper. Reading upside down was a skill I learned early on in my secretarial career and it's a skill that's paid off many times over the years.

The two pieces of paper looked the same to me from my vantage point, so I leaned back in my chair and blew smoke up towards the ceiling. I was being considerate, not blowing it directly at Jay.

"Here, you look." Jay shoved the two papers at me. "You tell me what the differences are."

Each sheet of paper looked identical and contained a list of about fifty names. The five columns across the page were headed: Name, Number of Options Granted, Exercise Price, Exercise Date and Expiry Date. I had to squint because the typeface was quite small.

"Do you want to tell me what I'm looking for?"

Jay sighed. "Come on Kate. Help me out here. Just look at it."

I hate comparing documents to look for differences so I used one of my lazy tricks. I put the two pieces of paper together and held them up to the light and carefully aligned the column headings and started reading down the first column. The names on each piece were the same. The second column had some differences because the numbers appeared jumbled. I quickly glanced at the other three columns and nothing appeared out of order.

"The differences are in the second column, number of options granted." I tried to hand the papers back to him.

"Okay, give the girl a kewpie doll. Where are the differences?"

I held the papers back up to the light and read off, "Richard Cox, Mary Dawson, Jay Harmon and Bill Heatherington." I put the papers down side by side and ran my finger down the list of names on the first page to Richard Cox's name. The column beside Rick's name had a number of 50,000. I found his name on the other list and checked the column beside it. The number there was 30,000. I found Jay's name on the first sheet and compared it to the other. The first sheet had a figure of 10,000 beside Jay's name and the second one had the number 1,000. Mary Dawson and Bill Heatherington's options had been changed by 9,000 options as well. I quickly glanced at the bottom of both pages to compare the totals They were different too. A difference of 47,000. I'm quite a mathematician when the need arises.

I handed the papers back to Jay.

"Which page did I just give you? In other words, which list did the directors' approve?" I asked.

"It doesn't really matter. What matters is which one did I print off directly from the stock option system?"

"The point being?" I asked. I can be incredibly slow sometimes. Jay stared at me waiting for my answer. "The list you printed off from the system is the one that's up by 47,000. Hey Jay, who's your fairy godmother?" I joked.

"Shut up Kate. The board approved 1,000 options for me, Mary and Bill and 30,000 for Cox. The list I printed off the stock option system shows 10,000 for us and 50,000 for Cox. It's impossible that Ev could have made the same mistake three times and added a zero and there's no explanation for the change to Cox's. Besides," he continued, "Ev would have noticed that the totals didn't balance. I knew I was getting a thousand options, because Cox told me. I would have put a down-payment on a house if he had promised me 10,000."

"Ev and I were the only two people besides Rick Cox with access to the system," he continued. "And I certainly don't input numbers. I just run reports. But if she and I are the only two with access to the system, who made the change?"

I did a quick calculation. "If the shares ever get up to $15.00, which we all admit is a pipe dream, and the exercise price is $10.00, Cox could make $250,000 before taxes. Not a small amount in my mind, but certainly peanuts to someone like Rick. You, on the other hand, could certainly make a dent in those student loans with a cool fifty grand. Mary and Bill could use the fifty grand but they're not still paying off loans," I teased. Mary and Bill were both financial analysts who worked in the finance department and like Jay, reported directly to Rick Cox.

"Get serious Kate. Work with me here. Are you sure you gave me the list the directors approved?"

"The finger points directly at you. You'd profit a lot more on a relative basis than Rick would. Rick spends a hundred K at lunch and doesn't think twice about it," I joked.

Jay stood up so fast he knocked over the chair. He took a deep breath and tried to calm himself. He scared me when he spoke. "Thank you F. Lee Bailey." He turned around and pulled on the door handle so hard I thought it would break off.

I stood up too. "Jay, hey. Calm down." He was gone. Those young guys can move fast. I started to run around my desk to catch up to him and thought better of it. Don't want to strain my heart, I thought.

I tucked in my blouse, straightened my skirt, dusted the cigarette ashes off my jacket and very primly walked out of my office. Who did I think I was kidding?

Jay was going into the kitchenette so I followed him in and closed the door behind me. He was facing the coffee machine and had his back to me.

"Hey," I kidded, "if you can't take a joke, you shouldn't have joined up."

He turned around and I could see he was still pissed off. As he brushed past me to reach for the door handle, he said, "Another one of your stupid sayings that I'm sick of Kate. Your sense of humour is sick. You make me sick."

I moved aside to let him pass. "Want to come over tonight and we'll do our nails?" I asked. He was gone. Again.

I waited a few moments and followed Jay to his office. He ignored me when I came in. I closed the door quietly and asked if I could sit down. He continued to ignore me so I sat anyway.

"Look Jay. I apologize. I know I can be too mouthy for my own good. You know I didn't mean anything by what I said. I was just joking." I thought that came out well but he still wasn't responding so I tried again.

"Stop being an asshole about this. I said I was sorry. I was just teasing. This is no big deal. I'm pretty sure I gave you the right sheet. If you notice in the bottom corner, Didrickson's initialled it. That means it's the list the board approved. You know how many times Cox fucks around with those lists before, during, and after a board meeting. Didrickson laid down the law and said the only lists I'm to use for stock exchange approval, are the ones he initials. I'd give a copy to Ev because she was never sure if she had the most up-to-date one."

"Look," I continued. "I'll get Harold to settle this. Give me those two lists. I'll ask him. The Great One has been known to screw up occasionally too. I'm gonna go see if he's in. Cox still breathing down your neck for the report?"

"Yeah, and it's not going to be a pretty sight if I don't produce it soon. This change of 47,000 throws the totals off whack. They're scraping the barrel looking for more room on the 10% limit to give out more options."

I took the papers off Jay's desk. I leaned over and almost touched my nose to his. "I was only teasing, okay?"

CHAPTER
nine

Didrickson wasn't in his office when I got back so I scribbled him a note to call me. I dropped the note on the seat of his chair so he wouldn't miss it.

I pulled out the bottom drawer of my desk and propped my feet up on it. Once I'd tried putting my feet on the desk but the chair was so cheap I fell flat on the floor when I leaned back.

I lit a cigarette and cursed the stock options. Nothing but a pain in the ass. Back in the good old days stock options weren't a problem. Because there were none. The previous owner of the company was such a tight wad he didn't believe in sharing the wealth. It was a different regime when Oakes took over though. He gave away the farm. He hired all of his old buddies from the last place he worked, tripled their salaries and gave them stock options. Rick Cox only made things worse. The man managed to make everything an administrative nightmare. He was responsible for rolling out the yearly stock option plan and crunching the numbers for the option grants. Oakes would make his recommendations on numbers of options for his cronies and Cox would play around with the rest left-over. And play around. And play around. The numbers were a constant moving target right up until the moment the numbers were given to the board to approve. The total options they issued could never change because of the 10% limit, but the individual's numbers were fair game. I think his formula for coming up with numbers was based on where the planets were in the sky on a certain day. Very scientific.

When Richard Cox joined the company as a full-time employee I had breathed a sigh of relief. I remember thinking that we were finally getting someone 'normal' at the helm. Cox was originally a member of the board of directors, appointed by the bank consortium. He had been a wizard at a Bay Street investment bank and actually brought some sanity to the place. The board woke up one day and appointed him the chief operating officer. The position was vacant because they had just fired the current chief operating officer. Actually, press reports said the guy resigned to pursue other business interests. Right. Cox was on-deck and the logical choice as replacement. Chris Oakes put up a fight but soon realized he was in a losing battle. A few months later, when the board gave Cox the additional responsibilities of chief financial officer because the incumbent retired, the battle lines were drawn. Oakes and Rick Cox had been openly feuding now for two years.

I wasn't the only one who was glad Cox joined the company. The company was re-organized, excuse me, re-engineered, and many people who had reported directly to Oakes ended-up reporting directly to Cox. But Cox's true stripes started to show after about three months of having the dual role of COO and CFO. What a let-down. The guy turned out to be indecisive, misdirected, unfocused and on a good day, a three-headed monster.

The rivalry between Oakes and Cox appeared to be heating up over the last month or two and I expected a show-down soon.

My phone rang and I tore my pantyhose on the corner of the drawer when I tried to get my feet back on the floor and swing my chair around. Kathleen, you are so graceful.

"Kathleen Monahan."

"Yes?" the voice on the other end demanded.

"Who's speaking please?" I knew it was Didrickson, and in fact his extension number lit up on the digit display on the telephone console, but I hate arrogant bastards who don't identify themselves on the phone.

"It's Harold. You left me a note to call you. I'm back."

"I'll be right in." I picked up the two sheets of paper with the stock option lists on them and headed for his office.

I handed him the list with his initials on the bottom and said, "I got this list out of the last board meeting file." Then I handed him the other one. "Jay printed this from the stock option system just before lunch. The numbers aren't the same. He's got to give a report to Rick Cox with the total options outstanding and he noticed the numbers don't jive."

He handed both back to me after he quickly glanced at the two. "Then the system is wrong. The one with my initials on it is the one that was approved at the board meeting."

"Thanks."

I called Jay when I got back to my office and told him Didrickson said the one with his initials was the final list. He said he would come down and pick up the lists.

My phone rang again. The digit display indicated it was Didrickson calling. "Yes," I answered. I thought I'd try his style.

"What exactly were the differences on those two lists?"

"There were four different entries. Rick Cox, Mary Dawson, Jay Harmon and Bill Heatherington. Cox had a difference of 20,000 and each of the others were increased by 9,000 each."

"I think you better give me those lists back."

"Sure. But Jay's on his way back down here to get the lists to finish his report to Cox. And he's the one who noticed the differences."

"Make him copies then." He hung up.

Yessir. Right away sir. I passed Jay in the hall on my way to the photocopier room. "Follow me. Didrickson wants the originals of these and I'll make you a copy."

The next couple of hours were spent creating paper. Agendas for the upcoming board and committee meetings, indexes for the binders of materials, drafting resolutions for the board to approve. Paper, paper and more paper. Baffle 'em with bullshit. Most of the documents I started on were full of holes, ready for Didrickson to fill in the blanks. I made sure a current date and time were printed on the draft documents. Didrickson would soon start passing the documents around to Oakes and Cox for their input and we needed to be sure we were always working on the same draft. Chris Oakes never focused on anything until the last minute and was usually working on draft #2 when the rest of us were working on #5. I especially enjoyed receiving his comments on the documents two days after the meetings were over.

I ran into Tom James when I was getting my fifth cup of coffee since lunch.

"Tom, nice tie," I said with a straight face. He puffed up his chest. It *was* a nice tie, but this was the way Tom and I started off every conversation. It was expected that I would compliment Tom on his tie, or his suit, or whatever, and I think I had now complimented him on this particular tie about sixty times. Our man of substance. I was surprised to see Tom in the office this late in the day. Normally, he leaves at lunch to go to his gym for a workout and if he comes back, it's only to impress Oakes.

"What are you doing in the office so late in the day?" I teased.

"I thought Oakes was out of town." Tom looked insulted. It didn't work with me.

"He was. He flew back this afternoon and we've got a meeting."

"Yeah? Good for you. Putting in overtime for this?" I laughed. Tom looked a little confused. He knew no-one got paid overtime in this organization and as the vice president in charge of human resources I could see his brain working to try and remember this.

"Forget it Tom," I said. I teased him because I could. Kind of like, why does a dog lick his balls? Because he can. Why do I tease Tom James? Because I can. He's such an easy target.

"So what's so important on a Friday afternoon? You and Oakes deciding on a tee time?" I grinned.

"We're going over the personnel stuff on the acquisition of Marshton Systems. Deciding on who goes where. Who keeps their jobs. You know." Tom puffed up his chest a little when he said this.

Oh, this was *good* dirt. Amazing what these guys will share with me. I live for this stuff. Actually, it's the only interesting thing in this job. The speculation. The rumours. The politics. My brain works a mile a minute trying to keep one step ahead of everyone by putting together everything they tell me. Bits and pieces, here and there. And before you know it, I know what's going to happen before they do. I do most of my speculation with Vee and between the two of us we re-organize the company on a monthly basis. The way *we* think it should work. And eventually, the powers that be catch up with us and everything falls into place. We joke that in another life we'll be management consultants. With the information that Vee's privy to working for the Chairman of the Board, and the information all the guys share with me, we know everything that's going on in the company. As much as it's a game with us to speculate and play around with the information, we keep the information between the two of us. We're professional enough to know that rumours have killed many a public company.

I like to think that the executives share information with me because they can trust me. I've been around and lived through a lot of history in this company and I've become the unofficial company historian of fact and fiction.

"So, who's in and who's out?" I asked Tom.

"Well, the technical staff stay. That goes without saying. We're trying to figure out now if there's any fit for the top guys." Tom very carefully added Sweet 'n Low to his coffee. No extra calories for this guy.

"What about Jerry Marsh?" I asked. Jerry Marsh was the majority owner of the company we had just acquired and the word was that he sold the company so he could retire.

"He'll stay around for six months to consult. Help with the transition," Tom said.

"In other words, he's playing golf and buying retirement real estate," I stated.

"We've got a lot of overlap in the finance and personnel positions. We promised them hefty severance packages when we bought them. Most of them'll be gone when we get their operations working in synch with ours," Tom said.

This was standard operating procedure. TechniGroup would buy up smaller companies who were in the same sort of business as ours. Usually they would have contracts that were making money so they were very attractive buys for us. We'd purchase the company, keep the technical people and ditch the rest of the staff. I'd seen dozens of people come and go over the last two years. The transitions could take up to six months while our people got to understand their operations. We'd take this time to train their technical staff to our products and internal procedures.

"What about Phil? Oops. Excuse me, Philip?" I asked.

"I can't see him lasting long. We don't need two operational guys. Rick Cox'll make mincemeat of him."

"Yeah, but I thought we'd promised him a job. We did a separate agreement for him to keep him on. Oakes was adamant about fitting Phil into the organization. Wasn't the plan to create some sort of position in operations, kind of on a smaller scale? Get Phil running a couple of the regions?" I asked.

"Cox is fighting it tooth and nail. He and Oakes had a major screaming match about it the other day. Cox was so mad I thought he was going to run and get his mommy." Tom laughed.

Tom and I both knew that Rick Cox had not been very involved in the acquisition of Marshton Systems. It had been a transaction that Oakes had pushed through without any input from Cox. God, what a pair. I wondered if other organizations had such team work at the top.

I took a sip of my coffee. "Well, the next week should be interesting."

"Have any arrangements been announced yet for Ev's funeral?" Tom asked.

"No, nothing yet. If I find out, I'll let everyone know. You know Tom, we've got a great gaping hole with Ev gone. It's going to take some time to get someone up to speed on her job."

"Jay can take it over," Tom stated.

Oh yeah, big promotion Jay. Maybe I'll be the one to tell him. Jay, you've been promoted. We hope you're up to the task. The job'll involve a lot of data entry work and we'll be glad to provide training.

"Right Tom. Jay'll be happy with that. Taking over a clerical job. Tom, you should look at some of the existing staff to see who can do the job. We need someone who can be trusted. If we get someone from inside, the learning curve won't be difficult."

Tom was flexing his forearms and staring at himself in the shiny surface of the paper towel dispenser over the sink. I grabbed my coffee and sighed. At least I'd had his attention for about five minutes. Par for the course. The man had the attention span of a two year old.

"Good luck at your meeting," I said over my shoulder as I left the room.

He didn't hear me. He was picking at a piece of dry skin over his eyebrow.

CHAPTER
ten

I'd had enough by five-thirty. Even a slave gets time off. I signed off my computer and caressed the monitor before I powered off. If I'm nice to the machine, maybe it'll be running next time I need it.

The office was quiet when I opened my door. On my way to Didrickson's office, I glanced into the area where the secretaries and paralegals worked. No one in sight. The rats had definitely exited on time. Harold was on the phone when I stuck my head in his door so I waited until he finished. He'd be in the same position when I got in on Monday. Phone glued to his ear, pen in hand, writing furiously. The guy takes better shorthand than I do. I'm sure he takes down every word said to him over the phone. He keeps copious notes and heads up each one with the date, time and person he spoke to.

Didrickson saw me standing there so he swivelled his chair. His back was to me and I overhead him say, "Okay Grace, I'll let you know as soon as I speak with Chris. Right." He swivelled back to face the desk and wrote something. "I'll call you if I need you before Monday." He hung up.

"I'm outta here Harold. Have a good weekend."

"Okay Kate. If Vanessa's at her desk let her know I'm still waiting to see Chris."

"He's probably still in his meeting with Tom." Harold's eyebrows went up. He doesn't ask how I know everything going on.

"They're meeting about the personnel changes for Marshton Systems," I said.

"Well, that won't last long. Tom can't concentrate more than half an hour at a time," he said with a hint of a smile.

Very good, I thought. The man's getting some humour.

"See you Monday," I waved.

I could see Philip Winston leaning up against the doorframe

of Vee's office as I turned the corner and headed down the hall. As I approached her office, I could see through the glass front that she was on the phone, furiously scribbling down information.

"Philip, how's it going?" I said.

"Kathleen," he said. At least *this* man got my name right. He stuck out his hand. The guy was so formal for someone so young. My mother would love him. I took a couple more steps and shook his hand. His aftershave filled my nostrils. God, I could chew this guy's neck. He smelled so good. I mentally slapped myself. Boy toy, boy toy, I chanted under my breath. Problem was, he knew he smelled good and he knew he looked good. Tom James was going to have a resident rival. I looked up at Philip who was tall by my standards. He was slim and his suit hung on his body perfectly. No doubt about it, I thought, he didn't shop at Wal-Mart. His tie matched the shirt, which matched the suit. I tried not to giggle as I wondered if his jockey shorts matched too. He didn't have a hair out of place on his gorgeous head. Amazing how anyone can look this put together at the end of the day. Maybe he hair sprayed his whole body.

He smiled at me and I noticed a dimple in his right cheek. After I finished chewing on his neck I was going for his bottom lip. I felt myself starting to blush and gave myself a mental cold shower.

"Philip, who're you trying to impress? It's five-thirty. Go on home," I urged. I said it like someone in charge. I've always believed that if you act like you've got authority, people will obey you. I tried this tact with all the new guys who got sucked in right away. Trouble was, most of them figure me out pretty quick and after a while they know I'm just joking. Philip on the other hand was still fair game.

"I've got one more meeting for the day," he replied. Obviously it was with Oakes or he wouldn't be hanging around Vanessa's office. Unless I interrupted him trying to put the make on her. If Tom James thought Rick Cox could make mincemeat of Philip Winston, wait until Vee got her hands on him. This woman had absolutely no time for men. Thanks to her ex and Chris Oakes, Vanessa was completely soured on the opposite sex.

The door to Oakes' office opened and we saw Tom James coming out. He stopped to button his suit jacket and straighten his tie when he saw Philip. Philip stood up a little straighter and buttoned his jacket and adjusted his tie. I watched in amusement as Tom lightly passed his hand over the side of his head to make sure his hair was smooth. Philip did the same. Mirror image. I'd have to follow these two into the bathroom some time and see what happens in front of the urinal.

Philip stuck out his hand as Tom approached and they shook. Tom grimaced ever so slightly and I guessed that Philip was giving him a bone-crushing handshake. I wouldn't be surprised if one of them lifted his leg and pissed on the doorframe of Oakes' office. Boys will be boys.

Philip went into Oakes' office and closed the door behind him.

"So Tom. How'd it go?" I asked. As if it were any of my business.

"Not bad. We've got everyone sorted out. I've got to start on the formal severance packages over the next couple of weeks."

"And Philip?" I asked. This was *definitely* not my business.

"Oh, he'll do fine. Oakes wants me to do up a package for the board on some options for him and draw up a formal employment agreement."

"Well, we've got options on the agenda for the next meeting so get me the information as soon as you can." I turned to go into Vee's office and Tom followed me.

"Hey, Vee," I said. She had her elbows on the desk and was resting her head in her hands. She looked exhausted. "Hey yourself," she said back.

"Yes Tom?" she asked tiredly. She looked at me and rolled her eyes.

"How'd the stock do?" Tom asked. It was a daily ritual for the executives to check with Vee on how the stock did for the day. They had to keep track of their fortunes.

"Down a buck. Not a very large volume of shares traded." She paused. "Anything else?"

"Um, uh, um. Nope. Have a good weekend ladies." Tom probably had something on his mind but got sidetracked when he saw a loose thread on his jacket sleeve. He was picking at it as he left Vee's office.

"Oakes is going to have a fit," Vee stated.

"Why? Just 'cause the stock's down? Again? Big deal. His excuse'll be something lame like the price of rice in China," I said. "Besides, the rest of us have nothing to worry about. He'll blame it all on you," I joked.

"That's okay. I've got big shoulders," Vee sighed. "At least the weather held today and his flights were on time." A couple of weeks ago Oakes' flight to the west coast was delayed because of fog. He blamed it all on Vee. She now had to check weather patterns at least four hours before any of his flights. The man was a lunatic.

"Harold asked me to tell you he was still waiting to see Oakes."

"I know, I know. Chris isn't interested in seeing Harold even though I told him it was urgent. He said 'tough'. What's the big deal anyway?" she asked. "It's Friday afternoon."

"Who knows? It might be something to do with the stock options. The list that was approved at the last board meeting doesn't jive with the information on Ev's system. Didrickson's probably just covering his ass again."

"Well, Harold better tread lightly. Chris and Rick are at it again. And Chris knows that Harold's siding with Rick. That isn't making Chris happy," Vee said.

The politics among the executives was heating up. What didn't help matters was Human Synergies, Inc. They had been hired by our board of directors to assist with the most recent re-engineering of our company.

Re-engineering is a term from the nineties to describe re-organization. You can't even find the word in a dictionary published before 1995. Re-engineering. How absurd. People are out there making millions on coming up with new words. "Hello, pleased to meet you. What do I do for a living? I'm a *synonymer*. Pardon? You're not familiar with that term? Basically, I make-up new words to describe mundane things. Yes, there's oodles of financial benefits." Gawd!

Human Synergies, Inc. had been hanging around for the last six months fine-tuning our re-organization. All departments had been renamed and reporting lines had reshuffled. All of that had gone relatively smoothly because we seem to reshuffle, rename and reorganize at least twice a year. What they hadn't anticipated was the in-fighting. The latest reorganization had divided the company in two. And the two camps were headed up by Oakes and Cox. All of the executives had clearly chosen sides and everyone seemed to be aware of who was siding with who. This was all unspoken, of course, but it was as plain as the nose on your face.

Human Synergies had reported to the board of directors at the last board meeting about their concerns on the lack of leadership and team effort among the executives. What a bunch of smug bastards. They had caused all of the unrest and fuelled it constantly with secret meetings and strategy sessions. They'd meet with individual executives to get input and word would filter back to the other members of the executive team. It reminded me of a group of adolescent girls in the seventh grade. They probably passed each other notes in meetings too.

"When is Chris ever happy?" I asked Vee. "I'll tell you when he's happy. When he's stirring up the pot, screaming at everyone and pulling their strings. The man would be miserable if he woke up every day next to Doris Day singing *Que Sera Sera*."

Chris Oakes' office door opened and he walked out with Philip Winston. Oakes had his overcoat on and his briefcase in his hand. He waved to Vanessa and headed down the hall. I jumped out of my seat and called after him.

"Chris. Harold needs to see you. He said it's urgent."

Oakes said something to Winston who continued down the hall towards the reception. Chris turned around and headed back to me. I thought he was going to say something to me as he walked past but he ignored me and turned around the corner towards Didrickson's office.

"Long live the King. Good night Vee," I said.

CHAPTER
eleven

Weekends were my favourite time. Two whole days to myself, away from the office. I was planning my Friday evening as I pulled out of the parking garage and eased my way into rush-hour traffic. The traffic was at a standstill and I took a couple of deep breaths to get my mindset into the weekend. Any other night of the week and my blood pressure would be rising because of the gridlock. Friday nights I didn't let it bother me. I used the time to plan out what I wanted to do and what needed to be done. The things that needed to be done were easy - housecleaning, laundry, grocery shopping. I could get those things done in a couple of hours and have the rest of the time for goofing off.

My mind was wandering when the gentleman in the pick-up truck behind me gave me a blast on his horn. I glanced in my rear-view mirror and saw him waving his fist because I hadn't jumped the intersection on a yellow light. I was in no mood to fight so I ignored him. Probably a good move, I thought, when he pulled out around me, squealed his tires and sped through the intersection still waving his fist. The only thing missing from the gentleman's truck was his gun rack.

I arrived home in record time for a Friday night. A mere fifty-five minutes. I could have made it in twenty if I'd used public transit but I couldn't give up my status symbol, my parking pass.

I parked my car at the back and dragged myself and my briefcase up the walk at the side of the house to the front. I lived on the third floor of an old house that had been converted into three apartments. I was dead tired as I walked up the front steps onto the porch and into the small lobby. I thought about having another cigarette before I tackled the stairs but decided I'd save that reward if I made it without coughing up a lung.

My apartment smelled stuffy and reeked of stale cigarette smoke. I dropped my jacket and briefcase in the front hall and headed into the living room to open some windows. I gave a nervous, sideways glance at the fishbowl to see if Snapper the Fourth was still alive. I hate facing death straight on and I wasn't up for any shocks. I was relieved to see he was swimming around as usual and fed him a few morsels of fish food. My luck was holding.

I grabbed an overflowing ashtray and dirty coffee cup off the desk and took them into the kitchen. No time like the present, I thought. I emptied the ashtray and started loading all the dirty coffee cups into the dishwasher. I tried to reach the window over the kitchen sink and found myself balancing on my stomach on the counter with my feet off the floor and one hand in the kitchen sink. I vowed to ask Santa Claus for about three more inches in height this Christmas.

I gave up my balancing act and hooked my foot around a small step stool beside the stove and dragged it over in front of the sink. I felt like the king in the castle standing on the top step of the stool and was able to unlatch the kitchen window and open it. I turned around and surveyed my domain and was disgusted to see dust bunnies on top of the refrigerator.

I decided to get out of my work clothes before I started on my manic cleaning routine and headed for the bedroom where I stripped off my clothes and peeled off my control top pantyhose. Now that's relief. The pain we go through to look good. After fumbling around in the pile of discarded clothes on the floor I found my sweatpants and an old shirt. Clothes were sorted into two piles, laundry and dry cleaning. I stripped the bed and added the sheets and pillowcases to the laundry pile. I was on a roll.

I considered myself lucky because I had a washer and dryer in my apartment. I loathe doing laundry and the chore became more hateful every time I had to schlep to the laundromat so a couple of years ago I made the plunge and bought an apartment size, stackable washer and dryer. Technology at its finest. A load of whites went in first and I grabbed the plastic dishpan that held all of my cleaning supplies and marched off to battle.

By the time I finished cleaning it was nine o'clock. I sat on the couch, lit a cigarette and looked around me. Beautiful. My stomach was calling and together we thought about dinner. My mind inventoried the food in the fridge but my stomach was yelling for pizza. I couldn't argue.

Tony's Pizzeria, in my opinion, was one of the best in Toronto. Alfredo answered the phone.

"Tony's Pizzeria," he said with a thick Italian accent.

"I'd like to speak to Tony," I said in a thick Irish brogue.

"Tony's not a-here, can I a-help you?" Alfredo replied.

"Hi Al, it's Kathleen." I dropped the phoney brogue. Tony had never existed but this was a game we played every time I called. Alfredo was Puerto Rican but had a great, just off the boat, Italian accent when it suited him.

"K-k-Katie, beautiful Katie, you're the only g-g-g-girl that I adore," he sang. I cut him off before he finished all three verses of the old wartime song.

"I'm hungry," I stated.

"The usual?" he asked.

"Oh yeah," I drawled and the saliva in my mouth started up as I thought about the sauce on the pizza, lightly spiced and the gooey cheese. "Just mushrooms and lots of cheese," I reminded him.

He sounded insulted that I had to remind him. "I know, I know," he said. He dropped his voice a little and said in his sexiest voice, "So when are you gonna let me take you out for a real meal?" This was another game we played.

I lowered my voice and whispered into the phone, "Ooh Alfredo, you name the time. Just let me know when your wife can line up a baby-sitter, or better yet, bring all the kids and your wife, and we'll make it a real party," I laughed.

"Pizza'll be there in about twenty minutes. Ciao baby."

I was chuckling as I hung up the phone. I headed to the kitchen to set the table and find my purse to pay the delivery boy. He arrived in about eighteen minutes and I tipped him generously.

I opened the top of the box and breathed in the aroma. I served myself a slice, put my napkin on my lap and dug in. Although I don't cook, I believe in the formality of dinner time so food prepared by someone else gets the same treatment in my house. I wolfed down two slices before I started to slow down.

After I ate, I curled up on the couch with a new book and covered myself with an old quilt. The breeze coming through the open French doors was chilly but I loved the crispness of the air. The apartment smelled clean and the breeze from outside was fresh. I was in heaven.

I studied the cover of the book. A woman with long, flowing auburn hair was locked in a passionate embrace with a man who looked like he could anchor the evening news on network TV. She was wearing a low cut, peasant-style blouse which exposed the tops of her breasts. I wish.

The book was a fast read and I skimmed through about three chapters before I stopped to light a cigarette. The story was similar to the dozens of other novels I had read - poor woman, rich man. They meet, they argue, they secretly pine for each other and eventually end up locking lips in a mad embrace at the end of a particularly nasty argument.

I thought about why I read these books. Always looking for my knight in shining armour and reading these books kind of kept the fantasy alive. Reading for me was pure escapism and I justified my habit by reminding myself I didn't drink or take drugs. Cigarettes and romance books. My two vices. Probably time to clean up my act.

I heaved myself off the couch and stood looking out the front windows to the street below. I was restless and had nagging feelings which I tried to pinpoint. I had frantically cleaned my apartment and ate my dinner like a stevedore. My planned and forced relaxation on the couch hadn't lasted long. As usual, I was avoiding things.

Evelyn's death hung over me. As trite as it sounded, it made me sad. Sad is an emotion that usually doesn't have any backbone and it's hard to define. My whole body started to ache with sadness, thinking about her. The more I thought about Ev, the more restless I became. I paced in the living room and ruined the nice look of the freshly vacuumed carpet. I couldn't understand her death. Why did she have to die? I had been avoiding thinking about her all day by keeping busy and now I didn't have anything to keep me occupied. The book bored me. I checked the TV Guide to see if there were any sports on the television and as usual, I came up empty. Friday night sitcoms and news shows. Forget it.

I phoned Danny. I hadn't talked to him since last night. The phone rang a couple of times before he answered.

"Hello." He sounded tired.

"Danny, it's Kathleen. How're things?"

"All right, I guess." The tone of his voice told me I would have to carry the conversation.

"Is there anything you need? How are your brother and sister?" I asked.

"They're fine. The neighbours have been in and out with food. There's nothing I need right now."

"Danny, when's the funeral? Have you set the time yet?"

"No, they're not releasing the body. The doctor said they have to do an autopsy to determine the cause of death."

I was surprised. "I thought she died from a reaction to nuts."

"When I spoke to the doctor this morning, he said the cause of death was undetermined so they had to do an autopsy. He said they're backed-up at the morgue so it could take a couple of days." He paused. "I just want to bury her." He started to cry softly.

I felt helpless and didn't know what to say. "It'll be okay Danny. Take it easy. Is there anything I can do? Is there anyone there with you?" I asked.

"Jonathan's here. Elaine left a while ago to go home. I'm all right Kate. I'll call you if I need anything. I gotta go."

I said good-bye to a dial tone.

CHAPTER
twelve

I thought I'd try my luck with Jay. See if he'd forgiven me.
"Yeah," he answered on the first ring.

"What telephone manners," I said. "How're you doing?"

"I'm fine thank you. And you?" he said like a five year old.

"Bored. Sad. Restless. I cleaned the apartment, ate dinner, tried to read for a while. Have you forgiven me yet?" I asked.

"For what?"

"Don't be a smart-ass Jay." I changed the subject. "What time did you get out of the office?"

"About seven. I headed for the hills when the yelling reached a fever pitch."

"Yeah? Who was yelling?"

"I don't know. It sounded like Oakes and Cox. I was working on that stock option report, trying to get it finished. I had a couple of questions for Rick but never got past his door. When I went to go in I could hear yelling in his office so I hightailed it out of there. They sounded busy."

"I'm surprised. I saw Oakes with his coat on when I left. What were they yelling about?"

"I didn't stop to listen Kate."

"Come on Jay. Didn't you put your ear up to the door?"

"Unlike you Kate, I believe in letting some people have their privacy. Besides, it was none of my business."

Ouch. "So Rick never got his report."

"Yes he did. I sent it to him on e-mail. Not that he'll read it but my ass is covered. There're still outstanding problems. I worked backwards and ended up using the stock option numbers you gave me from the last board meeting. There's no sense to why those numbers on the system were changed and I couldn't find any back-up for them. I'm sure it'll get sorted out when I talk to Rick about it. Why did Didrickson keep the originals of the two lists?"

"I'm not sure. And, he was anxious to see Oakes at the end of the day. Must have been something important for Harold to want to see Oakes. Maybe it was about the lists."

"Oh yeah, really Kate," Jay said sarcastically. "Didrickson is going to bother Oakes with a clerical error."

"Well, Mr. Smarty Pants, maybe Harold thought someone had been diddling with the numbers. Maybe he thought you had a fairy godmother too."

"Are you starting up again?" Jay's voice went up half an octave.

"Sorry. Really. Forget it. Listen, I talked to Danny. They haven't released Evelyn's body yet. He said they want to do an autopsy to determine the cause of death."

"It wasn't a reaction to nuts?" Jay asked.

"They're not sure." The sadness started to overwhelm me again. I slumped against the wall. "I gotta go Jay."

"Kate? You all right?" Jay asked quietly.

"Yeah, sure. I'll call you tomorrow." I could hear Jay calling my name as I hung up the phone but I ignored him and hung up anyway. I slid down the wall to a sitting position on the floor and hugged my knees and was suddenly so tired I couldn't move. The adrenaline had finally vacated the body. I had been up since five that morning.

The phone rang and I didn't answer. If I could just get up the energy to stand up and go to bed, I thought. I didn't even have enough fuel in me to crawl. The phone stopped ringing after five rings. My throat tightened up and I started to cry. Twice in two days. My crying was quiet at first and slowly changed to gasping sobs. I rolled on my side and hugged myself. I could feel the carpet beneath my cheek getting wet.

I stopped crying when the phone started to ring again. It seemed like I had been crying for a century but it must have been about two minutes. I ignored the phone and closed my eyes and fell asleep and dreamed that Jay was holding me. He was telling me it was okay, that he forgave me. He was stroking my hair and his arms felt good around me.

I opened my eyes and I was looking into Jay's. He was sitting on the floor in my hallway, holding me on his lap. His arms were around me and it felt good. My heart was in my throat the moment I realized I wasn't dreaming.

"Jesus Christ. You scared me Jay."

"Shut up Kate."

"How long have you been here?" I asked.

"Just a few minutes. I didn't mean to scare you."

I pushed his arms away and struggled to my feet. Jesus, I felt warm. Jay certainly throws off body heat, I thought. He got to his feet and leaned over and touched his nose to mine. "I was worried about you."

He was going to make me start crying again. "Do you want some coffee?" I asked, quickly changing the subject. I was great at changing the subject. "I'll make decaf," I pronounced as I hurried into the kitchen. I fussed about making coffee, feeling like a fourteen year old school girl. Calm yourself Kathleen. The man is like a brother. You've known him since you were six. I turned around to look at Jay who was leaning against the doorframe with this hands in the pockets of his jeans. He wasn't hard to look at. Jay was thirteen inches taller than me and had dark hair that hugged his head. His eyes were dark brown, almost black. His face was square and the most prominent feature was his nose. Not overly large, but noticeable because the slight bend in it where it looked like it had been broken and not properly re-set.

"If I remember correctly, I gave you a key to my apartment to check the fish when I was on vacation," I reminded him.

"I was worried about you. So sue me."

"Go and sit. I'll bring the coffee as soon as it's ready," I said. He shrugged his shoulders and turned around into the living room.

No doubt about it, I thought. The man was sweet. Very sweet. And you, Kathleen, are very vulnerable. You're feeling sad because of Evelyn's death, I lectured myself. Jay's a friend. A good friend. Good friends give you a shoulder to cry on. They even hold you to make you feel better. I was good at this. I was *very* convincing.

I held the two coffee cups in one hand and scooped up a couple of coasters from my desk before placing the cups on the coffee table. Holding two hot cups in one hand is no mean feat, but one of my many hidden talents I learned over the years serving coffee to executives.

Jay was sitting in the corner of the sofa with his long legs up on the coffee table. I sat at the other end of the couch and lit a cigarette. The silence was overwhelming.

"So. Another busy Friday night for you too?" I joked.

Jay put his feet on the floor and leaned over to take a sip of his coffee. He carefully put the cup on the coaster and looked over at me. He ran his hand through his hair a couple of times before he answered.

"Kathleen, do you have to joke about everything?" I noticed his use of my proper name. Things were getting serious.

"Jay, I save my humour for those close to me."

"You make a joke out of everything," he started.

I interrupted him before it became a lecture. "Listen Jay, if you're going to chew me out again for what I said in the office, about you having a fairy godmother, I already apologized."

Jay sighed. "Kate, this has nothing to do with that. What I'm getting at is that you can't have a serious conversation without turning it into a joke. Why is that?"

I thought about it and couldn't come up with an answer so I shrugged my shoulders. This was very reminiscent of getting a lecture from my mother.

This time Jay changed the subject. "I know you're sad about Ev. Do you want to talk about it?"

"Jay, did you take counselling classes at Western? I heard they have a new one called 'Death and the Helpless Friend'. No I don't want to talk about it. What's there to talk about? One of my best friends has died. Needlessly. Can you explain why?" I didn't give him time to answer. It was a rhetorical question and I was on a roll. "Why did she die? She wasn't old. She was healthy. She's gone and left her three kids and a grandchild. What's the sense of it all?" I looked at Jay. "She left me." My throat was tight and I couldn't swallow. There. I said it. Evelyn left me.

God, how does Danny feel, I thought. I don't want anyone to leave me again. I want my mommy. I'm 34 years old and I want my mommy. I reached over for my coffee cup and Jay grabbed my hand. He pulled me over to him and wrapped me in his arms.

"And people say you're tough," he said softly. I had a million smart retorts to that one but I didn't bother.

CHAPTER
thirteen

I woke up the next morning in my bed and I couldn't remember how I got there. Jay must have helped me, I thought. A peek under the duvet confirmed that I had my clothes on. The clock radio read seven thirty-six. I got up, took off my clothes and paddled into the bathroom to shower and brush my teeth. My mouth felt like the French Foreign Legion had marched through it, barefoot, after three months in the desert.

I dressed in jeans and a blouse, which I didn't tuck in. I put on some clean white gym socks and headed for the kitchen. The curtains above the sink were billowing straight out and I remembered that I hadn't closed any windows the night before. I pushed the step stool over in front of the sink and climbed up. I glanced at the top of the refrigerator and happily noted that the dust bunnies I had cleaned the night before hadn't reappeared. With my knees braced against the sink I leaned over and wrestled with the window.

I lit a cigarette while I waited for the coffee to drip through and wandered into the living room to retrieve the dirty coffee cups. The curtains in there were billowing too and it was cold. Jay's huddled body beneath the quilt on the sofa scared the life out of me.

"Christ," I cursed out loud. I hate being scared. I crossed the room to close the doors to the balcony and noticed something orange floating on the top of the fishbowl. Oh no, I thought. Not another one. I peeked in the fishbowl hoping it wasn't what I thought. Snapper the Fourth was doing the backstroke. I give up, I thought. I just fucking give up. I can't keep anything alive. Imagine what I'd do to a poor dog or cat if I had it long enough.

I picked up the fishbowl to head to the bathroom for the ceremonial burial. Jay was stirring on the couch. He must be frozen, I thought. I looked at his sleeping face and felt like I was intruding. There is definitely something very personal about observing someone in their sleep. I hurried out of the living room to do the dirty deed.

This time the ceremony was shorter. I intoned a few sombre words over the toilet bowl before wishing Snapper the Fourth farewell. "Bye, bye, big buddy," I finished off. I reached for the handle to flush and heard Jay cough behind me. The toilet flushed and I blushed at getting caught. He was leaning on the doorframe with his hands in pockets. The boy leaned a lot.

"Morning," I said.

"Morning to you too." He grinned. "I hope that was leftovers you were flushing." I held up the fishbowl. "Ah, Kate. Not another one. What's the Humane Society going to say?"

"Shut-up. I've given up. The goldfish of the world are safe. Kathleen Monahan will never own another one." I pushed past him into the hallway. "Clean towels are in the closet behind the door," I said over my shoulder.

I was on my second cup of coffee and third cigarette when Jay joined me. He helped himself to a mug in the cupboard over the coffee maker and sat at the table across from me. He pushed the ashtray to the side. He had the good grace, and good sense, not to comment on the number of butts in the ashtray.

"What time did I go to bed? I don't even remember going."

"You didn't go. I carried you and tucked you in." His grin this time had a bit of a leer to it.

"Hope you didn't strain your back," I said.

"Right, Kate. What are you? All of a hundred pounds, soaking wet? I carried you with one hand."

"Bless you my son. No, I'm not a hundred pounds. I wish. I'm a hundred and ten. Besides, it's rude to ask a lady her weight."

"What lady?" he joked.

"Well, was it good for you too?" I teased.

"Ooh. I almost needed a cigarette afterwards." We both laughed.

"What are you up to today?" I asked him.

"This and that. You?"

"Absolutely nothing. I cleaned the apartment last night and did the laundry. I only have to buy some groceries but that can wait until tomorrow."

"I think I'll do some of the same. I've got to go into the office tomorrow to finalize some reports for Cox. I'm going for a run this morning."

He finished his coffee in one gulp and stood up. He came around to my side of the table and squatted down beside me. I turned sideways in my chair and our eyes were level. It pissed me off that he got down to what he thought was my level because I was short. It was patronizing. I pushed my chair back from the table and stood up. He put his hands on his knees and pushed himself upright. Great. Now he was towering over me. I grabbed the step-stool and jumped up on it but was still about four inches shorter. I wasn't getting up on the counter.

"Will you cut it out?" Jay demanded. "I just wanted to say good-bye. God, you're irritating at times."

I put my hands on my hips. "Well. Good-bye. Have a good run. See you Monday." He took a step forward and stopped about three inches from me and leaned into my face. I was sure he was going to touch his nose to mine again but he didn't.

"Good-bye," he breathed into my face. And he kissed me. Very lightly. Very friendly. Almost brotherly. I was kidding myself. I blushed about four shades of red and purple and stepped down off the stool.

"Good-bye."

I was enjoying my Saturday afternoon, under the old quilt on my sofa racing through the novel I had started the night before. I was at a particularly hot and steamy part of the story when the phone rang. It was Didrickson telling me I was needed at the office to help the internal auditor on an urgent audit.

"What's an urgent audit? Did someone lose a bean?" When he didn't laugh, I realized he didn't even have a sense of humour on the weekends.

"She's auditing the stock option lists and needs your help pulling out back-up documentation."

"I'll be there in half an hour." I hung up the phone and finished the chapter I was reading while I leaned up against the wall beside the phone. I carefully marked my spot in the book and pulled on my windbreaker, grabbed my purse and headed downstairs to my car. The shit's hit the fan over the stock option lists, I thought. This should be interesting.

It proved to be a very long Saturday and ended up being a very long week. I didn't open my book for the next ten days.

CHAPTER
fourteen

The parking lot was surprisingly full when I arrived at the office. It never ceases to amaze me the number of people who actually *work* on a Saturday. Ninety percent of them were probably executives from our company who flee their homes to avoid their family duties. I've never seen them actually *working* on the few Saturdays I've been in the office. They seem to hang out and schmooze. And tell war stories.

I smiled at the security guard who stared back at me. He was wearing glasses that were so thick I think the bottoms were made from old Coke bottles. He looked old enough to have been a drummer boy in the civil war.

"How's it going?" I asked as I signed the security register. As he worked his lips into an answer I ran my finger down the sign-in ledger and noticed that Grace O'Grady had signed in at seven fifty-five a.m. I looked further down the list and saw that Didrickson had come and gone - in at eight-ten and out by nine fifty-five.

I held out my security pass with my picture on it so the old-timer could get a good look. It was turned upside down - I wanted to see if he was really on the ball.

"Fine, fine," he mumbled. The drool on the left side of his mouth was particularly attractive. I wondered if he had been taking personal grooming tips from Chris Oakes.

"13th floor please," I said. He stared back and I realized he must be deaf too. I tried to figure out how to hold up 13 fingers and gave up.

"13th floor," I shouted. He nodded and pushed a button on the console. He was asleep before I turned around.

The corridor had an eerie silence about it when I got off the elevator. Creepy. The reception area was dark and locked up tight so I turned down the hall to go in the back entrance. The smell of cigar smoke hit me as soon as I opened the door. Lovely, just lovely.

Chris Oakes was on the premises. Well, at least I'll be able to smoke with my door open. I made a mental note to check that there was a fire extinguisher handy. Chris had a habit of leaving burning cigars wherever he felt like it. He had once fallen asleep and started a fire in his bed in one of the poshest hotels in San Francisco. The cause, of course, was his cigar. He blamed the hotel. His ranting and raving in the lobby of the hotel almost made the front page of the newspaper. The hotel was very nice when they let us know that they didn't want him back. Ever.

I took a shortcut to my office so I could avoid executive row because the last person I wanted to see on my day off was Chris Oakes. I stripped off my windbreaker and tossed it on the guest chair and sat down in my chair. I swivelled around to turn on my computer and swivelled back to check my voice messages. I was getting dizzy. There were no notes on my desk from Didrickson with instructions or information so I figured he'd left me a voice message. The voice mail system told me I had two messages, both of which were hang ups. Love it, love it. Two less phone calls I had to return.

The only other place Harold would have left me anything was in his out-basket on his desk so I rummaged around in my desk for the keys to his office. The man was so paranoid about confidentiality he kept his office locked whenever he wasn't in. The cleaning staff were not allowed to clean his office in the evenings and the furniture in his office was always dusty. Every couple of days or so he would put his wastebasket out in the hall for the cleaners and every couple of months we'd have them in during the day to dust and vacuum.

One of my favourite jobs was shredding all his waste paper. I'd have to schlep the paper in boxes down to the photocopier room and stand in front of the shredder feeding it paper. The dust from the machine was incredible and typically, I would be wearing a black suit. I was waiting for the day that he asked me to eat the paper, rather than shred it to make sure it was properly disposed of. He caught me one day getting one of the secretaries to do the shredding and I almost lost my job. For his next birthday, I was going to buy him a personal Ollie North desktop shredder to save my lungs.

There was nothing of any importance in his out-basket so I locked his office and thought about where I might find Grace.

Grace O'Grady was our internal auditor and she was my hero.

Capital H. When I grew up, I wanted to be just like Grace. She was one of the smartest, toughest and funniest women I had ever met. Grace told it like it was and didn't care who she was telling it to. She had been hired out of retirement by the Chairman of our company's Audit Committee of the Board of Directors and she reported directly to him, and no-one else. Grace knew the dirt on everyone in the company and knew what closet every skeleton was in.

Her job was to make sure financial controls were followed, procedures were implemented, the i's were dotted and the t's were crossed. As a public company we had legal and financial obligations to our shareholders and Grace made sure we followed the rules. Her only disappointment was that the Chairman of the Audit Committee rarely acted on her recommendations. But she kept at it and took her job very seriously.

Grace was rarely seen around the head office because she was on the road most of the time visiting our regional offices and auditing their books and contracts. When she did make an appearance at our place, tongues started wagging and speculation on her presence was the main topic of discussion. She appeared for every board of directors meeting to make her reports but her presence today signalled to me that Didrickson needed her forensic abilities.

In the past Harold has asked for her assistance on some particularly sticky matters. Something sticky had obviously come up and that's why she was here. I couldn't wait to find out.

I stuck my head in a few of the offices to see where she had parked herself and was surprised to find her working at Ev's desk.

"Top of the mornin' to ya Irish," I said.

She looked up from the computer terminal. "And the rest of the day to you," she sang back. I stood in front of the desk.

"Harold said you needed my help."

"Sit down and I'll fill you in."

I sat on the edge of the guest chair. It didn't feel right to be in Ev's office and I felt myself getting a little edgy.

"I was sorry to hear about Evelyn. We're going to miss her. Can you let me know when the funeral is so I can make sure I'm around?"

"Sure. Nothing's been set yet but I'll let you know. Let's get a coffee and go down to my office. You can fill me in there."

She nodded and I knew she understood. Grace stood up and came around the front of the desk. She slung her arm over my shoulder and the two of us jammed our way through the door. She had on dungarees. Yes, dungarees. I know they went out of style in the fifties, but Grace still had an original pair. Dark blue jeans, wide legs, cuff rolled up three times. She was wearing a plaid, flannel shirt which was unbuttoned and showed a man's sleeveless undershirt underneath. What a fashion statement. A woman after my own heart. She probably wore white gym socks too. Grace had thick hair as white as snow and she wore it cropped short. I think she cut it herself.

She turned her head and smiled at me. "So, what's three miles long and has an IQ of thirty-seven?" she asked. The jokes were starting.

I smiled back. "I don't know."

"A St. Patrick's Day Parade." We both laughed. Grace was a lot like me and she laughed the hardest at her own jokes. She had toned the jokes down a bit to take into consideration people's feelings in the new millennium. Her only politically incorrect jokes now were aimed at her own heritage, the Irish.

We bumped into the kitchenette door and I let Grace go in first. "Age before beauty," I joked.

We caught up on old times while we waited for a fresh pot of coffee to brew. When I opened the fridge to get some cream for the coffee, I noticed there was still an awful lot of leftover food in the fridge from the Thursday party. I plugged my nose in disgust.

"Disgusting," I said. "Why doesn't anyone ever clean this fridge out?" I felt sorry for the person who had to do it. It wasn't so long ago that it had been one of my jobs but now that I was among the high and mighty, I felt the task was below me. I slammed the door and handed Grace the cream.

"Still smoking?" Grace asked me.

"Hardly at all," I replied and started craving a cigarette. "Have you started up again?" Grace was forever quitting and starting. She said the reason she quit was to save money so she only smoked OP's. Other people's.

"I quit last week. But I'll have one of yours. Come on." We headed back to my office.

When we were settled in my office puffing away, I popped the question.

"So. What's the dirt? What's going on?"

Grace took her feet off my desk, put her cigarette out and put on her serious face. The joking time was over. Down to business.

"There's a slight problem with the stock option system. As you know, because Harold told me you pointed it out, the information on Evelyn's system doesn't jive with the numbers that were approved by the board."

"Right," I agreed. "Evelyn obviously input the wrong information. You know how these guys work. Nothing's final. They fuck around with the numbers so much I'm surprised anything in Ev's system is right."

"Tell me what the procedure is. What information do you give Ev?" she asked.

"Okay. After a board meeting, Didrickson gives me the lists of numbers that have been approved."

Grace interrupted me. "Bear with me here. Where does Harold get the lists?"

"Rick Cox has responsibility for producing the recommendations to the board. When he hands out the papers at the board meetings to the directors, those are the numbers they approve."

"What do the lists usually contain?" Grace asked.

"They have the names, the number of options to be granted, the exercise date and the expiry date." I turned around to open my file cabinet. "I'll show you what they look like."

"Yeah, I know what they look like. Harold gave me the copies you gave him."

I shut the file drawer.

"Grace, I'm not sure how much you know or how much detail you want," I said.

"I'm just trying to get in my mind a step by step procedure. So, Rick Cox presents the numbers and board approves them. Then what?" she asked. I wondered if she had asked Harold these questions.

Before I could answer, Grace said, "I've asked Harold, I'm just checking for your understanding of the process." Jesus, she was scary. She could read my mind. I better not think too much about those dungarees.

"Then what? Um, after the board meeting Harold gives me the approved list with his initials on it. If it's initialled, it's the official list, as far as I'm concerned."

Grace thought for a moment. "How soon after the board meeting does he give you the list?"

"Depends. If the meetings are held out of town, he might give me the lists at the meeting because I end up carrying all the papers back to Toronto. If the meetings are held here, I usually get the list the next day or so when he does the minutes."

"What do you do with the lists?" she asked me.

"A couple of things. I'll make a copy and give it to Ev so she can enter the information in the system. I make a copy for myself because I have to get stock exchange approval for all options granted and I use it as my working copy. The original I keep on the file for the specific board meeting."

"In your experience, did Ev enter the information on the system in a timely manner?"

Whoa. In my experience. Grace was starting to sound like a prosecuting attorney.

"In my experience," I mimicked her, "Ev did her work as fast as you could give it to her."

"Listen Grace," I continued. "I'm sure there's a reasonable explanation for what's happened here. If we could get into Ev's paper files, I'm sure we'd find that the information on the system matches up to some paper. Ev just got a wrong list. One that Rick had created and then changed his mind."

"Kathleen, we opened Ev's files this morning. There's no paper back-up for the information on the system."

"So her filing abilities were like mine. Non-existent," I stated. "Big deal."

"Her files appear to be immaculate. She notes on each list the date and time she's entered the information. Her last paper back up is the same one you have on file."

I digested this little tidbit and wondered how much more Grace was going to share with me.

"So? What happened?" I asked and waited to see if she'd answer. There were a lot of things that Grace didn't share with me and rightly so. I usually figured it out though but I wondered if she'd help me along this time.

"The computer log shows that those correct entries were made the day after the last board meeting," she blurted out.

"And?"

"And the computer log shows that the more recent entries making the changes were made on the night Ev died."

Wow, I was impressed. Our computer system had a log? And it had information? Technology at its finest. But I started to get indigestion as I digested this tidbit.

"Is our computer log smart enough to show who made the entries?" I asked. I was treading gingerly here.

"Yes," she said slowly.

"Are you going to share that with me?" I asked.

"No. Sorry. I have to finish my investigation. Can you grab all your files relating to stock option grants and bring them down to Ev's office? I'd like to compare your lists to the ones in Evelyn's files. I think we should do a complete check."

Yuck, I thought. One of my favourite things, going through files. Especially my files which were always in a mess. I think I'd rather clip my nails in the Cuisinart than go through files.

"Sure," I said. "Give me a few minutes, I'll meet you down there." Grace stood up and grabbed another cigarette from the pack on the desk before making her exit.

"This should be fun," she said and grinned. Sadist, I thought.

CHAPTER
fifteen

The next couple of hours were very painful. Painful in the sense that Grace, thorough by nature and career choice, showed her true colours about "checking" my files against Ev's. She had her auditor's hat on and was all business. Because my files contain a jumble of papers in no particular order we decided to use Ev's as the starting point.

Evelyn's files were neat and orderly with all the papers ordered by date with the most recent information on top. All documents in the files were neatly punched with two holes in the top of each page and secured in the file with metal clips. I never believed in using those metal clips because I considered them a hazard. When a clip caught you under the fingernail and gouged out a hunk of skin, your files ended up with blood all over the papers. Not a pretty sight.

Grace was methodically taking each sheet of information from Evelyn's files and matching it to one in mine. This was time consuming because I had to rifle through at least three inches of paper each time to find the matching sheet. Grace would then check the computer system to see if the information was the same. A simple three-step process but because of the shape of my files it was taking too long. And it was embarrassing. Thankfully Grace didn't comment.

By six-thirty Grace was satisfied that the process I had described could be proven. I got the final numbers from Didrickson, gave them to Ev, and she entered it in the system. Easy. Grace was also satisfied that all stock option grants that had been approved by the board of directors over the last three years were safely entered in the computer.

"Good, good," Grace was mumbling to herself. She was scrolling through the information on the computer on a final check.

"We're finished?" I asked. She kept her attention on the computer screen and nodded. I lit a cigarette and took a deep drag. I was leaning back in my chair stretching my neck when I heard a light tapping on the door behind me. I turned around and Ray was standing there with a bunch of papers in his hands.

"Raymond," I said. "To what do we owe this pleasure? Good to see you up and about at this time of day."

"Ha ha," he deadpanned. "I've been up since eight when Grace called me. All these early morning wake-up calls are ruining my beauty sleep."

"Ah, the important life of a system administrator. Doesn't it feel good to be needed?" I joked.

"Yeah, just great. At least the system wasn't down this morning," he said.

I looked over at Grace who was still staring at the computer screen. "Grace," I said to get her attention. Boy, could she focus. She took a couple of more seconds and then looked up.

"You've got that information for me?" she asked Ray.

"All right here," he said as he passed her the papers. I held out my hand to take the papers but he passed them directly to Grace. Damn.

Grace started flipping through the sheets of paper which were stapled in the corner. "Educate me," she said. "What is all this?"

Ray walked around to the other side of the desk and I made myself small in the chair. After the last couple of painful hours I felt I deserved some compensation. If I sat here quietly I might be lucky enough to pick up some information.

Grace ignored me and started firing questions at Ray.

"This indicates what?" she asked and pointed to a line of text on the page. I thought about leaning forward and trying my reading upside-down trick but thought better of it. I had to keep myself invisible.

"That's the user i.d.," Ray said. "The numbers beside it indicate the date and time the user was on the system and the line underneath shows how long their session lasted."

"What's this?" Grace asked.

Ray studied the information beside Grace's finger on the piece of paper. "That shows which part of the system the user was logged onto."

"For example?" Grace asked.

"For example, if the user was using the accounting part of the system or the employee information system, these numbers indicate that," Ray said. "So, this information shows Ev was logged onto the computer, the date and time, and here it shows that she was using the stock option system."

"How far back does this information go?" she asked.

"The current system keeps it for a year. We have information stored off site for all the previous years."

"So you can tell every time a person uses the system?" Grace asked Ray.

"Of course. There's all sorts of information in the background that's transparent to the user. If I needed to, I could find out exactly what keys they punched while they used the computer."

"Good. That's what I needed to know. You told me this morning on the phone that the system showed that Rick Cox was on the system on Thursday night. Show me where the log confirms that."

Ooh. So the culprit was Rick Cox. I didn't know what to make of this little tidbit. First of all, I thought, Rick Cox using a computer was totally unbelievable. Out of the question. We may be a high tech company, but none of our executives were users. Well, maybe they used scotch but they certainly didn't use computers. In fact, one of the biggest laughs we had was when Chris Oakes was interviewed for the Globe & Mail business section and the picture that went along with the story showed him sitting in front of his computer, supposedly working away. The only keys he punched were on his telephone to use voice mail. Oakes could talk good computer. Cox on the other hand was a total technophobe. He had respect for computers because they meant money and money was his business. But to actually use a computer was beneath him. And probably rightly so. Unless you were a secretary or a finance type, using computers to generate information or gather information was below an executive. They had people to do that for them. Rick Cox using our internal computer system was totally unbelievable. He would have a user i.d. because everyone in the company did. But Rick actually logging on and creating or generating information? No way. He'd call someone at home and get them out of bed before he did that. I wonder if Grace understood this.

"Now explain to me levels of access," Grace demanded. "Who exactly has access to the different systems?"

"Select people are identified as users and depending on their job descriptions or responsibilities, they have access to different levels. For the stock option system, there are three people who are users. That means those three are the only ones who can input information, change information and gather reports," Ray said.

"And the three users are? You mentioned Rick Cox and Ev. Who's the third?" Grace asked.

"Jay Harmon."

"Jay. Oh yeah. He's one of the management trainees. He's working for Cox now, isn't he?" Grace looked over at me for confirmation. At least she knew I was still sitting there. I nodded rather than answer out loud. Better not to break her concentration.

"Show me some instances of Jay's usage of the system," she said to Ray.

He pointed to the first entry on the top page. "Here," he said. "Jay was the last person to log into the stock option system. See," he ran his finger across the page, "that's his user i.d., this shows the date and time he was on the system, this number here shows he generated a report. I don't know what the report was, I'll have to check."

"God. This is like learning a new language," Grace laughed. "What's this t.i.d.?"

"Terminal identification. That shows which computer the user was logged on to," Ray said.

Grace was now really intent on the information. She was a quick study and was flipping the pages. Ray backed up and sat on the credenza behind Ev's desk. We were both quiet while Grace did her reading. I glanced at some of the pages as they flipped by and all I could see was a jumble of letters and numbers. She turned back to the first page of the document and ran her finger down the page.

"There. That's the entry. Right?" she said.

Ray slid off the credenza and looked over her shoulder.

"Yup," was all he said.

"Translate for me," she demanded.

"User i.d. is Rick Cox's. He logged on at eight-nineteen p.m. He was on the system for about three minutes. This number indicates he was in the stock option system. The number beside it indicates what part, or sub-menu of the stock option system, but I'll have to check what that is. And the terminal i.d. says he was logged on to this computer. Ev's." He rattled off the information like he was reading a Dr. Seuss rhyme.

"Okay. And the two entries above it are Jay Harmon's?" Grace asked.

"Right. Both entries are almost identical. User i.d. is Jay Harmon's. Date and time. Stock option system. I'll have to check what part of the system. And the terminal i.d. is his own computer," Ray fired off.

"How do you know all the terminal i.d.'s?" Grace asked.

"I know all the terminal i.d.'s and all the user i.d.'s. Can't remember a phone number but I know all my users." Ray grinned.

"One last question Ray. How many people know that you can access this information? Do the users know that their usage is tracked and records are kept?"

Ray looked at me. "The technical types in this company would certainly know. They design these systems. The users though, I don't know. Kate, were you aware of this?" he asked me.

"Hell no. I suppose if I thought about it, it makes sense. But I just use the system. I don't know how it works."

Ray said to Grace, "And that's probably typical of everyone except the techies. People love having computers and using them but don't understand the guts of them."

"Well thank you for the lesson. I'll keep these records," she said. "I don't think there's anything else right now. Ray, go on home and if I need you I'll call you."

"You're welcome," he replied. "I'm at your service."

After he left Grace looked up at me across the desk.

"Well, I suppose you've figured it all out?" she said.

"Basically. Rick Cox logged on to the system and made the changes to his stock options and a couple of other people's on the night Ev died. What time does the log say he did the dirty deed?" I asked.

Grace looked at the sheet. "Eight-nineteen," she said. "Why?"

"No reason," I said and stood up. I needed to think. Something wasn't right here but I wasn't going to share my thoughts with Grace. Yet.

"Anything else?" I asked her.

"Not from you. Thanks so much. Your files were a great help," she said.

"Yeah right," I said. I gathered up all my stuff and headed for the door.

"Kathleen," Grace said. I stopped and turned around.

"I'll have to ask you to keep this information to yourself. What's happened here is very serious and the fallout is going to be messy."

"I know," I said. "Mum's the word."

CHAPTER
sixteen

Something was wrong and I couldn't pinpoint it. It was easy to see the mess with Rick Cox. That was obvious. But I had niggling thoughts. I thought about shaking my head to get my jumbled thoughts in order but knew I'd only make myself dizzy. I barrelled around the corner to head down the hall to my office and ran smack into Chris Oakes.

Ooof, was the only sound I made. I had been holding all my files against my chest with my arms wrapped around them and my head was down. The impact of running into him pushed the files into my chest and I now knew what a body check in hockey felt like. The files dropped at my feet and I took a step backwards to get my breath.

I looked up at Oakes and said "Sorry" and immediately wished I hadn't said it. Why should I apologize? The asshole should have been watching where he was going. And you Kathleen, should have been watching where you were going, my internal Jiminy Cricket said to me.

I bent over to scoop up my files.

Oakes said, "Call Vanessa and tell her to check her voice mail."

I stood up.

"I'm fine Chris. And you?" Jesus Christ, whatever happened to social niceties?

"Uh, uh, fine." The man was a master conversationalist. Inspirational. "Sorry about the files," he said. Now we were getting somewhere. I decided to forgive him.

"No problem. What's that about Vanessa?" I asked.

"Call her and tell her to check her voice mail," he repeated.

"Yeah, I got that part. Have you tried to reach her?" I asked.

"She's not answering," he pouted.

Is it any wonder, I thought. The man hounds her twenty-four

hours a day, seven days a week. She doesn't answer her phone on the weekends because of it.

"I'm sure she's checking her voice messages Chris. She always does," I pointed out. "Do you need something?" I asked reluctantly. I could be letting myself in for some work here, and immediately regretted offering my services.

Chris latched on right away. "I can't find something in her office," he whined. As if he'd ever been in her office. "I'm looking for a couple of memos I got last week."

"Let me put these files back in my office and I'll take a look for you. Which ones do you need?" I asked. I sighed. You stupid idiot, Kathleen. I mentally slapped myself for offering to help. I was never going to get back to my book. Oakes followed along beside me to my office. I glanced up at him as we walked and saw traces of shaving cream on his right ear lobe. Yuck. To think he'd gone through a whole day and hadn't noticed a hunk of dried something or other hanging off his ear. Double yuck!

"Some of the regional vice presidents sent me memos," he said. I said nothing. The regional vp's sent him memos every day. He'd better be a little more specific, I thought, or he's going to get about six inches of paper dropped on his desk. He obviously thought I was a mind reader because he offered no other information.

"Chris," I finally said. We were stopped outside the door to my office. "More specifics. Which memos?" I demanded.

"Vanessa knows," he stated. And he turned around and continued down the hall towards his office.

Great, I thought. Just what I need. A treasure hunt. I lobbed a mental grenade at his back and savoured the thought of him going up in smoke. I dropped the files on my desk in a heap and headed to Vee's office. As usual, her desk was neat as a pin and there wasn't a piece of paper in sight. I knew everything would be locked up because she took the confidentiality factor very seriously. I lifted the vase on the back credenza which was filled with a beautiful silk flower arrangement and found the key to her filing cabinet underneath. Confidentiality, yes. Security, so-so. I had no idea where to begin and I knew I'd have to call her to find anything.

I dialled her cellular phone number which a few select people had. The company supplied the phone but the number was secret so Oakes couldn't reach her. He was so thick he never thought to ask her for that number.

She answered on the third ring.

"Hello," she said.

"Hi, it's Kate. Enjoying your Saturday?" I asked.

"Yeah, it's great. Ashley's out at friend's for a sleep-over and I'm just veggin' out." Ashley was her daughter.

"Checked your voice mail lately?"

"No, and I don't plan to until tomorrow. Why?" she asked.

"I'm at the office. Oakes needs some memos and he's being very vague as usual. I need some help finding them."

"What the hell are you doing at the office?" she asked. "Catching up on your piling?" she joked. Everyone calls my filing, my piling. Because before it became a file, it was a pile.

"No, I thought I'd save that for you," I teased. "You haven't been that busy lately, so you can help me out." We both laughed. "I'm in your office," I continued. "He's looking for some memos from the regional vp's. That's all he said."

"He asked you to get them?" She sounded surprised.

"Yeah. Why? What's the big deal?"

Vee paused for a moment. "I'm just surprised. The memos are pretty sensitive." I was amazed. She obviously knew exactly what Oakes wanted.

"Well, he did say he's been trying to call you. I'm his last resort. So, you're holding out on me," I said. "What's in the memos?"

"I would've let you know eventually," she said. Vee and I share everything related to work. Besides giving us something to talk about, we keep each other informed.

Vee continued. "The memos he's looking for are in the third drawer of the filing cabinet, in a file marked Roosters."

"You're sure those are the ones he wants?" I didn't want this treasure hunt going on forever. I held the handset of the phone between my cheek and shoulder and unlocked the file cabinet as we talked. The file marked Roosters was near the back of the third drawer.

"Got it," I said and shoved the drawer shut with my foot. "I'll call you back if he needs anything else. I won't tell him I talked to you. The man is going to think I'm amazing because I found the file," I half bragged.

"Oh yeah. You'll get a big raise. Get serious Kate," she said.

"I know, I know. Just joking," I laughed into the phone. "I'm going to give him a test and see if he remembers my name twice in one day. Talk to you later." I hung up the phone and opened the file to take a quick glance and make sure there were memos in it from the regional vp's. There were exactly three sheets of paper in the file. Three separate memos from three different vice presidents. The top third of each sheet looked the same because the memos had been created on our standard company memo paper. To, from, date, subject. Standard stuff. The subject line on each memo said Rick Cox.

Interesting, I thought. Very interesting. Rick Cox's name was coming up at every turn. I quickly read each memo. The first one was what I thought a police report would read like: dates, times, names, places. The second and third memos were in a more narrative style but still covered dates, times, names and places. I slapped the file folder shut and headed into Oakes' office.

He was barely visible through the cigar smoke where he was sitting at a very large oval table in the center of the room. Oakes didn't have a desk. He worked at a table. I crossed the floor and my feet sunk ever so slightly into the plush carpet. His office was the size of a school gym but was sparsely furnished because he could never make up his mind on furnishings. He would order furniture and reject it as soon as it came in the door.

He was on the phone. I placed the file folder in front of him and turned around to leave the room. He called after me. "Kate."

Be still my heart, I thought. He remembered my name. I turned around and he went back to talking on the phone. I was near the door and couldn't make out what he was saying so I waited until he finally hung up.

"I need you to poll the directors and call a board meeting," he said.

Fuck, fuck, fuck, I chanted under my breath. Vee, you owe me one, I thought.

"There's a board meeting called for the end of the week," I reminded him.

"I know. I want one tonight," he said.

"Okay." This wasn't unusual. Chris called board meetings on a whim. The board members loved it. More directors' fees. Every time there was a meeting they got paid big bucks. If the meetings lasted all day or half an hour, they got paid for it.

"Subject matter?" I asked. The board members like to know in advance exactly what they're going to be required to rubber stamp.

He ignored me. "I only want the outside directors and Grace on the call. Don't tell Didrickson," he ordered. "There won't be any minutes taken." Great, I thought. Put me on the spot. When Harold finds out I knew about this, he's going to be extremely pissed with me.

Oakes looked at his $14,000 Rolex. "Set it up for an hour from now. Around eight-thirty." He picked up his phone and started dialling furiously. Yes, your majesty. Right away, your royal highness. I curtsied, but of course, he didn't see me. He was making love to his phone. I turned around and hurried back to my office. My mind was in overload with all the information I was taking in and I needed time to sort it out.

In the whole mess, Rick Cox's name came up at every turn. Rick Cox and the stock options. Rick Cox and the memos from the regional vp's. A board meeting with only outside directors. That meant Rick Cox was not to be invited. As an employee of the company he was considered an inside director. Outside directors were the big guns we put on the board to give us a good name. Besides Cox and Oakes, the only other two inside directors were senior members of our management team. Senior puppets. And both of those puppets had sent Oakes memos which were on the file called Roosters.

What the hell did Roosters mean, I thought. I couldn't remember seeing any reference to Roosters in the memos I had read. And then I got it. Very good, Vee. Cox, roosters. Cocks and roosters. Things were about to take an interesting turn.

CHAPTER
seventeen

I opened the top drawer of my desk and pulled out the list of directors. The sheet of paper had each director's name and beside the name were their various telephone numbers. Some of them had office, cellular, home, country home, ski chalet and hunting lodge telephone numbers. Beside two directors' names, in pencil, was the phone number of their current mistress. Below the director's information was their secretary's name and phone numbers. Oops. Executive Assistants, excuse me. It was very passé and uncouth to call someone a secretary nowadays. Everyone was an executive assistant. A junior clerk typist was an executive secretary. And most of them didn't even work for executives. Up until the time I became a full fledged paralegal, I called a spade a spade and referred to myself as a secretary.

I started at the top of the list. It was seven-thirty on a Saturday night and I had to track down six people. I decided to put their secretaries to work. They should all know if their bosses were available on a Saturday night.

Bill Frankford's secretary, Jessica, was the first on my list. Bill was a paper baron. At least that's the way Oakes described him when he was bragging about our directors.

"Hello," a voice answered.

"Jessica?" I asked.

"That you Kate?" she replied.

"Yeah. Hi. Sorry to bother you. Chris needs to get in touch with Bill. Any idea where he is? I thought I'd start with you before I tried his numbers."

"He's out at some social function and I don't know if he's got his cell phone with him. Want me to try him?" she offered.

"Please. Let him know Chris wants a board meeting at eight-thirty tonight. By phone. Call me back. If you get my voice mail leave me a message."

"All right. So they're keeping you hopping on a Saturday night, aren't they? Where's Vanessa?" she asked.

"I got roped into it because I was in the office. She's at home enjoying some peace and quiet," I said. I had to get a move on here to get in contact with everyone else, so I ended the conversation quickly.

I grabbed my Hilroy notebook that contained my doodlings and notes from each day and turned to a fresh page where I wrote down Bill's name and marked beside it, l/m. Left message. Oakes would no doubt want a status report within the next fifteen seconds and I'd have to let him know the situation with each person. If I heard back that Bill was able to attend the meeting, I'd scratch out the l/m and write okay.

I had the same luck with the next four secretaries I talked to. They were all at home and would get in touch with their bosses. Whit Williams' secretary didn't answer her home phone number in Dallas, so I called his house directly. Sue-Ellen, his wife, answered on the fifth ring. She sounded out of breath.

"Sue-Ellen, it's Kathleen Monahan at TechniGroup. How are you?" I started.

"Kathleen," she drawled. "How nice to hear from you." What a classy broad. I had probably interrupted her Saturday evening and she didn't act the least bit put out.

"Sorry to bother you Sue-Ellen. Is Mr. Williams in?" I asked. I used the Mr. because with Sue-Ellen it seemed right to be formal.

"Certainly Kathleen. Hold on just a moment." There was a slight knock as she laid the phone down and I could hear her calling his name. Whitney Williams was an oil baron. We had lots of barons on our board. He insisted that everyone call him Whit. I waited a few minutes and he finally came on the phone.

"Kate," he bellowed. "How's my favourite girl?"

"I'm just fine, Mr. Williams. How're things in Dallas?"

"Glorious, just glorious. I've got my grand-kiddies here for the weekend and they were just teaching me how to use the computer. I'm not sure I've got the hang of it yet, though," he said with a chuckle. The man was a charmer and I liked him.

"Sorry to interrupt your computer lesson. Chris asked me to poll the directors to find out their availability for a board meeting. Tonight. In about an hour," I said.

"Fine, fine. Is there a number to call in to or will you call me?" he asked.

"We'll call you," I said.

"What's the meeting about? Don't we have one set up for later in the week?"

"Chris didn't say," I said.

"Alright. Call me back," he said.

The red light on my phone was flashing indicating messages. Before I checked them I wrote down Whit's name and okay beside it in my notebook. All six names were there now and I dialled my voice mail. Two confirmations and I scratched out l/m beside their names and marked okay. I looked at my watch and it was seven forty-five. Not bad for fifteen minutes. Three okay's and three to go. My phone rang. It was Jessica.

"Hi Kate. Listen, Bill's at a black-tie function at the Four Seasons. He said he can sneak out and you can patch him in through his cell phone. He wasn't impressed that I called him in the middle of his shrimp cocktail," she giggled.

"Well, we can save him a few calories. I'll probably call him about the time they're serving the baked Alaska," I responded. I confirmed his cell phone number and marked okay beside his name.

While I waited for the other two secretaries to call me back I lit a cigarette and thought about everything. Rick Cox was in deep shit. And I think I knew what the board meeting was going to be about. Oakes was obviously about to make a power play and Cox wouldn't be around to defend himself. Couple of babies, I thought. Oakes obviously knew about Grace's investigation because he wanted her on the call for the meeting. And the most disturbing factor was the contents of those three memos.

The three regional vice presidents had sent memos detailing incidents involving Cox. One incident reported was on the west coast in a client meeting. The client was upset about the progress on their contract and Cox had chewed out our people in front of the client. Chewed out is probably mild. The memo said he was a raving lunatic and had embarrassed the company. Nothing about Cox embarrassing himself. I believed this story. Cox didn't give a shit who he chewed out. His ranting and raving put professional wrestlers to shame.

The second memo was about Cox ordering the controller of our international division to falsely report revenue. I didn't understand the mechanics of it but Cox was being accused of fraud. This story I didn't believe. He may be a lunatic but I had trouble believing he would do anything criminal. Most of his ranting and raving was because he was a perfectionist, and the fact that he believed the people around him didn't live up to his standards.

The third memo was just as bad as the others. It was from a female vice president who accused Cox of sexual harassment. She ended the memo threatening to charge Cox with sexual assault, and I didn't know what to think about this one. The harassment accusation I could understand. Harassment takes many forms and verbal abuse is one form as far as I was concerned. I could understand it if she'd accused him of verbal harassment. The sexual side, I wasn't so sure. Assault? Had I ever seen him get physical?

Regardless, Cox was history. Whether these stories were true was besides the point. Oakes had managed to get his people to write these memos and assuming that they were willing to confirm everything if asked, Cox was toast. Coupled with the stock option fiasco, Cox was *finito*. History. Oakes was victorious. Sure glad I'm not working for him, I thought selfishly. When he leaves, so does his secretary. I wondered if it was too soon to ask the office manager for his reserved parking spot.

I heard from the other two board members' secretaries in the next five minutes. It was five to eight when I headed back down the hall to Oakes' office to give him an update. I could have called him but I knew he wouldn't answer his phone. He never talks to a person, voice to voice, unless he initiates the call. His door was shut so I knocked before I opened the door. Grace was sitting across from him at the table and they both looked up when I came in.

"I've contacted the outside directors and everyone's on board for a call at eight-thirty," I said.

"Get everyone on the line," he replied. He started to speak again to Grace and I interrupted him. "Do me a favour then. When your phone rings at eight-thirty pick it up," I said. "If I have to get everyone on the phone I'll have to do it from reception. My phone only has the capability to patch in five others. I need to use the switchboard and I don't want to be running back here to make sure you pick up." He wasn't listening.

"I'll be sure to answer," Grace said. "Thanks Kathleen." It was a dismissal.

My stomach was grumbling and I knew there wasn't enough time to go out and get something to eat before I had to make the call. I headed for the kitchen and thought about eating some leftovers in the fridge but my stomach turned at the thought. Ptomaine poisoning was not on my agenda for the weekend.

I settled for a coffee with sugar to stave off the headache I felt coming on. I had another 20 minutes to kill so I grabbed my cigarettes off my desk and headed for the reception to familiarize myself with the switchboard. It'd been a long time since I used the system and I wanted to make sure I knew what I was doing. If I cut one person off on this call, Oakes would consider it grounds for firing me. I needed the job.

CHAPTER
eighteen

I picked up the phone and dialled Arthur Graves first because he was the least pushy of the directors and wouldn't mind being the first on the call and waiting for me to patch in the others. He answered on the first ring and I asked him to hold while I went to work. I was successful getting the next two and then ran into two busy numbers so I thought I might as well get Grace and Oakes on the phone and they could all chat while I got the other three. I dialled Chris' extension number and Grace answered. Her voice sounded hollow so I knew they were on the speaker phone.

I punched a button. "Mr. Oakes, I've got Mr. Graves, Mr. Frankford and Mr. Williams. Go ahead. I'll try the other numbers now," I said into the phone.

I was able to get two more directors and waited for a break in the conversation going on before I announced them and added them to the call. The last number kept giving me a busy signal and after about ten tries I wondered if I should go on the call and tell Oakes I was having trouble reaching the last director, but he'd probably bite my face off for interrupting. Jesus, this was pissing me off. The guy knew the call was scheduled for eight-thirty, I thought to myself. I tried one more time before having to admit defeat to Oakes, and the phone on the other end finally rang.

"Larry Everly," the voice barked. Ooh, what a charmer. Larry was an investment banker and he never let anyone forget it. He acted as if his participation on our board of directors was the single-most irritating factor in his life. He was impatient and pushy.

I sugar-coated my voice and said, "Mr. Everly, please hold for the conference call." I hit the button on the console to patch him through and waited for a break in the conversation to announce him but the pace of the conversation I overheard made it difficult to cut in.

Before I could announce Larry, he did it himself. "Chris, Larry here," he cut in. "What's up?"

"Well, we've got a serious situation here with Rick Cox," Oakes replied.

"I take it he's not on this call," Larry said.

"No he's not. There's just outside directors and myself," Chris continued. "I've filled in the other directors on the situation and I don't think we have any recourse but to fire Rick."

I realized with a start that I was eavesdropping and thought about hanging up. To hell with them. They don't pay me enough, so I considered this a bonus. I continued to listen.

"What'll that do to the stock price?" Larry asked. My, my, another one with a heart. No one was allowed to express a view on the stock price without bowing to Larry first. He was Mr. Dow Jones. Because it was a rhetorical question, Larry continued. "I'll tell you what it'll do to the stock price. It won't be pretty. And we can't afford any more dips in the price. The stock closed down a buck on Friday. Overall for the week, it was down one and seven-eighths." That was a dollar and eighty-seven and a half cents. I wasn't just another pretty face.

Larry continued. "If it goes down much more it's going to fuck the deal we're working on."

Whit Williams interrupted. "What deal's that, Larry?" he drawled.

Oakes' turn to interrupt. "I'll call you each individually and fill you in. I had a meeting with Jack Vincent this week. About the stock though, I don't think this'll have an adverse affect."

"Who're you kidding Chris?" Larry Everly demanded. "When a company fires its chief financial officer, it *affects* the stock price. When a company fires its chief operating officer, it *affects* the stock price. Rick is both chief financial officer and chief operating officer." He had yelled for emphasis when he said *affects*. I moved the receiver away from my ear.

Larry continued. "If you remember correctly Chris, the analysts like it when a company has a chief financial officer. It gives them a warm and fuzzy feeling," he said sarcastically. "The analysts are not going to feel warm and fuzzy if we fire Rick Cox."

"Well, then," Whit said. "We'll just have to get him to resign."

I was amazed that Larry Everly hadn't even asked what had gone wrong. But I knew that he and Chris Oakes were on the phone many times during the day and Vee and I sometimes wondered who in fact was running this company. Chris had probably filled Larry in before the conference call.

Larry must have read my mind because he demanded, "What happened anyway?" I almost laughed out loud and quickly caught myself. Cutting someone off a call would be nothing compared to getting caught eavesdropping on a board of directors meeting. Oakes would definitely have grounds to fire me. I had sat in on several meetings before but in those instances I had been invited to take minutes in Didrickson's absence. This was a *little* different.

"A few things. You know this has been building up for the past while," Oakes said in response to Larry's question. "The straw that broke the camel's back was the discovery today that he fiddled with the stock option numbers and granted himself a whole bunch more."

"He *what*?" Larry asked incredulously. "How can anyone be so stupid? Have you got proof of this?"

It was Grace's turn to speak. "Hi Larry. Grace O'Grady here. Yes, we've got proof. I've been in the office all of today going over things and my investigation points to Rick being responsible. In fact, our computer logs prove he did it." She sounded a little depressed as she reported this. She was certainly not flying high like Oakes and I could tell Grace was very disappointed in Rick.

"What else?" Larry demanded.

"We've got an accusation of fraud and a sexual harassment claim," Oakes answered.

"Sure he didn't murder the Pope as well?" Whit Williams asked.

"This all happened today?" Arthur Graves asked. I was impressed because I was sure Arthur would be asleep. He normally slept through most board meetings.

"No Arthur. The fraud and harassment charges have been lying around. The stock option mess came to light yesterday. One of the clerks discovered it," Oakes said.

Jay was going to be happy to hear he got a promotion to clerk.

"As far as I was concerned," Chris continued, "that was the straw that broke the camel's back."

Larry interrupted. "When did you find out about the fraud?" In typical male fashion, he was ignoring the sexual harassment issue. "This stock option thing is fraud too. Our shareholders'll kill us when they find out we didn't act on the first complaint. A chief financial officer has to be beyond reproach," he lectured.

"Uh, um. The other fraud issue was just brought up too," Chris lied. He had just told Arthur the other charges had been lying around and no one reminded him of this little slip up.

"Good," Larry said. Larry had now taken over the meeting and was in charge. "If asked, we can say both things came to light at the same time. Grace, have you looked into both charges?"

"I'm not aware of the other issue. The only thing I was asked to look at by Harold Didrickson, with Chris Oakes' approval, was the stock options," she said.

"Chris, you haven't investigated the other charge?" Larry demanded. Before Chris could lie again, Larry charged on. "Grace, investigate the other fraud charge. Let me have your report by Monday afternoon."

"People," Larry continued. "We'll issue a press release before market opens on Monday. Take the hit right away. Chris, get Rick into the office and have him sign a resignation. Grace, you should be present as a witness. The only way this goes out is as a resignation. Word it something like, Rick Cox wants to pursue other business interests. Get your PR people on it. Is everyone in agreement?" he asked.

There were a few murmurs of consent but Whit Williams piped up, "Now hold on a second Larry. We have to at least give the man a chance to defend himself. Accusing him of fraud is a very serious issue. We've got to look at the legal ramifications here. Has anyone consulted Harold?"

Chris answered. "I don't want Harold consulted. I'll call in outside counsel. Harold and Rick are too chummy-chummy for my liking."

Well. The cat was out of the bag. I knew Harold had been quietly and discretely aligning himself with Rick Cox and I guess I wasn't surprised that Chris Oakes knew it. I wondered how long Harold could hold on to *his* job. This was a fast lynching.

"And another thing," Larry said. "Get the Human Synergies people in to do damage control. This has to come across as a resignation and we'll have to get working on Rick's replacement."

"Uh, Larry," Oakes said. "I've been thinking about that. I'd like to talk it over with you."

Well. Chris Oakes was seeking someone's permission. I was glad someone had *him* by the short and curlies.

"Call me tomorrow and we'll discuss it," Larry said.

"Sure Larry." Oakes took back the meeting. "Okay everyone,

if there's nothing else I'll let you go. I'll be in touch about that other matter over the next couple of days. I'm looking forward to seeing everyone on Thursday for the quarterly meeting."

Everyone started saying good-bye and I hit the release button on the switchboard console. I quickly turned it over to the nightline, grabbed my stuff off the desk, turned off the lights and hightailed it back to my office before someone could ask me to do more work. It was late and I'd had it. I was going home.

CHAPTER
nineteen

I had every intention of going home and I almost went there in an ambulance. I suffered the closest thing to a heart attack I had ever experienced when I saw Rick Cox coming out of the kitchen as I hurried down the hall. The sight of him made me stop dead in my tracks. When did he come in, I wondered frantically. He certainly didn't get off the elevator when I was at reception. Maybe I was so intent on eavesdropping, I'd missed him. But he was one of those fitness nuts and had probably taken the stairs.

His presence frightened me so much my heart was in my throat. Not just his sudden appearance but knowing what was about to happen.

"Rick," I croaked out. I cleared my throat and tried to act nonchalant. "When did you come in?" I asked. I still felt like I had a fur ball in my throat so I coughed again.

"I just got here. What's this I hear about a board meeting?" he asked. Fuck, fuck, fuck. I thought quickly of a response but nothing came to mind. I'm not a good liar.

My eyes widened in mock surprise. He was dressed casually in chinos and an open-necked golf shirt and the muscles in his jaw and neck were moving. He must have been clenching his teeth.

"Cut the crap Kate. I know there's a meeting going on. And, I heard Oakes on the phone in his office. Who's on the call?" he demanded.

Who'd he think I was? The Amazing Kreskin? Who was I to know what was going on in this godforsaken place? I continued to stare at him, speechless. Sweat was pouring out of my armpits and down my back. At least offer me a last cigarette before the firing squad cocks their rifles, I prayed.

"Don't know," I mumbled. There. I said it. I lied. God was going to strike me dead. I could feel Sister Josephine pulling on my earlobe and sweet Jesus, it was painful. That was the last time I out-and-out lied. Six years old. I hadn't forgotten. I hope the poor dear wasn't turning over in her grave.

"Fine," he hissed. This man was pissed and I didn't want to be in his way. He hurried down the hall towards executive row.

Really Kathleen, you have nothing to worry about. The man's history. I headed towards my office and vowed to myself I wouldn't get interrupted this time. I was leaving. My phone was ringing when I got to my office and I automatically answered it.

"Kathleen Monahan," I barked into the phone.

"Yes ma'am. Security here. There's a Mr. Johnston here to see Mr. Oakes and I'm not getting any answer on Mr. Oakes' phone. Do you know if Mr. Oakes is in?" the security guard asked.

I sighed. "Yes, he's here. Please send Mr. Johnston up and I'll meet him at the elevator. Thanks." I dropped the handset back into its place on the phone from my standing height, hoping it would break. I couldn't answer a dead phone, now could I? The handset bounced once and settled on my desk. Fuck it, I thought. I should have brought my jammies. I knew I was going to be here all night.

Cleveland Johnston was waiting by the back door when I opened it and I smiled up at him. Cleve and I went back a long way and as tired and fed up as I felt, I was glad to see him. He leaned over and pecked my cheek.

"Katie, how are you?" he asked. I stood back to let him pass and the door swung shut behind us. Cleveland was the only person besides my brother who was allowed to call me Katie.

"Not so great. You're here to see Chris?" I asked. He nodded. "Want a coffee or something before?"

"Naw. I was at dinner when Chris tracked me down. I had just finished a coffee and brandy. My sister and her husband are in town and we were having a great time."

I was impressed that Chris had actually tracked someone down on his own.

"Well, Cleve, you know the way to his office. I was just leaving and I'm outta here as soon as I get my purse."

"Katie, can you stick around? I might need your assistance drafting some documents and if things turn out the way I think, it could be a long night."

"For you Cleve, anything." I couldn't say no to Cleve. Harold would want me to help out.

"What're we working on?" I asked him.

"I'll let you know." We had reached Chris Oakes' office

and I knocked on the door. I opened it a crack and peeked in not knowing what or who I'd find. I wondered if Rick Cox had barged in on Oakes yet demanding an explanation. Chris was sitting by himself at the table.

"Chris, Cleveland Johnston's here," I announced. I opened the door wider and Cleve winked at me as he passed.

I once had an enormous crush on Cleveland Johnston and was thinking yummy thoughts about him as I headed back to my office. There were voices coming from Rick Cox's office and I slowed down to listen. I couldn't make out the conversation but I think he was alone and talking to someone on his speaker phone. I hurried on because I didn't want to be caught eavesdropping. Didn't think of that while you listened in to a whole board meeting, did you Kathleen?

I slumped in my chair and put my feet up on the desk and thought about Cleve. We had first met about ten years ago when I was working as a legal secretary at Scapelli, Marks & Wilson, one of the largest law firms in the city. He was a junior partner and we had worked long nights together on some pretty hairy deals. Initial public offerings, cross-border transactions, junk bonds, you name it. It was the high flyin' nineties. Limos, expense accounts, posh hotels, fancy dinners. He was the brain and I was the brawn. Most of my work was strictly clerical and secretarial but we were a great team.

We were both single at the time but never had the energy to make anything of it. I had the energy now but he was married. I burned out before he did and moved on. He's still with Scapelli's but now he's the senior partner in charge of the securities department. Scapelli's were hired as TechniGroup's outside counsel when the company had first gone public and Cleve had worked on the file at that time. I was sure it wasn't a securities matter that had brought him here tonight to see Oakes. Chris was most likely having Cleve draw up the termination documentation to fire Rick. Cleve would want to make sure everything was nice and neat so when we had to disclose the termination package in our annual information form, the annual filing we made each year with the Ontario Securities Commission, we'd all be speaking out of the same side of our mouths.

I must have dozed off because the next thing I knew Jay was shaking my shoulder. The man was making a habit of waking me up lately.

I touched my hand to the side of mouth to make sure I wasn't drooling. My face was dry, thank God.

"Jay," I said. I tried to push my chair back and get my legs off my desk. This must be very attractive, I thought. I was having obvious difficulty so Jay helped by pulling on the chair. I put my feet on the floor and looked up at him. He looked like he'd seen a ghost.

"What are you doing here?" I demanded. I looked at my watch and saw that it was eleven p.m. I'd been asleep for over an hour and a half. My father always said a good soldier could sleep anywhere and I was proving his theory.

And where the hell was Cleve? If he'd left me here without saying so much as a good-bye, the man was in trouble. I focused on Jay. He definitely wasn't looking well.

"The fuck just fired me," he stated.

"I beg your pardon?" I was in shock. "What the hell happened?"

"Rick called me at home at nine-thirty and told me to get in here. I thought it was about the stock option report I was supposed to be preparing. I wish I never answered the phone."

Getting called into the office on short notice on evenings and weekends wasn't an unusual thing around here. Jay was a poor lamb heading for the slaughter when he agreed to come in.

When he didn't continue, I prompted him, "And?"

"Rick was calm. No ranting. No raving. I was surprised at how mellow he was. I figured he'd been drinking."

"What'd he say? Why'd he fire you?" I asked.

"He said that he was about to be fired by the board because of that information on the stock option system. You know, the different numbers I showed you yesterday." I nodded. Oh yeah, I knew. Rick Cox obviously had an ally on the board who had let him know what happened at the meeting.

"He said that Grace O'Grady had proof that the numbers had been changed by him on the system."

"Right," I agreed. Seen it with my own two eyes.

"But he said that both he and I knew that he never used the system so it must have been me. I asked him why he thought I would do something like that."

"What'd he say?" I asked.

"He said to benefit me. His numbers, mine and two others were changed. I'd benefit he said."

"But Jay, Grace said she had proof it was him," I said. I wasn't letting on that I knew everything. "If Grace had proof, it must be pretty solid. The proof must've shown that he was on the system," I prompted.

"He said it was me using his password. He's never used the system," Jay said.

"How would you know his password?"

"When I first transferred into finance Ray was away a couple of days and wasn't able to set me up with access to the stock option system. Rick gave me his password to log in."

"Right, but the system requires a password change every month, doesn't it?" I asked.

"Yeah, and that's where he thinks he's got me."

"How?"

"He told me to change his password every month. I change it to the name of the month. In March I changed his password to March. Same for April." Jay was leaning forward with his elbows on his knees and he hung his head.

"Can't you take the Nuremberg defence on this one?" I asked him.

"The what?"

"The Nuremberg defence. You were just following orders. That's the excuse all the Nazis used at the end of the war," I said.

Jay stood up and started pacing in my small office like a caged animal. "But I didn't do it," he yelled. "He can't just fire me. He's got no proof."

I felt helpless. Rick felt he was being falsely accused. So he fired the person who he logically thought was guilty.

"What the hell am I going to do?" Jay asked me. I didn't know what to say to him. He turned his back to me and slammed his fist against the door. "Fuck. Fucking cocksucker." I heard him take a deep breath. "I'm screwed. This isn't fair."

He turned around and smiled weakly at me. "He gave me thirty minutes to clear the premises. I was on my way out when I saw you sleeping in here so I just thought I'd let you know. I'm going to get drunk. You coming?" he asked me.

"I can't. Cleveland Johnston's here meeting with Oakes and he asked me to hang around. He needs me to help with some agreements. At least I think he's still here. Let me check. If he's gone, I'll go with you. Wait here."

I hurried out of my office and down the hall to Oakes'. With the amount of walking I do in these halls each day, you'd think

I'd wear off my excess pounds. The door to Rick Cox's office was open and I could see that he wasn't there. I could hear voices inside Chris' office and I put my ear up to the door to listen. I tried to decipher the voices but couldn't make out anything. I opened the door a crack and peeked in. Cleve was standing with his back to me looking out the windows. Oakes was talking. Shit. This could go on all night. I closed the door quietly and walked back to my office. This was going to be hard. I didn't want to have to make a choice between a good friend and this thankless job. In fact, there should be no choice. Fuck 'em. Jay was more important. Cleve could call his own secretary. I wasn't getting paid overtime.

Jay was gone when I got back to my office and there was a yellow post-it note on my computer screen where I wouldn't miss it. "Nose to nose" it said. "I'll call you later. Jay."

I shoved my cigarettes and lighter in my purse and headed out the door. I stopped and turned around to grab the note off the computer screen. I put in my shirt pocket. Fuck 'em all, I thought. They won't engrave on my tombstone, "She should have spent more time at the office." I pulled the door shut behind me.

CHAPTER
twenty

I hurried to the elevator to see if I could catch Jay. He wasn't in the main lobby of the building and had already signed out at security. The man moves fast. In typical fashion my car choked and coughed a few times before starting and I gunned the engine impatiently when it finally caught.

I could see Jay's car going up the ramp out of the building as I waited behind two other cars at the exit. The idiot at the head of the line had to get out of his car to put his pass in the machine and he turned and grinned sheepishly at us. Moron. I wanted to lean on my horn but better judgment prevailed. I wasn't sure what the statistics were on drive-by shootings in underground garages.

When I finally cleared the garage and came up to the street the only car I could see was the one that had been in front of me in the garage. Traffic was light, and it was twenty minutes later when I pulled up in front of Jay's place where he lived in a multi-storied apartment building. I rang his doorbell a few times and when I didn't get any answer, I hurried back to my car and lit a cigarette. I left the car idling while I thought about what to do. I could go home. The thought of sinking into bed and feeling the duvet settle around me was definitely an option. I could leave a note for Jay letting him know I tried. But that was wimping out. I had to at least make an effort to find him so I put the car in gear and pulled back into the street. He said he was going to get drunk so I thought I'd try the bars in the neighbourhood.

Luck was with me because I saw his car parked in the lot at Murphy's.

The sour smell of beer hit me as soon as I opened the door to the tavern. The cigarette smoke was thick and I felt right at home. It was relatively quiet for a Saturday night and there was a country song playing in the background. Most of the round tables were occupied with couples talking quietly and the dance floor was empty. All of the barstools were taken and I saw Jay sitting at the far end of the bar staring straight ahead. He was running his hand repeatedly through his hair.

I walked down the length of the bar and came up behind him. "You're brushing," I said into his back.

He turned around with a sad grin on his face. "Let me be," he said. He got down off his barstool and took my elbow. "Let's get a table." We found a small table near one of the front windows.

"What do you want to drink?" Jay asked me.

"Soda water with lime, please." Jay waved at the bartender who was leaning on the bar reading a newspaper. When the bartender didn't respond Jay got up and went to the bar to get me a drink. I lit a cigarette and waited.

When Jay returned and was settled in his chair I asked him, "So, why didn't you wait for me?"

He shrugged and took a deep drink of his beer, straight from the bottle. "My 30 minutes were up and I had to get out of the office," he said. "I thought you were too busy to join me." I listened for sarcasm in the remark but didn't hear any.

My turn to shrug. I picked up my drink and saw that it had a slice of lemon instead of lime. Not the time to get picky, I thought. I sipped my drink and smoked my cigarette and Jay stared out the window. Silence engulfed both of us. I didn't want to patronize Jay and I didn't want to mouth trite words. My hand reached for his across the table and his thumb lightly caressed the side of my hand.

"You want another drink?" he asked abruptly.

I shook my head. He came back from the bar with two bottles of beer and I wondered if he was serious about getting drunk because I certainly wasn't looking forward to it. I have a low tolerance for people when they get drunk. Not that I have anything against people drinking, I just totally lose interest when they reach that 'other' place. Drunks speak another language and think like aliens as far as I'm concerned. I had never seen Jay drunk and wasn't looking forward to it.

"You planning on getting drunk?" I asked him.

"Who're you? My mother?" he snapped back.

"Nope. Just asking. Just making conversation."

"Well just mind your own business," he said.

I gathered my cigarettes and lighter, and reached for my purse on the back of my chair. I stood up. I kept my expression neutral and refused to show him how hurt I was by that comment. I took a step around the table and leaned over and put my nose against his.

"Call me if you need me," I whispered into his face. He stood up abruptly and took my purse off my shoulder

"I do need you. Let's dance." He steered me toward the empty dance floor.

Oh yeah, this should be cute. I think the last time I danced was in the seventh grade when we learned folk dancing. The music from the jukebox was country and the singer was crooning softly. When we reached the middle of the dance floor Jay put his arms around me and started to sway to the music. I guessed we weren't going to polka.

When the song finally finished, Jay stopped moving but he didn't take his arms away. We stood like that for a moment and I looked up at him. He was looking down at me and I felt my throat tighten. He lowered his head and put his lips on mine. I didn't react to his kiss because I didn't think I should. He was upset and vulnerable. Just like I had felt the night before.

The music started up again and Jay put his hand on the side of my face. He shook his head and said, "I shouldn't have done that. Sorry."

I took his hand in mine and led him off the dance floor back to our table. I retrieved my cigarettes and lit one, dragging deeply. Jay was chugging his beer from the bottle. We were both uncomfortable with what had just happened.

I looked at him sitting across from me. His eyes stared back at me and I tried to figure out why I felt so uncomfortable. The man was like a brother to me and that was why this felt wrong. There was six years difference in our ages and we had known each other forever. The last couple of days had definitely changed things. I was changing the way I felt about him.

I tried to put the age issue aside. Six years. Big deal. He was 28 and I was 34. At least no one would say I was old enough to be his mother. I decided to take the bull by the horns.

"What just happened out there?" I asked him softly.

"I'm sorry," he said back. "I shouldn't have done that. Look, can we just forget it?" Forget it? I could still feel his lips on mine.

"You caught me off guard, Jay. I didn't know how to react."

He pulled his chair closer to the edge of the table and leaned forward.

"Kate, I'm pissed off about being fired. I'm scared shitless. I don't know if I can get another job in this city after being fired. I don't know what to do. I shouldn't have kissed you. I was way out of line. I apologize." He was rambling. "I'm sorry about this morning too. I don't know what got into me."

I took his hand. "Jay, you'll get another job. TechniGroup isn't such a great place. Besides, Rick Cox is getting fired. I think you should call Tom James and let him know what happened. If the board fires Cox for the stock option fiasco, then that'll prove that you didn't do it. Call James and explain what happened. Maybe he'll let you resign if they don't rescind the dismissal."

Jay slumped back in his chair and sighed. "This is so bogus. I've been set up. What the fuck is going on at that place anyway? Why can't everyone just get to work and forget about the shit that's constantly flying around? Oakes and Cox are such assholes. In a forty hour week, I'm lucky if I spend four hours producing meaningful work. Maybe I'm better off."

The fight was going out of him quickly. Probably the beers.

"You hungry?" I asked. My stomach was protesting. I hadn't eaten since lunch. Jay looked at his watch.

"It's one o'clock. Nothing's open. Come on back to my place and I'll cook you something," he invited.

His place? Good girls don't go to a man's place at one in the morning to be cooked for. I saw my mother shaking her finger in my face. I threw caution to the wind.

"Sure." It wasn't like I hadn't been there before. I'd spent many evenings at Jay's place watching Monday Night Football or the Maple Leafs on TV. I doubted though that there was anything on TSN at this time of night except drag racing or bass fishing. I followed Jay to the parking lot.

"I'll drive. You've been drinking and you can walk over in the morning and get your car," I said.

Jay looked fondly at his Saab. "I'm okay to drive and I don't want to leave it in this parking lot overnight. I'll be careful," he said. "You follow me."

My car started on the first try and I followed Jay the couple of blocks to his place. I grabbed the first parking spot I saw close to his apartment and waited in the outside lobby of his building for him to come up from the underground parking garage. We didn't speak in the elevator and I was starting to feel uncomfortable again. I stared at his back as he fit the key in the door to his apartment. My knees felt weak and there were butterflies in my stomach. I felt like I was sixteen again and about to receive my first kiss. Jay flicked on the light switch in the hall and reached over me to set the dead bolt lock on the apartment door.

"How about eggs and toast?" he asked.

"Sure. Sounds great." I took off my jacket and hung it in the closet. "Need any help?" I offered, but Jay knew better. I was just being polite. He didn't let me in his kitchen when the stove was turned on.

"No. Thanks. I can manage," he laughed and headed down the hall. The living room was at the end of the hall. The kitchen was on the left through the living room and his bedroom and bathroom were on the right of the living room. He left the living room in darkness and turned on a light in the kitchen.

"Make yourself at home," he said over his shoulder. I dropped my purse on the coffee table and said, "I'm just going to use the little girl's room."

Like the rest of the apartment, the bathroom was neat as a pin. Jay had been taught well by his mother. She showed no favouritism when it came to household chores and Jay was familiar with all of them.

I splashed cold water on my face and looked at myself in the mirror. A very round, pixie-like face stared back. My hair looked like I had been standing in front of a fan and I tried to remember if I had brushed it that morning. Once a day was my rule. I was stalling in the bathroom and didn't know why.

Our relationship had taken a definite turn today. Jay had shown some unbrotherly-like interest in me and I didn't know how to deal with it. I wasn't a neophyte when it came to relationships but the river had run dry during the last year. I hadn't been seeing anyone seriously in a long time. In fact, I couldn't remember the last time I'd had a date.

After my divorce from Tommy, it had taken me a long time to get back in the dating mode. At one time I'd been a real pro. At dating. I was quite the girl about town. When I worked at the law firm I met lots of interesting, fast men. Tommy was one of them. My autobiography will describe our courtship as whirlwind, our marriage as a disaster and our divorce as friendly.

Tom Connaught was an Irish-American from Phoenix who I'd met when our law firm was acting for his company on their initial public offering. We'd married shortly after the deal closed and he went back to Phoenix to look after his business. I was going to follow as soon as I could close up my apartment. Weeks stretched into months. I was flying back and forth to Phoenix every second weekend and when business allowed, Tommy would come to Toronto. My excuse was work. I always had one more deal to close. Half packed boxes sat in my apartment and I just never got around to moving. We drifted apart as fast as we had come together. Tommy still called me whenever he was in Toronto and it was times like this that I missed him. I hadn't been involved in a serious relationship since. It had been seven years since our divorce.

I turned out the bathroom light and went back to the living room. Jay was standing there with two plates in his hand. The living room was dark and the light from the kitchen silhouetted Jay's body.

I turned on a lamp on the side table and pulled the coffee table closer to the sofa. Jay sat down beside me and placed the two plates on the table. He had prepared scrambled eggs and toast. He pulled two forks and two knives out of his shirt pocket and handed me one of each.

"Eat," he ordered. I dug in. The food was good and hot. I sank back in the sofa when I was finished and tucked my legs up under me. I turned sideways and leaned against the back of the sofa and looked at Jay. He was sitting close to me and I could smell his aftershave.

"Thanks for the eggs. You could always get a job as a short order cook," I joked. He smiled and gathered up the two plates and returned them to the kitchen. I heard him rinsing the plates and I thought about leaving. He sat down closer to me when he came back and I threw caution to the wind for the second time that night. This time I kissed him. And he wasn't rude like I'd been. He responded. He tasted like beer.

When we came up for air I asked him, "Should we be doing this?"

He held me back at arm's length and said, "Why not? This isn't against the law Kate." I decided not to argue and my lips closed over his again. The man could cook *and* kiss. Definitely a keeper.

CHAPTER
twenty-one

I looked at Jay's sleeping face beside me the next morning and promised myself there would be no mental bashing. Although I hadn't thoroughly analyzed the pros and cons of a relationship with him, it had happened. And I was glad. Maybe it could be a stronger relationship because we'd known each other for so long. Many experts say solid relationships are based on friendship, I reassured myself. He definitely knew all my faults. And there were many.

I lightly ran my finger down the side of Jay's face and mentally pinched myself. What had happened last night after the kissing had been tender. I eased myself out of bed and went looking for a toothbrush. I used Jay's. Now that our relationship had reached a new plateau, I was sure he wouldn't mind. Besides, we exchanged enough spit the night before that using his toothbrush didn't seem out of line.

Jay found me sitting at the kitchen table smoking and drinking coffee. He was shirtless and wearing jeans.

"Hey," he said.

"Hey yourself," I replied. He poured himself a coffee and leaned against the kitchen counter. I felt shy and cursed under my breath. I'd never been at a loss for words with him before. The man was bringing out that feminine side that I'd always abhorred in other women. I was definitely not the cute type.

I looked at him and swallowed. Fuck it. Let's barge on.

"So. Are you okay with what happened last night?" I asked him. I tried to be cool about this. I wasn't looking for a marriage proposal but I did need to know where we stood. I needed to know if it had been a one-night stand for him. I wasn't sure how I'd feel about that, but I wasn't about to make a fool of myself either.

"Okay?" he laughed. "I'm great with it. You?"

"Great," I said slowly. "Is it likely to happen again?"

"Well, Kate. You were the one who initiated it. Are you going to do that again?" he teased.

"Depends on how drunk you get and if I think I can take advantage of you," I joked. I was feeling better. "Can I buy you breakfast?"

"Sure. Did you want to shower before we go out? You'll find clean towels in the closet in my bedroom."

"Yeah. Give me a few minutes." I stood up and he grabbed me around the waist and pulled me to him. He held me like that for a few moments and lightly kissed the top of my head. He slapped my butt and said, "Get a move on. I'm hungry."

We decided to walk because the day was gorgeous. Actually he decided to walk and I thought about my arteries. A couple of blocks won't hurt, I thought to myself. But I found I was enjoying myself as we set a brisk pace block after block. I had to remind him not to walk so fast because his legs were about ten times longer than mine. We finally found a place and we ordered large breakfasts.

When Jay was finished, he pushed his plate back and stretched.

"Ah," he sighed. He grinned and looked at me. "Good food. Good woman. What else could a man want?"

"Good job?" I teased.

"Don't remind me," he said. We sat quietly for a few minutes and I thought about Jay and TechniGroup. There were some screwy things going on.

"Do you realize what we've been through in the last three days?" I asked him. "Evelyn died, you discovered some fuck up with the stock options, Oakes called a board meeting and they're going to fire Cox, and Rick fired you." I ticked each event off on my fingers.

"I can't believe that Rick would screw around with the stock options. It's so bush league. What could he possibly gain?" Jay asked himself out loud.

"And," I said. "I think they've got a couple of other things on him too."

"Like what?"

"Fraud and sexual harassment."

"I beg your pardon?" he said. His eyes widened and his eyebrows shot up.

"You heard me. Fraud and sexual harassment," I repeated.

"Just how do you know this?" he asked.

"You know. I hear things."

"And the board knows about all of this? That's why they decided to fire him?"

I nodded my head.

"Fraud. I can't believe it. Won't believe it. He may be a raving lunatic but he's no criminal. I've worked with the guy and he takes his legal obligations very seriously. What kind of fraud?" he asked me.

"Something about falsely reporting revenue. I don't really understand it. You know me and financial statements," I said lamely.

"I admit some of our accounting treatment is questionable but the auditors always sign off on it. I can't believe Rick would falsely report revenue," Jay stated.

"He supposedly ordered one of the controllers to do it," I said.

"And the guy did it?"

"I don't know if he did. The memo said he ordered the guy to do it."

"What memo?" Jay asked.

"Nothing. Forget I said it. Look, I think the house of cards is about to come tumbling down. Once the public find out that Rick Cox is gone, our shares'll be in the toilet. The analysts'll have a heyday with this shit. Monday is not going to be fun."

"Yeah, well the bastards have pulled it off before. They'll say he resigned and we're seeking a replacement. Remember the last time?"

I remembered. We'd had a brief sojourn with a chief operating officer that lasted six months. We had touted him to the world as the second coming of Christ. Oakes had hand-picked him and he was going to save the world. The analysts loved it and the share price rose steadily for the six months he was around. I thought the guy was a perfect fit because he was as loony as Oakes. He didn't last long enough though, and when the board fired him they told the public he was resigning to pursue personal interests.

I should write a book. It probably wouldn't sell though because it would be so unbelievable. And now we were firing another chief operating officer who was going to 'pursue personal interests'. Our only hope was that the public and the analysts had a short memory. The other guy got fired almost exactly two years ago. This was becoming almost an annual event.

"Well, I have a feeling we'll have a replacement before you can say Bob's Your Uncle," I said.

"Yeah," Jay joked. "Maybe I should apply for the job."

"Well, you've always wanted the job," I reminded him. "Actually, I think Oakes wants to see Philip Winston in the position."

Jay snorted. "Yeah, right. He's got no more experience than I do. There's no way the board will allow that."

"The board'll do exactly what Oakes and Larry Everly tell them to do. The board members are there for one reason only. The money. The board fees. And their stock options. Having a conscience and thinking for yourself are not requirements for being on our board."

We sat silent for a few minutes, both of us thinking. I was thinking about stock options and how they had been the center of almost everything that had happened in the last couple of days. Evelyn and stock options. Rick Cox and stock options. Jay and stock options. Stock options had caused the demise of three people in three days. And two of those people were very close to me.

"Jay, have you ever known anyone who died?" I asked.

"My grandmother. And when I was in high school some guy killed himself. Walked in front of a train. I didn't know him well but everyone at school was upset about it. And Evelyn. But we still don't know why she died."

"Exactly. Why she died. Notice you didn't say how she died. Why. Do you think it could have anything to do with the stock options? Do you think someone planned it?"

"Kate, get real. Let me ask you a question. Have you ever known anyone who was murdered?" I shook my head.

"Right," Jay continued. "Neither have I. This is the real world. Not some movie about corporate America where they murder off people every twenty minutes. Our guys are stupid but I don't think anyone would murder one of the employees."

"You're probably right. Besides, they're all too stupid to have planned something like that. And the police haven't been knocking on the office door. So obviously no one suspects foul play."

Another thought occurred to me. Was someone smart enough to set up Jay and Rick Cox? But why? With Rick Cox gone the stock was going to take a hit. And all of the top guys were driven by the stock price. They were smart enough to know that when the stock price went down, so did the value of their stock options. Maybe someone hated Rick Cox so much they didn't care about their personal wealth.

Fuck it. I was spending too much time worrying about the office.

"Let's forget it, Jay. This shit is making my head hurt. It's a beautiful day. What do you want to do?"

Jay grinned. "Well, we could go back to my place. I won't make your head hurt."

It was a pleasant thought and I felt a blush starting at my neck and rising up my face. I grinned back.

CHAPTER
twenty-two

We were sitting on the sofa later that afternoon and the sky was starting to turn to evening. So far I'd had a perfect day. I was hoping it wouldn't end. I could remember as a kid those special Sunday's when my brother and I would leave the house after breakfast and play outside all day. One adventure after another. Games of baseball. Hide and seek. War. Road hockey. All the kids in the neighbourhood playing together. Mom wouldn't even bother trying to get us to come in for lunch and she would leave food on the front porch. If we remembered, we'd eat at some point in the day. When she finally called us in for dinner, we went reluctantly. Those days were perfect and I smiled to myself as I thought about them. The games Jay and I had played today didn't involve the neighbourhood kids but it had been just as much fun. I didn't want the day to end. I smiled again when I remembered that some of those neighbourhood kids had been Jay and his sisters. History was definitely repeating itself.

"Well, Mr. Harmon. Should I go home? It's time to be thinking about dinner and what to wear to work tomorrow. Not that you have to worry about what to wear tomorrow," I said.

"Oh sure. Rub it in. And I thought we'd agreed not to talk about work any more today," he said. "And no, you shouldn't go home unless you want to. We can eat here or go out. Whatever you want."

I thought about staying over at Jay's for another night and as appealing as that was, I knew I shouldn't push my luck.

"Well, if we stay here, you'll have to do the cooking. What've you got?"

"Do you care? Let me make dinner and you can see if there's anything on the TV." He got up and handed me the remote control off the coffee table. "Don't exert yourself," he laughed as he headed for the kitchen.

This man was definitely a catch. He cooked and I got to play with the remote. It doesn't get any better than this, I thought. I stretched out on the sofa and flicked through the channels. I could hear Jay in the kitchen behind me opening cupboard doors and making cooking sounds. I surfed the channels and settled on a golf game from Pasadena. I wasn't sure what was more exciting - watching golf on TV or watching paint dry. I flicked the remote a few more times and found some historical show about the castles of Germany. The scenery in the show was beautiful and some of the scenes looked vaguely familiar. My dad had been in the army and we had been posted to Germany for three years and I was sure some of what I was watching on the TV was on our home movies.

The smell of something interesting wafted in from the kitchen and my stomach growled. This was definitely not junk food.

"Let me know when you want me to set the table," I said over my shoulder to Jay. I don't think he heard me because he had the radio on low in the kitchen. I pushed the mute button on the TV and just watched the picture. I could hear the radio now and Jay had the station set to soft rock. The whole situation was very homey and domestic. The only thing missing was a dog and two kids. With my luck it'd be a barking dog and two snot nosed kids. I shook my head to clear the thought.

I had dozed off by the time dinner was ready and I woke up when Jay shook my shoulder.

"Hey, sleepy-head. Wake up. Come on, dinner's ready."

"How many times in the last few days have you had to wake me up?" I asked with a grin.

"A few. But who's counting? Dinner's served, madam. Let me show you to your table." He held out his hand and helped me off the sofa.

Not surprisingly, dinner was superb. Jay had prepared a pasta dish, the name of which I didn't ask. I hadn't seen it recently on the menu at McDonald's. I took my time cleaning up after dinner because I was reluctant to go home.

"Well," I said to Jay as I hung the wet dishtowel on the hook beside the refrigerator, "that's about it. I should be heading home."

"You can't stay?" Jay asked.

"I could but I shouldn't," I replied. "This has been a perfect day of domestic bliss, albeit in your home. And I don't want to overstay my welcome. Besides, you don't wear the same size underwear and pantyhose that I do and I'd have to leave early and go home to get ready for work."

Jay laughed. "You could call in sick and take the day off."

"I could. But Didrickson would probably fire me and then we'd both be out of jobs. Triple bypass surgery is the only excuse for missing work during a week when we're having a board meeting. What are you going to do tomorrow?"

"I think I'm going to take your advice and call the Tower of Jell-O. I'll plead and cry and see if Tom'll talk some sense into someone. Basically, I'm going to beg for my job back."

"Do you want me to talk to him?" I offered. I thought I might be treading on thin ice here because I knew how proud Jay was. But - a job's a job.

"No. I can handle it," he said.

"Will you promise me though that if you think I can help, you'll swallow your pride and ask me? I can bully Tom into anything you know. I can have him whimpering in a corner in two seconds. All I have to do is tell him his tie doesn't match his socks. The guy would be a basket case. Then I could swoop in and go for the kill. Make him promise to give you your job back for some fashion advice."

We both laughed. Jay stood up and put his arms around me.

"If it comes down to it and I think it's necessary, I'll ask for your help." He kissed me lightly on the forehead and then hugged me.

I looked up at him. "Walk a lady to her car?" I asked.

"Sure. But doesn't that smack of male chauvinism?" he joked.

"Not at all. It's polite and it shows manners. Your mom would be proud of you. Besides, I haven't used my car all day and I want to make sure it starts."

"Then I'd be honoured to escort you. Hang on while I get my apartment keys."

My car started on the first try. Damn. I think I was secretly hoping it wouldn't start and I'd have an excuse to stay. Jay leaned in the driver's side window and gave me a kiss. "You'll call me?" he asked.

"Sure," I said slowly. "When? When I get home? Later tonight? Tomorrow? You've gotta understand, I'm really rusty at this game and I'm not sure of the rules."

"Whenever. And I'm rusty too. If you want to call me when you get home, that'd be great. And then you could call me later tonight. And then again tomorrow. Let's make up the rules as we go." He smiled at me.

"No problem coach. Thanks for a great time, Jay." I put the car in gear. "Now get your head out of my car before I drag you down the street."

CHAPTER
twenty-three

By the time I reached the office the next morning I was in a complete panic. It was eight forty-five and I was late for work for the first time in recent history. I had slept like a well-fed baby the night before and my dreams had been wonderful. I slept through the alarm and then got caught in traffic.

My breath was short as I hurried down the hall to my office and I tried to calm myself. First of all, Kate, you're never late for work. Secondly, who cares? You work most nights well past quitting time. I continued to lecture myself as I hung my coat on the back of the door. Continue acting like a junior secretary who's required to punch a clock and you'll be treated like one.

The door caught Harold Didrickson on the foot as I tried to close it after hanging up my coat. I quickly caught the handle and pulled it back open.

"Sorry. I didn't see you there," I apologized. What the hell does he want, I thought. He never comes in my office.

"Kate. Have you got a minute?" he asked politely.

"Sure Harold."

He hesitated for a moment like he was on the edge of a high diving board. "I wanted to remind you that working hours here are from eight to five. If you're late, it doesn't set a good example for the other support staff," he said. With a straight face. I looked closely at him to make sure he wasn't joking. Of course, I thought, he doesn't joke around.

My blood pressure started rising and my right ear lobe started to burn. I thought about all the times Harold wandered into the office on his own sweet time and left early on those beautiful summer days to get in nine holes. Obviously though, he didn't consider himself support staff.

I thought about all the times I had stayed late into the night working on documentation for an acquisition. Or preparing for board meetings. All the times I'd traveled on weekends, on *my time*, to attend those board meetings to look after grown men and all their whims and fancies. Some times I'd worked so late I only had time to go home and shower because I had to be back at the office by eight. Or the times Harold had gone on vacation leaving me to deal with outside counsel, the auditors, bankers and underwriters on a crucial financing.

The miserable little prick was about to find out about my interpretation of work-to-rule.

"Eight to five?" I repeated. He nodded.

"Then remember that when I leave today at five," I said. "And for that matter, I'll be leaving every day this week, including Thursday when the board meeting is in full swing, at five." I opened the top drawer of my desk and slammed it shut for emphasis. He blanched.

"Can I get you a coffee, Harold?" I asked sweetly. His colour quickly returned and his cheeks turned pink. He quickly left my office.

Shit, fuck and damn. I was mad at myself for my reaction to his pettiness and then felt sorry for myself. I'll never get out of this stereotype of being a secretary. Always having someone to report to. Always looking after everyone else. I was sick and tired of it. Sick and tired of looking after grown men.

I grabbed my purse and went to find Vanessa. In for a penny, in for a pound - I was taking a coffee-break. If Harold could act like a spoiled brat, so could I.

Vee was coming out of Chris Oakes' office and I raised two fingers to my lips as if smoking. She nodded and pulled the door shut behind her. While she forwarded her phone calls back to the switchboard, I breathed deeply a few times to get my blood pressure back to normal. I was still spitting mad at Harold.

Vee and I didn't talk as we walked quickly down the corridor to the elevator and this time she had to trot to keep up with me. I viciously punched the button for the elevator.

"Well, who pissed in your Corn Flakes?" she asked.

"Short lawyer, big attitude," I told her. "He gave me shit for being late this morning. Perfect way to start the day."

The line-up at the coffee shop was out the door and Vanessa grabbed a table in the smoking area while I waited in line for coffee. By the time I got to the table I was seething.

I lit a cigarette and took a deep drag and watched Vanessa

struggle with the little containers of cream. Her nails were so long she couldn't get the lids off. I grabbed them from her and peeled back the covers and poured two creams in her coffee.

"There," I said. "Want me to drink it for you too?"

"Oh, take it easy Kate. Calm down. I thought we were on the same cycle. Is it that time of month again?" We laughed. I could never stay mad long and especially not around Vanessa. Laughter was the bond that kept us going.

"So," I said. "I hope you enjoyed your Saturday. Mine was one straight out of a Stephen King novel. It got weirder and weirder as the day went on. I didn't get out of here until after eleven."

"You're kidding. What happened? Why didn't you call me yesterday?" she asked.

"Um. I was busy yesterday." I wasn't sure about talking out loud about Jay and I yet. "Saturday though," I continued. "What a day from hell. I got a call from Harold in the afternoon to come to the office to help Grace with an audit. Then Oakes found me. After I called you and got the file he wanted he made me book a directors meeting. Then I had to get everyone on the phone for that. And then Cleveland Johnson arrived and I had to stick around in case he needed any help. Lotsa fun."

"Stop, stop. Hang on. Let's start at the beginning. Since when do you help Grace with audits? You're not turning on me and joining the finance department are you?"

"Right. I've always aspired to be a bean-counter. And I'd do so well in the finance group. I'm such a wizard with numbers. You know what Harold always says about me. Kate, you don't have a problem with math. You have a problem with arithmetic. He's such a sweet and inspiring little man. Anyway, there was a problem with the stock options. A big problem. I spent about four hours with Grace going over numbers. That's just background though. The dirt is, they're firing Rick Cox," I said.

Vee shook her head. "I knew it. I knew it. Oakes has been digging around for dirt on him for so long, I'm surprised he's lasted this long. Give it to me. What happened?"

I explained to her what had happened on Saturday night. "Didn't Oakes tell you this morning?" I asked her.

"He's not in."

"Oh. I saw you coming out of his office and I just assumed he was there. So the spineless wonder isn't going to stick around for the firing."

I lit another cigarette from the butt of the one I was finishing and glanced at my watch. It was time to get back upstairs.

"Anyway, the worst part is Rick Cox found out about the board meeting. Oakes didn't want any inside directors on the call and when I finished at the switchboard with the call I ran into him coming out of the kitchen. Somehow, he knew there was a board meeting. And someone on that call told him that he was being fired."

"Probably Arthur Graves," she said. "He's the one who pushed so hard initially to get Rick appointed COO. He and Rick are thick as thieves."

"Well, anyway, it gets better. Rick called Jay in to the office around nine-thirty and fired him."

"For what?" Vanessa was incredulous. "He fired Jay? What an asshole. He can't fire Jay. Jesus."

"He said that he thinks Jay was the one who screwed around with the stock option system because he, Rick, never uses the system and Jay has his password."

"Ohmigod. I can't believe this. Have you spoken to Jay?" she asked me.

"Yeah."

"And? What's he going to do? He should get a lawyer. They can't do this to him." Vanessa always felt the worst for the underdog. She couldn't stand to see people used and abused. Especially at the hands of Oakes and Cox.

"I think he might call Tom James and see if there's anything he can do," I said. "I don't think he should hold out any hope though. Besides, he's probably better off not here. This place is a zoo."

Vanessa gulped down the rest of her coffee. She slung her purse over her shoulder and said, "Come on. Dave Rowlandson told me we've got a press release going out and now I think I know what it's about." She looked at her watch. "The market's already open so they must be going to release it at the end of the day. Great. This'll be a day from hell."

Vanessa was always involved with the press releases because of Oakes. Dave Rowlandson, our public relations director had his own secretary but with press releases, Vee always ended up typing them. Oakes had final say on the contents of the press releases and he would make what seemed like zillions of changes before they were released. Because Vee was the only person who understood his hieroglyphics, she did the typing.

While we waited for the elevator in the lobby Vee said, "This should be fun. I'll have to be faxing drafts of the press release back and forth today. Chris is back in New York."

"Yeah? Meeting with you know who?" I asked.

"Yup. Jack Vincent himself. Chris went to New York yesterday. He's not due back until later today."

The receptionist was waving frantically at us when we got off the elevator. Vee hurried into reception and I followed.

"I've got Mr. Oakes on the phone," she said. She was very flustered.

"Calm down. I'll take it here," Vanessa said and pointed at the guest phone on a side coffee table.

The receptionist transferred the call to the other phone and sat down heavily in her chair. She held her head in her hands and started mumbling to herself.

I leaned on the marble counter of the reception desk and told her, "Don't take it so hard. The man only bites when he's standing next to you." She looked up at me with tears in her eyes.

"He told me if I didn't find her he was going to fire me," she sniffed. "He kept ranting about signing my paycheque."

"Don't worry about it. He's certifiable," I reassured her. I turned around and looked at Vanessa who was scribbling madly on a scrap of paper. She wasn't doing any of the talking.

"Okay, okay," she was saying. "Fine." She hung up the phone and looked up at me. "Press release has gone. They let it go before market opened. He wanted to know why I wasn't here to do the work. I told him he didn't leave me any instructions and that Dave said it was going out later today. I don't think he heard because he asked me three times why I wasn't here to do the work. Jesus, Mary and Joseph."

"Who sent the release out? The agency?" She nodded. Buckman & Bettles were our public relations agency.

"Call them and tell them to fax a copy over right away. I've got to see this," I said. Vee picked up the phone and dialled B&B and asked for Tony Player. Tony was the account manager at B&B who handled all of our stuff, and he and Vee worked closely together. Tony did all the slide shows for the company on presentations to analysts, or road shows, when our executives were trying to sell shares to investors. He also handled all the arrangements for our annual shareholders meeting. Usually when the executives were making presentations he traveled with them. If the press wanted an interview with Oakes, Tony set it up.

"Tony, it's Vee," she said into the phone. "I just heard from Chris that we had a release go before the market opened. Can you fax me a copy asap? Yeah, my private fax number. Thanks." She hung up the phone and said, "Come on. We'll pick it off the machine in my office."

The press release was waiting on the fax machine when we got back to her office. I read over her shoulder. It was our standard boilerplate release that went out every time we 'lost' another executive. Sorry to see him go. Pursuing other business interests. Standard quotes from Oakes. I glanced at the top of the page and noted that Chris Oakes was contact person. So, if the media, analysts or shareholders had any questions, they were to call Oakes. And he wasn't around. Vanessa was going to have her hands full today fielding calls and lying for Oakes. She'd take messages and he'd never return the calls. The red light was flashing on her phone console.

"The flood has started," I said pointing at her phone. "Have fun returning those calls."

"Right. I'll call them all back. But I have to call the vet first. Chris said that Baby was in getting groomed and I was to call them first. Must get my priorities straight," she said sarcastically.

Baby was Chris Oakes' dog. A miniature white poodle. Vee spent half her time arranging for dog walking, dog grooming and talking to the dog. If Oakes called her from home he often would say, "Here Baby. Say hi to Vanessa." Vanessa was supposed to talk to the stupid dog on the phone. And I thought I didn't get paid enough. I waved at her as I walked out of her office. No one would ever believe this shit, I thought. I should start taking notes for my book.

CHAPTER
twenty-four

Harold was on the phone when I walked into his office to retrieve the pile of papers in his out-basket.

"This is a voice message to Chris Oakes and Rick Cox," he was saying into the phone.

Now this was priceless. I put my purse on the guest chair in front of Harold's desk and thumbed through the pile of papers to do a quick check of what was in the out-basket in case I had any questions. Actually, I was eavesdropping.

"Rick," Harold continued. "I'll have a first draft of the board materials by eleven this morning and I'd like to go over them with you. Especially the numbers for the stock option grants. Chris, I'd like your feedback on the draft agendas." He punched a series of numbers into the phone to send the message and hung up his phone. I grabbed the pile of papers and my purse and headed out the door.

"I don't think Rick's in yet," I said over my shoulder. "And Chris is in New York." Ha! Gotcha. Harold had no idea that Rick had been fired. Ha! Serves the little prick right.

But the sick feeling started deep in the pit of my stomach when I thought of the ramifications of Harold not knowing that Rick had been fired. He had been siding with Rick in the corporate feuding and if no one had told him about the firing, maybe he was the next to go. And if he went, what happened to me? Shit. Time to set the little guy straight. I tossed around the idea of keeping Harold in the dark for a while longer but thought better of it. Besides, I couldn't wait to see his reaction.

I poured us both a cup of coffee and sat down in front of him. He was looking a little uncomfortable and I waited for him to speak first.

"Kate, I hope you understand my point about the hours of work," he started.

I interrupted him because he obviously wasn't going to apologize. "Forget it Harold. I have no problem with the hours of work. I do have a problem with the fact that you felt it was necessary to point them out to me. Have I ever left you to fend for yourself? Have I ever complained about working late on all the deals we do? Have I ever bitched about the traveling and serving coffee and arranging haircuts for those prima donnas on the board?"

He must have thought those were rhetorical questions because he didn't answer me. I continued to stare at him for a few moments and when he didn't answer, I said disgustedly, "Forget it. But I meant what I said about work to rule. Anyway, I thought you'd like to know that Rick Cox was fired. They've issued a press release that went out before market opened."

I watched his face for a reaction. It was slow in coming but it came. A look of absolute shock. And a little bit of terror.

"I guess you're reporting directly to Oakes now?" I asked. (Thought I'd rub it in a little.) He flicked his hand at me as if he was brushing away smoke or something in his face.

"When did this happen?" he asked me. I thought about how much I knew and how much I was going to tell him. He had little beads of sweat on his forehead. I gave in. I had my loyalties and as usual, I couldn't stay mad for long. Harold had been a good teacher to me over the years and usually he was fair to me. About as fair as making sure you feed your dog at least once a day.

I told him. "There was a board meeting on Saturday night. After I finished with Grace, Oakes cornered me and had me poll the directors for a conference call. He told me only outside directors and specifically said not to include you. Harold, you can't be surprised about this. You knew what Grace was going to find in that audit."

Harold was thinking and I didn't interrupt him. He got up and stood by the window and stared out.

"They called Cleve Johnson over after the board meeting. He must have done up the termination documents," I told him. Harold didn't visibly react to this and I picked up my coffee to leave.

"Close my door will you? And hold my calls," was all he said.

I spent the next hour mechanically dealing with the documents I had picked out of Harold's out-basket. He had marked up all of the draft documents I had given him for the upcoming board and committee meetings, so I made all of the changes on the computer and proofread the documents for mistakes. I printed clean copies and got everything ready to return to him when he opened his office door. Most times I don't let a closed door keep me out but I thought it'd be prudent to stay out of his way this morning.

Vee called me around eleven and let me know that her phone had not stopped ringing. Shareholders, analysts and the media had been calling steadily. I asked her what the stock price was doing.

"Down one and a half, so far. Trading at seven and five eighths," she said.

"Much volume?" I asked her. Sometimes if there weren't a lot of shares trading the stock would flatten out and the price would hold for a while.

"About a million shares so far," she said.

That wasn't good. On a typical day, not more than 100,000 shares traded. If the stock market had been open for an hour and a half and a million shares had traded it could get worse.

"Small or large blocks?" I asked her. Maybe someone with a million shares dumped them but then again, it could be five hundred shareholders holding 2,000 shares each. Five hundred shareholders dumping their shares could be a very bad sign.

"I didn't ask. But a lot of mom and pop shareholders have been calling. One old lady called to say she was sorry that nice man Mr. Cox decided to leave the company. She said he helped her up the stairs at the last shareholders' meeting and she thinks he's a prince. Too bad he had to resign she said." Vee chuckled. "And then she wanted to know why he didn't have to give two week's notice like everyone else so we could find a replacement. Little old lady shareholders should take their hard-earned money and put it in government bonds. Not this shit-hole," she said.

"You know Vee, since last week the shares are down over three bucks. Last Friday there was no visible reason for the shares to go down. Now there's a reason. I'd say the slide isn't over yet. They're trading now at just under eight dollars. Keep me posted if you hear anything."

My phone rang again as soon as I hung up.

"Kathleen Monahan."

"Katie, it's Cleve. How're you doing today?" he asked me.

"Well, Mr. Johnston. I could only be better if you were here talking to me in person. Listen, sorry about Saturday night. Something came up and I had to leave. Sorry if I left you in the lurch."

"No problem. As it turned out I had to go back to my office to use my precedents for one of the documents I had to create. I felt bad about keeping you waiting around so long. Anyway, I spent most of yesterday here at the office with Rick Cox doing up the termination documents and I need to find out if they're all right by Harold. I got his voice mail when I called his line. Is he in?"

"Yeah, he's here. In a meeting," I lied. "Where're the documents?"

"You should have them by now. I sent them over by courier first thing this morning. And Kate, can you have a look at the schedule attached to the agreement? We've set out what we think are Rick's stock options and he said you'd be able to confirm all the numbers and exercise dates. He didn't have a current stock option statement to verify the numbers."

Rick would be able to cash in on his stock options if the bottom didn't fall out of our share price. If someone leaves our company and has stock options that are exercisable they have ninety days to exercise them. It was standard to outline the available options in any termination documentation and also standard to set out what options were not available to them. The executive would acknowledge all of this information in the agreement so there would be no questions after the fact.

I thought it was odd that Cleve was dealing directly with Rick and not Rick's lawyer. Cleve was acting for us.

"All right, I can do that. I can get a current statement from Evelyn's file. I'll make sure Harold reviews the other stuff too."

"Is Evelyn the lady who died last week?" Cleve asked me.

"Yeah."

"We were really sorry to hear about that. Should our firm send some flowers or something?"

"I'll let you know. They're still doing the autopsy as far as I know. No funeral arrangements have been made. But thanks for asking Cleve. She was a good friend of mine. You know she looked after our computer system for the stock options."

He cleared his throat. "Uh, yeah, I know all about that. Chris told me."

"Did Chris tell you that someone got in to her system after she died and changed some numbers?"

"Yes."

"Did he tell you they think it was Rick Cox?"

"Of course, Katie. I didn't know how much you knew and I'm

not at liberty of course to divulge that information. I wasn't certain you were up to speed."

"Right," I snorted. "Listen, can I ask you something in confidence?"

He hesitated. "Uh, sure. As a friend or as the company's counsel?"

"Cut the crap Cleve. As both. As my friend and as the company's lawyer. Can you wear both hats?" He didn't answer so I continued. "Is Rick Cox denying he made those changes to the system?" I knew I was on very shaky ground here.

"Yes, Rick is maintaining his innocence in this matter."

"Shit, Cleve. You sound like a defence lawyer. Maintaining his innocence," I mimicked. "Did he tell you he fired someone else in the company for making the changes in the system?"

"Yes. He told me the circumstances," he said.

"Can he do that?"

"You mean fire someone for the screw-up?"

"Yes. The person he fired happens to be a friend who needs his job. And his reputation. I want to know how the board can accuse Cox, and fire him, and then Cox turns around and accuses someone else. Wouldn't my friend have a case for saving his job by proving that the board of directors of this company had proof that Rick Cox did it and fired him for it? How can Cox pass the blame and fire someone else? I could see it if they did it together or if the company had proof they did it together. But the board is firing just Cox for this fuck up." I was out of breath.

"Kate, Rick Cox is resigning," Cleve said slowly. "The Board is not firing him."

I was shocked.

"You fuck," I yelled into the phone. "You know damn well that a lynching occurred on a conference call on Saturday night and all of the board members were made aware of what Rick Cox did. They all agreed to fire him."

"Kate, I'm aware of no such thing. Chris Oakes made it clear that Rick Cox was resigning to pursue personal business. I met with Rick to ask him for his resignation. The company records will show that Rick resigned."

"Save it for the press you miserable shit," I yelled and slammed down the phone.

Jay was going to fry along with Rick.

CHAPTER
twenty-five

I had to get out of this place. The morons weren't only running the zoo, they were being advised by professional morons who they paid handsomely for their moronic advice. Rationally, I supposed, if I thought about it, I could understand where Cleve was coming from. Irrationally though, I wanted to spit in Cleve's face.

I forwarded my phone to voice mail and picked up the board documents that I'd been waiting to give back to Harold. I saw that his office door was still closed so I went into the bullpen where the legal assistants sat and headed for Jackie's desk.

She was bent over an open file drawer trying to jam a file folder into the already packed filing cabinet. She looked up at me helplessly.

"I know, I know," I said. "I promise we'll go through these drawers soon and get rid of all the dead stuff. Give you more room."

"Why don't I make a current list of everything in the cabinets and you can just mark on it which files I can dead store. That'll make it easier for you," she said. The girl was always thinking. Jackie had been in the department for about a year now and she was worth her weight in gold. She was keen and had a great work attitude.

"Great idea. And I promise I'll look at the list. Listen, I'm going out. Harold wanted these documents revised," I said. I handed the pile to her. "He doesn't want to be disturbed and I'm sure as hell not going in there. If and when his door opens, put these in his basket. And keep an eye open for a courier package from Scapelli's. Cleveland Johnston's sent over some urgent documents and Harold needs to look at them right away. In fact, if the package arrives, send Harold an e-mail telling him it's here. He might be checking his messages in there. Either way, wait until his door opens. And if anyone asks, I'll be back when I'm back."

"Uh, sure Kate." She hesitated a moment. "You will be back this afternoon won't you?"

"Don't worry Jackie. I won't leave you to be eaten up by the wolves. Yeah, I'll be back. I'm just going out for a walk. Clear my head."

"A walk? You're sure? But you don't walk Kate."

"Maybe I'm starting. See you later."

I came out of the office and stood at the corner of King and Bay Streets. I was confused about which way to go. I'd never deliberately gone for a walk. Sure, I'd walk to get something to eat, or walk to my doctor's office four blocks over. But to walk for the sake of walking was something new to me. I turned left and hiked south on Bay Street. At Front Street I looked right and left. Nothing interested me either way and the looming Union Station just depressed me even more. I continued down Bay through the underpass towards Lake Ontario and Queen's Quay. I mentally patted myself on the back as I passed two sidewalk vendors selling hot dogs. I dodged a few homeless people panhandling for money. My pace was by no means brisk, but I walked as fast as my short legs could carry me, although walking briskly wasn't something easily accomplished at lunchtime in this area of the city. The sidewalks were teeming with people and I managed to hit every red light. The road was torn up as usual at the entrance to Lakeshore Boulevard, and I stepped carefully over the construction debris littering the street.

There was less traffic noise and things were more peaceful when I finally reached Queen's Quay. The sun was bright and the reflection on the lake hurt my eyes. I found an unoccupied bench facing the lake and I sat down heavily. I rummaged in my purse for sunglasses and cigarettes. I wasn't out of breath and felt good. I wasn't sure if the walk could be considered aerobic exercise because I hadn't worked up a sweat. But I had walked. And I reminded myself as I lit a cigarette, that I hadn't walked for exercise, I had walked to get away from the office.

I leaned back on the bench and tilted my face to the sun and thought about quitting. The job. The so-called career. I wondered if there were places to work out there that treated their employees like people. Places that realized that the workers *were* people. I laughed out loud when I realized that those types of places only existed in brochures describing working conditions in communist countries. I knew I was cynical but I had earned the right. I had been watching grown men play at being powerful executives now for so many years it was a joke.

How important was it all, I asked myself. In the whole scheme of things, how important was the business our company was in? In two years, we'd be selling customers something completely different because technology changes so quickly. Our executives clearly didn't care about our customers. Look at how many of our former customers have us tied up in litigation. We weren't working on a cure for cancer. We were selling technology. Big fucking deal. I flicked my cigarette butt into the grass.

So Kate, if you quit, what'll you do? I had always been cocky enough to think I could get a job anywhere. Enough people had told me they wanted to hire me. I could make a list as long as your arm of the number of high-powered executives in this city who had patronizingly told me what a fantastic job I did. "Hope they pay you well, Kate," several had said to me.

Right. I made excellent money for a secretary and I had surpassed the salary ceiling for that field of work. But you're not a secretary Kate, I reminded myself. You're a paralegal. And paralegals make less money than secretaries. There was no way I could go to a law firm and make the money I was making at TechniGroup. I was making more now than many junior associates in law firms.

I mentally kicked myself for not going to law school when I had the chance. I had the applications filled out and had taken the LSAT exams and was ready to take the plunge. There was enough money saved to get by and Mom and Dad had promised to help if things got rough. But then I met Tommy. Whirlwind romance. Every time he'd kissed me, the thought of law school got further and further from my mind. By the time the dust had settled and we were divorced I had no more ambition. I'd quit the law firm and started doing temp work in the city. There was a different job each week and I had started to really enjoy not getting attached to the people I worked with. Like a homeless person wandering the streets, only I wandered the offices of Toronto. It was a great healing time for me.

I was ready to settle down again when they offered me a full-time job at TechniGroup. And now I had the seven year itch. Seven years at TechniGroup. I knew there wasn't anywhere else for me to go in the company in terms of advancement. But who was I kidding? There's only so far you can go as a secretary or for that matter, a paralegal. You work with one of the top dogs and you do all their dirty work. Day in and day out. Most times the work was interesting but after a while, it was the same. If I went to another company I'd be doing the same thing after six months. Working for one of the senior people and as soon as I got the hang of the company and all the inner workings, I'd be back in the same boat. What a vicious fucking circle. Maybe it was time to get into a whole new field.

I put my elbows on my knees and cupped my face in my hands and stared out at the lake. Shit, this was depressing. I felt my shoulders getting heavy and knew that if I didn't shake out of this mood I'd be in sad shape by the end of the day.

The assholes were getting to me and I was feeling sorry for myself. If my mother were here she'd jack me up and tell me to snap out of it. "There's always someone worse off than you," she'd say. And she'd be right.

I had a job. A nice apartment. A car that worked most of the time. I had friends. And family. And what did I care about those idiots at TechniGroup? I cared about what they were doing to Jay. And how he was going to get fucked worse than Rick Cox. At least Cox'll get a very generous severance package. And his stock options. Jay'll get nothing.

I smiled to myself when I thought about the severance for Rick. Right now we were telling the public he resigned. But when we disclosed the terms of his settlement package, as we were obliged to do under securities laws, we'd have to disclose the fact that we paid him severance. Any shareholder in their right mind should ask the question, why pay severance when someone resigns? I'm sure the company was banking on the fact that shareholders had short memories. The company would part with over a million dollars just to get rid of Rick Cox. And Jay is on the street, without a reference and no severance. I was starting to get pissed off again and being pissed off felt a lot better than being depressed.

I started walking back over to Bay Street and dreaded the thought of the long walk back to the office. Fuck it, I thought. I'd had enough exercise to last me a month. I hailed a cab.

CHAPTER
twenty-six

Jackie was standing outside my office door wringing her hands when I got back. She looked worried. "Kate, thank God you're back," she said anxiously.

Great, another crisis. Well, they'll just have to take a number and get in line. I opened the door and waved her in.

"What is it Jackie?"

"There's a police officer in the reception waiting to see you. The receptionist has been calling every five minutes looking for you."

"A police officer? Why? Did anyone say what he wants?"

"No," Jackie said. "And it's a she. Do you want me to go get her?"

"No. Thanks. I'll go."

Thoughts of disaster ran through my mind as I walked quickly to the reception area. God. Please don't let it be something awful. I'd never had a police person call on me before. I had no idea what to expect. My mouth was dry and my mind was racing.

She was sitting in one of the guest chairs in the reception thumbing through a magazine. As I came in, the receptionist said my name and the police officer stood up. She was very petite and almost as short as I was.

I held out my hand and said, "Hi. I'm Kathleen Monahan."

"Hi. I'm Constable Gina Lofaro." She shook my hand.

Gina had very short, very curly black hair. Her skin was almost see-through and she looked like a china doll. Beautiful dark eyes and a perfectly shaped nose. She could be a model, I thought. Being a police officer on the streets of Toronto must be one tough job and I quickly got past her delicate beauty. She obviously didn't get the job because of her looks.

"Is there somewhere we can talk?" she asked me.

"Uh, sure." I turned around to the receptionist and asked her if the small meeting room was empty. She nodded.

I pointed Constable Lofaro to the closed door on the opposite side of the reception area. I opened the door and turned on the lights and sat down on one of the chairs at the small, circular meeting table. I looked up at her anxiously as she closed the door behind her.

"Is there something wrong? Has there been an accident?" I asked her. My voice was shaky and my knees felt weak. I put my hands in front of me on the table.

"No, no. Everything's okay. Danny Morris asked me to talk to you."

My knees started to knock.

"Danny?" I croaked out. I cleared my throat. "Danny? Evelyn Morris' son? Is he all right?"

"Yes, he's fine. So to speak. Let me start at the beginning." She pulled out the chair opposite me and sat down. She pulled out a small notebook from her breast pocket and flipped it open.

"As you are no doubt aware, Evelyn Morris died on Thursday night. An autopsy was performed and the coroner has ruled her death accidental. The autopsy report noted that there were very high levels of peanut oil in her digestive system. The report also noted that Mrs. Morris was severely allergic to nuts." She looked up at me.

"We all knew Evelyn was allergic to nuts," I said.

Constable Lofaro wrote something in her notebook.

"Mr. Morris came to our station this morning after he received the results of the autopsy. He's asked us to look into the matter. He was adamant that his mother wouldn't knowingly eat anything with peanut oil in it. In fact, he said that it was a rule at the office that nothing was brought in by the staff or the caterers for social events with peanut oil in it. Is this your understanding as well?"

I nodded my head.

"What can you tell me about last Thursday night?" she asked me. Her pen was poised over her notebook.

I described to her what had happened.

"Did you see Mrs. Morris eat anything?"

I shook my head. "No. As I said, I was only in the room for a short time. She could have eaten before I got there. She certainly wasn't looking good when I arrived but I remember her saying she was hot."

"Tell me about the food. Did you use the same caterers?"

"No. It was a potluck. I think Mr. Oakes, our chairman, asked the staff to bring the food. This wouldn't have happened if it was catered. The firm we use has strict orders about the use of peanut oil and they knew about Ev's allergy. I can't imagine who would bring something to the office with peanut oil in it. I think someone told me the message that went out to the staff about the potluck reminded everyone about Ev's allergy. She shouldn't have eaten anything. She shouldn't have taken the chance. How could she be so stupid?"

Constable Lofaro looked up from her notebook. "She probably trusted everyone. Listen, we're looking into this because Mr. Morris has asked us to. He's understandably very upset. Is there anything else you can tell me?"

My conversation with Jay the day before at the restaurant came to mind. Evelyn and stock options. Rick Cox and stock options. Jay and stock options. Fucking stock options.

"No," I said and shook my head. I wasn't about to speculate with the police.

She closed her notebook and asked, "I don't suppose any of the food from last Thursday night is still around?"

"Well, it was stinking up the kitchen on Saturday night. I'm sure it would have been cleaned away though by now. We can go and take a look if you want," I offered.

She put her notebook back in her breast pocket and stood up. "Sure, let's take a look."

She followed me across the reception and down the hall to the large boardroom where the party had been held last Thursday night. I opened the door a crack to make sure the room was not being used. A few overhead pot lights were on and I noticed that the room had been restored to its status as a boardroom. Not a party room.

"Come on," I said over my shoulder to Constable Lofaro.

We walked through the room to the other side and I opened a door into the kitchenette that was well hidden in the dark cherry wood paneling.

"This is the room where the caterers normally work from if we have a function in the boardroom. The day after the party last week, the counters here and the fridge were full of the leftovers from the party," I told her. There was no food on the counters and when I opened the fridge, it was empty except for cream and milk.

"Well, they must have finally cleaned it out," I said.

"Do you know how often they pick up the garbage?" she asked me.

"Every day I think. They come every night to take away the garbage. But the cleaning staff aren't allowed to touch anything on the counters and they certainly wouldn't touch anything in the fridge," I said.

"Do they come on Friday's or Sunday's?" she asked me. "At the station," she explained, "the cleaning staff take Friday nights off and clean on Sunday's. What happens around here?"

"Friday's. I've never seen them here on a Sunday."

"Have they been around today?"

"Not that I know of. They come around six-thirty or seven at night. It's far too early."

"So," she said. "If you said the food was stinking up the kitchen on Saturday night, the food would have still been here this morning. On the assumption that the cleaning staff don't come around until Monday night. Right? Is there someone we can ask?"

"Sure." I picked up the phone on the wall beside the refrigerator and dialled the office manager's extension. She answered right away.

"Linda. It's Kate. Did the cleaning staff clean out the fridge in the kitchenette off the main boardroom over the weekend?" I asked her.

"No, Kate, I did. Someone complained this morning about the smell so I emptied everything into green garbage bags. It was disgusting. And I threw out everyone's Tupperware containers."

"So where is it now?"

"I called the building maintenance people to come and haul it away. Why? Did I throw out something of yours? I'm sorry if I did Kate. I just couldn't bring myself to empty each container and then wash them. Christine is away today so I had to do it. Usually, that's her job."

Christine was the office clerk who got all the nice jobs like cleaning the sour milk out of the fridge and washing out coffee cups with science experiments in them.

"No, it's all right Linda. I was just curious."

"Well," she said. "I had to lug the garbage bags out to the service elevator. The lazy pokes at building maintenance told me to leave the stuff there. It's probably stinking up the service elevator bay now."

"Thanks Linda. I'll have a look."

I went to hang up the phone and Linda said, "Kate, are you nuts? You're going to go through the garbage? Did you lose something?"

"No, no. Never mind Linda. Thanks for your help." I hung up the phone and turned to Constable Lofaro.

"The officer manager said she emptied everything into green garbage bags this morning and put it out by the service elevator. Do you want to see if it's still there?" She nodded.

The service elevator was at the opposite end of the hall from the back door where I usually entered the office. There were large double steel doors with small windows in them about three quarters of the way up the door. It was hopeless trying to see through the windows so I opened one of the double doors and the smell, or rather the stench, wafted out of three garbage bags piled in the corner.

"There's the stuff," I pointed out.

She glanced at the bags and looked at me. I knew what was coming.

"No. Please," I begged. "Take my word for it. I know that smell. Don't make me do it."

She laughed. "Come on. Plug your nose. Help me out here. I'll open one bag and you can confirm it's garbage from your office."

"Why can't Linda do it?" I whined. I had a weak stomach at the best of times and this certainly wasn't going to help. The only saving grace was the fact that I hadn't eaten lunch and my stomach was empty.

I plugged my nose. "Okay. Let's do it. Hurry up." I breathed through my mouth.

She untied the top bag and I glanced in. I could see a jumble of Tupperware containers and serving platters. There was loose food around the sides of the bag and I eyed one of the brownies I had been so eager to stuff into my mouth last Friday. I was going to puke. Right here. Right now. I made a mental note to never eat brownies again.

I nodded at Constable Lofaro and hurried out the door. I left her there to tie the bag back up. I was breathing deeply when she came back out.

"Hey, that was nothing," she said. "The food's only a couple of days old. No maggots, yet. Buck up," she laughed.

"You sound like my mother," I said. "How can you do that?" I asked her.

"Do what? Look in a garbage bag? Big deal. At least I didn't find a dead baby."

I held up my hand. "Stop right there. Stop it. I appreciate you have a pretty disgusting job at times. But I've got a weak stomach."

"You're over-reacting," she said.

"I know," I agreed. "Kate Monahan's school of over-reaction. My parents said I should have been an actor. So you've found out one of my deep dark secrets. Keep it to yourself, okay?"

"No problem. Look, because the food is still around, I'm going to take it in. We'll have the lab do some analysis on it."

"What will they look for?" I asked.

"Peanut oil, obviously. That and other things. I'll hand it over to one of the detectives. Thanks for your help Ms. Monahan," she said and held out her hand.

"Kate. Call me Kate. Listen, do you know if they've released Evelyn's body to the family?"

"No, I don't know. They probably have though if the autopsy's been done and the report released. You'd have to ask Mr. Morris."

"You're right. I'll call Danny right away. We're all anxious to know about funeral arrangements. We miss her so much, you know." I was blathering again and I stopped myself. "Do you want some help lugging those bags?" I offered.

"No, I'll be fine. Do you know if this elevator goes to the underground parking garage?"

I nodded. "Great," she continued. "I'm parked inside so I can just take this elevator. Thanks again." She opened the door to the service elevator bay and disappeared behind it.

I stood there and thought about how strange it was that the police were now involved in Evelyn's death. I remembered my conversation with Jay yesterday and how we both agreed that no one suspected foul play in Evelyn's death. Well, Danny thought enough about it to go to the police.

I opened the door to the elevator bay and saw that Constable Lofaro was still waiting for the elevator. With my nose plugged, I told her, "This elevator could take days. Someone might be using it to move in or out of the building you know."

"I'll wait a little longer," she said. "Was there something else?"

"Yeah," I said. I paused for a moment. "Do you have a card? With your phone number on it? Just in case I think of something else."

She dug in her pants pocket and handed me one.

"And how can we get in touch with you after office hours?" she asked me.

"I'm in the book."

CHAPTER
twenty-seven

Suddenly I was very tired and realized that my whole body was trembling slightly from the aftershock of finding out what the police wanted. My psyche had steeled itself for a disaster - a personal shock - and when that didn't happen, my body didn't react and get back to normal as quickly.

Harold's door was still closed as I went past and none of the legal support staff were in their area so I closeted myself in my office and lit a cigarette.

The red light was flashing on my phone and I knew I had to get back to work. I had accomplished little today and if things kept going the way they were, I wouldn't feel too good about leaving at five. And I was leaving at five. Harold may have a short memory, but I didn't.

I grabbed my notebook and dialled into my voice mail. THIRTEEN new messages, the computer voice intoned. Thirteen new messages in two hours. It certainly wasn't a record for the most messages received in two hours but it was close. I guessed things had been busier than I thought.

I worked my way through the messages, making notes about who I had to call back. Harold had left me three, describing things he needed done. None of them mentioned Rick Cox or the papers from Cleve.

Two of the messages were from Danny and one was from Jay. I decided to call Danny first.

The phone rang a couple of times on the other end and when Danny answered he sounded out of breath.

"Hello."

"Hi Danny. It's Kate. How're you doing? You sound out of breath."

"I was upstairs. Cleaning out Mom's room. Trying to sort through her things."

God, that must be an awful job, I thought. It would tear my heart out. I hoped he wasn't calling to ask me to help him so I quickly changed the subject.

"You left me a couple of messages. What's up?"

"I just wanted to let you know that they've released her body and I've made the funeral arrangements. There'll be visitation tomorrow afternoon and tomorrow evening and we'll bury her on Wednesday morning. We'll have a service in the chapel at the funeral home before we go to the cemetery. I'd like it if you could come by, Kate."

"Oh, Danny. Of course. I'll be there. Tomorrow afternoon and evening. Both. If you want. Anything. Are you doing okay?"

"I'm getting there," he said. He did sound a lot better than he had on Friday night when I last talked to him. "We're all getting there. Little Sarah is still pretty upset. She keeps asking if Grandma's an angel now."

My throat tightened up.

"Well, I'll be there. Which funeral home, Danny?"

"The Hillson Memorial Home, on Clark. It's near Exhibition Stadium."

"I know the one. I'll see you tomorrow afternoon. Call me in the meantime if you want anything," I said.

"Uh, Kate. One other thing. I went to the police this morning," he said quietly.

"I know Danny. Why'd you do that?" I asked him softly.

"Because it didn't seem right. The autopsy said she'd died from an allergic reaction to peanuts. And they ruled the death accidental. But the coroner told me she had very high levels of peanut oil in her system. It didn't make any sense. First of all, we both know mom wouldn't eat anything she suspected might have peanut oil in it. Secondly, if she couldn't confirm the ingredients in something, she just didn't eat it. You guys all knew about her allergy didn't you? She trusted you. And look what happened." He started to sob. "Someone did this to her. I just want to know why. This wasn't accidental. I'm sure of it."

"We'll let the police decide that Danny. It had to have been an accident," I tried to convince him. "Who would want to kill your mother? Think about it. If there was anything wrong here at the office she would have told me or you. She didn't have anything to hide. Danny, I think this was just a horrible accident."

"Did the police come and see you? I told them to talk to you."

"Yes, a police officer came by a little while ago. She took away some food to have it tested. We'll know better when they get the results if it was something she ate at the party."

"It had to be something she ate at the party. Peanut allergies kick in right away. It's not like food poisoning you know," he said.

"I know. Look, I'll see you tomorrow, okay?"

I hung up after we said good-bye and put my head in my hands. This day was an emotional roller-coaster. I thought about leaving Harold a message that I was sick and going home but thought better of it. If Danny wanted me at the funeral home tomorrow afternoon, I'd only be in the office for the morning. And with the funeral on Wednesday morning, I'd be so behind by Wednesday afternoon, I'd never catch up.

I wondered if I should let anyone here at the office know that the police were now involved. They'd probably find out soon enough though. If Constable Lofaro had been waiting for any length of time in the reception, everyone would've known about it because tongues wag very quickly around here. Except for Harold there wasn't one officer of the company I trusted to take the situation seriously.

Before I did anything else I called the office manager again. I got her voice mail and left her a message. I asked her to send a broadcast e-mail message to all employees letting them know about the funeral arrangements for Ev. I also asked her to send some flower arrangements to the funeral home.

I made a quick call to Vee to find out about the stock price and was shocked when she told me it was down two dollars so far for the day.

"That brings us close to seven dollars," I said unnecessarily.

"I know. We're getting close to the price the shares were at four years ago when Oakes joined us. If the company lasts and we keep our jobs, I hope the shareholders fry his ass at the next shareholders' meeting," she said vehemently.

"Gee, Vanessa. Don't beat around the bush. Just come out with it and let us know how you really feel," I joked. She laughed reluctantly.

I returned some more calls and actually got some work done. Harold had asked me in one of his messages to call all of the out-of-town directors to ask them where to send their packages of materials for the board meeting on Thursday. Is the man in his right mind? If the materials haven't gone out by now, and past history was any indication, the board members wouldn't receive any material until they were seated at the table and the Chairman called the meeting to order. It was Monday and there was no sign of the documents being ready in time to send out today. If we sent them Tuesday by overnight courier, the directors wouldn't receive the packages until noon on Wednesday at the earliest, and by then, most of the out-of-town directors would be on their way to Toronto for the meeting on Thursday morning. This was a lame exercise we went through every time there was a meeting, and I was sick of playing the game.

Jackie could make the phone calls and take the heat from the directors' secretaries. They got tired of playing the game as well and would usually get pretty snippy with me. Or, if they were feeling particularly benevolent that day, they'd put me straight through to Mr. Director himself who would proceed to chew me out for not getting the documents out on time. No way. I was tired of going through the motions and being made a fool of.

I dialled Jackie to find out if Harold's door was open yet and she said she hadn't seen him all day and that as far as she knew, the door hadn't opened.

"So he still hasn't received those documents I gave you this morning?" I asked her.

"Nope. And the courier package from Scapelli's is still sitting here. Want me to bring them back in to you?"

"Please." I wanted to get a look at Rick Cox's severance package.

The courier package was a large envelope taped up very tightly. The front and back were stamped in red: "Confidential. To be opened by addressee only." Harold Didrickson was the addressee so I opened the envelope. What the hell, I thought. Some secretaries have very strict orders about opening confidential material but I had never received any such orders from Harold. I believe he trusted me.

The documents inside the envelope were very interesting. The company was kicking in section 4(a) of Rick Cox's employment agreement. The 'termination without cause' section. And termination without cause entitled Rick to three times his annual salary. I flipped to Schedule "A" of the document where they attached a copy of the actual employment agreement. Section 1(a) of the employment agreement stated that his annual salary was $550,000 a year. And that was a couple of years ago. If I remembered correctly from last year's annual information form, Rick's salary had gone up considerably.

I continued reading the main document. He was going to receive just over $2,000,000 in severance and was entitled to his exercisable stock options. I was too sick to do a quick calculation on what he'd make on those. Son of a bitch. I must get me fired one of these days. And then I remembered, I didn't have an employment agreement, and, I'd be lucky if the company gave me two weeks notice. They could get rid of me for not putting my dirty coffee cup in the dishwasher.

Well, well, well. I'm sure the two million dollars would smooth Rick's transition. Make him feel a little better about getting fired for fucking the company. Jay wouldn't be getting anything.

I picked up the documents from Scapelli's and all the other stuff for Harold that had accumulated over the day. I got the keys to his office from my desk drawer. I had decided to barge in if the door was locked.

Which it was. I knocked and when I didn't get any answer, I went in. Harold was lying on the sofa in his office with one arm over his eyes and I couldn't tell if he was sleeping.

"Harold," I said softly.

"I asked you not to disturb me," he said.

"Well, I wasn't sure if you were in or not," I lied. "I went out for lunch earlier on and I didn't know if you had gone out." I dropped the documents in his basket.

"What part of do not disturb don't you understand?" he asked me snidely. What a prick.

"The disturb part. I don't understand disturb, Harold," I retorted. "Disturb means to bother. I'm not bothering you. I'm doing my job. And if you're finished your little nap, maybe you should do yours." I looked at my watch. It was four-thirty. That meant it was six o'clock in Newfoundland. Good enough for me. Harold continued to lie on the sofa with his forearm covering his eyes.

"And," I continued. "It's quitting time. I'll see you tomorrow for the morning. I'll be out tomorrow afternoon and Wednesday morning. If anyone's focused on the board materials by tomorrow morning, I'd be glad to get working on them. If not, it'll have to wait until Wednesday afternoon. If I come back from Evelyn's funeral. The family may need me."

"I expect you to be here on Wednesday after the funeral.

There'll be a lot of things to get ready for the board meeting. We need you to do up a stock option report in the morning.   I understand Jay's no longer with us and you'll have to do it." He said all of this in a monotone.

I walked over to where he was lying and looked down at him. He removed his arm from over his eyes and looked up at me. He looked like shit. But didn't we all these days.

"In mourning for Rick?" I asked him. I knew I was treading on thin ice here and didn't care. He'd shown absolutely no emotion when Ev died and I had no sympathy for him.

He sat up and put his elbows on his knees and looked up at me.

"Kate. You're a smart girl. Think about the effect Rick's departure is going to have on me. Ergo, the effect it's going to have on you. Have a little sympathy here."

A hot flash coursed through my veins and I tried, I really tried, to keep my temper in check.

"Sympathy?" I said quietly through clenched teeth. "Sympathy? You want to know where to find sympathy? It's in the dictionary. Look it up. It's between shit and syphilis."

I slammed the door behind me on my way out.

CHAPTER
twenty-eight

I made one last call before leaving for the day.
"Hi. It's Kate," I said.

"Well I know that," Jay said. "How's your day been?" He sounded awfully chipper for someone who'd lost his job. Well, he probably had every right to feel chipper. He was out of this hell-hole. I guess I'd feel chipper too if I didn't have to come back in the morning.

"My day's been so-so. Actually, pretty rotten. But that's boring and I'm sure you don't want to hear anything about it," I said. "How's your day been?"

"Not bad, all in all. Why don't I tell you all about it over dinner tonight?" he asked.

"Dinner? I guess I have to eat. And I couldn't think of anyone nicer to eat with. Where should we meet?"

"How about somewhere close to home? Any ideas?"

"Yeah. I feel like Italian. How about Tony's? We could meet about six-thirty."

"I thought Tony's was just take-out," Jay said.

"He's got a few tables. And he's got other things besides pizza. You'll like it."

"Okay. Fine by me. See you there about six-thirty," he signed off.

I turned off my computer and left my desk in its usual mess. I decided to leave by the reception area, just to let everyone know I was leaving early. No sneaking out the back door this time. I asked myself if I was being petty and bitchy and decided I wasn't. If everyone else can act like babies, I could act like a toddler.

Traffic was lighter than normal and I realized it had been a long time since I was out of the office at ten to five. I arrived home in thirty minutes and took a leisurely shower. I dressed in jeans and a loose blouse. Because this was almost like a date, I put on clean, white sweat socks. I arrived at Tony's fifteen minutes early.

"To be punctual, is to be princely," my father used to lecture. I had tried over the years to be late for things and just couldn't do it. If I was five minutes early, I got palpitations of the heart and considered myself late. Fifteen minutes early was just right by my father's standards. I could drive around the block a few times but I saw a good parking spot in front of the Pizzeria and grabbed it.

Alfredo was on the phone behind the counter when I walked in. I glanced to the left and saw that none of the six tables were occupied.

"Are Monday's always this slow?" I asked him when he hung up.

"No darling. I just had a feeling you were coming in so I cleared the place. We did the same for the Pope you know, the last time he was in Toronto." He came around the front of the counter with a menu in his hand and gave me a bear hug.

"Are you taking out or eating in?" he asked me.

"Eating in. With someone. He's meeting me here in a few minutes." I headed over to my favourite table at the back, beside the window. I couldn't remember the last time I'd eaten here with someone. Usually, I eat alone and read the newspaper.

"With someone," Alfredo mimicked me as he followed me. "And it's a him. Ooh. Someone special Kathleen?"

I sat down and hooked my purse over the back of the chair.

"Yes, Alfredo. It's a him. And is he someone special? None of your business," I teased. "Now can I please have a drink?" We both laughed.

"Right away." He was singing the Katie song as he made his way back to the counter.

I stared out the window and watched the traffic as I waited for Jay. I knew I had really pushed Didrickson to the limit today. Twice. I had never talked back to him like that. Most times I was my usual sarcastic self and most times I got away with it because I knew when it was appropriate. And I didn't think my sarcasm had any menace to it. It was mostly teasing.

But today he had made me angry twice. And both times I let him have it back. My parents had brought me up to respect authority and I know now that my mother regrets teaching us that. "Blind respect for authority will get you nothing but trouble," my mother says now. "Let them earn your respect first." My father on the other hand still believes in blind obedience. That's what made him a first class, infantry soldier.

I still have trouble defining the line between blind respect and earned respect. But I had learned over the last couple of years that just because someone is in a position of authority, doesn't mean they *deserve* to be in that position.

Usually, I'm a good soldier. And I admit that I'm a soldier. I do what's asked of me to the best of my abilities. But even a good soldier gets tired of the assholes.

I noticed Jay's car drive by and I yelled at Alfredo for my drink.

"Come on. The service in this place is going downhill. All I asked for was a measly soda water. Did you have to go to the restaurant down the street to get it?"

"Hang on. Hang on," he yelled back. He was bending down behind the counter and he was triumphant when he stood back up. "Found it!"

He paraded to my table with a soda water in one hand and a round, red glass ball with a candle inside. He placed the soda in front of me and fumbled in his pants pockets for some matches to light the candle which he put in the middle of the table.

"Please Alfredo. Let's not make a big deal out of this. And you better not make a fuss when he comes in or you'll lose your best customer. Please," I begged him. I hated being the center of attention.

"Sure, sure. Don't you worry. We'll make this a very," he strung out the word verrrrry, "romantic dinner."

"I didn't say I wanted a romantic dinner. If I wanted romantic, I'd go somewhere else. Somewhere nice," I teased. "I want food. Good food. Come on Alfredo. Don't embarrass me," I pleaded.

"Ah, Cara Mia," he crooned.

"Cut the phoney Italian shit, Alfredo. Now go away. Get," I ordered him. We were both laughing so hard I didn't notice Jay standing behind Alfredo.

I leaned sideways and smiled at Jay when we both realized he was there. He was wearing jeans and a faded Levi jean jacket with a white T-shirt underneath. Very sexy. He looked good enough to eat. "Come on Jay. Take a seat. Let me introduce you to my great-grandfather Alfredo. Alfredo, this is Jay Harmon." They shook hands and Jay sat down. Alfredo continued to hover.

"Jay, Alfredo has decided to make my life miserable this evening. Please order something to drink so he'll go away," I told him. I smiled up at Alfredo very sweetly.

"I'll have a beer. Labatt's Blue," Jay ordered.

"Right away, sir. And I'm not related to her," he said over his shoulder as he headed back to his counter.

"So," Jay started. "Tell me about your day. How were things at the office?"

"You don't want to know how things were. Things were shitty."

Alfredo arrived with Jay's beer and hovered.

"Can we wait a little while before we order?" I asked him. "I know there's a line-up out the door and down the street, but please sir, we'll tip big."

"All right, already. D'you want another soda water?" he asked.

"Not right now. Thanks. I'll yell when we're ready to order, okay?"

I looked over at Jay and he was smiling.

"You don't spare anyone do you? But that's one thing I adore about you Kate. You treat everyone the same."

I smiled back at him and thought about yesterday afternoon at his apartment. I leered at him and did my best Groucho Marx imitation. "Well not exactly the same, if you know what I mean."

"So, please. Tell me what happened today," Jay insisted.

"Well, I left the office at ten to five. Traffic was light coming home. I made it in thirty minutes. I went for a long walk at lunch down to the lake." Jay's eyebrows went up.

"A long walk? I'm impressed. Are you turning over a new leaf?" he teased me.

"No. For a moment I thought I was. But I took a cab back to the office," I replied.

"That's all very nice. But what happened when you got in this morning?"

"I had coffee with Vee."

"Are you avoiding the subject Kathleen? I just asked what happened today at the office."

"And I don't especially want to talk about it right now."

Jay took a long drink of his beer which Alfredo had poured into a tall pilsner glass.

"All right," he said. "Let's talk about my day. I got up. I went for a run, not a walk. I had coffee by myself. I didn't get caught in traffic. There. That was my day," he laughed. "Now tell me about yours. And stop being cute. I'm not going to drag it out of you."

So I told him. About being late and getting chewed out by Didrickson. About the press release going out before the market opened. About the continuing slide of the share price. About my long walk at lunch. About meeting Constable Lofaro. And the smelly garbage. About my talk with Danny. I left out the part about my conversation with Cleve and Rick Cox's severance package. I didn't want to rub dirt into his wounds.

I was fairly long-winded and by the time I finished my story, two more couples had come in for dinner and had already been served their pizzas.

"So, that's it in a nutshell," I said. "Hey waiter," I yelled at Alfredo. "Can we get some service over here?" Alfredo shook his fist at me from behind the counter.

Jay picked up the menu and glanced at it. "I've only had pizza from here. What else is good?"

"Everything. I'm having pizza. It's my favourite. I could eat it morning, noon and night. Now tell me about your day."

"Like I said, Kate. I ran, I drank coffee and I didn't get stuck in traffic. I played a little on the Internet."

Alfredo took our orders and returned with more drinks.

"The Internet? You're not turning into a geek on me are you?"

"No," he answered. "You're only a geek if you surf the net all day and all night. I have other plans for tonight."

He grinned and continued. "I found some interesting things on the net. I was looking up information on the companies we've acquired over the last few months."

"Yeah? What would the Internet have on those companies that we wouldn't know already? We cover off almost everything on due diligence. I even know the size of most of the major shareholders' boxer shorts by the time we're finished with them," I said.

"Well, because most of the companies we acquired were American, and publicly traded, their public information is filed on EDGAR through the Securities & Exchange Commission. All of their old 10-K's, prospectuses and stuff like that are on the web. And as you know, those documents contain facts about the company, their officers and shareholders. And their products. You just have to take the information a couple of steps further and it's magic. Amazing the stuff you can dig up."

This was interesting.

"So what amazing stuff did you come up with? Come on. Give."

"Nope. I'm still researching a few things. I could only get so far on the net and ended up at the library in the reference stacks. Bear with me though. If things lead where I think they're going, we could be in for a very interesting ride."

"Bear with you? Whaddya mean? Come on Jay. You know I live for this shit. You can't hold out on me," I said. Jay was grinning like the Cheshire cat. I grinned back.

"Me?" he asked. "Hold out on you? Now why would I do that? You and I both know that I follow your example. I share all the information with you." He looked a little more serious now and his tone suddenly changed. "Just like you do with me Kate."

"Right Kate?" he asked me when I didn't answer.

"Sorry. I thought it was rhetorical. Yeah, I share everything," I said quietly. My bluff and blarney was disappearing. I peered at Jay in the candlelight to see how serious he was. He was serious, not angry, but I wasn't sure what he was getting at.

"Okay, buster. What didn't I share with you?" I asked.

"Two million in severance? You can't tell me you didn't know that. And by the way, it's not the two million. It's the severance. The son of a bitch got fired. Fired. And the press release said he resigned. And he got severance?" Jay was angry now.

"Hey, don't get mad at me," I said defensively.

"I'm not mad at *you* about the severance. I just get extremely angry whenever I think about it. And I'm thinking about it right now and I'm angry."

Alfredo chose that moment to arrive with our food. Timely, I thought. The man is very timely.

I dug into my pizza and after a few mouthfuls I put down my fork and asked Jay, "How did you find out about Rick's severance? Will you share that with me?"

He finished chewing what was in his mouth. Good manners. "Sure. I'll share. Tom James told me. He told me everything."

Why wasn't I surprised?

CHAPTER
twenty-nine

"Tom James told you?" I repeated. I was incredulous. Tom was a senior officer of a public company and was bound by confidentiality. The severance arrangements for Rick Cox were confidential information. Tom shouldn't be sharing that information with anyone, especially an ex-employee of the company. Granted, the information would eventually become public knowledge but eventually was a long time off.

Jay nodded.

"When did you talk to Tom?" I asked.

"I took your suggestion and called him today. I told him what had happened with Rick and asked him if he could do anything about it. He said he'd look into the situation."

"I guess that's not all you talked about," I said.

"No. Tom told me what had happened with Rick. And he told me about the severance. Boy, the guy has loose lips. He told me that Oakes had been wanting to get rid of Rick for a long time. He said there was bad blood."

I shook my head. Unbelievable. I wondered how much Tom told his barber.

"What did he mean when he said he'd look into the situation?" I asked Jay.

"He didn't get specific. Tom said he'd call me back in a couple of days."

"Don't hold your breath. Besides, you don't want to work at TechniGroup anyway."

"Wrong Kate. That's easy for you to say. You have a job. I don't. You may not want to work at TechniGroup. I do. At least it pays the rent. Right now I have no job and no money coming in. And no references. How do I explain to a future employer why I left TechniGroup?"

"Lie to them," I said laughing.

"Stop being so damn flip about everything. I personally don't see any humour in the situation. It wasn't so bad you know, working there. I was getting well-rounded experience. I was exposed to a lot of things. The salary wasn't bad and I had some stock options. All in all, not a bad place. Just because you dislike it so much doesn't mean everyone else does." Jay was getting visibly angry again.

"I'm sorry," I apologized. "What're you going to do about a job?"

"I'm getting my resume together. I've called a couple of my friends from university. I'm putting the word out that I'm looking. But, the wheels turn slowly," he said.

"I know. Look, if there's anything I can do, let me know," I offered. "I could at least type your resume. It's one thing I do well."

"Thanks. I'll probably take you up on that."

Jay looked down at his plate of food which had quickly turned cold. He turned around and waved at Alfredo.

"Let's go. I've suddenly lost my appetite." He pulled his wallet out of the hip pocket of his jeans.

Alfredo arrived at the table and looked down at us.

"Ready for some coffee?" he asked. He gathered up the plates.

"No," said Jay. "Just the bill."

Alfredo raised his eyebrows and glanced at me.

"Nothing personal Alfredo. The food was great. We've got to go," I explained. "Do up the bill for us, please."

I gathered up my things and headed for the counter to pay. Jay was right behind me and he snatched the bill from Alfredo's outstretched hand. I looked at Jay beside me and said, "Let me pay."

"No way, Monahan," he said under his breath. He laid two twenties on the counter and took my elbow to steer me out the door.

"Thanks very much Alfredo," he said over his shoulder.

Outside on the sidewalk he said to me, "Kate, when I ask you to dinner, I pay. Okay?"

"Yessir, Mr. Caveman," I snapped. "Want to beat your chest now and drag me off by the hair?"

"What the hell is that all about? I asked you to dinner. I pay. If you ask me to dinner, you can pay. I resent the Mr. Caveman remark, Kathleen," he said. "It was totally uncalled for." He looked hurt.

Open mouth, insert foot, I thought.

"Sorry," I apologized again. I had been doing that a lot tonight. Apologizing. It wasn't often I was called upon to be sensitive and I probably needed a refresher course.

"You're right," I continued. "Totally uncalled for. Won't happen again." We were facing each other and I looked up at Jay with my best sexy smile.

"Can I make it up to you?" I offered. And I meant it. I admitted to myself that I liked where our relationship was going. And if I kept up the snide remarks there wouldn't be a relationship.

"How?" Jay grinned at me.

"Coffee at my place," I offered.

"How can I refuse? Should I drag you by the hair to your car or can you make it on your own?"

I drank too much coffee that night and it kept me awake. Jay and I had talked for a long time. I looked over Jay's sleeping face to the clock radio on the other side of the bed. The red fluorescent numbers read three-twenty. Lovely. If I didn't get to sleep soon I knew I'd be a basket case in the morning. I was wide awake now thinking about our conversation and some of the disturbing questions it raised.

I'd been sitting on the sofa and Jay was standing in front of the French doors looking at the park.

"Do you think Danny was right in going to the police?" I asked Jay.

He shrugged his shoulders. "I don't know. Put yourself in his place Kate." He turned around and came and sat down beside me.

"He's grieving and angry. Anger is one of the offshoots of grief. He can't believe his mother's dead. But the logic isn't there for me. Yes, Evelyn died at the office where everyone knew about her allergy. But it has to be an accident. Who in their right mind would want to kill her?" he asked.

"No one who kills is in their right mind. You know, I didn't tell anyone at the office that the police had come about her death," I told him.

"I wouldn't worry about it. If the police find anything, they'll all find out soon enough."

We sat quietly for a long time. Jay turned on the television and pushed the mute button. He flicked through the channels and I stared at the images on the screen. Jay settled on the Weather

Channel and he put the remote control on the table in front of him. We watched the satellite pictures and I tried to read the announcer's lips. Across the bottom of the screen were several digital clocks showing the local time in Halifax, Toronto, Winnipeg, Calgary and Vancouver. The clock showed nine-fifteen in Toronto and eight-fifteen in Winnipeg. The minutes ticked by.

When the clocks showed nine-nineteen in Toronto and eight-nineteen in Winnipeg I sat up straighter. 8:19.

"Jay, what time did Evelyn die last Thursday?"

"Um, around eleven-thirty I think. Why?"

I ignored his question. "What time did we leave the office to go to the hospital?"

"I can't remember. Around eight or eight thirty. Why?"

Eight-nineteen set off some bells in my head. I tried to remember the sequence of events that night.

I remembered the paramedics rushing Ev on to the elevator. I remembered trying to call Danny from the phone in my office. I remembered waiting for Jay in the lobby of the building. I remembered my frustration because he was taking so long. And then I remembered looking at my watch. It had said eight-twenty. Or it could have been eight-nineteen. I'm never that accurate when reading the time from my watch because it's not digital.

Okay, I thought. I was waiting for Jay in the lobby of the building at eight-nineteen. Or eight-twenty. What was the significance of that? It was really bugging me and I couldn't pin it down. I got up off the sofa and poured myself another coffee in the kitchen.

I leaned back against the counter in the kitchen and sipped my coffee and methodically went through the events of the last few days. Eight-nineteen had been significant in another discussion I had participated in, or listened to, sometime in the last few days. The light bulb finally went on in my head when I remembered it was during the discussion between Ray and Grace. Ray had been helping Grace read the user information from the report Ray had printed out. The system had shown that Rick Cox had logged on the system at eight-nineteen. I remembered now asking Grace to repeat the time to me. Something must have seemed wrong to me at that time as well.

But eight-nineteen was significant to me because I remember waiting for Jay in the lobby of the building at that time. And I remembered that it was five minutes or more before he showed up. And Jay had Rick's password to the system. I felt sick when I realized it could have been Jay who signed on the system while I was waiting in the lobby. While Ev was dying. Maybe Rick's protests of innocence weren't so far off base. Had anyone seen Rick at the party, I wondered. If he wasn't in the boardroom at the reception, he could have been logged on the system. The log report showed that whoever had logged on, had been at Evelyn's terminal. In her office. While she was dying.

My mind protested this line of thinking. Rick Cox had been accused, tried and found guilty. I knew Jay. And I knew Jay would never have done what they accused Rick of. No way. He was too honest. Besides, I didn't sleep with dishonest people. I couldn't and wouldn't believe that Jay would have anything to do with this whole mess.

I sensed Jay's presence in the doorway and looked up guiltily.

"A penny for your thoughts," he said quietly. He was leaning against the doorframe with his hands in his jeans pockets. "The Weather Channel was getting boring so I thought I'd join you. You look confused. What're you thinking about?" he asked me.

"Nothing," I lied. "Just thinking. About Ev. And the funeral. I have to go to the visitation tomorrow afternoon. I've never done this before, you know. I wonder what it'll be like."

"Not pleasant," Jay said. "Funeral's never are. I'll go with you. We can find out together."

Jay came over to where I was leaning against the counter and put his arms around me. I hugged him back very tightly. I felt guilty about putting Jay at the scene of the crime, so to speak. But the dirty deed had been done at eight-nineteen and Jay had had the opportunity.

"I have to ask you a question," I said into his chest.

"Shoot," he said back.

I took Jay's hand and led him back to the living room.

"Sit down," I said.

He sat on the sofa and looked up at me. "It's too early for a marriage proposal Kathleen," he said. "And besides, I wanted to be the first to ask."

"Don't joke about that Jay," I said. "And this wasn't going to be a marriage proposal." I sat down beside him.

"Let me take you back through a sequence of events as I remember them," I continued. I looked down at my hands and said, "Last Thursday night, after the paramedics disappeared on the elevator with Ev, I went back to my office to try and call Danny. When I couldn't reach him I left. I went to the lobby of the building and waited for you. It seemed like forever before you came down in the elevator. I remember looking at my watch and deciding that if you didn't show up soon, I was leaving without you." I looked at Jay. "You said you were just going to get your jacket. What took you so long?"

Jay looked back at me. "I can't remember. I went back to my office and got my jacket. I met you in the lobby. That's all, I think."

I stared at him and measured his words. There was no hedging. He sounded honest.

"Then what took so long?"

"I don't remember Kate. What's this all about anyway? Why am I getting the third degree?"

"Because. I know some things that're bothering me. And I'm trying to figure something out."

"Well maybe I can help figure it out if you tell me what you know," he offered.

I lit a cigarette and dragged deeply. I felt the smoke seer my lungs. I have to quit this filthy habit, I thought. I took another drag.

"Okay. I know some things that I'm not supposed to know. I hear things. I'm privy to confidential information. Sometimes, I'm amazed at how much I know. But then I remember that people speak in front of me and forget that I'm there. It's like I'm invisible. Because I'm a lowly support person, they don't think I can understand what they're talking about. So they talk around me and ignore me. You understand?" I asked him.

"Yeah. I understand. Can you be a little more specific?"

"I'm getting there. The other thing I wanted to say is that the confidential stuff I hear, has to stay confidential. Sure, I talk about it with Vanessa, but she's bound by the same code I am. We keep our jobs because we're discrete. And we're expected to keep things that we hear, confidential."

"Kate, I understand confidentiality. And you should know that people talk in front of you not because they think you don't understand. It's because they trust you."

"Well, I'm about to break that trust. I know we have a relationship. Or at least I hope it becomes a relationship. I keep forgetting it's only been a couple of days." I smiled at Jay.

"Anyway, I shouldn't share any confidential information with you.   Especially since you're an ex-employee of the company," I said quietly. I wasn't about to put my foot in my mouth again and rub it in because he didn't have a job. I was consciously practicing sensitivity here. "Even if you were still working at the company," I continued quickly, "I wouldn't be in a position to share this stuff with you."

"I understand all that Kate. So what's the big deal? Did you discover the secret to the atomic bomb in Harold's out-basket?"

We both laughed.

"No. Nothing quite so serious. Did I tell you what Grace and I were doing at the office on Saturday?" He shook his head.

"We were checking the stock option records. My records against Ev's. And she had Ray print-off a report that shows when everyone uses the computer system. The report shows every time someone logs on, what terminal they're using, what part of the system they log on to, stuff like that. Did you know they had those sorts of records?" I asked him.

"Sure. I knew. I learned a lot about the internal system when I was working in with some technical guys on one of my rotations."

"Well, anyway, Ray's report shows that Rick Cox logged on to Ev's terminal at eight-nineteen on Thursday night. He logged into the stock option system and was on the computer for three or four minutes. That's the confidential information I shouldn't be sharing with you."

"Rick told me that they had a report showing he logged on. So where do I come in to this?"

"I remember waiting for you in the lobby. You said you were going to get your jacket but it was taking so long. I looked at my watch and it said eight-twenty or something. I waited another five minutes."

Jay thought for a moment. "So, you're thinking that because I was taking so long it could've been me?"

"Admit it Jay, if anyone knew to ask me the right questions, I could theoretically put you at the scene of the crime. You knew Rick's password. So you could've logged on to Ev's terminal and made those changes. Help me out here. What took you so long?"

"Admit it?" he demanded. "Who the hell are you? The Gestapo? What the fuck is this Kathleen?" Jay stood up from the sofa and looked around for his jacket. He was going to leave. I'd done it again. He stormed down the hallway towards the door.

"Jay. Please." I got off the sofa and hurried after him. I grabbed his arm.

"Jay. Come on. Just listen to me. I'm not accusing you of anything," I said to his back. "Please." I tugged on his arm and he turned around.

"I have all this information, in bits and pieces. So I put some of the pieces together. I wasn't going to say anything but it was bugging me. I'm not accusing you," I repeated. "So work with me here. Let's figure it out. What if someone did lace Ev's food with something? What if the police start asking questions? Won't they find out about Rick getting fired and start putting two and two together? There's definitely a link here with the stock options. Please, Jay. Don't make me apologize again tonight. I seem to be starting off every sentence with you saying, I'm sorry. I am. But look at it from my point of view. Think. What took you so long?"

Jay took a deep breath before he answered. "I was pulling myself together. I left you and went to my office. I closed the door and put on my coat. And I sat down for a while. I was in shock. It's not every day I have to perform CPR on a friend."

I took a step towards him and put my arms around his waist. He hugged me.

"I was so scared," he said.

"And you're too macho to admit it?" I asked him.

"No. I'm not too macho. I learned how to cry from my sisters. There's no shame in it. I needed to be strong for you. I needed you to lean on me."

"I'm leaning on you now Jay. And not just figuratively," I said into his chest. "So why couldn't you tell me that?"

"Thursday night was the first time I was going to be allowed to do something for you. You had actually asked me for help. You wanted me to take you to the hospital. Call it macho. Call it what you want. I was going to look after you. I had to pull myself together."

I stood back and looked at him.

"You did help me Jay. Thank you." I held out my hand to him. "Don't leave. Especially don't leave mad."

He took my hand and looked hard into my eyes.

"Kathleen Monahan, I helped you because I love you."

My throat tightened. "It's too early to say that Jay."

"Not for me it isn't. I've loved you forever Kate." And he kissed me. Just like in one of my favourite Harlequin romance novels.

CHAPTER thirty

I made sure Harold Didrickson wouldn't have any excuse to chew me out for being late on Tuesday morning. I arrived at the office at seven-fifteen. I hadn't slept well and had tossed and turned for what seemed like forever. I tried waking Jay with a kiss just before six but he just smiled in his sleep and turned over. I left him sleeping and dragged myself out of bed.

I put on a black Chanel-style, light wool suit with white piping on the collar and cuffs of the jacket. It was a little heavy for the warm spring we were having but it was the most appropriate outfit I had for a funeral home. I planned on going straight to Hillson's from the office for the visitation.

I was powering up my computer and having my first cup of coffee of the day when I heard a tentative knock on my door.

"Yeah," I shouted. "Come in."

The door opened at few inches and Harold's face appeared. I looked at my watch.

"You're in awfully early Harold. It's only seven-thirty. Come in."

Harold came in and shut the door behind him. He sat down in the guest chair across from me.

"A couple of things Kate," he started. I grabbed my notebook and a pen and looked at him.

"First of all. About yesterday. Let's forget about it okay?" He looked at me expectantly. I figured this was as close to an apology as I was going to get. It must have been difficult for him to say that much. I thought about letting him stew for a while longer and then remembered that I'd said some pretty nasty things to him too.

"It's forgotten Harold." I felt simply magnanimous. Like the governor granting a pardon at the last minute. "Don't worry about it."

He nodded. And looked relieved. Jesus, did he think I was going to bite him, I wondered. I had heard people say that they were scared of me and I always laughed it off. I doubted that Harold could be scared of me. He was a mean son of a bitch when he wanted to be.

"That's good. Anyway, I know you'll be out of the office this afternoon and again tomorrow for Evelyn's funeral. And something pretty important has come up that I need your help on."

"No problem. Aren't you going to Ev's funeral?" I asked him.

"Of course I am. But I'll be here this afternoon. I'll probably go to the visitation this evening." He looked a little offended that I would suggest he wouldn't go to her funeral.

He continued. "We've got a lot to do before Thursday."

"I know," I interrupted. "I left the board agendas and draft materials in your basket yesterday. If you can look at those this morning, I can get them out to Oakes for comments."

"The agenda's totally changed," he told me. "If Oakes can make up his mind about what's to go on it, we'll do something about it. In the meantime, we've got other things on the burner. Do you have a copy of the master list we use for due diligence when we're acquiring a company?"

I dug the list out of a file in the cabinet behind my desk and passed it to him. Harold went down the list and left check marks in the left margin beside several items. He finished and handed the list back to me.

"Start getting these things together. *You* do the work. *You* do the photocopying. How long will this take you?"

I had no idea what he was talking about. I looked at the list and saw that he had checked off about seven or eight different items.

The list was a generic one that we would give to a company, or their lawyers, when we were taking a serious look into acquiring that company. Due diligence materials we called them. Documents of their's that we wanted to see and review. Minutes of meetings, historical financial statements, business plans, press releases, policies and procedures. Materials they would provide to us for our people to look over before making big decisions like whether or not to buy their company.

"You want me to get these things together for *our* company?" I asked him. Harold nodded.

"This is a change. Are we on the other side now?"

"Yes. Someone is looking at us. And I must emphasize Kate, that this is extremely sensitive and confidential. I understand their lawyers will be contacting us today and I know they'll want at least this material. I don't know what else. This'll at least get us started."

"Okay. I'll get right at it. How far back should I go?"

"Last five years. How long will it take you?" he asked.

"Well, most of the financial information will be easy. I'll just get the annual reports. And I've got a start if I use the materials we'd pulled together three years ago when the Germans were snooping around."

We had gone through a very thorough, I called it painful, due diligence process then. I had spent many long nights getting the material together and indexed for the German's lawyers. I still had all the documents in binders in one of my filing cabinet drawers. It had remained good reference material.

"I've got at least two years of the last five in those materials. I'll get working on the past three years," I continued. "I should have everything by noon. Is that okay?"

Harold stood up to leave. "Noon is great. What time are you leaving?"

"Probably around two. Danny, Ev's son, asked me to be there for the whole afternoon."

"You leave when you have to." He shut the door behind him when he left.

I lit a cigarette and chewed on the information Harold had just shared with me. I had wanted to ask him who was looking at us but knew he wouldn't have told me. I'd find out soon enough on my own.

I wanted to call Vanessa and get the dirt but I knew she wouldn't be in for at least another ten minutes so I dug out the binders of due diligence materials from three years ago and started getting the material for Harold together. It was going to be another interesting day.

It was ten after two when I arrived at the funeral home and parked my car in the large lot behind the building. I saw Jay standing beside his car when I pulled in and I was glad to see him there. He had agreed to meet me and I had planned on hiding in my car if he wasn't there when I arrived. I knew this wasn't going to be pleasant and I didn't want to go in alone. Jay was dressed in a dark, navy suit and was wearing sunglasses. He reminded me of an FBI agent.

The last time I'd been in a funeral home was when the original founder of our company had died, and that time I paid my respects to his wife and made a beeline for the door. The wife and his sons had been clinging to each other, sobbing. It had broken my heart and I didn't know what to say in the situation. Funerals don't usually call for smart remarks and jokes and that was the only way I knew how to handle myself.

Jay opened my door for me and I got out. I brushed the cigarette ashes off the front of my jacket and slung my purse over my shoulder.

"Hi," I said. "Did I keep you waiting long?" We'd agreed to meet at two.

"No. Just a few minutes. No problem." He put his arm around my shoulder and we walked around to the front of the building. It was built in the style of a southern plantation home, with white brick and large stone columns across the front of the building. We walked up the steps onto the veranda and Jay opened the large front door.

Inside it was very quiet and I could hear Muzak playing softly in the background. There was an easel set up at the left of the lobby with a listing of the deceased's names. I looked for Evelyn's name and saw that she was resting in the Evergreen room. I held Jay's hand tightly and we wandered down the main hallway, glancing at the brass plaques beside the door of each room. We passed the Whispering Pines and the Grand Oak rooms before we came to the Evergreen room.

We stood outside the room for a moment before entering and I looked in. I could see the coffin set up at the end of the room on the left, and I could see Danny and his twin brother, Jonathan, standing together at the foot of the coffin. At the other end of the room were several wing-back chairs and coffee tables, and I saw Evelyn's daughter sitting in one of the chairs with her daughter on her lap. There were other people standing around in small groups. It was very quiet.

I was perspiring and could feel a small rivulet of sweat running down my back between my shoulder blades. My mouth was dry and the blood pounding in my temples was giving me a headache. I can't do this, I said to myself. My hand was wet in Jay's and he pulled me through the door. I followed reluctantly.

The next five minutes were ones I'd just as soon forget. Jay led me over to Danny and his brother and I can't remember what we said. Actually, I can't remember if we said anything. We just sobbed.

Danny was a very large man and I tried to hold him the best I could. It was hard but I stood on my tiptoes and wrapped my arms around his shoulders. I shook Jonathan's hand and nodded my head. I kept nodding my head because I didn't know what to say. Sorry just didn't seem enough in the situation.

I found my way over to where Elaine, Evelyn's daughter was sitting and I started crying again when I looked at little Sarah sitting on her lap. Little Sarah was ten now, but Ev had always called her Little Sarah.

Elaine and Sarah stood up when I approached and Sarah gave me a hug. She was almost as tall as I was.

Sarah said to me, "You shouldn't be crying so much Kate. Grandma said you were the toughest person she knew. So don't cry. She's an angel now and she can see you." She smiled at me and I smiled back through my tears. I gave Elaine a hug and made small talk for a few minutes before excusing myself.

Outside on the veranda I lit a cigarette and breathed in and out. In and out, trying to calm myself. I looked at my watch and saw that it was only two-thirty and wondered how I was going to make it through another hour and a half. I felt emotionally spent. I had lost a very good friend, but Danny, Jonathan and Elaine had lost their mother. I ground out my cigarette and was going back in when I saw Gina Lofaro walking up the steps of the veranda. She looked different and I realized it was because she wasn't in uniform. There was an older man with her.

"Constable Lofaro," I said.

"Ms. Monahan. Kate. Hello," she said. "This is Detective John Leech. John, this is Kate Monahan."

I guessed that he was about fifty and it showed on his face. The age lines were deeply etched in his face and were especially noticeable beside his mouth. He had steel gray hair cut in a brush cut. He held out his hand and we shook.

"Pleased to meet you Miss Monahan."

I looked at Gina and wanted to ask why they were here but didn't know if that would be rude.

She answered my unasked question. "We're here to pay our respects. And talk to Mr. Morris about the lab findings."

"Um," I cleared my throat. "I'm not sure if this is a good time to be talking to Danny. It's pretty emotional in there."

Detective Leech nodded his head. "Yes, ma'am. We know. We'll try and pick a good moment." He took Constable Lofaro by the elbow and led her to the front doors.

"Miss Lofaro," I called after them. Gina turned around and looked at me. "You got a minute?"

"You go ahead, John," she said to the detective. "I'll be just a minute."

"I'll wait," he said. "I've never met the family." He stood by the door and Gina came over to me.

"Did they find anything in the lab analysis of the food?" I asked her. "I don't know if you can tell me, but I need to know. Evelyn was my best friend. You understand, don't you?"

"Actually, Ms. Monahan, nothing's official yet," she said.

"Kate. Please call me Kate," I said.

"Kate. And unofficially, yes, we did find something," she reluctantly told me.

My stomach sank. So there had been something in one of the dishes. Someone had made a mistake and Evelyn was lying in there. Dead. Someone had made a *stupid* mistake and Evelyn had paid for it. I wanted to wring someone's neck.

"What did they find?" I asked her. "Which dish was it?"

"Actually," Officer Lofaro said. "It wasn't just one dish of food. It was everything. Everything was laced with peanut oil. We found it in almost everything."

I was shocked. I couldn't digest this information.

"Everything?" I repeated in a whisper.

"Yes," she said. "And please. Keep this to yourself. There's going to be an investigation. Detective Leech is from Homicide." She turned around and joined Leech at the door.

Homicide. Evelyn had been murdered.

CHAPTER
thirty-one

Nothing had changed when I walked back into the Evergreen room. Everyone was talking quietly. Sarah was still sitting on her mother's lap. Danny and Jonathan were still standing shoulder to shoulder talking to another relative. Evelyn was still in the closed coffin. Everything appeared the same but I knew it was different now. Evelyn had been murdered. At least that's what the police thought. Danny must have thought so too and that's why he went to the police.

I looked around for the police officers and saw them standing near the head of the coffin waiting to speak to Danny and Jonathan. My headache was full blown now and it felt like my head was about to explode. The Detective and Constable Lofaro approached Danny and his brother.

Jay came up beside me and said quietly, "Where did you disappear to?"

"I went out for a cigarette," I said. I looked at him, blinked hard a few times, and tried to smile, but my face hurt. My temples were pounding now and my back was cold where the sweat had dried. I thought my ears were ringing but realized it was the dull Muzak in the background.

"Are you feeling all right?" he asked me.

I nodded weakly and thought I was going to throw up. Signs of a major migraine coming on.

"Can you take me home?" I whispered. I knew from experience that if I didn't lie down soon, in a dark room, I'd embarrass everyone around me when I threw up.

"Sure," Jay said. "Just let me tell Ev's family that you're not feeling well and we're leaving."

I waited outside and when Jay came out he put his arm around my shoulder. I shrugged him off because I couldn't stand anything touching me when I felt this way.

"Sorry," I said. "I'll explain later." I kept my head level and hurried down the walkway to the parking lot. Every step pounded up through my legs to my head as I walked. Definitely a migraine. My body became incredibly sensitive to everything when I felt like this.

I gingerly sat in the passenger seat of Jay's car and gently laid my head back on the headrest. Jay got in the other side and started the car. Before he put the car in gear he reached around me to do up my seatbelt.

"Are you sick Kathleen?" he asked me.

I nodded and a sharp pain shot up the back of my neck to the top of my head. I gasped with pain.

I closed my eyes and asked Jay if I could borrow his sunglasses. The light was seeping through my closed eyelids.

"Just take me home. It's just a migraine. I have to lie down."

I felt every start and stop on the way home and I thanked the lord that Jay had a decent car with good shocks.

When we finally arrived at my apartment, Jay helped me undress all the while asking me what he could do for me but I couldn't answer. I knew if I opened my mouth it wouldn't be pretty. The pillows felt good under my head and the cotton sheets were cool under me. I kicked off the duvet because I couldn't stand the weight of it on my body but then I started to shiver. Jay disappeared and returned with a glass of water and a bottle of Extra Strength Tylenol.

I couldn't shake my head no, so I whispered, "Tylenol Three's. In the medicine cabinet. Prescription." I didn't get many migraines, usually a couple of times a year, and about two years ago I'd gone to the doctor who'd prescribed the stronger painkillers. I didn't like taking them because they upset my stomach but they usually did the trick with the pain in my head.

I took two and closed my eyes. It was dark outside when I woke up and discovered Jay sitting in my mother's old rocking chair beside the bed. I glanced at the clock and saw that it was eight-thirty.

To test the pain level, I opened and closed my eyes a few times. My head was still sensitive but the Tylenol 3's had done their work.

"Hey," I croaked out. "You the night nurse?" I smiled at him.

He smiled back at me. "Yup. I've got the midnight shift. At your service. How're you feeling?" he asked.

Bless his pointed little head. He was genuinely concerned.

"I'll be fine. It was just a migraine. Lie down beside me?" I asked him. He complied and gathered me in his arms. He stroked my hair and put his hand on my forehead.

"No temperature. You'll be fine," he proclaimed.

"Thank you Nurse Ratchet."

"Do you get migraines often?"

"Couple of times a year," I told him. "Brought on by stress. The funeral home was a little much for me today." I paused. "The police were there, you know."

"I know. I saw them on the six o'clock news. Harold called. And so did Vanessa. This has been a busy place."

"You saw who on the six o'clock news?" I asked him.

"The Detective who was at the funeral home. I saw him there but didn't know who he was until I saw him on the news."

"Then you know?" I asked. "That Evelyn was murdered?"

"Yeah. They said on the news they were investigating the death of Evelyn Morris as a possible homicide. They interviewed Danny. How did you find out?"

"Constable Lofaro told me they were investigating it as a homicide. All of the food at the reception the other night was laced with peanut oil. Everything." I told him.

"Jesus," Jay whispered. "Then it definitely was no accident. Who the hell would do something like that?"

"Why did Harold and Vanessa call?" I changed the subject.

"Vanessa called because she didn't see you at Hillson's. I told her you were in bed with a migraine. She was surprised that I answered the phone and I told her I had driven you home. Harold on the other hand, didn't ask why I was answering your phone."

"Harold wouldn't ask if the Queen of England answered my phone. He never asks personal questions. What did he want?"

"Wanted to know what time you'd be in the office tomorrow after the funeral. He asked if I'd tell you to check your voice mail. He'd leave you a message."

"Fuck voice mail. I don't check it after hours," I declared.

"Are you going to tell Vanessa about us?" Jay asked me.

"Of course. I want to tell everyone and I'd love to get up on the top of the CN Tower and broadcast it to the world."

"Broadcast it to the world? I don't think that's such a good idea. I'm an outcast at TechniGroup right now."

"I know it's only been a couple of days, but this feels right Jay. For me anyway."

"And you know how I feel. I told you last night. I love you." He said that so easily. I wanted to say it back but the last time I responded quickly to someone when they told me they loved me, I ended up married to him.

So I hedged a little bit and told him, "I feel the same."

The news that Evelyn's death was being investigated as a homicide was a big item on the ten o'clock news.

A reporter was interviewing Danny in front of his home. He looked scared and sounded mad.

"I was convinced it was no accident," he was saying to the reporter. "I had to go to the police and beg them to get involved." The reporter removed the microphone from in front of Danny's face and looked straight at the camera. Danny's image faded away.

"This news comes quickly on the heels of a press release issued by TechniGroup earlier in the week which detailed the resignation of Richard Cox, the company's chief financial officer," the reporter told Toronto. "Mr. Morris informs us," she continued, "that Mr. Cox was his mother's boss." She finished her story with a brief description of the company's business.

Great. I couldn't wait to see what the stock opened at in the morning.

We were sitting in the dark and I was sipping a very hot Cup of Soup. One of the many gourmet delights I kept hidden in my kitchen cupboard.

I asked Jay if he had heard what the stock had closed at today.

"No change," he said.

"Well, that's comforting for now. Tomorrow'll be interesting. With that reporter reminding everyone about Rick Cox and now the news about the police getting involved, it'll be like October 1987 all over again." I thought about the possibility of Oakes jumping out of an office window and remembered that they were all sealed tight. "I wonder how much of a hit the stock'll take," I said.

"As if I care," I answered myself. "If one of those sons of bitches is responsible, I hope the stock goes to a negative. Can that happen?" I wondered out loud.

Jay laughed. "Not that I know of," he said.

"Why's Didrickson so hot about what time you'll be in tomorrow?" Jay asked after he muted the sound on the television.

I thought about the news that Harold had told me about the possible buy-out. I was sworn to secrecy and wasn't supposed the share the information with anyone. I looked over at Jay and he was staring at me, waiting for an answer.

"Confidentially? What I tell you goes no further?"

Jay nodded.

"Pinkie swear?" I asked him. He held out his baby finger and linked it with mine. This was an old ritual all the neighbourhood kids had. It was a stronger promise than swearing in blood.

"We're being looked at. Someone out there is interested in buying TechniGroup. Didrickson's got me getting material together for due diligence. I imagine he's heard from the other side now on what documents and material they're going to want to look at. He needs me there to be his personal photocopy slave."

"Interesting," he mumbled. Interesting? This was big news.

"Hey," I prodded. "Interesting? No other comment? Come on. Let's speculate. Who do you think it might be? The Germans again?"

"I don't know," he replied distractedly.

"Hey. Earth to Jay. Over here." I poked him on the shoulder. He looked at me.

"What? Sorry. What'd you say?" he asked me.

"Who do you think it might be?" I repeated. "The Germans?"

"I don't know," Jay said. "But I do know this. Whoever it is, will get a nice price for the company. If the stock keeps dropping they'll get the place for a quarter of what it's worth."

I thought about that for a moment.

"Maybe someone wants the stock price to keep dropping and that's why everything has been happening. Maybe that's why Rick got fired and Evelyn was murdered," he said.

CHAPTER
thirty-two

"And that only happens in books," I said. "You're dreaming in Technicolor, Jay. Rick Cox got fired because he fucked up. And because they got him for fraud and sexual harassment too. Remember you asked me how I knew about the fraud? Well, I saw the charges in different memos from a couple of the regional vp's. Oh, and by the way, the pinkie swear covers those memos too."

"Okay, I'll give you that. On it's own. Rick got fired because of apparently legitimate reasons. But why was Ev murdered? And I'll go on the record right now. I agree that it was murder. You say they found peanut oil in everything?"

I nodded.

"Well, then," he said. "Why would there be peanut oil in brownies? Or in a ham and cheese casserole? I'll tell you why. Because someone wanted to make damn sure that whatever Evelyn ate, would kill her."

Jay continued. "Those two unrelated incidents will no doubt drive the stock price down. And then you hear that we're a target of a takeover bid. And," he pointed his finger at me, "tell me why the shares were down over a buck and a half last week, before any of this news got out? Can you explain that?"

I laughed. "No, Your Honour. I can't. And I'd forgotten about that." Less than ten days ago the shares had been over $11.00 and now they were trading around $7.00. And with the news on the street about Ev, the slide wasn't about to stop.

"You have to agree," Jay said. "That the two events together are cause for concern. Once the police find out about Cox, and they will find out, they'll want to know what the two had in common. I'll tell you what they had in common."

"Stock options," I interrupted him. "And, let's not forget about the other variable in this formula."

"And that is?"

"You. You got fired too. Because of stock options. The common element. I wonder if the police'll be knocking on your door?"

"Damn. I hadn't thought of that." Jay looked concerned.

"But you've got nothing to worry about," I reassured him.

"You're right. But no one likes being questioned by the police," he said. "My mother definitely won't be impressed."

"She won't be impressed when she finds out you've been fired. Have you told her yet?"

Jay shook his head. "I'll tell her when I land another job. What she doesn't know won't hurt her."

The funeral the next day wasn't a merry affair by any means but I did a lot better than the day before. Jay and I sat shoulder to shoulder in the chapel at Hillson's and I held his hand tightly in mine. There were dozens of people from the office at the service and if they'd didn't know about Jay and I by now, they'd soon figure it out when they saw how closely we were sitting together. I felt safe with his shoulder touching mine. I didn't acknowledge anyone and stared straight ahead like a zombie. I blocked out everything and tried not to listen to anything that was said during the eulogy. It was a trick I learned as a child. Don't listen and what they say can't hurt you.

"Midget," they used to taunt me. "Shorty pants." It was something to laugh about now, but as a kid, it used to hurt me through and through. I was very conscious of my size and when the other kids started to tease me, I just wouldn't listen. I would sit on the curb with my hands over my ears, blocking out their taunts.

Evelyn was buried at the Thorncliffe Cemetery. We stayed back from the crowd around the graveside and I hung on to Jay's arm. When they started lowering her coffin into the ground I turned around quickly and started back to the car. The rest of the crowd soon followed us and when the front cars in the funeral procession pulled out, Jay followed.

"Do you want me to drop you at the office?" he asked me.

"Sure, but my car's still at Hillson's. I'll have to get it eventually," I replied. I had no feeling in my arms and my neck felt like rubber. I wanted to lie down and go to sleep and never wake up again. My best friend had just been put in the ground and the sadness overwhelmed me. I wanted to go to the office about as much as I wanted to have a root canal without Novocain.

"I've got some things I want to do downtown. I can hang around and take you back after work," he offered.

My mind wandered and I wondered if Evelyn was watching me, just like Sarah told me. My eyes looked up at the clouds. I've got a prince, I told her silently. You'd be happy for me, Ev. My eyes filled with tears for the first time that day and I quickly wiped them away with the back of my hand and turned to look at Jay.

"Thank you. I'll take you up on that offer."

We didn't talk on the way back downtown and I gave Jay a quick peck on his cheek when he pulled up in front of the building.

"I'll be here at what time?" he asked me.

"Is five-thirty too late?" I had no idea what awaited me upstairs.

"Five-thirty it is. See you then." I waved as he drove off and I made my way slowly in to the building.

This is the last place I want to be, I thought as I punched the button for the elevator. When your best friend dies, you should be at the home of her relatives, participating in the grieving process. I had given my regrets to Danny before the service and he looked almost relieved that I wasn't going back to his place after the burial. He probably didn't want anything to do with any of us now that there was a full-fledged investigation going on.

I caught a whiff of Vanessa's perfume and turned around. She was standing behind me waiting for the elevator.

"Why didn't you say something?" I asked her.

"Didn't want to invade your personal space," she replied. "You definitely had the walls up today. I noticed it at the funeral home and the graveside. You alright?"

"Yeah. I guess so. I'm getting there." We got on the elevator when it arrived and I punched our floor. I backed into the corner and watched the numbers of the floors flash by on the indicator.

"You need to talk Kate, you know I'm here," she said softly.

"I know Vee. And I know I'm not the only one grieving for Ev. I know she was a good friend of yours too. If I drank, I'd say let's go out and get drunk." I grinned at her.

"You could always start. I'd be glad to introduce you to my bedmate, Chardonnay. Hey, you wanna do that tonight after work?

Ashley's over at her dad's place. I don't have to go home. We could get something to eat, too."

"I'd like that Vee. But Jay's picking me up after work," I told her.

"Oh," she said.

We arrived at our floor and got off the elevator.

"I can't get in touch with him because I don't know where he is," I told her. "But we could go as a threesome."

"No. That's all right. Some other time," she said.

"Vee. Get serious. Jay doesn't bite. And it's not as if the three of us haven't eaten together before," I reminded her. We were standing in the elevator lobby and I steered her along the hall towards the back door.

"We've eaten together before when you two weren't so obviously a couple," she said. "I don't want to butt in."

"Shit Vanessa. This is stupid." I flashed my security pass at the black box beside the door. It clicked and she pulled the door open.

"So maybe we are an obvious couple. But you're still my friend. We'll hoist a few to Ev. Let's meet at six at Bigliardi's."

"Bigliardi's?" she said. "That's an old fogey's place."

"Yup. And it was Ev's favourite restaurant. And I'm sure they serve Chardonnay." I went through the door ahead of her and waved over my shoulder. "Six. And don't be late."

CHAPTER thirty-three

It was quiet in the legal department area when I got to my office. Everyone was probably still in traffic coming back from the funeral. So, I took the opportunity to check my voice mail. My friend, the voice mail lady, told me I had six new voice messages, one of which was urgent. Probably Harold, I thought. You could send someone a message and tag it urgent and the computer voice would intone, "Message Three is URGENT."

Everything was urgent in Harold's book. And then I remembered I hadn't listened to my messages last night after Jay told me that Harold wanted me to. I scrolled through the messages and got the urgent one. As I suspected, it was from Harold.

"Kate, this is Harold. We've received the list from the other side. I'll leave it in my basket. I'd appreciate it if you could start getting the documents together that they want as soon as possible." Click.

"Oh Harold," I said out loud into the receiver, "you forgot to say thank you."

I got the keys to his office from my desk and retrieved the dreaded list. The letterhead was that of a well-established law firm who were renowned as the masters of the take-over bid. Scapelli's often competed with them for business. As counsel to TechniGroup, Cleveland Johnson was probably rubbing his hands together, salivating at all the work about to come his way. Well, I thought, the miserable shit can rub his hands together all he wants. If we get taken-over, his firm will lose our business to the Bay Street firm who were representing the company about to bid on us. Put that one in your pipe and smoke it Cleve. Ah, what goes around, comes around, I chanted. I was still mad at Cleve and was being bitchy.

The list of what they wanted to look at was a long one. The total document was ten pages long and Harold had marked all over it. Harold had put a check mark beside most items but others had

NO WAY written in capital letters beside them. I guessed that the other firm was on a fishing expedition and until they made us an offer, we weren't going to show them our panties until they showed us their's. The time to lift our kilts would be after we had a firm commitment of an offer in hand.

I sighed as I sat down at my desk. It was eleven-thirty and I planned on being out of the office by five-thirty. I lit a cigarette and started going through the list. Most of the documents they wanted existed, but it was going to take some time getting it all together. I wondered how much time I had.

I flipped to the last page of the document and saw that the lawyer who wrote the letter had indicated in the penultimate paragraph that he expected the documents by close of business next Monday. If that was going to pose a problem, blah, blah, blah. No problem, I thought. I'd gotten a good head start yesterday morning when Harold was decent enough to give me a head's up.

Some of the items would be trickier than others, though. The ones that stuck out immediately were the requests for information covering the last three years on stock option grants and the employee stock purchase plan. Not my responsibility, I thought. Harold had written "Finance" beside several of the items meaning that the finance department would be responsible for those items. Lists of customers. Accounts receivable. I wrote "Finance" beside the requests for information on the options and the stock purchase plan. They could whistle Dixie if they thought I was going to dig up all that shit. Evelyn, Jay and Rick were the keepers of that information. In a pinch and with the thumbscrews tightening, I could pull together the stock option stuff. But there was no way I could come up with the employee stock purchase plan information.

I dug in the drawer of the file cabinet where I kept supplies and pulled out a new box of legal-size file folders. I marked 1(a) on the first one and inserted the copies of the annual reports I'd already retrieved the day before. I highlighted the item on the list with a yellow marker. I marked 1(b) on the next file folder and inserted the last five years' proxy statements to shareholders. I checked that one off the list with the yellow highlighter.

I continued going through the list and putting documents in files where I already had the information. I created several new documents on my computer for requests for things that didn't already exist on paper. The lawyers wanted to know things like number of outstanding shares at certain dates, the names and dates of all companies we'd acquired over the last five years, the number of shares that had been paid to those companies as the purchase price. The list went on and on. By the time I was finished I had a pile of full file folders about a foot high on my desk. I went over the letter from the Bay Street lawyers again and saw that I was more than half way through.

Jackie snuck her head around the door at that point and told me Harold wanted to see me.

I stood at the open door to his office and waited while he talked into his Dictaphone. He finally noticed me standing there.

"Kate, come in. " I gave him the marked up list from the lawyers.

"Everything highlighted in yellow, I've done. I'll need some input from you on the rest of things I'm responsible for. Whenever you've got a minute."

"I'm impressed. Great job so far," he said. A rare compliment.

He continued. "We'll have to put that aside for a while though. The board meeting's in the morning and his Royal Pain has finally focused on the agenda. Can you help me out here?" He handed me a stack of papers that had been lying in front of him. It was all the material for the director's meeting.

"And, Kate. You do the books." We always put the director's materials in binders with tabs separating each item. "This stuff is really sensitive. And I'll need them by five-thirty when I head over to the Toronto Club for the dinner. Oakes wants them to have the stuff to read overnight before the meeting in the morning."

"They'll be amazed. They're actually going to see things before the meeting," I said. Harold grinned.

"Maybe, just maybe, we're finally getting things right after all these years," he said.

"Let's not hold our breath. Oakes hasn't signed off on all of this yet." Chris always had to see the final product and nine times out of ten, he made more changes.

"Not this time. He's out at some meeting and said to let the stuff go. So. Go for it," Harold said.

"No way," I laughed. "Three whole hours? I get three hours to do a proper job? Now I believe there is a God."

I got up to leave and noticed that the location of the meeting had been changed from the last draft of the agenda that I had prepared. The original agenda had the office address as the location for the meeting but Harold had scratched that out and changed it to the Four Seasons Hotel.

"Christ Harold. Could they have picked a location further from the office?" I asked him. "What's wrong with our boardroom?"

"Oakes is hiding. There've been press people hanging around since the news about the investigation into Evelyn's death. He doesn't want anyone to know about the board meeting. The Four Seasons is very hush-hush by the way."

"I know, I know," I said over my shoulder.

"And Kate. One more thing. As soon as you're done with those books bring them in. I've got a meeting at four that I want you to participate in."

I stopped and turned around. "With who?" I asked.

"Detective Leech from the Police Department. He wants to talk to us about Evelyn."

CHAPTER
thirty-four

The agendas for the meetings had changed drastically since the first draft. Originally, this meeting had been planned as a regular quarterly meeting where the directors would get together and rubber stamp the financial statements and several other administrative things.

Most of those items had been crossed off the board agenda. Some of the new items on the agenda were "Presentation by Jack Vincent re Strategic Partnership", "Amendments to Employment Agreements", "Grant of Stock Options to Senior Executives and Directors". Jack Vincent had been allotted all the time for the meeting of the Investment Committee.

The Investment Committee of the Board had a meeting scheduled for the morning, as well as the Compensation Committee. Each of the items from the board meeting agenda appeared on the relevant committee agenda. Traditionally, acquisitions and investments were initially approved by the Investment Committee before presentation to the board and similarly, compensation issues like salaries, stock options and such were discussed and approved by the Compensation Committee before rubber-stamping by the board.

In my view, the committees were a joke. It had started out that the committees each consisted of three outside directors, with the intention that they were to be independent of the board, and not include inside directors. But Oakes attended each of the committee meetings and instead of three outside directors, each committee now had five. And, because most of the directors were from out of town, everyone ended up attending the committee meetings, rather than sit around and twiddle their thumbs. Besides, for every committee meeting they attended, it was more money in their pockets. So, by the looks of the agendas, the afternoon session of the board of directors would be a repeat of the morning sessions of the committees.

Not that they ever stuck to the agendas. Oakes would take over the meetings, and ramble and pontificate. Then about ten minutes before the end of a meeting, Harold Didrickson would have to put his foot down and have the board approve the items that a board was supposed to approve. Like financial statements. Or grants of stock options.

In one of Harold's finer moments, he described the board meetings to me as a cluster fuck. He said everyone talked at once over Oakes' voice because Chris would just ramble on. A couple of the directors were avid deer hunters and would trade macho stories about their latest kills, and two of the other ones were scratch golfers and would catch up on their latest scores.

Tomorrow's meetings were going to be interesting, I had to give them that. If Jack Vincent was making an appearance, my guess was it was about the company that was looking to take us over. Jack would be acting as the go-between for the two companies and if the deal went through, Jack would no doubt continue being a very, very rich man. I wondered what his fees were going to be for this one. I recalled that we had paid him several million dollars for the deal that fell through a couple of years ago. Several million dollars for a deal that fell through. Nice work if you can get it.

Detective Leech was right on time. I escorted him to Harold's office when he arrived at four o'clock. On our way down the hallway I pointed to the kitchenette and offered him coffee.

"It's fresh," I offered, thinking about all those TV shows I'd seen where the cops were always complaining about three-day old coffee.

"Fine," he said. "I'd like that."

He stood formally by the door inside the kitchen while I poured. I held up the container of cream and he nodded.

"Sugar?" He nodded again. Wow, what a great conversationalist, I thought.

"So you want to see Harold and I about Evelyn," I said as I stirred the cream and sugar into the coffee. I had my back to him and couldn't see if he nodded, because he certainly didn't speak. I turned around. He was standing with his hands tucked deeply in the pockets of his overcoat.

"We'll be talking to quite a few people. Mr. Didrickson and yourself are on the list," he said. Two whole sentences.

I handed him his coffee and opened the door.

"After you," I offered. This time he shook his head. He reached over my shoulder and held the door and I went ahead of him. And they say chivalry is dead.

I led him into Harold's office and after making the introductions, I closed the door and took a seat. Detective Leech looked at Harold who was standing behind his desk, and at me, sitting in one of the guest chairs.

"Perhaps I was misunderstood," he said. "I do want to talk to both of you, but separately. Ms. Monahan, perhaps I could speak with Mr. Didrickson first and then I'll find you."

It wasn't a question.

"Sure, no problem. Harold knows where I'll be," I said as I closed the door behind me. I felt like I'd been sent to sit in the hall outside the principal's office.

Detective Leech knocked on my door ten minutes later. I was chain-smoking my second cigarette. He took a seat and waved his hand in front of his face. The smoke was a little thick, so I butted my cigarette in the ashtray in my bottom drawer and kicked the drawer shut with my foot.

"So," I said. I pulled my chair closer to the desk and folded my hands together in front of me.

"So," he replied. He reached inside his jacket pocket and pulled out his eyeglasses and put them on. They were half glasses like the grandmother wore in Little Red Riding Hood. He flipped open his very small, spiral-bound notebook. With his pen poised he asked me to tell him about what had happened last Thursday night. I wasn't about to tell him that I had already relayed all that information to Constable Lofaro because he might make me sit in the hall again. So, I told him.

He took copious notes during my description of the events and didn't interrupt. When I finished he flipped through the pages of his notebook and re-read his notes. Without lifting his head, he peered at me over his glasses.

"What time did you say you joined the party?"

"I didn't say. I can't really remember. Probably about seven-thirty."

"Did you see Mrs. Morris eat anything while you were there?"

"No."

"Did you yourself eat anything?"

"No."

"Who do you recall seeing at the reception?"

"Well, almost everyone," I said lamely. "Are you asking if I saw someone specific?"

"No, I asked who you recalled seeing at the reception," he repeated. Well, excuse me, I thought.

"You want a list?"

He nodded without looking up.

I opened the top drawer of my desk and took out our internal phone list that had all of the employee's names on it. I started at the top of the list and read out loud the names of the people I could recall seeing. Leech was writing furiously so I spoke faster. When I reached the D's on the alphabetical list, he held up his hand and motioned me to stop, just like one of those officious traffic cops, directing morning traffic downtown under the Lakeshore Boulevard. He continued to write for a moment and then looked up at me.

"Are there many more names?" he asked.

Get a grip Mister and learn shorthand, I thought. I'd only given him about twenty names so far.

"Quite a few. Why don't I just give you this list and I'll mark on it who I remember seeing at the party," I offered. I beamed at him, giving him my Sunday best smile. Anything to help the local constabulary, I thought. And get this asshole out of my office.

"Okay," he said. He put his notebook on my desk and folded his hands on his lap, waiting.

"Now?"

"I'll wait," he said.

I sighed and picked up a pen and went over the list fairly quickly. A few names here and there stopped me and I had to think hard about whether or not I recalled seeing them at the reception. The names of a couple of deadbeats who'd pissed me off over the years also made me stop and think. A good chance for revenge, I thought. I could put a tick beside their name and put them at the scene of the crime. That's one of the best things about revenge. You can always think about it but never have to act on it. I finished up and handed Detective Leech the list.

He folded the list in half lengthwise without looking at it and put it in the inside pocket of his suit jacket. He picked up his notebook and I stood up. I was anxious to usher him out because he was giving me the heebie-jeebies.

"Just a couple of more questions, Ms. Monahan," he said as he opened his notebook again. Fuck.

"Did you know Mrs. Morris well?"

"Yes."

"Did she have any enemies here at the office that you were aware of?"

"No."

"Is there any reason why, that you can think of, that someone would want to harm Mrs. Morris?"

"No."

He flipped his notebook shut and shoved it in his overcoat side pocket. "Thank you. If there's anything at all that comes to light that you think might have some bearing on our investigation, please call me." He passed me a business card that was rumpled and used. He probably took them back from unsuspecting people after he arrested them. I took it by the corner and laid it on my desk blotter. I noticed the address was the same station as Constable Lofaro.

He stood up. Thank God. I wasn't sure why this man was rubbing me the wrong way, and then I reminded myself that he was only doing his job. Maybe I resented someone so cold and apparently uncaring, investigating the death of my best friend.

"I'll escort you back to reception."

"That's fine. I know the way."

"Sorry. Security, you know," I told him. I marched down the hall and he hurried to keep up.

"Sign him out," I told the receptionist. I offered my hand because I could feel my mother standing behind me reminding me of the art of social graces.

"Thank you for your time, Ms. Monahan," he said as he shook my hand. His hand was dry and I could feel calluses on the palm. "And," he said as he looked into my eyes, "I understand from Mr. Didrickson that you and Mrs. Morris were great friends. I'm sorry for your loss." With that, he turned and headed for the elevator.

I was pleasantly surprised that it took a stranger to offer me condolences. No one else besides Jay and Vanessa had understood or told me they were sorry. I made a mental note to be nicer to the Detective if I ever saw him again.

CHAPTER
thirty-five

Vanessa was furiously punching her phone when I stopped by her office. I sat down in one of the guest chairs and flipped through a magazine she had in her basket. It was a trade magazine, all about the world of high tech. The cover story was about the next chairman of Elite Technologies. Elite was the latest and greatest in high tech companies and had been founded by a handful of young, preppie programmers who had left Microsoft or IBM or Apple, I couldn't remember. It was the latest darling of Wall Street and was in the news almost every week. I checked the inside index and found the page number for the cover story.

I glanced at the pictures accompanying the story and read the captions underneath. The writers had compiled a list of who they were touting to be the next president of Elite. The preppie programmers had finally decided that they didn't like managing their company, they liked the development side so the word was out that they were looking for a business-minded, technical-type to captain their ship for the next while. Business-minded, tech weenie. What an oxymoron! I recognized a few of the faces in the article and remembered a few years back when IBM was searching for their next president and the Wall Street Journal had done a similar article.

Some joker at our PR firm had taken the Wall Street Journal article that had about six or seven pictures of likely candidates in it, and had pasted a picture of Chris Oakes in one of the spots. They had rewritten the caption under the picture and faxed it to Oakes, anonymously. The fax looked amazingly real and Oakes bought it. He actually believed it was his picture in the Wall Street Journal. He walked around the office showing everyone. I remember actually being embarrassed for the idiot. No one had the heart to show him a copy of the real Wall Street Journal which happened to be sitting in his in-basket.

I tossed the magazine back in Vanessa's basket and stared at her, willing her to look at me. She was writing in her book and firing off instructions to someone on the end of the line. As I listened, I realized she was talking to someone at the Toronto Club where the directors were scheduled to have dinner that night.

"Right. Right. And the cigars. Don't forget the cigars. Thanks." She hung up and slumped back in her chair.

"They don't pay me enough for this shit," she said.

"Stop your bitching. You love it," I teased her.

"Just about as much as I love my ex," she shot back. She looked at her watch and sat back up in her chair. "I'm not going to make dinner tonight. Oakes wants me to deliver some shit over to the Club before the dinner. No way I can make it back by six."

"We'll wait for you. Whatever Oakes wants, give it to the maitre d' and hightail it out of there. Why can't you just send it over by taxi?" I asked her.

"It's stuff he needs to sign. A letter agreement with Jack Vincent."

"Ooh. Are we getting ready to mortgage the company again to pay little Jack his fees?"

"Whatever." She brushed me off.

"Not interested? Or not sharing?" I asked her.

"Not interested. We'll talk later. I'll be at Bigliardi's as soon as I can. Thanks for waiting for me," she said. She stood up and started gathering up the papers on her desk. "Everything done for the meeting tomorrow?"

"I've got all the books together. How about you?"

Vee and I were a team when it came to the director's meetings. I got the materials for the meetings together and she looked after the physical requirements. If they needed laptops, projectors, conference telephone systems, TV monitors, or whatever, Vee looked after that.

I made sure all of the directors got to the meeting. Vee looked after them while they were there. Booking limos, hair appointments, golf tee times, you name it. Every one of their wishes was our command. Some of the tasks we performed for them were mundane, some were ridiculous and most were useless.

Like the time one of the directors who was very overweight, came out of the meeting with this hand on the back of his pants. We were out of town and holding the meeting in the penthouse suite of a very swank hotel. Vee and I were sitting at a large table outside the meeting room.

"Got a stapler?" he asked through his teeth that were clenched around a cigar.

"Yes," I said and held it out to him. He disappeared down the hall to the men's room. When he returned he handed me the stapler and turned around and lifted up the back of his suit jacket.

"Can you tell?" he asked me. The idiot had torn the seam on the seat of his suit pants and had stapled it back together. On the outside.

"Not at all," I deadpanned. "Great job."

Vee and I laughed so hard we both had to run to the ladies room. Even funnier though was the next morning when he showed up for a committee meeting wearing the same pants. And they still had the staples in them.

Harold was packing the director's binders into a large legal briefcase when I wandered past his office.

"Everything in order?" I asked him when I stuck my head in the door.

"Fine. Thanks," he said. He closed the flaps on the top of the briefcase and threaded the leather handle through the hole in the top. He snapped the two buckles shut.

"Have fun then." Although he wouldn't admit it, I knew Harold secretly looked forward to these dinners. The great, secret, male enclave. Farting and belching. Cigar smoke. Brandy. Hangovers in the morning. Ah, he probably thought, it doesn't get any better.

"Kate, I'd like a word," he said. "Come in and close the door."

"Should I get my book?" I offered. If he was going to fire off instructions about work tomorrow or things that needed to be done, I had to write it down. I was never any good without my notes.

"No, no. Uhm," he cleared his throat. Harold was obviously uncomfortable about something and I knew he was going to talk about something unrelated to work. I closed the door and sat down.

At the best of times, it was hard for Harold to say good morning to me. He never asked me how my weekend was. Once, when I returned from a two week vacation, beautifully tanned and visibly relaxed, he hadn't even asked me how my holiday was. At first I thought it was because he was ignorant. After a while though, I realized it was because he was very shy and didn't like to pry. And, he didn't really care.

I didn't consider passing the time of day or asking how one's weekend was, prying, but Harold did. And, we were not allowed to ask him anything personal. I knew he had a beautiful wife and two gorgeous children, but that was the extent of it. If he attended company functions, it was alone. He wasn't like everyone else who bragged about their kids and had pictures of them plastered all over the place. I often wondered what he was like at home.

"Kate," he started. "I know this is none of my business." He was red in the face. I looked at him blankly. I had no idea where this was going and I was starting to feel as uncomfortable as he was obviously feeling.

He ran his index finger under his shirt collar.

"May I ask a personal question?"

If it was about my secrets on how to keep a goldfish alive, I wasn't sharing.

"Sure. Shoot."

"Are you involved with Jay Harmon?" he blurted out.

Well. Word gets around fast, I thought and then I remembered that Harold had two eyes and had seen us at the funeral. Our first date in front of probing eyes, I thought bitterly. What business was it of his?

"Yes," I said through a closed mouth. My hands curled into fists on my lap and I felt the sweat starting to bead on my palms. Calm down, Kathleen I told myself. You and Jay are both over twenty-one and single. You were going to announce it proudly from the observation skydeck at the CN Tower. Maybe he's going to tell me how happy he is for the both of us. Not fucking likely.

"Well, that puts me in an awkward position," Harold said.

"How so?"

"Confidentiality. The deal that's about to happen. You know," he said.

"No I don't know, Harold. How about you tell me?" I thought about the pinkie swear the night before and the information I had shared with Jay. Sister Josephine was about to tear my right ear off. I knew it.

"I don't need to remind you of your role in this company and the information you are privy to," Harold said. I made a mental note to remind him not to end his sentences with a preposition.

"No, you don't."

"Mr. Harmon was fired on Sunday and that puts us in an even more awkward situation," he informed me.

"Get to the point, Harold."

"I'll be unable to have you work on this deal with me unless you can give me assurances that I can rely on your discretion and trust that you'll keep everything confidential."

"Fine. I get the point. You know, and I know, that I need this job Harold. You also know that you can trust me. I may be sleeping with the man," I said as I stood up, "but I *don't* talk in my sleep."

We stared at each other across the desk.

"Will that be all, sir?" I asked. I emphasized the sir. He nodded.

I didn't slam the door on the way out. It would have been a useless gesture. I knew Harold was right and I was mad at myself. I shouldn't have told Jay anything, pinkie swear or not. I had broken a confidence, a trust that Harold had in me.

This time I didn't make a mental note. I swore to myself that my days of sharing information were over.

CHAPTER
thirty-six

"I'm Luis. Something from the bar?" the waiter asked us. He was an older gentleman, outfitted in a very formal, black tuxedo. A starched white towel folded over his arm completed his ensemble.

Luis took our orders and left us. I looked around and took in the scenery. Bigliardi's was small and dark, with cozy tables set randomly around the restaurant. The restaurant was renowned for their steak and my stomach grumbled.

We were seated at a small table for four against the wall. Jay was beside me.

"Just for the record Harmon, tonight is my treat. Vee and I are having a farewell dinner to Evelyn and you're my guest. All right by you?"

"All right by me," he agreed.

I smoked a cigarette and we sat quietly for several minutes until Luis returned with our drinks. I held my soda water and said, "To Ev." I took a sip.

"To Ev," Jay repeated. "How was the rest of your day?"

"Shitty and I don't think I want to talk about it," I told him. I was embarrassed and feeling guilty about my talk with Harold. Embarrassed because he felt he needed to raise the subject and guilty because I knew I was in the wrong. If I refused to talk about my day with Jay, I wouldn't let anything slip.

Jay didn't respond, he just sipped his beer. The silence was awkward and I let my eyes wander the room deliberately avoiding looking at Jay who was handsome in a solid navy blue suit. I wanted to curl up on his lap and go to sleep. Into oblivion.

I looked at my watch and prayed that Vee would arrive soon.

"So," Jay said. "Too bad about the Leafs. We're almost through another season and it's not looking good. I doubt they'll get a playoff spot."

"Yeah. Too bad." Small talk. I hated it. My right ear started to burn.

"Where the fuck is Vee? It's six-twenty. That asshole Oakes has probably got her working." I mashed my cigarette out in the ashtray. A younger version of Luis appeared and replaced it with a clean one.

"Another beer," Jay ordered tersely. He scurried away and I looked at my watch again.

"Jesus, Kate. Wind down. Take it easy." Jay put his hand over mine. My hand was balled into a fist and Jay worked at prying my fingers out of the fist. Very gently.

I could feel the heat from his body, he was sitting so close to me.

He leaned over and whispered in my ear, "What's the matter, Kate?" And then I burst into quiet tears. Jay's hand tightened on mine. I hated myself. Crying in a public place. I kept my head down and I tasted the tears that ran down into my mouth. I grabbed the napkin that Luis had placed on my lap when we sat down and tried to wipe my eyes with it but it was so stiff from starch I felt like I was wiping my face with a piece of cardboard.

I didn't see Vanessa arrive at that moment but I knew she was sitting beside me when I caught a pleasant draft of her perfume. Now I was really embarrassed. I heard her order a vodka tonic. Jay passed me a clean tissue and I cleaned myself up.

I smiled weakly at Vanessa beside me.

"Hi."

"Hi yourself," she said back. More small talk. "You okay?"

I nodded. "Fine. Just fine."

Luis returned with Vee's vodka tonic and I surprised everyone at the table.

"I'll have a Canadian Club with gingerale on the side." I couldn't remember the last time I'd had a real drink. Maybe seven or eight years ago. I looked forward to it. I felt I deserved it.

The drink relaxed me and we ended up enjoying the rest of the evening. We made a pact among the three of us that we wouldn't talk about what was going on at the office. We were here to honour Ev so we told Evelyn stories. At one point Vee and I were laughing so hard Jay had to shush us.

"Everyone in the restaurant's staring at us," he laughed.

"Fuck 'em," I slurred, pretending to be drunk.

Vee agreed. "Yeah, fuck 'em." Her slur wasn't faked. She'd

had some wine with dinner and she was now into the liqueurs. Something brown and thick served over ice. The thought of it made me shiver.

I waved at Luis and asked for the bill. Time to get out of here. Hit the dusty trail. Tomorrow wasn't going to be a picnic. We'd be on call all day for the directors' meeting. I had no idea if I was going to be expected to run back and forth between the office and the Four Seasons. I remembered that I hadn't cleared that point with Harold. Normally he'd want me on the premises, wherever they were holding the meeting but I'd received no instructions.

Jay and I put Vee into a cab and waited for the valet to bring his car around. A taxi pulled up in front of Bigliardi's and five or six Japanese gentlemen poured out. Jay and I backed up against the wall beside the entrance to avoid getting trampled.

Jay put his arm around me and I huddled close to him. I was feeling very sleepy and I was watching the Japanese. They were trying to convince their cab driver to get out of the car and take their picture in front of the restaurant. As I watched the Japanese another taxi arrived.

I just about missed them in the crowd of people in front of the restaurant. When I realized who was passing right beside us I just about fell over.

I elbowed Jay in his side and whispered loudly up at him, "There." I pointed. "Can you believe that?" I was amazed. Jay looked around and then down at me.

"What?" The valet arrived with Jay's car and suddenly the sidewalk in front of the restaurant was empty. Jay started towards the valet and was holding out his hand to pass him a tip. The valet opened my door and I slid in. Jay got in and fastened his seatbelt.

"Did you see that?" I demanded.

He looked in the side mirror for traffic coming up behind us and eased the car into the street.

"What?"

"Not what. Who. Didn't you see who got out of that second cab?"

"No. I was thinking about how tall I was compared to those Japanese guys."

Jesus.

"Tell me pretty Kathleen. Who got out of the second cab?" He looked over at me and smiled. "Dini Petty?"

"No. I don't think Dini travels around the city in a cab. You'll never guess."

"I don't want to guess. Who was it?"

"Rick Cox and Philip Winston."

Jay went right through a red light.

CHAPTER thirty-seven

"Shit, Jay," I yelled. "Are you trying to kill us or just put us in the hospital for the next three months?"

"Stop over-reacting. The streets are deserted. Nothin' coming either way," he said as he checked his rear-view mirror. The streets may have been deserted, but he was still checking for cops.

I relaxed my shoulders and sat back in my seat. I stared out the window and breathed deeply. He was right. I always over-react and I've probably given myself high blood pressure because it.

"Rick Cox and Philip Winston?" Jay questioned me. "Sure you weren't seeing things?"

"Ah ha. You weren't trying to kill us. You were listening to me. Yeah. Rick and Philip Winston. Can you believe that?"

"I can't believe Philip Winston would be caught dead in Bigliardi's. Sure he didn't have his grandmother with him?" He laughed.

"You didn't see them get out of that cab?" I asked him.

"No. I was watching the Japanese and thinking I should move to Tokyo. I'd be big man on campus there."

I thought I heard him giggle.

"How many beers did you have tonight? Should I be driving?"

"Forget the beers I drank. You actually had a drink. I don't think I've ever seen you have a drink of hard liquor. Or wine or beer for that matter. Why is that?"

I paused thinking of a good answer.

"Oh God. I'm sorry," Jay said. "I shouldn't pry."

Now I giggled.

"I'm not a recovering alcoholic if that's what you think," I reassured him. "Although sometimes their twelve-step program sounds like a good path to sanity. You've known me all my life Jay. I think you'd know if I'd had a drinking problem."

Jay slowed the car and carefully came to a full stop at a red light.

"I don't drink for various reasons. One of them is I normally can't stand the taste of alcohol. Another is I don't like the feeling I get when I drink. I can feel the effect immediately. But most of all I don't want to lose control. I need to be in control of my wits at all times," I told him.

"Somebody who's so dead set against drinking must've had some pretty bad experiences with it. Did you get really hammered on cheap wine or lemon Gin?" he asked. He looked over at me.

"Keep your eyes on the road," I told him. "No, nothing awful ever happened. In fact, I've never been drunk. Never had a hangover."

"Yeah right."

"Believe it or not. I don't care if you do," I snapped.

"Just joking Kate. As you would say, can't take a joke, you shouldn't have joined up."

"I know."

"So, are you out of control now?" he teased. "Seeing things? Like Rick and Philip?"

"No. I'd just like to know what those two were doing together. In fact, next time I see Philip, I'll ask him."

"You will not."

"Will too."

"We sound like two little kids. Philip's probably sucking around after Rick's job and he's getting some pointers from him," Jay said.

"As if. Rick didn't have two minutes for Philip. In fact, I heard that he was dead set against the acquisition in the first place, and had no time for Philip. Tom James told me."

"Tom James'd say anything."

I put my head back against the back of the seat and stared out the window. My head was starting to ache and I wanted to go to bed. To sleep. I was exhausted emotionally and physically.

I thought back to Evelyn's funeral that morning and had trouble remembering details of it. And then I remembered that I'd forgotten to send flowers and suddenly felt sick. How could I have been so stupid? Oh Ev, you know I love you. Why didn't someone remind me? Because you're always so frigging efficient, no one needs to remind you, I yelled at myself.

I felt tears well-up in my eyes and took a few deep breaths. This was no time to feel sorry for myself and I didn't want to cry again today. I had cried so much now since Evelyn had died, I wondered if I had any tears left. My throat was tight and I willed myself to stop. Quit it. Stop your whining. I closed my eyes.

I was disoriented when Jay stopped the car and I opened my eyes and looked around. I realized we were back at Hillson's. Jay had parked next to my car in the dark parking lot. Shit, I thought. I can't do this. I don't have the energy to drive home. I had completely forgotten that my car was here.

"I'll follow you home," Jay told me.

"No. I'll be fine," I said.

I fumbled with my seatbelt and groped in the dark for my purse on the floor. Jay looked over at me.

"You don't want me to come over?" He sounded a little hurt.

I shook my head because I couldn't speak. I didn't feel up to having a guest. In fact, I just wanted to put on my sweat socks and crawl under the covers. And never come out. But how could I tell Jay that? He'd certainly seen the emotional side of me in the last few days and he was probably good and sick of it. He took my hand in the dark and put it to his lips.

"I'll still follow you home. Just to be sure you make it all right," he told me.

I hurried out of the car and almost tripped as I stumbled over to my car. I yanked open the door and jammed the key in the ignition. The engine coughed a couple of times and then turned over. I put the car in gear and left the parking lot.

I watched Jay's headlights in the mirror all the way home. Waves of exhaustion continued to pour over me and I thought about all those poor bastards who fall asleep at the wheel. I understand now, I thought.

I saw Jay parked on the street in front of my house when I came around the side and up to the porch. I waved at him as he pulled out and drove off. The tears started again on my way up the stairs.

I dreamt I was back in the desert searching for Evelyn. I couldn't find her and I remember running around for what seemed like days, searching and searching. I was frantic.

I consciously woke myself up and stared at the clock. Normally, I slept well but since Evelyn had died my sleep had been fitful at best. This has got to stop, I told myself. Grieve for Evelyn and move on. Remember her. Never forget her. The pain would heal over time, I told myself. I tried to recall things I'd heard about the grieving process. Anger. Feelings of loss. Despair. I had never suffered the loss of a friend or a close family member and all of this was new to me.

I was feeling the loss, that was certain. And despair was right up there. I looked at the clock and knew if I didn't get back to sleep soon, I'd be functioning like a zombie in the morning. I'd have to deal with my anger then.

The alarm went off at five-thirty and I dragged my sorry ass out of bed. I put the coffee on before I showered because I knew I was going to need at least three cups before I hit the road. My head felt thick from lack of sleep and I took two Extra-Strength Tylenol's to try and clear the fog.

I turned the showerhead to pulse and let the hot water pound at the back of my neck. By the time I had dressed I was feeling a little more human. The air that wafted through my open bedroom window had the smell of spring to it so I put on a light cotton summer dress and said to hell with pantyhose.

I slipped my feet into white, low heeled sandals and practiced my dagger look in the mirror in preparation for the snotty comments I'd get when someone realized I was wearing white shoes before the Victoria Day weekend. No one had ever accused me of being a fashion hound.

I poured myself a coffee and wandered into the living room where I could hear the birds singing. I opened the French doors and breathed in the warm air. I loved this time of the day. No traffic sounds. No sounds from neighbouring houses. No kids screaming outside.

Despite my lack of sleep I was feeling better today. Some of the dreadful weight I'd been feeling in my shoulders that I associated with depression was lifting.

I poured myself a coffee for the road in a plastic mug someone had given me from Tim Horton's and glanced at the clock. It was almost six and I wondered if it was too early to call Jay and apologize for last night.

I dialled his number and the answering machine picked up right away. It was doubtful that he was on the phone this early so I assumed he had turned on the machine deliberately.

"It's me," I said into the machine. "Call me sometime today.

I want to apologize for my behaviour last night. Miss you." I hung up.

I hated talking into machines. I was only good at leaving my name and number.

I thought about my message. Damn it. I didn't want to apologize, I wanted to explain. I had said sorry so many times lately, I was turning into a wuss. Begging forgiveness was not something I usually did.

I quickly dialled Jay's number and said into the machine, "Correction Harmon. I don't want to apologize for last night. But I do want to explain. Please call me."

CHAPTER
thirty-eight

Shit, shit, shit. Let that be a lesson to you Kate, I told myself. Checking your voice messages from home is sometimes not such a bad thing. I checked my watch again and prayed that everyone else would be late.

I had been proud of myself for arriving at the office earlier than everyone else but had panicked when I listened to my messages. Didrickson had ordered me to be at the Four Seasons for seven-thirty to make sure the breakfast and meeting room arrangements were in order.

Those are Vanessa's responsibilities, I thought as I flagged a cab in front of the building. Everything'll be in perfect order but Harold obviously needs me to hold his hand. As Corporate Secretary of the company he took his duties seriously. He at least wanted the meetings to look organized even though they typically fell apart as soon as Oakes took center stage.

The meeting area on the top floor of the Four Seasons was empty except for a busboy laying out the food and a person who was obviously the floor captain. I introduced myself and checked out the arrangements.

Several small, round tables with fresh, white linens draped over them were placed around the room and I saw a separate table against one wall with a fax and small photocopier on it. The breakfast buffet was laden with fresh fruit, muffins, croissants, cereals, yogurt, coffee, tea and juices. I asked the busboy to bring in several Diet Cokes for Larry Everly who always made a point of letting everyone know he didn't poison his body with caffeine and refused to drink coffee or tea. He obviously had never checked the label on the Diet Coke. He could swallow about five or six cans before coffee break.

I pulled open the heavy double doors that led into the meeting room and wasn't surprised to see the room in perfect order. Each place setting had a fresh pad of paper on the blotter, pencils, pens, and a carafe of water. There was a projector on a mobile cart in the middle of the room hooked up to the laptop on the podium.

Samuel Welch and Arthur Graves were piling their plates with food at the breakfast buffet when I pushed open the doors back into the ante room. I didn't need to check my watch to know that it must be exactly seven-thirty. The agenda that went out noted that breakfast would be served at seven-thirty and the meeting would start at eight. You could always count on Sam and Arthur to be on time, especially where food was concerned.

"Gentleman," I greeted them. "Welcome."

They both offered me big smiles, and Sam put his plate down and gave me a big hug. Some people would consider a hug not very professional and certain huggee's would probably scream about sexual harassment, but Sam was a true gentleman and I considered him a friend. Arthur and I shook hands.

Both men were the longest-standing directors on our board. Sam had been a senior vice president at the brokerage firm that were the underwriters of TechniGroup's initial public offering years ago. It was a tradition back then to appoint a representative of the underwriters to sit on the board. Sam had retired after a big shake-up at the brokerage firm but he kept active by being a member on the boards of directors of many companies. He was the current chairman of our compensation committee. Sam's hair was pure white and I couldn't help but notice how much older he was looking these days. He was sixty-nine years old and certainly looking his age today. His light gray suit hung well on his square body and I noticed that his tie, the handkerchief in his breast pocket and his suspenders were a matching set, all brightly coloured in a red and blue paisley. I wondered what he looked like on the golf course where he probably wore matching shorts and T-shirts, like a little boy.

Arthur and Sam sat at one of the small tables, and Sam pulled out his Globe & Mail before digging into his breakfast. I stood beside the buffet and smiled at Arthur who was delicately buttering a muffin. Arthur was a classically handsome man who got better looking with age. He looked about twenty years younger than Sam but was in fact only ten. Arthur's hair was a dark brown with not a speck of gray and I often wondered if he coloured it.

Arthur had oodles of money and his occupation in our shareholders' proxy and annual report was listed as "private investor". He had loaned mega dollars to the original founder of the company almost ten years ago and had been a member of the board since then. I think he was bored with our company now and most times his boredom showed when he would nap during the meetings. Arthur was a quiet man and I was sure Chris Oakes' bluff and bluster turned him off. With the exception of Larry Everly, Arthur was the one director of our company who directly held the most shares. Amongst all the other shareholders of our company, Arthur probably held close to one percent of the issued and outstanding. Very wealthy.

Vanessa's voice came to me from the hallway and I gulped down the cold coffee in the bottom of the cup I was holding and headed for the door to meet her. She came barrelling through the door at a fast clip speaking into her cell phone. I wondered how she did that. Talking on the phone was definitely a sit-down affair for me. If I stood while I was on the phone, I didn't move. But then again, I had trouble walking and chewing gum at the same time. She took the phone away from her ear and flicked the off button with her long thumbnail.

It was quarter to eight and I was amazed at the energy she was throwing off. Vanessa was a hyperactive adult and she was constantly on the go. I could see that today would be no exception. I peered at her, looking for traces of a hangover. She looked yummy in a short-skirted lavender suit with a white lace teddy showing discretely at the top of the buttoned jacket. Her high heels were the exact colour of the suit and I immediately felt like a frump when I looked down at my low heeled sandals and cotton dress. Her hair was perfect as usual and I congratulated myself for not having a jealous bone in my body.

"Vee, you're embarrassing me. You look like you're dressed to go gardening. You should have called me. I could have dug something out of my closet for you," I teased her.

"Shut up," she shot back. She looked down at my sandals. "How many times have I told you that you don't wear white shoes before Victoria Day?"

"I heard on Oprah the other day that it's now acceptable to wear white all year long," I lied.

"Not in my lifetime," she said.

She glanced at the double doors to the meeting room and back at Arthur and Sam. "Anyone besides Frick and Frack here yet?" she asked.

I shook my head and heard voices in the hall. I grabbed her by the arm and led her over to "our table" before the other directors piled in. I'd greet each one on my terms, not like a servant standing at the door. I was glad it was spring because they wouldn't be handing me their overcoats when they arrived.

I told Vanessa to empty her briefcase. If she had anything for me to distribute to the directors, I wanted it now. While she fumbled around I noticed that Bill Frankford, Whit Williams and Neil Adam had arrived. There was some serious macho back slapping going on and several guffaws. I saw Neil Adam look my way and I busied myself with nothing.

"Katie, Katie," he bellowed. I gritted my teeth. The man was becoming far too familiar and I was sick of him already. Neil was the ex-Liberal Premier of one of the Atlantic provinces and still acted like he was on the campaign trail. He was a snake and because of him I had stopped voting.

He lumbered across the room with his hand outstretched. I steeled myself and felt a unpleasant shiver go up my back.

"Mr. Adam," I said and held out my hand. He grabbed it and pulled me close. He caressed my arm with his free hand and it brushed against my breast. Pig. I looked up at his little eyes set in his fat, sweaty face and felt my stomach turn.

"Katie, Katie, how many times do I have to tell you? We're like family. Call me Neil." I pulled my hand out of his and took a step back. His aftershave was overpowering and I knew that within the hour he'd smell sour from sweat. Neil was huge and his weight had billowed to about three hundred pounds after he lost his home riding in the last provincial election. No doubt about it, the man repulsed me. I gave him a weak smile and saw him eyeing Vanessa, who was bent over the fax machine and giving the world a beautiful view of her rear end. Neil had already forgotten about me and was on his way to rub her tits.

"Get a haircut," I told him and he touched the back of his head. I laughed to myself and checked his rear view to see if there were staples holding his pants together today.

Bill Frankford and Whit Williams were standing by one of the windows with coffee cups in their hands. They were in a deep conversation and I didn't interrupt them. Larry Everly and Chris Oakes were missing and would probably be late. The only time Chris showed up on time was when we were out of town for a meeting and he was staying in the same hotel where the meetings were held.

Harold had arrived unnoticed and was sitting with Arthur and Sam. Sam's nose was buried in his newspaper, and Arthur and Harold were laughing. It was a rare sight to see Harold in a good mood and I sidled up to the table and waited for a break in the conversation. Harold finally stopped talking and looked up at me.

"Need anything?" I asked him. He shook his head sharply, dismissing me, and continued talking to Arthur. The urge to curtsy came over me but I got him another coffee instead. I placed it very gently in front of him and beamed. He ignored me and I tired of the game.

I eased myself into a corner and enjoyed the view out the windows. I would play invisible now until someone had a mundane request.

"Over there," I heard someone say. "By the window." Let the games begin, I thought to myself. Someone must need their nose wiped or their wife called. I turned around and saw Detective Leech heading my way.

CHAPTER
thirty-nine

Detective Leech wanted to see Mr. Oakes. Now. He'd had an appointment to meet him last evening and when Oakes broke that he made another one for this morning. Oakes never showed up.

"He should be here any minute Detective," I told him. "But I don't proclaim to have any say over his schedule. His secretary is the master of his day."

"His secretary wasn't in. So I thought I'd try you," he said hopefully.

"You're mistaken if you think I can make magic when it comes to Oakes' schedule," I said. I pointed to Vanessa on the other side of the room. "His secretary is over there. You should talk to her." He glanced in Vee's direction and I asked him how he had found us. "The location of this meeting is supposed to be confidential." He shrugged and dismissed me with a wave as he walked towards Vee.

I heard more voices and saw the rest of the gang arrive. Oakes and Larry Everly looked like twins dressed in old-fashioned, light-blue and white striped seersucker suits. I knew white shoes were a no-no before the long weekend in May but this was ridiculous. There should be a law, I thought. Larry's ferret eyes were scanning the room while Chris spoke into his ear.

Jack Vincent was standing behind them with his hands clasped in front of him. His briefcase rested on the floor between his feet.

I leaned back against the wall and took in the scene before me. The noise level had risen and conversations were taking place all around the room. Vanessa had her hand on the Detective's arm and was gesturing at Oakes with the other hand. She was talking rapidly to him.

Larry Everly was trying to get everyone's attention. He

obviously wanted to get the show on the road. People were reluctantly picking up their briefcases and heading into the meeting room.

Chris was shaking hands and patting everyone on the shoulder. I spied some shaving cream on his ear and smiled. Vanessa led Detective Leech closer to the crowd and I fumbled in my dress pocket for a cigarette. I took a deep drag and waited for the scene to unfold.

As the last director before Oakes passed through the double doors into the meeting room, Vanessa hurriedly presented the Detective to Oakes. I couldn't hear the conversation but Oakes was pointedly ignoring him and looking past him into the meeting room. The Detective spoke sharply at Oakes and Chris walked away. Vanessa threw her hands up in the air.

I was glad to see that Chris Oakes treated everyone equally. Like a bug that needed squashing. But he was never prepared to do the squashing. He left that up to Vanessa.

The room was suddenly quiet because Chris had pulled the double doors closed behind him. I heard Vee apologizing to Detective Leech.

"I'll wait," he said. "What time do they normally break for coffee?"

Good luck, I thought. Chris' coffee break time was reserved exclusively for harassing employees on voice mail.

Vanessa led Leech out the door towards the elevator bay. If anyone could handle a disgruntled civil servant it was Vanessa. I found an ashtray and butted my cigarette and waited for her to return.

I spent the next hour quietly, listening to Vanessa on the phone and reading the discarded Globe & Mail which I hated because it didn't have a very good sports section and the movie reviews were too highbrow. The busboy busied himself clearing away the dirty dishes.

I was bored and thought about all the things I could be doing at the office. I hated this part. Waiting around. Fiddling my thumbs. I checked at the office for messages and was disappointed that there wasn't one from Jay. I slumped in a chair and put my feet up and smoked several cigarettes and wished I had a pack of cards in my purse.

When I heard voices in the hall I sat up and put my feet on the floor and tried to look busy. I was surprised when Detective Leech walked back in the room with Cleveland Johnston.

I stood up and went to stand by the window. The only exit out of the room was by the door that was filled with the two men. I kept my back to them and recalled my last conversation with Cleve. I was stilled pissed off at him and was embarrassed to see him here although I shouldn't have been surprised because I remembered typing his name on the list of attendees for the meeting. He was supposed to give the directors a resounding speech reminding them of their duties to the shareholders of the company at the time of a takeover bid.

I watched Cleve and the Detective talking to Vee in the reflection of the window and felt my stomach sink when Cleve walked towards me.

"Detective Leech a friend of yours?" I spoke at the window without turning around. Cleve stood closely beside me and my shoulder touched his arm. I moved away slightly.

"We met on the elevator coming up."

I lit a cigarette and blew the smoke against the window. It wafted right back at us and Cleve waved his hand to clear the smoke.

"When are you going to quit that disgusting habit?" he asked me.

"On my list of disgusting habits, Cleve, smoking rates at the bottom. There're other things I want to quit first," I told him.

"Like what?" he asked.

"Like useless friendships," I snapped.

"Our friendship is useless?"

"You catch on quick, counsellor."

"Thanks for not calling me a miserable shit. I prefer counsellor," he quipped. "And, if you're having trouble drawing a line in the sand to delineate between friendship and my relationship with TechniGroup as a lawyer, let me outline it for you."

"Forget it. I don't want to know because I already figured it out. The company comes first, then our friendship. I understand that Cleve. So call me when the take-over bid happens and we have new corporate lawyers. You'll be off the file then." With that I turned and marched out of the room.

There were several more surprises that day but when I thought about them collectively, they weren't that surprising.

I was sitting in my living room with all the lights out sipping a decaf coffee. I had left the hotel when the meetings adjourned about four-thirty and returned to the office to fetch my car. I felt exhausted when I got home and fell into a deep sleep on the couch. It was now eleven and I wondered if I'd be able to get back to sleep. Sitting around a nice hotel suite all day, doing practically nothing was more exhausting than being run off my feet at the office.

Cleve Johnston had hung around for the rest of the meetings and had avoided me the whole day for which I couldn't blame him. I had been out of line and I knew it. But fuck it, I thought. Sometimes friendship has to rule.

Chris Oakes had surprisingly kept his appointment with Sherlock Holmes at the coffee break. Their interview had been short and Detective Leech left shaking his head. You'll be okay, I wanted to yell after him. He had the look about him of someone who had just been returned to earth after being poked and prodded by aliens. I wondered who had done the interviewing because giving someone the third degree was an art that Oakes had perfected himself. If he could concentrate long enough, I reminded myself. I almost ran into the hall after Detective Leech to beg him to cuff Oakes and drag him out.

Not that Chris Oakes was any stranger to handcuffs. Vanessa had reported to me one day that yet another limo driver had called and quit. She was upset because there weren't many more limousine services in the city that would serve us. If Oakes wasn't firing them, they were quitting. The latest driver had quit because when he arrived at Pearson Airport to drop off Oakes, Oakes wouldn't get out of the car because he was on the car phone talking to someone. The conversation dragged on and on, and the police knocked on the driver's window a few times motioning for the driver to pull away. The driver waved over his shoulder a few times at Oakes who pointedly ignored him. Finally, the driver got out of the car and explained to the police that his passenger wasn't moving.

The police tried gesturing to Oakes through the passenger window but he ignored them too. Chris finally caught on that he had to hang up the phone when the police officer reached behind him and pulled out his handcuffs which he waved at Oakes through the window. Oakes quickly hung up the phone and got out of the car. The driver got a fine that we ended up paying. The saying that no man is above the law didn't seem to apply to Chris. He was in his own world and he had his own rules. I hoped that one day his attitude would catch up with him.

Tom James and Philip Winston had showed up at the directors' meeting during the coffee break. I knew Tom would be needed for the compensation committee meeting but I had no idea why Philip was there. I waved at Tom and motioned him over to where I was standing.

"What's Mr. Winston the Third doing here?" I asked.

Tom shrugged. "Chris wants the board members to meet him."

"Why?"

"Figure it out Kate." I looked over at Philip, grinning from ear to ear, shaking Arthur's hand. "You're looking at one of our new senior officers."

"Senior officer of what?" I asked him.

"Confidential," Tom whispered.

"Oh, fuck off Tom. Confidential my ass. I'll be doing the minutes of the meeting and I'll find out soon enough."

Tom leaned over and whispered in my ear. "Oakes wants to put his name up for chief operating officer."

"Larry Everly's obviously bought in," I stated.

Tom nodded and walked away.

So, I wondered. What the hell had Rick and Phil been up to the night before? Philip was taking over the chief operating officer side of Rick's job but I couldn't possibly fathom why Rick would be meeting with Philip. Rick had been fired and was the latest untouchable in our company's leper colony of cast-offs. Philip was shaking everyone's hand and moving about the room. When he headed my way I wiped my hand on my dress, waiting for the inevitable handshake.

"Kathleen," he pronounced as he walked up and held out his hand.

"Philip," I boomed back and gripped his hand. "So, I understand congratulations are in order."

He nodded and grinned.

"You're sure you're up for the challenge?"

"I think it'll be a good fit. I've got big shoes to fill and I hope to live up to the board's expectations," he pontificated.

"Save it Phil. You sound like a press release." I had made him uncomfortable and he looked around for another hand to shake. Time to go for the kill, I thought.

"So, how was dinner last night?" I asked sweetly.

He was looking across the room and my question obviously didn't sink in right away.

"Fine, fine," he mumbled. He started to walk away and I grabbed the sleeve of his suit jacket.

"Rick give you some good pointers?" I asked. Now I had his attention.

"Pardon?"

"I asked you if Rick gave you some good pointers. You know, where the best place is to go for lunch. Which secretaries in the office have the cutest buns. When and how to avoid Oakes. You know. Inside stuff."

He was staring at me and I knew, that he knew, that I knew.

"Rick who?" he asked innocently and walked away.

CHAPTER
forty

My phone rang and I hurried down the hallway to answer it, hoping it was Jay. I hadn't heard from him all day and was anxious to talk to him.

"Hi, it's me," Vanessa said.

"Oh, hi," I said, slightly disappointed.

"Excuse me," she said. "Expecting someone *else* to call?"

I laughed. "Hoping is more like it. I just thought it was Jay calling." I looked at my watch. "What are you doing up so late?"

"Calling you."

"I gathered that Vee. Get to the point," I urged. I hoped she didn't have something work-related for me to do.

"They've taken Rick Cox in for questioning in connection with Ev's death," she announced. I was dumbfounded.

"Taken him in?" I repeated. "What does that mean?" They had *questioned* me even though the Detective said it was an interview. Only my questioning was done in the comfort of my office.

"I don't know what it means. I don't think they've arrested him."

Neither of us spoke for a moment.

"How did you find out?" I asked her.

"Oakes. He called and I made the mistake of answering the phone. It was late and I thought it might be my ex calling about Ashley. Oakes was gloating. He's drunk and he was rambling but I made out that they had taken in Rick."

I wondered how Oakes had found out.

"Some reporter called Chris," Vee answered my unspoken question. "I guess those bloodsuckers hang out at the police stations waiting for news."

"Jesus. What happened with our stock today?" I asked out of the blue.

"Down another buck."

And the slide continues. News of Rick's 'questioning' certainly wasn't going to help the share price, I thought grimly.

"Thanks for calling Vee. I'll see you tomorrow." We hung up.

I paced up and down the hallway by the front door and thought about the latest revelation about Rick Cox being 'taken in'. I couldn't put the pieces in place but I figured the police must be putting two and two together now. I tried to think like they would and came up with all sorts of possibilities.

One of the reasons Rick was fired was for fiddling with the stock options. Evelyn's job had been stock options. So maybe the police think that Rick needed Ev out of the way so he poisoned her. But why would Rick need Ev out of the way? He didn't need Evelyn dead to be able to sign on to the stock option system and make changes. Certainly if Ev were alive she would have found out and done something about it. If Rick had been guilty of wanting Ev out of the way, why would he then be so stupid to ask Jay to generate reports from the system? Jay wasn't dumb and he would no doubt find the same changes. In fact, he *had* discovered that someone had screwed around.

Maybe Rick didn't think the changes would be discovered so quickly by someone other than Ev. Maybe Rick would kill Jay next, I thought irrationally. Stop it. We have no proof that Rick killed Ev. The police are just questioning him.

I grabbed the phone and dialled Jay's number. The machine kicked in right away and I slammed the phone down without leaving a message. I hadn't spoken with Jay since this time last night. He hadn't returned any of my calls. He must be really angry with me, I thought. I made a mental note to tell on him, next time I saw his mother. Rude. He was downright rude.

I wondered what he had done all day as I got undressed for bed. Probably slacking off and playing on the Internet. I missed him and was mad at him for not calling me. I stood in front of the mirror on my dresser and practiced a pout but decided the look didn't suit me so I flicked off the light and crawled into bed.

My sleep started off with very pleasant dreams of Jay. And then I was back in the desert running around in circles looking for Ev and Jay.

I woke up in a sweat and was surprised that it was morning. I kicked off the duvet and let the cool air from the window wash over my body. I wondered if I could burn off calories while dreaming of running. Not a bad thought.

In spite of being awake, I still felt lost, and my chest felt hollow. I got out of bed and shuffled down the hall to my phone to check my voice mail at the office. I didn't have an answering machine at home and deliberately left the phone at the point farthest from my bedroom so it wouldn't disturb me. I wished now I had an answering machine. What if Jay had tried to call? I felt like a schoolgirl again, waiting for someone to telephone and ask me to the prom. There were no messages on my system at the office so I tried Jay's number again. The machine was still on and I hung up the phone slowly.

"Well, fuck you Jay Harmon," I said out loud. Fuck you and the horse you came in on.

I showered and dressed quickly and went to work.

TechniGroup made the front page of the paper that morning. They ran about a quarter of a column outlining the recent events and at the bottom of the column it was noted in bold print that there was a further story in the Business Section.

Wow, free press. You can't buy publicity like this I thought. Dave Rowlandson and Tony Player were probably frantic at this point and would be huddled together charting out the damage control.

When something like this happened, where the press reiterated all the bad news, it was bound to have a continuing adverse affect on the stock price. My prediction came true when the stock opened down half a dollar.

The office was buzzing with speculation and the many employees who held stock through the employee stock purchase plan weren't impressed with the latest slide in the price. In fact, not impressed understated the issue somewhat. If it was possible to have a mutiny in a corporation, I'm sure we would have had one on our hands that morning. I wanted to remind them all that they were shareholders and that they did have a voice. Collectively, their voices could be heard at the annual shareholders meeting. They weren't dumb though. They all knew that their shares in total couldn't make a difference when it was time to vote for the directors.

I closed my door and got to work on the stack of materials from Harold's out-basket. I started at the top and worked my way through. Mostly mundane tasks. I saved the minutes of yesterday's meetings for the last. Harold had been a busy little beaver because there were two full tapes of dictation. He must have been up all night dictating.

I ate at my desk and worked straight through staring at my phone every couple of minutes, willing it to ring. Jay still hadn't returned my calls and I was starting to get a little worried. I tried his number again and when the machine kicked on, I hung up quickly.

I pulled the Dictaphone transcription machine closer to the side of my computer and plugged in the first tape. The machine was set to broadcast from the little speaker in the front because I couldn't stand to wear earphones. I pushed the right hand side of the floor pedal to activate the machine and listened to Harold's voice. He talked and I typed. His voice droned on through all the standard verbiage that appears at the beginning of all minutes of meetings. Who was present. Who chaired the meeting. The fact that the corporate secretary was present. Resolutions to approve the minutes of the last meeting. His voice droned on and I went into automatic. I found myself typing things before he said them. This must be what it's like to work in a factory, I thought.

When he said, "New heading. Strategic Alliance with Morgenstern," my ears perked up. This next part would be about Jack Vincent's presentation. I wondered who the hell was Morgenstern? I'd never heard of a company by that name. It turned out to be a code name because Harold mentioned in the minutes that it was agreed by all directors to refer to the possible acquiror as Morgenstern. Typically, because of confidentiality, any time a deal was about to take place and either of the companies involved were a public company, code names for the companies were used, to guard against leakage of information that could possibly affect the public stock price. Envision very high-priced lawyers, sitting around an exquisite boardroom table about to enter into negotiations for a huge, take-over bid. First item on the agenda - what code names are to be used. By the time that issue was settled, the legal fees were into the six digits.

I typed along in automatic pilot and remembered reading a Herman Wouk novel when I was a young teenager. The girl's name in the book was Morgenstern. Marjorie Morgenstern. It was a great novel about a Jewish girl in her late teens growing up in New York City. The name Morgenstern was Yiddish or German. And I remembered she had changed her name when she became an actress to Marjorie Morningstar. I couldn't make any connection with the code name and I shook my head and tried to concentrate on what Harold was saying. I checked the computer and saw that I had typed two full pages and couldn't remember doing it. I pushed the page up button on the computer and re-read everything I'd typed. Boring.

Everything so far in the minutes was non-committal. Generic stuff. The first side of the tape ended and I flipped it over. It was the start of the minutes of the compensation committee meeting. Harold talked. I typed. My fingers were working and I closed my eyes. I wondered if it was possible to be blind and be a dicta-typist. I typed along for awhile and checked what I had done. Not bad, but I'd definitely need a proof-reader.

I snapped out of my trance because Harold was talking directly at me on the tape.

"This next section Kate, covers the employment agreements. Can you please pull out the agreements for Chris Oakes, Tom James, Roger Smith, Roy Dunleavy and Patrick Hanks and draft amending agreements incorporating the changes I'm about to dictate here." He continued on with the minutes.

The board had agreed to amend the employment agreements of the top executives by amending the change of control clause. I was familiar with it because it had been a disclosure issue a couple of years ago. Change of control happened when another party became the majority owner of the company's shares. Each executive's employment agreement had a clause covering termination of their employment due to a change in control. In other words, how the company would have to compensate the individual if there was a change of control and they lost their job. A majority shareholder was all it would take. Right now our largest shareholder was Larry Everly's company and they held only 6% of TechniGroup's shares.

Now why wasn't I surprised? We *know* there's going to be a change of control because someone, code-named Morgenstern, was knocking at the door. We also know that top executives usually lose their jobs in a takeover. So, let's belly-up to the bar and cover our collective asses. Let's make sure we get paid a shit-load of money to lose our jobs. This definitely sucks, I told myself.

I stopped typing and turned around to my desk, and pulled my notebook towards me where I made a note to amend the employment agreements and disgustedly turned back around to my machine. The clock at the bottom of the screen told me it was only three-thirty so I stopped for a cigarette break and started to feel depressed. These guys certainly have horseshoes up their asses.

I knew that if the takeover happened, Oakes would be walking around like a peacock. Bragging about how he had pulled it off and 'won' the game. It was all a game to him. When Chris had first started working at TechniGroup I was convinced that he wasn't driven by personal gain. He couldn't have been because he never seemed to care about the share price which stayed steady for a long time. After the aborted deal with the Germans fell through and the stock was on a rollercoaster, it didn't seem to bother him. A hefty portion of his compensation package was tied to stock options and he'd never made a move to cash in on any of them. He had some very low exercise prices because his stock had been granted to him when the shares were trading at around $6.00. On paper he was a multi-millionaire. Well, he was last week before the stock took a shit, I thought with glee. This thought made me a little happier and I ground out my cigarette and got back to work.

I was even more depressed though a few minutes later when Harold dictated in the minutes that the board had approved the grant of 150,000 additional stock options to each of the senior executives. The exercise price would be the closing price of the shares on the date of grant. That was yesterday and the shares had closed at about $7.00. If a takeover bid was imminent, you could bet your sweet bippy that Morgenstern would be paying a little more than $7.00 a share.

I wondered to myself what would happen to stock options on a takeover bid. That area of the law was cloudy to me and I wasn't sure if unexercisable stock options would be acknowledged and paid for in a takeover. The options granted yesterday wouldn't become exercisable for one year.

The minutes of the directors meeting were a rehash of everything that had been discussed and approved at the two committee meetings. The only additional item was the appointment of Philip Winston the Third, to the position of Chief Operating Officer.

"Make sure you type his name in full Kate, with a comma and the roman numeral three," Harold reminded me.

Harold droned on and I was surprised to hear that the board also appointed Winston a director to fill the vacancy created by Richard Cox's resignation. I choked a little as I typed the word 'resignation'. The board was happy to have Philip joining the team, blah, blah, blah. They approved the grant of 250,000 options to Winston and the exercise price was to be set on the date his employment agreement was signed.

Harold spoke at me again, "Kate, give me a copy of a standard executive employment agreement and I'll fill in the blanks. It can wait until Monday."

CHAPTER
forty-one

My eyes were glazing over and I was having trouble concentrating while I proofread the minutes of the meetings. I've never believed in the spell check feature on the computer because it always misses my glaring errors, like "there" instead of "their", or "your" instead of "you're". Try and convince a tech-weenie who believes that the only thing a computer can't do is breed, that the computer doesn't have a brain. That's why I made the big bucks. Proof-reader extraordinaire.

My phone rang and I eagerly answered it, hoping for a break in the monotony.

"I have a favour to ask," Harold said.

"Shoot." I never understand why he asks for favours when he knows I'm here to work and I don't care what I do. Sometimes I wished he'd ask me to pick up his dry cleaning because it would be an excuse to get out of the office. But Mr. Fair Didrickson would never ask anyone to do something he considered beyond the scope of their duties.

"I know it's almost quitting time," he said and I groaned inwardly. I couldn't face working late tonight. "But I was wondering if you could attend at Rick Cox's house and have him sign some documents. I know he lives near you and I thought on your way home... " he trailed off.

Well that certainly answered one of the day's mysteries. The police obviously hadn't arrested Rick. "He's at home and ex-pecting me?"

"Yeah. I spoke with him earlier this afternoon. I've got the documents in here. I said someone would be there before six."

I didn't need any more encouragement to turn off my computer and pack it in for the day.

Rick Cox lived in an older home off Avenue Road in Rosedale, the richest residential area of Toronto. Lots of old money. And, lots of new money too because I knew of many executives and Bay Street lawyers who owned mansions in Rosedale and whose families certainly hadn't started out there. The streets in the area were tree-lined and the houses were set well-back from the street. I cruised slowly down the street glancing at house numbers looking for the one that matched the address I had quickly scribbled on a piece of paper. I had been to Rick's house only once before and that had been at night. I recognized the house and double-checked the number before I pulled into the empty driveway and parked my car. There was a garage at the far end of the driveway and the yard at the back of the house was fenced.

The house was a very formal, old colonial and large windows dominated the front. The walkway which ran parallel to the front of the house was long, and paved with red, interlocking brick in a circular pattern. The sharp heels on my pumps slipped between the cracks of the bricks a couple of times. The third time it happened the heel stuck in the crack and I stepped right out of my shoe. I cursed as I bent over in a most lady-like fashion and yanked on it and cursed again when the lift on the heel came off and exposed the steel tip of the heel. I couldn't find the piece when I tried to stick my finger between the crack in the bricks. Great, I thought.

Me and my shoe clicked and limped up the sidewalk and I admired the neatly trimmed lilac and forsythia bushes which were strategically planted in the formal garden in front of the house. Hired help, I thought.

I tucked the large brown envelope with Rick's severance documents firmly under my arm and straightened my suit jacket as I approached the front of the house. I wasn't looking forward to seeing Rick and I hoped that his wife or one of the kids answered the door. I couldn't leave the envelope and run because my instructions were to get Rick's signature on everything and return the documents to the office on Monday. If his wife answered the door, I thought, I'll give her the envelope and tell her I'd wait outside while he signed.

The door of the house was open a few inches when I stepped onto the small front porch. I listened for sounds inside and rang the doorbell and waited. When no one came to answer the doorbell, I stuck my face in the opening of the door and called out Rick's name.

I looked at my watch and saw that it was only ten to six. There was no car in the driveway and I couldn't imagine that they had gone out and left the house open so I pushed the door open a little wider and called out again.

"Hello. Rick?" I waited for a few more moments to give him the benefit of the doubt. I listened for a toilet flushing or water running but heard neither.

I stepped off the front porch and angrily marched around to the back of the house to see if anyone was in the backyard and the shoe that hadn't lost its lift got stuck immediately between the bricks in the walkway. I swore out loud, not caring who heard. "Fuck." I took off both shoes and walked in my pantyhose-clad feet and made a mental note to charge the company for lifts for my shoes and one pair of pantyhose. This was definitely above and beyond the call of duty.

The gate to the backyard was locked and I yelled over the fence.

"Hello? Anyone?" I tried peering through the minute cracks in the fence to see if anyone was there and all I could see was blue. The shit has a pool too, I thought miserably. With all his severance money, he'll be able to enclose it and swim all year round.

On my return trip to the front of the house I made up my mind to leave the documents and come back on the weekend to fetch them before returning to the office on Monday. I pushed lightly on the open front door and glanced around the marble-tiled foyer for a table to lay the documents on. The foyer was pristine and the only furnishings were a large chandelier that hung above the circular staircase and some very old-looking paintings hanging on the walls. To the left of the foyer the door was open to the room I remembered as Rick's study. I called out once more and when no one responded, I scurried across the marble floor to the study.

The room was dark because the heavy, green velvet drapes were drawn. Rick's desk was on the far side of the room and an eerie, greenish glow surrounded the high back of the leather chair behind the desk. The chair was turned around and the tall back faced me. I realized that the green glow must be coming from a computer screen behind the desk. Rick must be in the house if the computer is on, I thought with a jump.

I turned around and faced the foyer and called Rick's name once again, but I heard nothing. I took a deep breath and reminded myself it was unlikely that I would be arrested for trespassing. The man expected you and was supposed to be here, I told myself.

I hugged my shoes to my chest and crossed the room to the

desk and laid the envelope in the middle where he wouldn't miss it. It was then that I knew something was wrong. I could see an arm hanging limply beside the chair.

Someone was sitting in the chair and I hadn't seen them because of the high back.

"Rick," I croaked out in a whisper but didn't expect an answer. My bare feet were stuck to the floor and I was frozen to the spot.

Move, I urged myself. He might need help. I tried reaching across the span of the desk for the chair to turn it around but my arms weren't long enough. I grasped my shoes tighter to my chest and slowly walked around the desk.

Rick Cox was staring at the blood spattered computer screen. The bottom half of his face was gone and in his lap was a gun. I tried to scream but the only thing that came out of my mouth was a hoarse moan.

I couldn't remember the house number or the street name when I called 911 from the phone on Rick's desk. The dispatcher assured me help was on the way. She tried to keep me on the phone but I hung up and I hurried outside. I was suddenly very cold and shivering violently as I ran to my car for the cigarettes I had left on the dashboard. I grabbed the pack and stood against the side of the house smoking and waiting for the police. My legs started to tremble and I looked down at them and willed them to stop. I stared at my bare feet and wondered where my shoes were. My big toe was sticking through my pantyhose and I thought irrationally that if Vee were here I could use some of the nail polish she always keeps in her purse to stop the run that was moving slowly up my shin.

I was on my second cigarette when a police cruiser silently glided into the driveway. The police probably felt that no sirens were necessary because I had told the dispatcher he was dead. I had made certain of that when I touched the limp arm hanging over the side of the chair. The arm was cold and I knew there was no need to check for a pulse. I had stared at the half of his face that was still recognizable and felt bile rising up in the back of my throat.

CHAPTER
forty-two

I tried to convince the police officers that there was no need for me to go back in the house but they insisted.

I had pointed wordlessly to the front door when they got out of the cruiser. One officer headed for the front door and one approached me.

"You made the 911 call, ma'am?" I nodded.

"You want to tell me what happened?"

I tried to speak but something was caught in my throat. I swallowed furiously a few times and still nothing came out.

He carefully took me by the arm and led me back up the walkway to the front of the house. I followed alongside him meekly. When we got to the front porch, my voice returned.

"I really don't want to go back in there," I told him.

"We understand that ma'am," he said. I wished he'd stop calling me ma'am. I looked up at his face and realized that anyone who looked as young as he did probably called everyone over 25, ma'am. I wondered if he'd started shaving yet. His lips were moving and I willed my brain to pay attention.

"I'd just like you to walk us through what you found," he was telling me.

I couldn't look at the body again so I mutely pointed at the open door of the den and ran.

It was getting dark when Detective Leech showed up and knocked on my car window. I was huddled inside in a fog of cigarette smoke. His knock scared me and I jumped an inch off my seat before I rolled down the window. He waved his hand in front of his face when the smoke wafted out.

"It won't be much longer now, Miss Monahan," he told me.

"How come you're here?" I asked him. "Mr. Cox killed himself. It was a suicide. You're a homicide detective. Why are you here?"

I was starting to feel hysterical and my breath was coming in short gasps.

I had been left sitting here, cooling my heels for an eternity. The body was still in the house and official-looking vehicles had been arriving in a steady stream. I had been watching everything through my rear-view mirror and knew that even if they said I could go, there was no way I could move my car.

"Why don't you come out of there and get some fresh air," the detective asked me as he pulled the door open. I had my skirt hiked up around my waist and was sitting cross-legged with my knees touching the steering wheel. I had been hugging myself and smoking.

I stumbled out of the car and tried to stretch the kinks out of my knees. Leech put his hand on my shoulder and looked down at me.

"Is there someone you want to call? Someone to come and take you home?"

"I look that bad?"

He nodded. "These situations are rough for the toughest types. You've had a shock. I've got a few questions for you but you could call someone in the meantime," he said and offered me a cell phone he had pulled out of his coat pocket. When I didn't take the phone he put it in my hand and wandered off.

Who would I call? I couldn't bother Vanessa because I knew she had Ashley this weekend. I tried Jay's number knowing that the answering machine would pick up. This time I left a message.

"It's me. Friday night about eight. I, um, I'm at Rick Cox's house. He's dead." I stopped talking and started feeling angry. I pushed the power off button on the phone. What a lovely situation. I had no one to call because I had no friends. My family didn't live in the city and my pathetic life was catching up with me. I went looking for Detective Leech determined to get this over with and get the hell out of here.

I was lying on the sofa, shivering under my quilt. When the Detective had finished with me I drove the short distance home in a trance where I tried warming up in the hot shower. I finally gave up when the water started to turn cool. I put the kettle on to boil and found a box of teabags at the back of my cupboard. Comfort and warmth were needed and whenever I was sick as a child my mother gave me tea.

The living room was dark and the soft light from the streetlights washed over me where I huddled on the sofa clutching the hot mug in my hands, trying to get the image of Rick's face out of my mind. The hot tea burned the back of my throat as I gulped it down.

I slid down on the sofa and pulled the quilt over my head. I couldn't shake the ice-cold feeling in my bones so I breathed hard under the blanket hoping my hot breath would warm me. When the phone started ringing I willed it to stop. Even though I had been trying to reach Jay I couldn't bring myself to talk to anyone.

When the phone stopped ringing I tried some relaxation exercises to calm myself down. I knew I'd had a shock. But I never thought my body would react like this. My mind was fully cognizant of everything around me and in fact, the sounds of the street from outside seemed sharper and clearer.

I talked to my body starting at my toes. Relax. Then the feet and the ankles. Relax. My body parts and I had a great conversation but I realized the technique wasn't working when I reached my shoulders. I still felt tense and cold.

A hard knocking on my door scared the shit out of me and I yelped. I reached an arm out from under my quilt and felt around on the coffee table in front of me for my watch. I held it up in front of my face and turned it slightly to let the light from outside show me the time. Eleven o'clock. There was another knock, this time softer. I reluctantly crawled out from under the quilt and went to the door.

"Who's there?" I asked through the door.

"It's Jay," came the muffled reply.

I undid the chain lock and opened the door a crack and saw that it certainly was the long-lost Jay. I pulled the door wide open and turned on my heel and walked back to the living room. Jay followed me and he stood and watched as I sat down on the sofa and pulled the quilt around me. I stared at him and didn't speak.

He looked like a giant from my vantage point and I craned my neck up.

"Are you okay?" he asked me kindly.

"Do you know how many times in the last week people have asked me if I was okay?" I barked at him.

"Well, you just answered my question," he said. "Can I sit down?"

I shrugged and he sat anyway.

"I got your message," he said quietly.

"Which one of the fifteen?" I asked snidely. My mouth was working but the rest of my body was still on standby, I realized, as I started to shiver again. I pulled the quilt tighter around me.

Jay looked at me without expression and I chastised myself for biting at him. He didn't owe me anything and it was probably time I started to realize it. A few rolls in the hay and a few terms of endearment whispered in my ear had started me down the relationship road. I felt like a fool for getting sucked-in to the love whirlpool.

"I got your message about Rick Cox. Can you tell me what happened?"

I was about to tell him to go down to the police station and read the police report but stopped myself.

"I was supposed to deliver some documents to his house."

"And?"

"I found him dead in his chair at his desk."

"My God. How did he die?"

"Shot."

Jay took a deep breath. "Kathleen. Work with me here. Am I going to get one word answers out of you for the rest of the night?"

"I don't think you'll be here for the rest of the night, Mr. Harmon. You got my message because I didn't have anyone else to call. I felt sorry myself at the time because I realized I had no one else to call. But I'm over that now. I don't need friends. And I certainly don't need you. So you can just fuck off and die."

I felt my body warming up with rage and felt better. I was about to add Jay Harmon to my miserable-shit list.

Jay stood up. "Coffee?" he asked me.

I pulled the quilt over my head and felt tears fill my eyes. I told myself they were tears of rage and vowed I wasn't going to cry. I had done enough of that to last a lifetime in the last week. Rick Cox was nothing to cry about.

The sounds of water running in the kitchen told me that he was making coffee. I heard cupboard doors open and close and I counted to ten. The man had nerve. He disappears from my life for forty-eight hours. He doesn't call. And then he comes over as casual as you please and offers to make coffee. I threw the quilt off and stormed into the kitchen. He was leaning. With his hands in his jeans pockets. Shit.

"You," I said as I pointed my index finger at him. "You piss me off." I took a couple of steps closer to him as the rage built. I poked him in the chest with my finger and repeated myself. "You piss me off. You disappear for two days and then think you can casually walk back in here? You think everything'll be fine?"

I took a step back and looked up at him. He made me so mad, just standing there, running his hand through his hair.

"Where the hell have you been?" I demanded.

"Around."

"Around?"

Jay shrugged and turned around to the coffee machine. He pulled a couple of mugs out of the cupboard above him and put them on the counter. I tugged at the back of his T-shirt.

"Doing what?"

Jay impatiently pushed my hand away from the back of his shirt.

"Some thinking," was all he said. He picked up the two cups of coffee he had poured and led the way back into the living room.

CHAPTER
forty-three

I followed him slowly and quickly came to the realization that it was none of my business. If Jay wasn't willing to share with me his reasons for disappearing for two days, then that was his business. We hadn't had time to reach the point in our relationship where it was a requirement to know each other's whereabouts. And besides Kathleen, I asked myself, who said he disappeared? It dawned on me that the rebuff I had given Jay the other night when I didn't invite him back to my place had backfired. As usual, my mother would say, I had been thinking of only myself. I had been tired and depressed and wanted my personal space to myself. And in my usual, selfish fashion, I had neglected to share that with Jay.

I turned on the Tiffany lamp on my desk and closed the drapes in the living room, all the while feeling more and more uncomfortable with the situation. Jay was sitting on the sofa with his feet on the coffee table. I watched him as he picked up his coffee cup and took a slow sip. He stared at me over the rim of the cup. The silence between us was deafening and for once I had no smart remarks to make.

I picked up my coffee where Jay had placed it on the table and sat on the chair at my desk facing Jay.

I finally broke the silence.

"I apologize," I said quietly. "My behaviour was uncalled for."

Jay shrugged. "You reacted as expected."

I thought about that and wasn't surprised. Jay knew me better than I gave him credit for.

"The message I left the other day. About explaining." I looked at him expectantly wanting a pardon before I made the not-guilty plea.

I faltered when he didn't respond. "I needed to be alone. I'm sorry if you took that the wrong way. I understand now why you haven't called me in a couple of days."

"I understood Kate. But it made me angry. I'll admit that. When you're involved with someone, you expect them to be open. And honest. So, do you mind if I make the first stab at honesty here?"

I wasn't sure if I wanted to hear this but I nodded mutely anyway. Jay put his coffee cup on the table and stood up. He ran his hand repeatedly through his hair and paced behind the sofa.

"You're a very emotional person Kate," he told me, as if I didn't know. "You say what you mean and you mean what you say. Some people appreciate that. It's a characteristic I admire." He paused. "But what gets in the way of you being an emotional person is *your* inability to see other people's emotions. I mean, understand their emotions."

Very succinct. He had just told me in a roundabout way that I was selfish. I sat silently and swallowed and felt a blush rise to my face.

"What was that you said to Harold the other day? Something about sympathy and where it was in the dictionary?"

My face was beet red now and I straightened my back and looked straight at him. The lyrics from some long-forgotten song played in the back of my head. *Hit me with your best shot. Fire away!* Jay's pistol was cocked and I steadied myself for the shot.

"Sympathy and empathy go a long way, you know. You never seem to take other people's feelings into consideration. You're not the only one who has suffered this last week. You're not the only one who lost a friend. And, just in case you need reminding, there've been traumatic things happening to the people around you." He took a deep breath and sat down heavily.

I had been told, in no uncertain terms, and I felt about six inches high. I was speechless and for good reason. I didn't know what to say.

"I've known you all my life, Kate. I've always admired your toughness, your strength. But if we're going to have any sort of relationship, be it together as a couple, or just friends, you need to... " he trailed off without completing the thought. He held up his hand like he was stopping traffic.

"Forget it. I'm not about to dictate how you should behave. I'm a big boy and I accept you the way you are."

I was glad he stopped because I didn't need any more hints. I had been selfish and I admitted it. My failure to acknowledge what Jay had been through hit me in the face.

"I'm sorry," I told him. I lit a cigarette and wandered around the living room. My hand caressed the fabric of the drapes and I pulled them apart and stared out at the street. If he could be a big boy, I could be a big girl and face reality. When you live alone you become the center of the universe. The reality was that I was the center of my universe and I grudgingly acknowledged to myself that I was self-centered. Was it any wonder that I was still living alone at the mature age of thirty-four?

Jay was standing beside me now and I admitted to myself that I liked the feeling of him being there. He tentatively put his arm around my shoulder and I knew I was forgiven.

Jay woke me early next morning and tossed my sweat pants in my face.

"Put them on," he ordered. "We're going for a walk."

When I groaned and tried to roll over, he pulled the duvet off me and tossed it to the end of the bed.

"I'll allow you one cup of coffee and we're off."

"Walk? I already walked once this week," I protested.

He laughed. "You should walk every day Kathleen. Get some exercise. Take your frustrations out on the pavement instead of everyone around you. It's good for the attitude."

It was a cool spring morning and I practically had to skip to keep up with him as we headed towards the park. He finally slowed down around the pond and I took this as a sign. I grabbed the first empty bench and sat down.

"Who said you could stop?" he said and grinned at me. "We're just getting our heart rate up. You have to sustain that rate for at least twenty minutes for the workout to have any effect."

"I'll wait here for you. My heart rate's been up since we left the house. Go on." He put his hands on his hips. "Seriously," I told him. "You need it more than I do," I teased him.

"Wait here then," he said as he jogged off.

I leaned back on the bench and stretched my legs out in front of me and thought about lighting a cigarette. I breathed deeply instead and enjoyed the feeling of the fresh air in my lungs. It was surprisingly quiet in the park and I looked around me. Up the slight incline in front of where I was sitting I saw a newspaper box.

Digging in the pocket of my sweatpants for change I ran up the little hill and dropped the coins in the slot.

The article I was looking for was below the fold. *"Toronto Executive Found Dead".* There was a small picture of Rick Cox in the middle of the story and I recognized the photo as the one that appeared in our last annual report. With the paper tucked under my arm I returned to the bench to carefully read the story.

Richard Cox, who earlier this week resigned as chief financial officer of TechniGroup Consulting Inc., was found dead yesterday in his Rosedale home of an apparently self-inflicted gunshot wound. Cox is survived by his wife and two daughters.

One securities analyst interviewed for this report, speculated that there was more to Cox's resignation than was disclosed to the public and TechniGroup's shareholders. An employee of the company, who asked that his name be withheld, told the writer that it was common knowledge at TechniGroup that Cox's leaving was not a resignation. When asked if Cox had recently exhibited signs of depression, the employee was unable to comment.

Police report that Cox was found by an employee of TechniGroup who was delivering some papers to his home. Police declined to release the employee's name.

The story went on to recount the recent slide in TechniGroup's stock price and the reporter, who obviously didn't hold any stock, speculated that this latest turn of events would not bode well for TechniGroup's shareholders.

The report finished by reminding the readers that Cox had been questioned by the police regarding the mysterious death of a TechniGroup employee.

I wasn't surprised that they had interviewed a securities analyst for the story because it was the analysts who ultimately drove the price of publicly-traded stocks. Securities analysts were the barometer of the stock market. What surprised me though was the fact that the analysts on the street knew that Cox hadn't resigned. Someone had been talking in their sleep.

CHAPTER
forty-four

Jay appeared on my left and slowly came to a stop in front of me. He lifted one leg onto the bench and re-tied his running shoe before contorting his body into all sorts of ungodly stretching positions. I stared at him with an admiring look and then shook my head.

"You really enjoy running, don't you?"

He nodded and clasped his hands behind his back and arched his shoulders. His soaked hair clung to his head and I could see rivulets of sweat running down his neck. There was a large, dark, wet spot on the front of his T-shirt.

"You should try it," he panted as he bent over and grabbed his hands behind his knees. The only time my hands see the back of my legs was when I was shaving them.

When he finally sat down, I handed him the newspaper folded to the story about Rick Cox and watched his face for reaction as he read the article. When he finished he laid the paper on the bench beside him and said, "The employee who asked that his name be withheld was probably Tom James. The man can't keep his mouth shut."

"You're probably right. What I find more surprising though is the speculation on the street that Rick didn't resign."

"It's more than speculation, Kate. It's all over the street. Everyone knows that he was fired and they think they know why."

"All over the street? Who told you?"

"A friend," he replied cryptically. "Some of my best friends are analysts, you know."

I laughed. "Nothing to be ashamed of," I jokingly told him. "It's their mothers who should be ashamed."

"What's the poop on why he was fired?" I asked.

"The rumours are saying it was because he cooked the books."

"I guess they're partly right."

"I think the street started that rumour because it's the most logical one, Kate. When a CFO gets fired, it's the logical conclusion."

"Well, if those rumours take off, we'll have the enforcement goons from the Ontario Securities Commission knocking on our door."

Jay picked up the paper again and looked at the picture of Rick. He shook his head slowly and said, "I can't believe it was suicide. Rick believed he didn't do anything wrong. That's why he fired me. And he wasn't the type."

"What's the type? From everything I've ever heard, some of the most apparently sane people kill themselves. You know, it fits here. Successful businessman with a beautiful wife, two kids, a dog and station wagon gets fired. His reputation is going to be in shreds. How well did we really know him?"

Jay snorted. "I worked with him every day for almost a year. The man was a bully with an ego almost as big as Chris Oakes'. Someone who loved themselves that much doesn't eat a pistol for lunch."

A picture, forever frozen in my brain, flashed before my eyes of Rick Cox minus his chin and lower jaw. I shivered and wrapped my arms around myself.

"Maybe his suicide had nothing to do with losing his job. Maybe," I said and turned towards Jay on the bench, "maybe, the police had something on him about Ev's death. What if he did it?"

"No way, Kate. He had nothing to gain by killing Ev. Nothing. I had more to gain than he did."

"Don't say that." I touched his shoulder. "Don't say things like that out loud."

We walked silently back to my apartment, each of us lost in our own thoughts. As we approached the house, I could see someone sitting on the top step of the porch. The beige overcoat was familiar, even from a block away, and my stomach sank when I realized it was Detective Leech.

Jay and I stood side by side at the bottom of the steps and looked up at Leech. Beside him on the step were my shoes evenly lined up with their toes touching the edge of the step.

"Detective," I acknowledged him.

"Ms. Monahan," he nodded at me. He looked curiously at Jay and waited for an introduction.

"Detective Leech, this is Jay Harmon. A friend of mine."

Leech pushed himself to a standing position and held out his hand to shake. Jay reached up and when he realized their hands wouldn't meet, he walked up the first two stairs.

"Thanks for returning my shoes," I told him.

"So they are yours," was all he said. He picked them up in one hand and put them under his arm. I approached Leech holding out my hand in hopes of retrieving my shoes and sending him on his way. My hopes were dashed when Leech backed up the stairs and pointed at the front door.

"I was hoping for some time to talk to you," he told me.

I reluctantly led the way and offered coffee when Leech was ensconced in the living room. He shook his head and motioned for me to sit down. Jay had excused himself and I could hear the shower running.

Leech tried balancing both of my wayward shoes on the palm of his hand and then held them out to me like a cannibal offering salt.

"Yours?"

I nodded.

"How did they come to end up on Mr. Cox's desk?"

"The heels had got caught in between the cracks on his walkway and tips of the heels came off. The lifts. I took them off and carried them. I guess I left them on the desk when I found Rick. Mr. Cox." Detective Leech had taken out his small notebook and was making notes while I talked. When I finished talking he looked at me without speaking as if expecting me to continue. The man was making me nervous.

I shrugged and held up the palms of my hands. "That's it. That's all. A very simple explanation," I babbled. I wondered if they thought the shoes were the weapon Cox had killed himself with.

"You told the responding police officers that you had heard nothing and seen no one. How long were you at the house before you discovered Mr. Cox's body?"

I thought about that for a moment and replied, "No more than a couple of minutes."

"And he was expecting you?"

I nodded again.

"What time did you arrive?"

"I can't remember exactly. I think just before six." I remembered that Leech had asked me these same questions last night.

"Why are you asking me all of this? We went over it last night." I hoped I sounded as exasperated as I felt.

Jay was standing in the doorway rubbing his head with a towel listening.

"Last night was a shock to you and you must admit, you were pretty shaken up. In fact, I was surprised you left on your own. Wasn't there someone you were trying to call?" As he said this he looked over at Jay.

"No, I was fine," I told him quickly.

"Well, I thought it might be prudent to go over some facts. See if you remembered anything since last night," he told me.

"And," he continued as he flipped his notebook to a fresh page, "my other reason for being here was to ask you if you knew where or how I could contact Mr. Harmon here. So, I've killed two birds with one stone." He laughed at his stupid joke and I stared at him.

"Mr. Harmon, if you've got a moment. I've been anxious to talk to you now for a couple of days."

Jay had dropped the towel around his shoulders and was running his hand through his hair, trying to comb it.

"Jay. You can call me Jay."

"Well, is now a good time?" Leech looked directly at me when he asked Jay the question. It was a look of dismissal but I waited to hear Jay's reply.

"Sure."

I picked up my shoes off the floor where they sat beside Leech and discretely left wondering which room would be the best to eavesdrop from. I stood at the back of the kitchen but it was too obvious because it opened on to the living room. I thought about standing at the end of the hall and pretending to be on the phone. There was no way I could go back through the living room to sit on the small balcony, so I gave up and decided to take a shower. I heard Leech's raised voice and stopped.

"We've been unable to reach you by phone. And twice in the last two days, we've sent an officer to your apartment and you weren't there. We'll need a statement from you accounting for your time over the last seventy-two hours. And, Mr. Harmon, I want times, places, and the names of people who can verify they saw you."

I hurriedly walked to my bedroom and quickly closed the

door. I stood and stared at the back of the door and frantically dug in my pockets for a cigarette. When my hands came up empty I realized that my cigarettes were in the living room on the coffee table, where I'd left them last night.

The police hadn't asked me to account for my time. I didn't have to give them times and places. The issue of where Jay had been for the last two days was one I dropped last night. We hadn't talked about it anymore because I had decided it wasn't any of my business. Now the police were asking him where he'd been. In the old Nancy Drew books I used to read, they called this an alibi.

CHAPTER
forty-five

There was a light knock on the bathroom door and I ignored it. I closed my eyes again and slid further down in the tub and felt the hot water and bubbles gathering around my neck.

"Kate," Jay's muffled voice said through the unlocked door.

"Yeah. Come in."

I felt his presence standing over me and without opening my eyes I asked him if Leech was gone.

"Yes."

Hiding in the warm bathtub had made me feel better, but just for a few minutes. Visions of the police dragging Jay down the stairs in handcuffs had danced before my closed eyes. Newspaper headlines blared about his arrest.

"What'd he ask you about?" I probed.

"My job. Why I was fired. Where I've been the last couple of days."

"Was he happy with the answers?"

"Somewhat. He's preparing a written statement and I have to go down to his precinct and sign it."

I hadn't been asked to sign any statements. My stomach sank and I opened my eyes. Jay was sitting on the edge of the bathtub with his back to me.

"You know Kate, the way he questioned me, it was strange. He didn't come out and say it, but I don't think they're convinced that Rick's death was a suicide. He asked me if I owned a gun. He asked me where I was yesterday in the late afternoon. He asked me when was the last time I'd seen Rick. And he went back to the night Ev died and asked me to give him the details of what had happened." Jay sounded despondent as he rattled this off. His shoulders were hunched and he was leaning forward with his elbows on his knees.

I stood up in the tub and reached around him for the towel

hanging on the rack. With the towel held primly in front of me I asked him to get up so I could get out of the bathtub.

"Sorry," he mumbled and left the bathroom without looking at me.

I was more perturbed now than I had been when I overheard Leech demanding an alibi. I dressed quickly and found him sitting on the balcony on a kitchen chair that he had moved out there.

"How did you answer Leech when he asked for an explanation of your whereabouts in the last seventy-two hours?" I had decided a flank attack might be better than firing from the hip. No more demands like last night, from me.

Jay shaded his eyes from the sunlight with his hand and peered up at me. My arms were crossed against my chest and I quickly dropped them and consciously eased the muscles in my face. I tried my best not to look like a schoolmarm.

"I told him the truth. I hadn't left Dodge City."

"And when he didn't even crack a smile, you realized he was serious."

"Yeah. Dead serious. I told him what I'd been doing. He recalled seeing me at the funeral. I told him that after the funeral I spent the afternoon downtown at the Public Library. Dinner at Bigliardi's with you and Vanessa. Slept in my own bed, alone, so I didn't have any witnesses. Thursday I had lunch with that friend I was telling you about, the analyst. Dave Smithson. That afternoon I was back at the library, doing more research. Slept alone, again," he sighed. "I tried wrenching his heart strings with that one but he wasn't budging."

I smiled but didn't interrupt.

"Friday I went to Ottawa. I had to go and see my mom."

"How is she?"

"She's great."

"And how did she take the news?"

I knew that had to have been a difficult trip for Jay to make. His mother was incredibly proud of her offspring's accomplishments, and rightly so. As poor as his family had been, his mother had insisted that they all attend university. Jay and his sisters all had graduate degrees and they were supporting their mother now. Jay was the last to graduate, and when he secured his job, he and his sisters had finally insisted that their mom quit her job and move out of the old neighbourhood in Centertown Ottawa. They had bought her a nice condominium overlooking the Canal and provided her with more money than she knew what to do with. She was the queen of Tuesday night bingo at the Glebe Community Centre now and Jay had told me that she placed pictures of her kids around her at the bingo table for good luck. The fact that Jay had been fired under questionable circumstances would not have gone over well with Mrs. Harmon.

"She was rightfully indignant, at first. And then when she listened to what had actually happened, how Rick had accused me and then fired me, I could tell she was going to box my ears," he laughed. "I think she's worried about me not getting a paycheque and she wouldn't believe me when I told her I wasn't destitute. I had to show her my passbook from the bank to prove that I had money in savings. She was ready to give me money because she told me she never spends half of what we give her."

He leaned the chair back on two legs and put his feet up on the railing of the balcony and stared at his bare feet.

"You know," he continued quietly, "mom wanted me to move back home. I told her this wasn't a complete disaster, yet, and that I'd get another job. Besides, who wants to work in a town where the only jobs are with the federal government and all they do is whine about the Senators not winning the Stanley Cup?"

Jay dropped his feet and the front legs of the chair hit the floor. "Traffic was heavy on the 401 and it was late when I got back. I checked my messages as soon as I got home, around ten-thirty and came over here right away."

My breath came out slowly when I realized I had been holding it all along. These were all reasonable explanations of his whereabouts. We'd discuss why he didn't call me, some other time.

"Did Leech ask if you slept alone last night?" I said with a laugh.

"No." He grabbed my hand and pulled me down on his lap where I curled up and put my head against his chest.

"Why were you doing all that research? Checking out companies in your job search?"

"No. As corny as it sounds, I was looking for the truth."

"Ah, the eternal search for truth. Tell me old wise one, what'd you find?"

He thought it would be better if he showed me.

The file Jay retrieved from his car was about an inch thick and he sorted the various sheets of paper in piles on the kitchen table. He held up a few sheets stapled in the corner and passed them to me.

The top sheet read *University of Western Ontario, Richard Ivey School of Business, MBA Graduates, Class of 1998.* Listed below, in alphabetical order were the names of the graduates. Jay's name was highlighted in yellow on the second page.

I smiled and passed it back to him. "Adding this to your resume?"

He didn't answer and handed me a single sheet of paper that had a section in the middle highlighted. I read in small type in the top, right-hand corner *Who's Who 2002.* The highlighted section read *Oakes, Christopher Earl, B.Comm., MBA: Chairman, CEO and member of the board of directors, TechniGroup Consulting Inc., B.Comm, University of Illinois, 1973, MBA, Richard Ivey School of Business, University of Western Ontario, 1975.*

The section went on to describe Chris' past jobs, the charitable foundations he graced with his presence, and his marital status, or lack thereof.

All of this was old news to me so I handed it back to Jay. He exchanged the *Who's Who* photocopy with another single sheet which I immediately recognized. It was our company's standard biography sheet which had a picture of Oakes and a couple of paragraphs describing his background. The few words describing his academic past were highlighted. I didn't bother reading any of this and I looked expectantly at Jay who silently offered me another piece of paper.

This one looked vaguely familiar. It was a photocopy of a trade magazine feature article about Chris Oakes that had been written about three months after Chris joined our company. The blurred photocopy didn't do justice to the original photo that had appeared in the magazine. The photo had pictured Oakes sitting at a desk with an active computer screen behind him. The article had described Oakes as a real computer wizard and it talked about how he used the computer at all hours of the night, sending e-mails and messages to his employees and executives. The article was a joke because Oakes didn't even have a desk, let alone a computer in his office. Chris could no more operate a computer than I could fly a jetfighter. He was just like Rick Cox - a technophobe and ashamed to admit it. I remember when I read the article I thought they should have been referring to voice mail, not e-mail.

Jay had highlighted several paragraphs that described Oakes' academic achievements.

I handed this back to him and said, "So?"

"The coup de grace," he replied and handed me more papers. This set looked similar to the first one Jay had handed me. *University of Western Ontario, Richard Ivey School of Business, Class of 1975.*

"Do you see Chris' name anywhere on that list?" Jay asked me. I flipped the pages to find the O's and carefully read the names.

"You won't find it on there," he told me as I read. "I checked the years before and after 1975, and his name doesn't appear. I called the registrar's office and they told me he was registered and dropped out in his first year."

"So, the man's a liar. Why hasn't anyone discovered this before now?"

"I don't know. Maybe when someone reaches his level, they forget to check references," Jay said.

"Well, Sherlock. What other goodies have you come up with?"

"When I discovered that he'd dropped out of Western, I knew something was fishy in Denmark. I realized then that there was a missing link because his resume of his past jobs only starts after his alleged graduation from MBA school."

"He was probably slinging hamburgers," I offered. "Not exactly something you want on your resume."

"Well, Kate. I've discovered he *wasn't* slinging hamburgers," he announced.

CHAPTER
forty-six

Jay had uncovered a squirming can of worms and when we put all of the information together it led us down a dangerous path.

Chris Oakes hadn't been slinging hamburgers between 1973 and 1975. He had been the treasurer of a small textile company in Hamilton, Ontario. The path that led to this revelation was quite convoluted, and after Jay spread out more papers on my kitchen table, he explained.

Jay was standing in front of the wall in the kitchen tracing imaginary lines across his fictional whiteboard. I was glad he didn't have a marker in his hand because I was sure he would be writing all over the wall.

"Oakes wasn't the only officer of the company I checked out," he was telling me. "I pulled the background dossiers on all the senior guys, and all of the directors, and discovered a few interesting things. First of all, most of the directors' paths have crossed some time or another in the past fifteen years. They've either served on the same boards, or were members of the same charitable foundations, or went to school together. All of their backgrounds as they've reported them checked out. Except one." He paused for effect.

"You want me to guess?"

He nodded his head and said, "Sure. But you'll never get it on the first try."

I was never one to back down from a challenge. "Can I ask one question first?"

"Come on. Just guess," he said impatiently.

I wanted to know if it was an officer or director of the company who didn't check out but when Jay wasn't amenable to the game, I guessed.

"Larry Everly," I pronounced.

Now it was Jay's turned to look surprised.

"You're right. How did you know?"

"Ah ha! So I was right," I rubbed it in. "But it was just a wild guess. I just don't like the man. Most of the directors are harmless old men who are puppets. Everly on the other hand, isn't old, and he isn't harmless. He's a snake. So, what didn't check out about him?" I asked eagerly.

He pulled out a sheaf of papers from the bottom of a pile that were paper clipped together and tossed them at me. I removed the paper clip and saw that it was a copy of each of the directors' biographies. Stapled to each biography was a copy of each director's entry from *Who's Who.*

"Take out Larry's and check out what he said was his first job."

"Bittman Brothers," I read out loud. "1973 to 1975." My face was a question mark.

"A small, family-owned, Wall Street brokerage house," Jay told me and tossed more papers at me that were photocopies of excerpts from the *Survey of Industrials*, a directory that is released each year listing various industrial companies. Jay had photocopied an excerpt from the 1973 edition and highlighted a company called Weinstein Textiles. Weinstein Textiles were described as a manufacturer of industrial strength textiles located in Hamilton, Ontario. Revenues, number of employees and a list of the company's officers followed. Chairman of the Board and President was a Mr. Robert Weinstein and on the same list I found the names of Christopher Oakes and Larry Everly. Chris Oakes was named as company Treasurer and Larry Everly was District Sales Manager.

"Well, well, well," I said smugly. "Mr. Everly must have been carrying a big load back then, commuting daily between Hamilton and New York. It must have taken a toll. Did you check it out?"

Jay nodded. "Of course. I called around and discovered that Bittman Brothers had been gobbled up by one of the larger brokerage houses in the mid-seventies. I managed to track down the son of one of the founders of Bittman Brothers who's still in the business and he told me that Larry Everly never worked there. In fact, he knows Larry because Wall Street's a small world. Told me they'd have been lucky to have Larry working there. He said if he remembered correctly, Larry was in the Toronto area during those years, working for some sort of manufacturing company. So, I searched the *Survey of Industrials* and found Larry Everly. And Chris Oakes."

"Your research skills amaze me," I complimented him as I flipped the pages and saw the identical information for 1974 and 1975 directories. In the entry for 1975 Oakes still held the position of Treasurer but Larry had been promoted to Vice-President of Sales.

"What happened after 1975?" I asked Jay.

"I couldn't find any more references to Weinstein Textiles. It appeared to have disappeared off the map."

I tried to digest the information. From 1973 to 1975 Oakes had said he was at school getting his MBA, and Larry was supposedly working on Wall Street. Treasurer and Vice President of Sales were legitimate jobs, so why did they both feel it was necessary to lie about those two years?

"Larry Everly knows damn well that Oakes is a fraud," I said.

"And," Jay pointed out, "Oakes knows that Everly is a fraud."

"Disgusting," I stated. I pushed my chair back and made some coffee. "Where does all this information get us?" I asked Jay as I spooned the coffee into the filter.

Jay was silent for a moment and then he said, "It gets us nowhere. All it does is create more questions."

"Yeah. Like what happened to Weinstein Textiles? Why would it just disappear like that from the reference books?"

"Because you stop paying to have your company listed. From what I understand the *Survey of Industrials* sends out a renewal form each year to the companies that are listed in it asking for updated information and a fee to have their company listed again. So," he said slowly, "I called them. Asked them what had happened in 1976 and why Weinstein hadn't re-listed."

"And?" I asked hopefully, leaning against the counter.

"They told me I was out of luck. Their records weren't computerized back then and there wasn't any way they could check back."

"Oh," I said disappointedly.

"But," Jay said brightly. "All those research skills I honed in university paid off. I did the next best thing."

This was like pulling teeth.

"You've had the answer all along haven't you?"

Jay smirked. "I got the answer but then I hit a dead-end. I started checking out obituaries. I started with this year and worked my way back." Once again, Jay paused for effect.

I shifted my weight to the other foot and crossed my arms against my chest. My body language said, you better tell me, and tell me fast.

"Okay, okay. Robert Weinstein died around Christmas in 1975." He dug around in his papers and came up with a microfiche copy of a small obituary. He handed it to me.

> Robert Weinstein, Chairman and President of Weinstein Textiles Inc. passed away suddenly on December 17, 1975. Survived by his loving wife Sadie and son Robert Jr.

I handed it back to Jay who was holding yet another goodie. This time he read it out loud: *Robert Weinstein, Chairman of Weinstein Textiles died of an apparent suicide on Thursday night. Mr. Weinstein will be fondly remembered by the many people who had been employed for decades at the textile plant. It was reported that Mr. Weinstein had been despondent recently over the bankruptcy of Weinstein Textiles. He is survived by his wife Sadie and their ten year old son, Robert Jr.*

Something was bothering me and I thought about it as I poured coffee. The name Sadie Weinstein was very familiar to me and I couldn't remember where I'd heard it before.

"Have you ever heard the name Sadie Weinstein before?" I asked Jay as I handed him a cup. He shook his head.

Jay sat down at the table and started rearranging his piles of photocopies. I wandered through the living room and back into the kitchen all the time trying to remember. I played some mind games and envisioned lists of names. Names of friends and family. Names of friends of friends and friends of family. When that didn't get me anywhere I switched to work. Names of people at the office, people outside the office at law firms and accounting firms. I was impressed with the number of people I knew but still didn't come up with any Sadie Weinsteins. And then I remembered typing the name so I knew she was related to something I had done at work.

"Jay," I said, trying to get his attention. He was reading something intently and had ignored my wandering around.

When he looked up at me, I said, "I know her name. And it's an odd enough name that I doubt I'm mistaken here. I've typed her name on my computer and for the life of me, I can't remember why."

His eyebrows went up slowly. "You've typed her name? On the computer at work?"

"Do you see a computer here at home? Yes, at work."

"I'll be right back," he said over his shoulder as he exited the kitchen quickly and I heard the front door close.

When he came back he yelled for me from the front door. I found him on his hands and knees in the front hall plugging his laptop computer into the wall jack for the phone. I watched him in silence as he typed a few commands into the computer.

The modem inside the computer emitted the scratchy sounds of a phone dialling and Jay looked up at me from where he was kneeling on the floor and asked, "You know Kate, it'd be nice if you joined the twentieth century and got a high speed connection and maybe a computer at home!"

He passed me the computer and I logged on to my system at work.

I clicked the mouse a few times to get to my file manager, clicked on the search button and typed in *Sadie Weinstein*. We waited while the computer searched the hundreds of subdirectories and documents on my computer.

The computer finished its search and told us there were three occurrences of the name and that they were in the directory *acquisitions*, subdirectory *marshton*. I had a directory, or file, on my computer containing all the documents we created for all the companies we purchased. Subdirectories were created with the name of each company we acquired. All relevant, computer-generated documents were filed there. *Marshton* was the name of the company we had just acquired.

I reached up to the small telephone table beside me and grabbed the pen and pad of paper I kept there for taking messages. I stared at the screen and wrote down the three documents where her name appeared. I clicked the mouse a few more times and a document appeared on the screen. I knew by now what the document contained and wasn't surprised when the screen showed her name in third place on the list. All shareholders of that company were listed in order of their holdings.

"There it is," I pointed to the screen. "Sadie Weinstein. She owned twenty-one percent of the shares of Marshton Systems."

CHAPTER
forty-seven

"Well, well, well," I said slowly as I watched Jay pack up his computer. "Isn't it a small world?"

I looked at the address I had written down on the piece of paper and picked up the phone and dialled information for Sadie's number.

"And just what are you going to do with her phone number?" Jay asked me.

"Nothing right now," I told him. "If she's not home, I'll be able to call her later."

"You're not going to her house?"

"Not me. We." I handed him the piece of paper. "It's not that far from here. Are you driving?" I dug in the front hall closet for my jacket and pulled it on.

"No way." Jay was shaking his head. "Let's figure this out first."

"I don't think we *can* figure it out without talking to her. Do you think it's a coincidence that she was a major shareholder of a company we just bought?"

"Weirder things have happened," Jay said.

"Like finding out that Oakes and Everly are both liars and that they worked for the same company back in the seventies?"

"That's weird," Jay agreed. "But the fact that there are a couple of anomalies in their resumes is not a big deal in the whole scheme of things."

"And," I continued, ignoring him, "the widow of the owner of *that* company now shows up as a shareholder in an acquisition we just did?"

"Maybe it's not a coincidence. But what are you going to ask her? How are you going to approach this?" Jay demanded.

"Well, I hadn't quite thought of that yet," I said dejectedly.

Jay helped me off with my coat.

"And what's the purpose?"

"You tell me Jay. You're the one who started it. Why *did* you dig up all this information? What're you planning to do with it?"

He turned around and walked back to the living room and I followed him.

"What're you trying to prove?" I asked again.

Jay sat on the edge of the coffee table and I stood in front of him.

"They've ruined my reputation Kate. I was fired for no just cause and I've got no recourse." He looked up at me and there was pain on his face. "Understand?"

I nodded. "Just how hard is it going to be for you to get another job? Without a reference?"

"Not hard. The reality of the situation is this. I'm a graduate of Western and could probably have a job tomorrow after making a few phone calls."

"So what's this all about?"

He shrugged. "Petty revenge?"

"You're asking me Jay? Is it or is it not, revenge?"

He took a while before he answered. "Maybe it started out like that. I was determined to ruin their reputations in the same way they ruined mine. And then I actually found something."

"But as you so succinctly pointed out to me, what you've found out is not such a big deal. Some lying on their resumes."

"Interesting though, don't you think?" Jay said with a little smirk on his face.

"I agree. So let's take it one step further. Let's go and see this Sadie Weinstein and see if there's more. Just for the helluva it."

As it turned out, Oakes and Everly would have been happy if they'd only been exposed as having lied about their education and past job histories.

Mrs. Sadie Weinstein's house certainly didn't reflect the fact that our company had recently paid her the hefty sum of $3.5 million for her shares. She lived in a rundown neighbourhood in downtown Hamilton. Her home looked neglected and the white picket fence surrounding the front yard was leaning precariously, in obvious need of a fresh coat of paint. The small gate in the middle of the waist-high fence was hanging by one hinge and the small patch of grass that was her front lawn was choked with weeds.

Jay leaned around me and peered out the side window of the car at her house.

"Doesn't look like anyone's home," he said.

The house was dark and showed no signs of life. I opened the car door slowly, reluctant to proceed now that I'd dragged Jay here. He'd only agreed to come along after I told him that I was going, regardless of whether or not he would do the chivalrous thing and escort me. I know he thought this was a stupid move but thankfully, he kept his thoughts to himself.

I had no idea what I was going to say to Mrs. Weinstein, if she answered the door. Deceit wasn't one of my strong points and I had desperately formulated numerous opening lines on the drive to her house. I stumbled on the uneven front step and cursed when a sharp pain shot through my shin. The light fixture beside the front door was missing the light bulb and I searched in the darkness around the doorframe for the doorbell. No light reached inside the porch which had an overhanging roof so I knocked loudly on the door.

I heard a muffled sound inside the house and said, "She's there." When Jay didn't respond I turned around to find myself alone on the porch and Jay still sitting in the car. I waved at him and wasn't surprised when he stayed in the car.

The sound of several chains coming unlocked got my attention and I turned eagerly to the door.

A small voice questioned me. "Who's there?"

"Um," I replied brilliantly. "Miss Monahan." A perfect response, I thought. She's really going to open the door to Miss Monahan, serial murderer.

"From TechniGroup", I added quickly, finally formulating my plan of attack. When the door still didn't open, I spoke at the door, "Mrs. Weinstein, I'm from the company that recently sent you some money for your shares."

The door creaked open a crack and I could see it was still fastened by one chain.

"I'm sorry dear, I don't know what you're talking about," a clear voice said.

"Our company," I explained, "sent you a cheque, for a very large sum of money a couple of weeks ago. I'm here to make sure you got it."

"I'm not interested in buying anything tonight," Sadie said and closed the door.

I quickly knocked again and said loudly, "Mrs. Weinstein, I'm not selling anything. Really." I dug in my purse for my wallet and found one of my business cards. "Mrs. Weinstein, please. Just open the door a crack and I'll pass you one of my business cards."

The sound behind me of a car door closing gave me the strength to push on. I couldn't fail at this because I couldn't stand for anyone to tell me, *I told you so.* Jay had been against my coming here and I had to prove to him that this wasn't a wild goose chase. I saw him coming slowly up the front walk.

Please, I prayed. "Mrs. Weinstein, please open the door. I'm not here to harm you," I reassured her.

The chain came off and the door opened to reveal a very tiny, old woman. So tiny in fact, she was shorter than I was. Her pure white hair was permed and it surrounded her head like a perfect 1970-style afro.

She took my proffered business card and read out loud, "Kathleen Monahan, Legal Administrator. Irish."

I nodded my head. Sadie looked around me and pointed, "Who's that?"

"Oh," I said and stepped aside. "This is Mr. Harmon, also from TechniGroup."

Jay came forward a couple of steps and offered his hand. "Mrs. Weinstein, very pleased to meet you." She timidly held out her hand and Jay gently shook it.

"Mrs. Weinstein," I said. "We're from TechniGroup, a company that recently bought Marshton Systems and our records showed that you owned a substantial number of the shares of Marshton. When the transaction closed, cheques were sent to the shareholders of Marshton. Did you receive the cheque?"

While I said this her face became more confused and she slowly shook her head.

"No. No, the only money I get is my Canada pension and old age security and some money from my son."

I pulled out a sheet of paper from my purse and said, "Our records also show that you had requested the cheque to be sent by courier, to this address. That was about two weeks ago. You don't remember?"

Jay nudged me and said, "I'm sure Mrs. Weinstein would have remembered receiving a cheque for that amount of money. We obviously have the wrong person, and we're sorry for taking up your time." He took my arm and tried to lead me away but I held up the scrap of paper.

"This address is *your* address, Mrs. Weinstein. There couldn't be a mistake," I told them.

Sadie took a step back and said, "I think there's been a mistake." A steady breeze was whipping across the porch and she wrapped her arms around herself and rubbed her upper arms. "It's cool tonight," she told us. "Why don't you two come in and we'll try and sort it out."

Jay started to decline but I kicked him lightly on his ankle before I followed Sadie into the dark house. There was light at the end of the hallway and I could see it was the kitchen. Sadie led us into a room to the left of the hallway and turned on a floor lamp with an old-fashioned tasselled lampshade.

"You sit," she ordered us. "I'll make some tea. You like tea?" she beamed up at Jay. "Such a handsome boy," she said as she patted his arm. "Sit, sit," she reminded us again as she hurried out of the room.

I did a three hundred and sixty degree turn in the living room and admired all of the antiques. It was almost impossible to believe that all of these beautiful things existed inside a house that from the outside appeared ready for demolition. Every surface was covered with lace doilies, pictures and knick-knacks. On closer inspection, I discovered that most of them weren't dime store knick-knacks, but original Royal Doulton, genuine Hummel, and other delicate English bone-china figurines.

Jay was sitting stiffly on an overstuffed sofa that was covered in a faded, cabbage rose pattern.

"Look," I said as I held out a Hummel figurine. "It's an original Chimney Sweep."

"Put it down," he hissed. "You shouldn't be touching her things."

"Party pooper," I mumbled under my breath as I gently replaced the Chimney Sweep in his position of honour on a low, Duncan Fyfe coffee table. Every surface was spotless and all of the objects had obviously been lovingly cared for over the years. The baby grand piano in the corner of the room took my breath away.

"Have you ever seen a piano in mahogany?" I asked Jay as I sat down on the bench. "I've only ever seen them in black. It's beautiful," I purred as I passed my hand over the closed cover of the keyboard.

The closed top of the baby grand was covered in dozens of pictures in ornate frames and I tried in the dim light to focus on the figures in the pictures.

Sadie pushed a rosewood teacart into the living room and sat herself in a small, armless Queen Ann chair.

"I'll pour," she declared to no one in particular.

The pictures on the piano were mostly black and whites and several obviously dated back to the early part of the century. I picked up a small, oval frame that fit in the palm of my hand and a very young, incredibly beautiful, Sadie peered back at me. I recognized her in several other pictures, standing arm-in-arm with a strapping, handsome man who was twice her size.

"Miss Monahan," I heard her calling me. "Milk and sugar?"

The pictures on the piano top were arranged in rows by size and a large, eight by ten, colour photo in the back row caught my eye. The only part of the picture visible from my vantage point was the person's hair, which was perfectly arranged. I got a funny feeling when I realized that the hair seemed very familiar and laughed out loud. Familiar hair?

I stood up and reached carefully over the rows of pictures to the one at the back and gingerly picked it up. The familiar, and perfect hair, was on the head of the very familiar, and perfect face of Philip Winston, the Third.

CHAPTER
forty-eight

M y heart was pounding and I realized I was holding my breath. I'm sure if someone had taken my picture at that moment they could have placed it in the dictionary as an illustration beside the word dumbfounded.

Jay's voice brought me back and I jumped at the sound of it. "Kate."

I hastily replaced the picture. "Sorry," I apologized. "I was just admiring all of your beautiful things, Mrs. Weinstein." I sat primly on the sofa beside Jay and folded my hands in my lap.

"So tell me," Sadie started. "Are you sure you're not with that Mr. Ed McMahon from the Johnny Carson show? I've seen pictures on the television of the nice people they send around to tell people they've won the jackpot."

I looked at Jay with a question mark on my face.

"Publisher's Clearing House," he told me. "Mrs. Weinstein thinks we're here to tell her she won the jackpot because you told her about a cheque she was supposed to have received."

"Oh," I said stupidly and looked at Sadie who smiled at me over the rim of her teacup. "No. But if you're the same Sadie Weinstein that our company cut a cheque for the other day, I'd say you've won more than the jackpot. You really don't remember receiving a package by courier about two weeks ago?"

"No," she said. "I don't remember ever receiving anything by courier."

We were obviously going nowhere on this so I changed tactics. "Did your husband own Weinstein Textiles?" I received a sharp jab in my side from Jay for that one, but I pushed on. "Was your husband Robert Weinstein?"

Sadie paused for a few moments and then replied softly, "Yes. But what has that got to do with a cheque?"

"I'm not sure Mrs. Weinstein," I told her honestly. "Can you tell me what happened to your husband's company?"

"It went bankrupt. We went bankrupt," she stated flatly. "At Thanksgiving 1975."

Even though the light was low in the room I could see her eyes brimming with tears.

"What happened?" I questioned her.

She dug in the pocket of her housedress for a hankie and dabbed at her eyes. "Somebody was stealing money from the company and by the time Robert discovered it, it was too late. There was no cash left to pay the bills. Or pay the employees."

I looked at Jay who was staring at Sadie and silently willed him to look at me. When he finally turned his head to look at me I whispered, "How far do we want to take this?"

He shrugged and hung his head and I pushed on. For him.

"Did they ever discover who was stealing the money?" I asked.

"My husband knew," she said sadly.

"Did the police catch the person?"

"The police were never told."

"Why?" Jay asked.

She shrugged her shoulders and pondered the question. When she finally answered, I had to strain to hear her say, "Pride. My husband was too proud."

"Too proud to admit someone stole from him?" I asked.

She nodded slowly. "And he still lost the company. He tried to make a recovery but within two weeks the banks foreclosed."

And where was his pride then, I wondered silently. Jay's hand slipped into mine and I gave it a squeeze.

I took a deep breath and pushed on because as painful as this was for Sadie, I needed answers. Pride is a wonderful thing to wear on your chest when you're facing adversity and there are lights at the end of the tunnel, like being a scholarship student because your mother didn't have any money. I needed answers for Jay because I didn't want to see his pride lead him down the same road that took Robert Weinstein's business and ultimately, his life.

"Do you know who stole the money?" I asked Sadie.

"Robert never told me," she said as she shook her head. "But I wasn't stupid then, and I'm not stupid now," she said defiantly. "He never told me, but I know."

Jay and I waited expectantly for her to tell us but she wasn't forthcoming. So, I tried another avenue.

"Do you remember Mr. Christopher Oakes and Mr. Larry Everly who worked for your husband back then?"

Sadie sat up straighter in her chair at my question and I could see her shoulders stiffen. When she didn't answer me I knew she remembered them. I wished I had brought pictures of them to show her for confirmation but like Sadie, I wasn't stupid. I knew that the two men by the names of Oakes and Everly that I work with were the same two who had worked at Weinstein's in the seventies. Her reaction to their names was unexpected and I needed to know why.

"Mrs. Weinstein, please," I pleaded. "Do you remember Mr. Oakes and Mr. Everly?"

She stood up and grabbed our teacups from the coffee table and Jay jumped up to help her. I knew this was a dismissal and I also knew I wasn't leaving until I had the answers so I tugged anxiously on the waistband of Jay's jeans. He ignored me. Sadie smiled weakly at Jay bent over the teacart and she caressed his cheek.

"Such a nice young man. So handsome," she said. "Your mother? She's still with us?"

Jay nodded mutely.

"She must be so proud. Sons are special to their mothers, you know," she told Jay. "Come. I'll show you a picture of my son. My Robert. We named him for his father. The most beautiful boy," she said as she led Jay over to the baby grand in the corner. "He comes to see his mother every week. He pays my bills even though he doesn't have much money of his own." She handed Jay the picture of the man we knew as Philip Winston and I watched helplessly.

Jay held the picture in both hands and I saw a look of absolute shock quickly pass over his face.

"Yes," he said as he passed it back to Sadie. "Very nice. Robert, you said?"

Sadie gave the picture a light kiss before she reverently laid it back on the glossy piano top.

"Robert. For his father."

I quickly crossed the room and put my hand in Jay's. "What does Robert do Mrs. Weinstein?"

"Oh, something or other in downtown Toronto. He's an accountant. He's such a hard worker. Such a good boy to his mother." She touched the frame of the picture and chose another one beside it and held it out to us. I took it from her hand and Philip Winston at about age ten stared back at us.

"That was his school picture the year his father died. Robert Jr. had such a hard time after it happened and I wondered if he'd ever be the same," she said through tears. She took the picture back from me and held it against her chest.

"He found him," she whispered. "Robert found his father. After school." Sadie was weeping openly now and my throat tightened. "I'd gone out to do some shopping. Robert wanted me out of the house because he said he was meeting someone. I never saw him alive again. Young Robert found him dead. He didn't speak a word until after Christmas that year. I thought I'd lost both of them," she sobbed.

I felt incredibly awkward and uncomfortable and had no words of comfort. Jay on the other hand, stepped forward and put his arm around her shoulders.

Sadie sniffed into the Kleenex Jay offered her and wiped her eyes. "After almost thirty years, I still cry every time I think about it." She straightened her dress and patted Jay's arm again. "About the cheque and the money, I don't know. Maybe Robert saw it in the mail. I'll phone him later and ask him." She pulled my card out of her pocket and waved it at me. "I'll tell him you were here asking and that he should call you. All right?"

I had led myself down this garden path and found myself stuck in an old English-style maze. I didn't know my way out of it but what I did know for certain was that I didn't want Philip, excuse me Robert, knowing we had been here. I tried to snatch my card back from Sadie but she had already tucked it back in her pocket.

CHAPTER
forty-nine

"He's blackmailing them," I declared through a mouthful of Big Mac. "Pure and simple, Philip Winston is blackmailing Oakes and Everly." I snatched the napkin from my lap and quickly wiped some Special Sauce that was running down my chin.

"For what? Blackmailing them for what?" Jay said as he carefully folded the little bag that had contained his French fries. I watched him fold it into a tiny square and heard it plop when it hit the bottom of the take-out bag that was sitting between us on the front seat of the car.

Jay turned sideways in the seat and faced me. "Just because Oakes and Everly used to work at his dad's company, doesn't mean Philip has any reason to blackmail them."

"Come on Jay. Were you born yesterday? Didn't you see Sadie's reaction when I mentioned Oakes and Everly?"

"Yeah. So what? Maybe the mention of their names brought back sad memories. You saw how she reacted when she was holding that picture of Philip when he was young. It was an emotional reaction Kate. Read her emotions."

"I'll do you one better, Mr. Know-It-All. I read body language. And her body language when I mentioned Oakes and Everly didn't indicate sad to me. It was fury. Those two guys had something to do with that company going bankrupt. And that something was stealing. Oakes was treasurer. You tell me, Mr. MBA. If anyone in a company has access to the money, it's the treasurer. Right?"

Jay angrily turned around in his seat and jammed the key in the ignition.

"Mr. Chauffeur is taking you home. Mr. Know-It-All and Mr. MBA are off for the night." The tires squealed as we pulled out of the parking lot at McDonald's and I felt like a teenager again. Hot guy. Hot car. Burning rubber. I hit the automatic window button and stuck my head out the window to feel the wind in my hair. It wasn't quite the same feeling as being in a convertible, but it was close.

The car silently cruised to a stop beside the curb and Jay turned off the ignition and extinguished the lights. We both remained in our seats and neither of us made a motion to get out of the car. The green digital clock on the dashboard read ten-thirty.

"Well?" I said hopefully. "Figured anything out?"

"Nope. I just keep going round and round the mulberry bush with this. We've got all sorts of loose ends and I'm not sure where they lead." Jay ran his hand through his hair a few times and continued, "I'm not sure that I want to know where they lead, Kate. I started this whole thing as petty revenge. But now, we've opened a can of worms and... " he trailed off.

"You're right, it's a mess," I agreed with him. "But I think this could potentially be more than a can of worms, Jay. This could be a big basket of snakes."

"Then I want to stop right now," he stated. "That's it, that's all. No more."

"You can't be serious Jay," I argued. I held up my hand and ticked off on my fingers what we had. "One, we've got Oakes and Everly for lying. Two, we've got Philip Winston lying about his name. Three, we've found out that Oakes and Everly used to work for Philip's father. Four, Philip's father's business went bankrupt because someone was stealing from it. And five, I think I know who was stealing from it."

"You forgot six and seven, Kate. Evelyn and Rick Cox. The police think someone deliberately poisoned Ev and so far they're convinced Rick shot himself. That's two dead bodies."

Jay's hand found mine in the darkness and he held it tightly. "Kathleen, enough is enough. I'm dropping this. The more I talk and think about it, the more scared I get. And," he said as he put his arms around me and hugged me close to his chest, "I never planned on you getting involved. This was a stupid lark. It wasn't supposed to turn out like this."

"I'm not dropping it Jay," I said defiantly. "I'm not. What if all of this has something to do with Evelyn's death?"

"Then the police'll figure it out. Please Kate," he pleaded with me. "I don't care anymore about this job. Now that I know more about the idiots at the top, I'm glad I'm not there. The two most powerful guys are liars and the one I had any respect for fired me and then killed himself. Enough is enough."

I sat silently in his arms for a few moments and felt my insides start to boil with indignation. I pushed his arms away and sat back against the door. "Don't quit on me Jay," I told him. "Maybe the police'll never figure out what happened to Evelyn and I happen to think we're in possession of relevant information. How it ties together, I don't know. Yet."

"No," he shook his head. "Let them do their job. Drop it."

"I won't." I wanted to stamp my feet but they barely touched the floor of the car. "Someone's going to pay for Evelyn's death. I'm not sure how or why, but I'll figure it out. On my own if I have to." I got out of the car and stood on the curb with my hands on my hips.

Jay leaned over and placed his hand on the seat and spoke to me out the open door. "I'll wait until I see your lights on," he said quietly.

"You're not coming up are you?" I said with a sinking feeling. He shook his head. "Just because I said I won't drop it? Are we being a little juvenile?" By we of course, I meant him. "This is a difference of opinion here, Jay. Not something earth-shattering like finding out you vote NDP."

Jay leaned over awkwardly to pull the door closed. "The juvenile chauffeur is going home. I need a change of clothes and I have to see Detective Leech first thing in the morning to sign my statement. Let's take a few hours to cool our heels and I'll call you in the morning. Okay?"

I nodded silently. "Please Kate. Let's forget it." I helped him close the door by slamming it.

My dreams that night were somewhat pleasant compared to the nightmares I'd been having of aimlessly wandering the desert, looking for Ev.

My dreams took me back to the old neighbourhood. Jay was there but now he was the same age as I was. It was a trip down memory lane. The softball diamond, the tree-house in Mr. McKinley's backyard, a barbecue in our backyard on Canada Day and my dad setting off fireworks. All the neighbourhood kids were in my dreams that night.

I struggled awake slowly when my dreams took me to the swimming pool. We were horsing around in the water, tossing a heavy ring to the bottom of the pool and racing to see who could pick it up. I was at the bottom of the pool and couldn't get back to the surface because I was out of breath. I was struggling in the water and getting nowhere. I wanted to scream for someone to help me but I couldn't open my mouth. My legs and arms were flailing and I felt myself sinking back to the bottom of the pool.

I finally came awake but the weight of the water was still on me and I couldn't breathe. My arms were over my head and there was a terrible weight on my stomach. I opened my eyes with a start and stared into a black, woollen face. A hand had my arms pinned over my head and the black face had his other hand over my mouth and nose. I whipped my head back and forth and struggled helplessly.

The black face came closer to mine and I tried to focus. I was getting a little air through one nostril but I desperately wanted to gulp a deep breath. The black face was someone wearing a wool ski mask. Only his eyes were visible through the one hole in the mask. I choked on a sob and felt the terror all the way down to my bowels.

"What?" I tried to scream through the leather glove that was covering my mouth and nose. He continued to stare at me, wordlessly, and I closed my eyes and started to pray but my mind couldn't remember how.

The weight on my body finally lifted and I opened my eyes to see the person standing beside the bed, his one hand still pinning mine over my head. He slowly removed the other hand off my nose and mouth and I gratefully gulped the air. My body shook from fright and my sobs were loud. He stood there staring at me, not speaking and I prayed that whatever he was going to do to me, he'd get it over with quickly. I closed my eyes again and willed myself to another place.

I took myself back to the softball diamond in my dreams, where I had spent most summer evenings of my childhood. I felt the stranger's breath now on my face and suddenly I was back under the bleacher seats at the ball diamond, and Tommy Gardner's breath was on my face. Tommy had me pinned down in the dirt, with both of my hands over my head. He had a glob of spit hanging from his mouth and he was about to let it go. Right on my face. I kicked up with my feet and used all of my strength to push the bully off of me.

The stranger's breath was hot on my face and without opening my eyes, I struggled to get away from him. My fighting instincts came back and I pulled my feet up and tried to kick at him. He let my hands go and I flailed out at him, scrambling back in the bed to get away from him but I wasn't fast enough. His fist slammed into the side of my face and everything I'd read in books about seeing stars came true. I cried out and put my hands over my face waiting for the next blow.

"Stay out of it," was all the stranger said in a low, gravely voice. And then he was gone.

CHAPTER
fifty

I stumbled to the telephone, hugging myself and sobbing. I was almost embarrassed to call 911 but the dispatcher on the other end of the line assured me and reassured me. I knew I hadn't dreamed any of it because the side of my face continued to throb and the steely taste of blood remained in my mouth.

When the police knocked urgently on the door I was still standing in the hall, dressed, or undressed, in my nightwear. White sweat socks and panties.

"Miss," the voice said from the other side of the door. "Police."

My hands shook as I undid the chain and opened the door. I wrapped my arms around my breasts to hide my nakedness and backed up against the wall.

"He's gone," I said in a whisper. One police officer quickly passed by me down the hall with his gun drawn, and the other one stayed back with me.

"I need to put on some clothes." I tried to read his name tag through my teary eyes but everything was a blur. He nodded silently and then said, "In a minute. Don't worry. My partner's just checking everything. Is there another exit or is this the only door?"

"There's a fire escape at the back. Out the laundry room door." I realized then that Mr. Black Mask must have exited through the fire escape because it was doubtful that he would have chain-locked my front door behind him on the way out.

The other police officer reappeared at my front door with his gun holstered. "No sign of anyone," he told his partner.

"Can I get dressed now?"

An hour later they were still there. Checking for fingerprints and asking me questions. A couple of other very tired-looking, plain clothes officers had shown up and they confirmed that a pane

254

of glass on the back door had been broken and he had gotten in that way.

I called Jay because I couldn't bear the thought of finishing off the night alone. I prayed he'd hear the phone and wake up because I didn't want to talk to his machine.

"Hello," a very sleepy voice answered. A wave of relief washed over me.

I lost my voice when I heard his and couldn't speak. My throat started to close and he said again, "Hello?"

"Jay," I whispered.

"Kate?" His voice sounded more awake now. I nodded stupidly and realized he couldn't see me.

"Jay, can you come over?" I asked weakly.

"What's the matter?" he demanded. "Are you all right?"

"Yeah. I'll be fine. Someone broke in my house tonight. The police are here."

"I'll be right there." I nodded again and hung up the phone.

The police were convinced it was a random act and told me I was lucky to be sitting there telling my story. I knew it wasn't random because of what the black mask had said, but I was too frightened to share it with the police. He had scared me sufficiently. I lied and told them he had said nothing.

When Jay arrived he wasn't alone. Detective Leech followed him in and I was certain I could see the collar of the Detective's pyjama top peeking through his trench coat. I wondered who the hell had called him.

I was back in a familiar position, huddled cross-legged on the sofa under my quilt.

Leech spoke before Jay. "My, my, my, Miss Monahan. We seem to be running into each other quite frequently."

"Not by choice, Detective. Rest assured," I said tiredly.

"Can I get anything for you Kate?" Jay interrupted. "Coffee?" I nodded thankfully and Jay headed for the kitchen.

Detective Leech took a chair across from me and said, "You should put something on that eye. You're gonna have a beautiful shiner tomorrow." I touched my cheek gingerly.

"Why're you here?" I asked him.

"Dispatcher's a friend of mine. She remembered that you had placed another 911 call just a few days ago."

"Well, this has nothing to do with the other one," I lied.

Leech looked at me with disbelief on his face and wandered

off without saying anything to talk to the other officers. I rested my head on the back of the sofa and closed my eyes. Sounds of voices in the laundry room filtered through my jumbled thoughts and the smell of coffee brewing reached my nostrils. My right hand shot out from under the quilt and I placed it over my nose and mouth, shutting off my breathing passages. I felt my fingernails digging into my cheek, and my thumb and index finger squeezed the end of my nose. The image of the black, mask-covered face appeared before my closed eyes and I felt the fear rising up again. The fear came from my gut and my intestines turned to Jell-O. My eyes filled and I felt a hand gently take mine away from my mouth and nose and when I opened my water-filled eyes, Jay was kneeling in front of me, holding my hand.

"Don't do that, Kate," he said. "You're leaving an imprint of your hand on your face. Here." He placed a dishtowel with ice in it on the side of my face and I winced at this new pain sensation. I tried to push it away but Jay held it there firmly. "It'll swell up. Just leave it there a minute or two."

"He's right, Miss Monahan," I heard Leech say. "You need ice on that."

"Fuck you," I said under my breath. I'd had black eyes before and proudly wore them like a badge of honour. When Kate Monahan had a black eye, everyone knew she'd been fighting. I wasn't proud though of this black eye. I'd never even landed a punch.

I looked at Leech and asked him if they were finished.

"I'd just like to ask you a couple of questions, hear it from the horse's mouth, so to speak," he said with a weak smile.

When I didn't smile at his lame joke, he asked me if the intruder had assaulted me. That, I considered a joke.

"Whaddya call this?" I said pointing to the side of my face.

"I meant sexually assault you," he said quietly. He looked embarrassed as he asked the question.

I shook my head and re-lived the feeling of the stranger's weight on my body. The fact that he hadn't raped me sent renewed waves of relief through me and I sobbed out loud.

"No, he just punched me." Jay sat down beside me on the sofa and my hand found his.

"I'm sorry, Miss Monahan. We're just trying to figure this out. It appears that nothing was stolen and you weren't sexually assaulted. The apartment wasn't trashed. So, the question is, why did he break in?"

Jay opened his mouth to speak and I squeezed his hand tight and dug my fingernails in to stop him.

"I don't know. Maybe he had every intention of raping me and stealing my things," I lied. "I got away from him and maybe because I was going to scream he ran off." I knew what he wanted and he had succeeded. He intended to scare me off and it had worked.

The uniformed officers appeared in the living room and told Leech that they were finished. I thanked them and Leech took his time getting out of the chair.

"You," he said and pointed at Jay. "I'll see you in the morning to sign your statement. In the meantime, Miss Monahan, I'd suggest you get some ice on that shiner and get some rest."

I nodded again, feeling like a string puppet. Jay and I sat silently while they all trooped out and when the door finally closed, Jay said to me, "You lied, didn't you Kate?"

The man knew me better than I gave him credit for. I just hoped the Detective couldn't read me as well.

CHAPTER
fifty-one

"What happened?" Jay asked when they left. I threw off the quilt and went in search of my cigarettes. I realized I hadn't had one since earlier that afternoon when Jay and I had sat at the kitchen table. My head felt dizzy when I took my first, deep drag. I placed both hands flat on the kitchen table to steady myself.

Jay had followed me to the kitchen and I heard him saying behind me, "I'm so sorry. I should've been here. This wouldn't have happened if I'd been here." He might've been right, but on the other hand, I shuddered to think what could've transpired if Jay had been there. I couldn't remember if Mr. Mask had a gun or another weapon, but if he had, he probably wouldn't have hesitated to use it on Jay or myself. I don't know how he would have subdued both of us without a weapon.

I straightened up and turned to face Jay.

"It's over. Forget it. Don't beat yourself up over this," I told him.

"Who was it?" Jay asked knowingly.

"I don't know, and that's the truth."

"Then tell me what happened," he demanded.

"I woke up. Someone was sitting on me, holding my hands and covering my mouth. He didn't say or do anything."

"What did he want?"

"I told you, I don't know."

"Kate, this has something to do with everything else that's going on. I'm not stupid. Please," he begged me. "I told you earlier that I'm sorry I got you involved in this stupid vengeance thing. And now this happens. I feel responsible."

Just forty-eight hours ago we had promised each other to be honest and I remembered that now.

"He told me to stay out of it," I said quietly. "That's all he said. And then he left."

258

Jay shook his head slowly and stared at me.

"I'm calling the police back. This has gone too far."

"No Jay. No police. No more police. I'm dropping it. He scared me sufficiently. In fact, he terrified me. I know now what it feels like to be drowning."

I stood there feeling terrified and reliving the feeling of that hand over my mouth and nose. The walls of the kitchen felt like they were closing around me and I was having trouble breathing, again. I butted my cigarette in disgust and tried to calm myself by taking deep, lung-cleansing breaths. In through the nose, out through the mouth.

I ended up on the balcony, overlooking the street trying to get myself back together. Feelings of helplessness overwhelmed me and I stood there with my hands on the railing, wanting to scream. Rage finally overtook the helplessness and I vowed to myself that if and when I met Mr. Black Mask, face to face, I would personally pound his face to a pulp. I didn't like being vulnerable and although I'd never portrayed myself as a damsel in distress, the events of the last ten days had made me feel my size, and my sex. I was a small woman, but I was determined not to let my size be my downfall.

When Jay finally convinced me to go to bed, sleep evaded me. My bed no longer seemed like my special place, where I could hide and feel safe. Jay helped me strip the linens and remake the bed so there were no reminders of what had transpired there a few hours ago. But the cool crispness and scent of the clean sheets didn't help and I laid wide awake, staring at the digital clock.

I was curled in a ball with my back to Jay so I couldn't tell if he was sleeping. I listened to his rhythmic breathing for a long time and when he offered to hold me, I gratefully turned around, into his arms.

"Thanks for being here for me," I said into his chest. "I appreciate it."

He responded by hugging me tighter and telling me to go to sleep.

I dragged myself to the office on Monday morning but feelings of dread overwhelmed me, and I didn't know if I was going to be able to cope.

I had rested all day Sunday and my physical energy returned

by the end of the day. Jay insisted on taking a long, leisurely walk after dinner and after a luxurious, steamy bath, my body felt normal. I couldn't let Jay out of my sight for the whole day and I although I knew it was ridiculous to be feeling this way, I admitted to myself that I needed something to cling to.

I woke up Sunday morning to the sound of the shower and had a momentary panic attack until I reoriented myself. The bed was warm beside me where Jay had been lying. The clock read nine-fifteen and I huddled under the duvet waiting for Jay to finish in the shower. When he reappeared in the bedroom he was dressed in the same clothes he was wearing the night before.

As he fastened his watch around his wrist, he said, "I've gotta go to sign that statement for Detective Leech."

Another panic attack came over me when I thought about being alone in my apartment. I threw off the covers and told Jay I'd go with him and stayed close to his side for the rest of the day.

We avoided talking about the events of the night before for most of the day but Jay finally brought it up that evening on our walk.

"Kate, I don't think you should go to the office tomorrow."

I admitted to myself that I'd been having the same thoughts because I was sure that my masked attacker was someone who I worked with.

"I'll see how I feel tomorrow," was all I said.

"We have to talk about this Kate. You can't avoid it."

We turned around and started walking back to my apartment. Jay wasn't about to let the subject drop and he stood in front of me.

"You must have some idea of who broke in. I certainly have some thoughts on the matter."

"Drop it Jay," I said and tried to sidestep around him but he grabbed my arm.

"No. I won't. All of this is tied-in to things at TechniGroup. And I don't think you're safe going to the office."

He was right, but I wasn't about to hide from the world.

"Jay, I'll be fine. Really. Hiding in my office and doing my work is something I've perfected over the last week or so."

"Call in sick," he suggested.

"It's too busy."

"Oh, really? And the work won't get done without you there? The world stops because Kathleen Monahan takes a day off?" he said sarcastically.

I yanked my arm out of his hand and defiantly shot back at him, "I'm a big girl and I can take care of myself."

"Right," he snorted. "Just like last night. You really took care of yourself then, didn't you?"

"I tried," I said very quietly, and started walking home.

"I'm sorry," he was saying behind me. "You did fine. I shouldn't have said that but this whole situation is scaring me to death. I can't bear the thought of something happening to you."

His hand found mine and we walked silently the last few blocks. The evening air smelled like spring, my favourite season of the year, and the odours and sounds gave me renewed strength and resolve.

At the front of my house I sat on the first step of the porch and motioned for Jay to sit beside me.

"You know," I told him, "a famous man once said that the only thing we have to fear is fear itself."

But now that I was at the office building I found I couldn't get out of my car. It was like there was a huge magnet in the seat and it was sucking all the power and energy out of me. When I looked in the rear-view mirror the image that came back at me wasn't a pretty one. One half of my face looked like Marlon Brando's in the Godfather. A magazine article had said that he stuffed his cheeks with cotton for that role.

The white of my left eye was bloodshot and the top of my cheekbone and surrounding eye were purplish-black. I couldn't wait for the green and yellow stage. Jay had suggested make-up to cover it up by I laughed him off.

"People will notice the make-up before they notice the black eye," I told him.

Before falling asleep the night before, I had made myself try and remember something about my attacker. Rather than push the memory away, I needed to know who it was. The few words he had spoken gave me no clue to his voice because I was sure he had disguised it. I couldn't remember his height in relation to anything and besides, everyone seemed tall to me. I recalled that he had been totally clothed in black, or very dark, clothes, and the only part of his body that was visible were his eyes. If his eyebrows had been exposed, I was sure I would have recognized him.

The fear and terror I had felt could only be described as all-encompassing. Those two emotions had taken over everything and my will and desire to survive the situation, alive and in one piece, overcame any reasonable thought process of getting a description of my attacker. I promised myself that I would never find myself in the same situation, ever again.

CHAPTER
fifty-two

I stayed in my office most of the day and avoided people. The few who saw me on my way in and commented on my face were told that I had taken a nasty fall down the stairs. No one had reason to disbelieve me. I had trouble avoiding Vanessa though and when she finally came barrelling in my office, wanting to go for coffee, I lied to her too and mumbled about falling down the stairs.

Harold called and asked me to see him and I reluctantly went in his office. He was standing with his hands behind his back looking out the window. When he turned around and saw me he didn't react to my black and blue face but said, "Vanessa told me that you had a fall. Are you okay?"

"Sure," I said.

"That's good. I want you to know that I'm extremely sorry for what happened the other night."

I had a moment of anxiety until I realized he was referring to me finding Rick Cox's dead body. What had happened to me on Saturday was not something I wanted anyone to know about, yet.

"You've got nothing to be sorry about Harold. Shit happens."

"Things are really fucked up here, Kate," he told me. I was shocked at his cavalier use of one of my favourite words. Harold didn't swear unless he was very angry and right now he was acting quite calm.

I wanted to answer that he didn't know how fucked up things *really* were but I waited for him to continue.

"The stock's understandably going to go down again today when everyone remembers what happened on Friday night. But, the other party appears to be still interested in this buy-out, so we're supposed to push on."

"All of my stuff is done," I told him, referring to all of the due diligence materials I had compiled the week before. "How soon can we expect an offer?"

"Their board is meeting this morning and depending on the outcome of that, we'll hold a conference call this afternoon with our directors. Vanessa has them all on standby."

"Isn't that kind of quick? They haven't had time to go over all the due diligence materials."

"Oh, they can make an offer and back out if certain things aren't to their liking. There are time limits but they can do it."

"Can I ask a stupid question, Harold?"

He grinned. "If you don't mind a stupid answer, Kate."

I smiled. "What happens to the stock options?"

"Well, a couple of things," he said. "First of all, the other company will buy out all existing, exercisable options. The holders will get paid the difference between their exercise price and the buying price. Say for example, the other company offers $12.00 a share for our shares and an executive has options with an exercise price of $6.00. That's a difference of $6.00 per share and that's what they'll get paid."

Simple enough for me. Most of the senior executives were holding about 500,000 options, so at a gain of $6.00 a share, they'd rake in $3,000,000. *Before* taxes, of course.

"What happens to unexercisable options?" I asked, thinking about all of the options that had just been granted to the senior officers and to Philip Winston the Third. Unexercisable options are options that are usually worthless until they have vested, or matured. The vesting or maturity period is normally one year in our company.

"They'll probably take those up too. You know, if this deal goes through, there'll be a lot of work to be done just on stock options alone. With Ev and Jay gone, somehow I get the feeling that I'm about to become an accountant as well as a lawyer," he said.

"Well, you'll make your mother proud. She won't have to lie anymore and tell people you work at the post office," I laughed. "Now she can brag that you're an accountant."

Harold laughed with me and it felt good.

"I'll help with the stock option stuff if it comes down to it," I offered. "What're we doing in the meantime?"

"Waiting."

"I can wait. I don't mind," I told him. "But before we wait, can I ask one last thing?"

He nodded.

"No take-over is clean. How many of us are going to lose our jobs?"

"That's hard to say, Kate. First of all, it'll be at least six months before any of that happens. And that's six months from when the deal closes. If it closes. And, usually on a takeover, the senior executives lose their jobs first."

My stomach sank. Harold was a senior executive and I was tied very closely to him.

"My point exactly, Harold. Senior executives leave, so do their support staff."

"Well, we'll see. If it does happen, you know you'll never have a hard time getting another job. There are few people in this world with skills like yours, Kate." He was stroking me and patronizing me but I didn't mind. Besides, I thought to myself, I think I'd rather work in a Siberian coal mine than stay here.

Before the day was out our shares had dropped another seventy-five cents to $4.75 and the 'other side' came in with an offer for all of the outstanding shares of TechniGroup at $12.00 a share. The offer was a well-guarded secret, and no-one but the directors of both companies supposedly knew about it. An announcement was to be made before the market opened the next day and in the meantime, I was tempted to put in a buy order before the market closed and make myself some fast cash, because once the announcement was out about the proposed take-over bid, the shares would rocket up in price and trade around the $12.00 bid price. It was just a fleeting thought though because somehow I couldn't picture myself in jail for making a couple of thousand dollars profit on inside information.

Needless to say, Harold was a happy man and I was sure he would do everything in his power to make sure the deal closed because he stood to make about three and a half million on his stock options. That kind of money makes it easier to look for another job. I had a few thousand shares I'd bought over the years on the employee stock purchase plan and maybe, just maybe, I'd have enough left over after Revenue Canada took their bite, to buy me a new car - or at least get the locks fixed.

Before my departure that day at five-thirty, I turned off my computer and tidied the mess on my desk. Other than meeting with Harold, I had avoided contact with everyone else. Admittedly, I was hiding and as the day progressed, feelings of cowardice crept around me. My work for the day had ended about an hour earlier but I was loathe to run into people leaving the office at quitting time, so I continued to hide in my office, chain-smoking and thinking.

Jay and I were in possession of information that could adversely affect the take-over bid. Larry Everly and Chris Oakes were frauds and that information alone could cause enough of a scandal, but I wasn't sure if it would be enough for the other side to back off on their bid. I knew that our company was in bad shape and a take-over bid was probably the best thing for it. New faces, new leaders, lots of cash. The perfect recipe for short-term success in the high tech world. But even if the information about Oakes and Everly was disclosed or somehow found out, I was cynical enough to know that some people would ignore it or at the very least, continue to hide it.

I had no idea who the 'other side' was and I asked myself if I knew, would I do something with the information?

So what's the big deal, I wondered. The other company wasn't buying Oakes and Everly, they were buying our company. The two of them would be history because our board of directors would be replaced and Oakes especially would be laughing all the way to the bank. He'd be terminated without cause, and the change of control clause in his employment contract would kick in and he'd be paid three times his salary plus all his stock options. Everly's company would get back all the money they'd invested and he'd get to keep his job.

I wondered though what would become of Philip Winston, a.k.a. Robert Weinstein. Would the new company keep him? The fact that he'd changed his name wasn't grounds for dismissal. Anyone could change their name so long as they didn't do it for criminal purposes.

Philip must know that Oakes and Everly were working for his father at the time of the bankruptcy. But that information didn't help me figure out why he was here at TechniGroup. With everything we'd found out in the last couple of days, I seriously doubted that it was a coincidence that Philip Winston was now our Chief Operating Officer.

A glance at my watch told me it was five-thirty and probably safe to the leave the office without running into anyone, so I packed up and headed down the hall towards reception. I deliberately avoided leaving by the back door because that exit route would take me past the executive offices.

I knew I was being stupid about avoiding everyone but it made me feel safe from the unknown. I had barely functioned all day, acting and reacting like a shell-shocked veteran. Unable to identify my attacker but sure that he was someone I knew had made it impossible for me to act normally. When I pushed the button for my floor in the parking garage elevator, I finally faced the fact that it could only be one of three men who had attacked me. Chris Oakes, Larry Everly or Philip Winston. I'd known it all along and I was sure Jay knew as well.

I'd been unable to bring the thought to the forefront of my mind and address it because I didn't want to admit it. The intrusion in my house and my bedroom had been the ultimate act of employee bashing. Indignation rose inside me as I stormed down the dimly lit hallway off the elevator to the parking garage.

The invisible legal secretary had stumbled stupidly across some information that the high and mighty executives had been trying to hide. After all my years of blood and sweat for this fucking place, I thought angrily. I yanked hard on the door to the parking garage. One of those bastards had not only invaded my personal space, he'd punched me in the face. I made up my mind then and there to quit my job the next morning. And find a reporter to tell my story to.

Righteous indignation felt much better than fear and cowardice and I was feeling somewhat better when I opened the back door of my car to put my briefcase and purse on the floor of the back seat.

I tried very hard to keep those feelings of indignation when I realized Philip Winston was sitting in the front passenger seat of my car. The fear quickly took over again when he crooked his index finger at me and told me to get in. I backed away from the open door of the car and looked over both shoulders for some help.

Philip quickly got out of the car on the other side and put his arms on the roof of the car. "You know Kathleen, you should lock your doors."

As if I need to be told that now, I thought.

"They don't work," I said lamely and he grinned at me.

I felt sick.

CHAPTER fifty-three

"Get in," he repeated.

"I don't think so, Philip," I told him. "If you needed a ride, you should have asked the office manager for petty cash to take a cab."

When he slammed his hand on the roof of the car, I knew he had no sense of humour.

"Get in the damn car, Kathleen," he growled.

"Fuck you," I replied, backing further away. There were two exits out of the garage and I knew that both would be useless to me if Philip meant to keep me here.

"I just want to talk to you," he said.

"So talk."

"Not here."

"Then leave me a voice message or send me an e-mail. I have no intention of getting in the car with you Philip," I said as I swallowed my fear.

Philip walked to the back of the car but stayed on the other side. He held up his hands to show me they were empty and said, "Please. I just want to talk."

"No. You're scaring me. Now get away from my car." Sweat was forming on my shoulder blades and my lips were dry. My feet were rooted to the asphalt and I wondered to myself if I had it in me to scream when the time came. It was then that I saw the look in his eyes change and my bowels turned to liquid. I recognized those eyes and knew that he was the one who'd attacked me.

I turned to run but of course, he was much faster than I was. His hand grabbed the collar of my blouse from behind and the force pulled me back against him. I swung around and landed my closed fist on his cheekbone with as much force as I could muster. I remembered to keep my elbow tucked and my feet firmly placed on the ground, just the way my dad used to coach us.

The punch had little or no effect because Philip quickly locked his arm around my neck and dragged me back to the car. I tried kicking him but he was nimble and avoided me.

He led me around to the passenger side and shoved me in the open front door. I looked helplessly around for someone, anyone, but the parking garage was empty of people. Philip hurried around to the driver's side and tried to fit his large frame in the seat. He grabbed at me again as I opened the door but this time he hurt me when his fingers dug into my neck.

The pain was almost paralyzing and I whimpered, "Please, you're hurting me." I tried to push his hand away but it was firmly locked on the nerve in my neck. He finally found the mechanism under the seat with his other hand and he pushed the seat back enough to get his feet inside the car. He slammed his door shut first and reached around me to pull the other door closed.

He put his face very close to mine and said, "Promise to sit still and I'll let go." I nodded and when he released my neck I rubbed it with my hand.

I stared at him and said, "You told me the other night to stay out of it and I am. What do you want?"

"It's too late now," he said.

"Too late for what?"

"Give me the keys," he said and held out his hand.

"They're in my purse in the back seat." Without taking his eyes off me his hand snaked down between the seats and he found my purse on the back floor. He pulled it through the opening between the seats and started going through it.

"Here," I said as I tried to grab it from him but he brought his elbow up to stop me. When he finally found the keys he flung my purse at me and jammed the key in the ignition. I hugged my purse to my chest and prayed. And thought about my escape route.

The engine coughed a couple of times but Philip finally had success on the third try. I couldn't even rely on this piece of shit when it counted the most, I thought.

"I thought you wanted to talk. Where are we going?"

He put the car in reverse and didn't answer me. He drove the car carefully up the circular ramp to the exit and I thought about jumping out of the car at the booth where I knew he had to stop to put my card in the machine to get out of the garage.

"Where's your pass?" he demanded.

"What makes you think a lowly little person like me has a parking pass?" I said snidely.

"Because as Chief Operating Officer, I've been going over everything. I agree. A lowly little *secretary* shouldn't have a parking pass. But your name was on the list. Now where is it?" he growled at me.

Personally, I preferred lowly little person to lowly little secretary, but I let the comment pass.

"On the sun visor," I pointed. There was one car ahead of us and Philip slowed down as we approached the booth. He put his hand inside his suit jacket and withdrew a small, ivory handled pistol. Or gun. Whatever. He held the gun in the palm of his hand where I could see it.

"Any thoughts you might have had about getting out of the car, have just passed, am I right Kathleen?" he said.

"Fuck you, *Robert.*" The gate ahead of us went up and the other car passed through. "Go ahead and shoot me," I declared bravely. "Because you can't think for a minute you'll get away with this. Whatever it is you plan on doing to me. Let me out of the car and we'll forget this happened," I lied.

I watched him take the parking pass off the sun visor and fit it in the slot of the machine. I leaned down and tried to get the parking lot attendant's attention through the window on the driver's side but his back was to us. I grabbed the handle of the door and yanked on it. Gun or no gun, I decided stupidly, I was getting out of here. Philip had different ideas though, I realized too late. His hand came up and the handle of the pistol hit me on the side of the head just above my ear. I saw stars again but this time there was blackness immediately afterwards.

The world felt like it was spinning and the dizziness was reminiscent of the one time I'd had too much to drink. The side of my head was throbbing and the spinning sensation was making me nauseous. My eyes opened slowly for a brief moment before I lost consciousness again.

The next time I came to I heard insistent voices, far away. My head was still throbbing but the spinning sensation was gone and I realized that was probably because I was lying on my back. Without opening my eyes, my hands touched the surface on either side of me and I felt a soft blanket beneath me. The sound of a door opening made my hands stop moving and I kept my eyes tightly shut.

I heard Philip say in a whisper, "She'll be fine, mother. Look, she's breathing and has colour in her face." The door shut quietly behind them and when I heard their voices in the hall again, I struggled to sit up.

"But she's bad, mother," Philip was saying. "Very bad. We can't let her leave just yet." Footsteps in the hall told me they were leaving.

The room I was in was dark but a little light showed under the doorframe. My eyes took a few moments to adjust to the darkness but it took my brain a few moments longer to get back in working order. Philip had said "Mother", so it was safe to assume that I was at Sadie Weinstein's house. A very stupid move on Philip's part, I thought. I stood up gingerly to make sure I wasn't going to fall over and when I felt steady enough on my feet I searched the room. Not surprisingly, the door was locked from the outside but the window I finally found behind the heavy drapes wasn't.

The room that was holding me prisoner was on the second floor of Sadie's decrepit house. Without thinking about the consequences, I hurriedly opened the window and was thankful to see that the porch roof was only about three feet below the windowsill. The drop from the roof below me to the front yard though, was quite a bit further, and I tried not to think about it as I eased my way quietly out the window. Panicked at the thought of Philip coming back, I quickly pulled the window shut behind me. My pumps felt slippery on the rough shingles of the slanted porch roof and I took them off and tossed each one like a grenade into a bush I spied at the side of the yard. I turned around and crawled backwards, crab-like, to the side edge of the roof, scraping the palms of my hands and knees.

When my feet went over the edge of the porch roof I laid down on my stomach and pushed myself over the edge. I had no idea what was below me but a drop of ten or twelve feet couldn't be as bad as being shot, I thought, as I let go. My feet hit the ground and I bent my knees to absorb the shock and fell backwards on my ass. The pain that shot up my tailbone made me forget the throbbing in my head. The fall knocked the wind out of me and I gasped, trying to catch my breath. In spite of the pain though, adrenaline made me scramble right back up. I grabbed my shoes from the bush where I'd lobbed them.

Silence surrounded me and I listened for sounds from the house hoping that they hadn't discovered my escape. I could see my car parked on the street but without my keys, it was useless to me, so I straddled the fence between Sadie's house and her neighbour's, and took off running.

CHAPTER
fifty-four

Vanessa was peeking out the front window of her house when the cab arrived and she hurried outside to pay the driver. I'd never been so glad to see a friendly face and I felt like sobbing.

The woman behind the bullet-proof partition at the self-service gas station had been understanding. She couldn't pass the phone through the small opening but she handed me the receiver and her tinny voice through the speaker offered to dial the number for me. There was no answer at my place or Jay's and this time I didn't hesitate to call Vanessa.

When Vanessa followed me through the front door, I told her I needed her car, her cell phone and some cash. She looked at my bloody knees and said, "Not so fast. How about a clean pair of pantyhose too?"

I shook my head.

"Well, you can have whatever you need. Come on in and I'll make you some coffee."

I followed her into the kitchen which was off the hallway at the front of the house and sat on a bar stool at the counter. She talked and moved about the kitchen efficiently making coffee and getting cups, and cream and sugar from the cupboards. I lit one of her cigarettes and put my elbows on the counter.

"What happened?" she asked me.

"I got mugged," I lied easily. "They stole my car and my purse."

"Did you call the police?" she asked calmly and I knew she didn't believe me.

"No. I called you."

"Where's Jay?"

"Don't know. What time is it anyway?"

"Quarter to ten," she replied as she dropped a full coffee cup in front of me. About a third of it slopped over the edge. "You're bullshitting me, Kate."

I tried changing the subject. "How's Ashley?"

"Fine. Asleep in bed. Every time she spends the weekend with her father she comes home exhausted. And don't change the subject."

I felt guilty but wanted to protect her. We'd been friends forever it seemed. The fewer people I cared about that I dragged into this mess, the better.

"Okay, I won't change the subject. Where's Chris?"

"How the hell should I know? I'm not his keeper."

"Yeah, right Vee. Is he in town or out?"

"In," she replied tersely. "Has this got something to do with where we work?"

"Correction. Where *you* work. I'm quitting tomorrow," I told her.

"Oh, now I get it. Harold gave you shit for coming in late again and you got down on your knees to beg for forgiveness. That would explain the blood on your knees."

"Save the sarcasm, Vee. This is serious but I'm not getting you involved. Now, are you going to give me your car and phone?"

Her car keys and cell phone were on the counter near the wall and she cupped both of them in her hand and slid them angrily across the counter at me. I caught them before they ended up on the floor. A couple of twenty dollar bills hit me lightly in the face and she said, "Don't forget the cash."

"Friends?" I asked her sheepishly.

"Always. But let me help you Kate," she pleaded. "This is too scary. First Ev and then Rick. And now you, showing up at my door with blood on your hands and knees. You're a mess. And that black eye has something to do with this. I know it. You didn't fall down any stairs, did you?"

I ignored her reference to my shiner. "You are helping me Vee. And seriously, I can't get you involved." I held up my scraped hands and said, "I ended up like this tonight because I was stupid enough to get involved." I casually felt the lump on the side of my head left there compliments of the butt of Philip's gun, but didn't tell her about it.

"Somebody hurt you," she said, sure that the cuts and scrapes had been caused by someone else. "At least call the police."

I slid off the barstool and gathered up the keys and cell phone in one hand, and the cash in the other.

"I plan on calling the police," I told her. "But in the meantime, *please* don't tell anyone I was here."

Alfredo placed the Diet Coke in front of me and I drank thirstily. I smiled up at his friendly face, glad for the presence of a friend.

"Hungry?"

"Not really. I just needed a place to hang out for a while. Lost my keys," I told him.

"Your friend was here looking for you, earlier."

"Which friend?"

"Your boyfriend. Mr. Jay Harmon," he winked.

"What time?" I had been trying to reach Jay because he had a set of keys to my apartment. I got furious again thinking about the possibility of losing my purse with all my treasures in it, including my original Frank Mahovlich hockey card which I kept hidden in a secret compartment of my wallet.

Alfredo looked at his watch and said, "About an hour ago."

Jay's machine kicked in when I tried it again on the cellular. The message said, "Kate, if that's you, leave me a message and the time. Jesus Christ, I'm worried." I hadn't thought to listen to the message on the machine when I called before.

"I'm at Alfredo's. I mean Tony's Pizzeria. It's about ten-fifteen. I'll wait here until eleven. Jay, I lost my keys to my apartment." I paused for a moment and when nothing else came to mind I pushed the power off button on the cell phone.

While I waited I thought about the events of the evening. Philip Winston, or Robert Weinstein to those blood-related to him, was definitely a wacko, and I decided to avoid him at all costs. He was definitely bad for my health.

He was bad for my career as well, but I was resigned to the fact that I was quitting tomorrow. Enough of the funny farm for me. I wondered what Harold's reaction would be when I handed in my notice. The thought, though, of going into the office, turned my blood cold. Maybe I could get Harold to meet me somewhere outside the office, where I could break the news to him. Of all the executives I was working with, Harold was about the only one I trusted.

I picked up the cell in one hand and tried dialling with the thumb of the same hand. I'd seen Vee do this several times and was impressed with her dialling prowess. The phone on the other end rang only twice before someone answered.

"Hello."

"Harold. It's Kate."

"Yes, Kate," he said slowly. "How are you?" He actually sounded concerned, even interested.

"Uh. I'm fine."

"Where are you?" Now that was a little *too* interested for me. On a good day, Harold wouldn't ask me how I was, let alone where I was. I started to feel uneasy.

"Oh. Out and about. Listen, can I meet with you first thing tomorrow morning?"

"Sure," he said like he was talking to a three year old. "If it's important, we could meet tonight," he offered without demanding to know why. When I placed the call I had the hope in the back of my mind that he'd force me to tell him why and then I could resign over the phone. I thought I knew Harold, but this solicitous side of him was something new to me.

"It's important. But tomorrow morning would be fine. How about Shopsy's Deli at Yonge and Front?"

"Fine, fine. Where are you now Kathleen?" The fact that he'd now asked me twice where I was made my knees start to shake.

"None of your damn business Harold. Why are you so interested all of a sudden?"

"Listen Kate. I talked to Philip tonight. He told me what happened and he knows he made a terrible mistake. We want to meet with you to make sure you're all right."

I jammed my index finger into the power off button on the cell phone and dropped it on the table like a hot potato. *Jesus Christ.* Now who could I trust?

I gave Alfredo the number of Vanessa's cell phone and made him promise to give it only to Jay. I couldn't stay at the pizzeria because I felt like a sitting duck so I got in the car and drove aimlessly around. When the phone on the seat beside me finally rang, I quickly pulled over to the curb and answered it.

"Yes," was all I said.

"Kate, it's Jay. Where are you?"

"I'm not exactly sure right now. Where are you?"

"At Tony's Pizzeria. I called there but Alfredo said he didn't recognize my voice but if I showed up in person, he had a message for me. I feel like James Bond."

"Wrong Jay. This is turning out to be more like Mission Impossible. Can you meet me?"

"Sure. At your apartment?"

"No," I said quickly. "Not my apartment. Or yours. How about the bench were I sat the other day while you went jogging?"

"You mean down at the park? Why all the cloak and dagger stuff?"

"I'll tell you later. How soon can you meet me there?"

"Kate, it's too dangerous to be alone in the park at night. Meet me at the pub where we danced. You remember?"

"That's a better idea." I looked out the window of the car to get my bearings and it took a moment for me to remember where I was. "I'll be there in five minutes."

CHAPTER
fifty-five

It turned out that Jay had a very protective side to him and as much as I'd dreamed of having a knight in shining armour to fight my battles for me, I had a helluva time holding him back.

"I'll kill him," was all he said through clenched teeth when I finished my story.

"Very nice, Mr. Harmon, but I don't think your mother'd be impressed. Besides, when we turn him over to the police and I charge him with kidnapping and assault, he'll go to jail."

I grinned at Jay but he didn't get it.

"He's so pretty Jay, so perfect. They'll love him in the Kingston penitentiary. I'm sure those convicts have had a long, cold winter and they'll welcome him with open arms."

This at least got a laugh out of Jay, but he quickly turned serious again.

"Let's go then," he said as he stood up.

"Where?"

"To the police."

"Hang on," I told him as I pulled his arm and made him sit down again.

"There's more to it. There has to be. *Why* did he kidnap me? What's he trying to hide? Think about it Jay. So his mother told him we were at the house and maybe he knows we figured out he's using another name. That's not a major crime. He's hiding something else. I'm sure, in fact I'm convinced, that this is all tied-in to Ev's death and Rick's death. And now Harold's involved. What the hell is Harold doing messed up with all of this?"

"Maybe Harold doesn't understand what he's involved with. You didn't let him explain what he wanted to talk to you about. Maybe Philip gave him some cock and bull story."

I snorted at this. "You didn't hear his voice Jay. He was very concerned, very solicitous. Does this sound like the short lawyer with a big attitude who we've all held so near and dear to our hearts these last few years?"

"Okay," he sighed. "I'll take your word for it. I just have trouble believing Harold's involved. I'm feeling like the last virgin at a pool party at Hugh Hefner's mansion."

I started to chuckle but he interrupted, "You know. You're determined to hang on to your innocence and virginity, but in the back of your mind you *know* it's all about to end. You're thinking, do I just give in and enjoy it or do I fight to keep it? That's how I feel about finding out Harold's just another snake. Disgusted."

"You're turning into a cynic Jay."

"It comes from associating with you," he joked.

"Stick with me Harmon, and you'll become more than just a cynic."

"In the meantime, we have to do something."

"After I return Vanessa's car."

When Vee answered the doorbell her cordless phone was tucked between her ear and shoulder. She silently motioned us in and Jay and I followed her in to the kitchen where we both sat at the counter on the barstools. The clock on the wall told me it was eleven-forty and because of the hour, I knew she could only be talking to one person - Chris Oakes.

Vee covered the mouthpiece of the phone and told us, "He's rambling." She rolled her eyes at the ceiling and mumbled something into the phone.

"This could take a while," I whispered to Jay and placed Vee's car keys, cell phone and money on the kitchen counter. "She's talking to Oakes."

I slid off the stool and waved good-bye but Vee once again covered the mouthpiece and said, "Hang on. I'll get rid of him."

"Chris," she said patiently into the phone. "Chris," she repeated in a singsong voice. "Goodbye." She pushed a button on the phone and put it on the counter.

"It'll take him a few minutes to realize I've hung up and then he'll call back," she told us.

"I thought you didn't answer the phone at home, just in case it was him," I teased her.

"Normally I don't, but I thought it might be you, so I'm holding you personally responsible for the crap I've just listened to."

"In one of his abusive modes?" I asked knowingly.

She shook her head. "No. In his morose mode. Drunk and rambling. When he's sober I have trouble following him but when he's drunk, it's worse."

"Why do you put up with that garbage?" Jay interrupted.

"Because I have two mouths to feed," she quickly retorted. "And it'll be something I can tell my grandchildren one day. How the big executive, with all the money and power in the world, goes home at night and has nothing better to do than drink, and watch Star Trek re-runs. He has no friends because he abuses anyone who gets remotely close to him. No one."

"I thought I read somewhere that he was married," Jay said.

"He tells everyone that. Cynthia was a woman who lived with him for a while but she's long gone now. She told me she woke up one day and realized that all the money in the world wasn't going to keep her there. Cynthia was nothing more than a decoration for Chris." Vee placed her elbows on the counter and put her face in her hands. None of what she was telling Jay was news to me but he was hanging on to her every word.

"The part of that whole story that amazed me," I interjected, "was the fact that they never once slept together."

"Come off it girls," Jay said. "How could you possibly know that?"

"How many times do I have to tell you, we're invisible," I said. "People tell secretaries anything and everything. They think we're stupid and they say anything in front of you. Because it doesn't get repeated, they tell you more. Before you know it, you're a confidante. The boss thinks you're stupid, we call it discrete. Want to know how many blow jobs Tom James's wife gave him last year?"

"That's disgusting. And no. I don't want to know," Jay said.

"None," I told him anyway and Vanessa laughed. "And just for the record, Tom, the great Tower of Jell-O, didn't tell me directly about his sex life, or lack thereof. He was lamenting with one of the directors one day. In front of me. Unbelievable."

"I agree," said Jay. "So Oakes told you Vee that he and this Cynthia never slept together?"

"Yup," she nodded. "One night, on the phone. Told me that they had separate bedrooms and that they'd never once had sex. Cynthia went up a few notches in my books after that." She looked at me and we both visibly shivered. "Yuk. Just the thought of getting into bed with that sorry excuse for a man, makes me sick."

I nodded my head in wholehearted agreement.

"So what was the great one rambling on about tonight?"

"Who knows Kate? It never makes any sense. Tonight he was crying over how much he misses Rick Cox. When he started on about that I just about hung up. He's sick," she stated emphatically. "Sick. The whole time Rick was with us, Oakes had a vendetta against him. All he wanted to do was to get him fired. You saw those memos he had the vice-presidents write. All garbage. And then Rick goes and does something stupid and gets himself fired anyway. But then Oakes got totally incoherent. Mumbling away about how it was an accident. Just an accident. Over and over again. *She* was an accident he kept saying and I wanted to remind him that Rick was a *he* but I couldn't bother wasting my breath. *She* was an accident. And then he put the dog on the phone. Say hi to Baby, Vanessa. That's when you guys arrived and saved me."

She was an accident, he'd said. *She* might be a slip of the tongue once or twice with someone drunk, but to repeat it over and over again, meant only one thing to me. *She* was Evelyn. The son-of-a-bitch meant Evelyn.

I slowly picked up the telephone that was lying on the counter between us and punched in Oakes' home number from memory. The phone on the other end rang three times and when it was answered I could hear a dog barking loudly in the background.

"Who're you calling?" Jay asked me and I quieted him with an upheld hand.

"Um," was the answer I got from the other end.

"Chris," I said firmly into the phone. "Kate Monahan here."

"Uh," was the reply which I took for a hello.

"Chris," I said again. "Is that Baby I hear in the background? How is Baby?" Baby was the only living thing that could stand to be around Chris Oakes and for that reason, he worshipped the dog. Talking about the dog always got big points.

"Baby," he slurred into the phone. "Baby's fine. You wanna say 'ello?"

"No. No thanks Chris. I just had a quick question." The man was clearly drunk and I knew I could go for the jugular and get a few quick answers. Knowing that I was never working for the company again gave me the bravado to be bold. "You were saying earlier that *she* was an accident. She was an accident," I repeated.

"Ohm," he mumbled.

I looked at Vee and Jay who were staring in disbelief at me.

"Chris," I said loudly to make sure I had his attention. "When you said *she* you mean Evelyn, didn't you?" There was silence at the other end of the phone and I wasn't sure if he'd passed out or was just ignoring my question. "Evelyn. The lady who died. Was *she* the accident Chris?"

I heard a sob from the other end and I felt the blood rush to my ears. He'd done it.

"You bastard," I yelled into the phone. "Evelyn. She was the accident wasn't she, Chris? Answer me," I demanded.

"She," he hesitated. "She shouldn't have died. It was an accident. I'm so sorry."

CHAPTER
fifty-six

"The bastard," I whispered to no one in particular. "He did it. He killed Evelyn." My eyes filled with tears of anger and the dead phone hung limply from my hand. Jay got up from where he was sitting and put a hand on my shoulder.

"Kate, he's drunk. You can't believe anything he said." I shrugged his hand off my shoulder and looked at Vanessa who was leaning against the wall hugging herself.

"Vee, he did it. He said he was *sorry*. That it was an *accident.*" I was yelling. "The only accident that ever happened in that sorry son of a bitch's life happened the day he was born."

Vee was shaking her head now. "No. No way."

"Don't Vee. Don't defend him. This'll turn out to be just another quirk in his miserable personality. The capability of killing someone."

"He couldn't have Kate," Vee said with disbelief in her voice.

"Are you defending him?" I demanded.

Vanessa hesitated before answering. "Yes. And no," she said slowly.

"Yes?" I repeated.

She nodded.

"He just as much admitted to me that he was responsible," I said angrily. "And you're defending him?"

"He's drunk Kate. You should know better than to believe anything he says."

"Stop it. Stop defending him." My blood was boiling and anger was bubbling up in the back of my throat. I took a step towards Vee and Jay stepped between us.

"Cut it out," he said.

"What is going on Kate?" Vee asked me. "I don't understand. You show up here tonight looking like you've been through a battle and you don't have the decency to tell me what happened. You just demand my car and money. And now you're accusing Chris of murder! Care to fill me in?"

"I can't fill you in," I answered her. "Because I don't know myself what's going on. What I will tell you is that Philip Winston hit me over the head and knocked me out and tried to lock me up in a room at his mother's house. I got away and came here. Why'd he do it? *I don't know.* And now Chris as much as admits that he had something to do with Evelyn's death. Why? *I don't know.* Maybe you know. Maybe *you* have some idea." My breath was coming in short gasps now and Vee was just staring at me.

"Me?"

"Yeah you. Everyone else at TechniGroup seems to be involved in all of this. Why not you?"

"Get out. Get out of my house," she said as she pushed past me. "How dare you?"

"How dare I?" I yelled at her. "My friend Evelyn is dead and I came close to it the other night. Like it or not, we're all involved in this and it's all about to come tumbling down around us. Because I'm not giving up until I find out what is going on."

"It's time to get the police involved," Jay interjected. "This has gone too far." He tried to take my arm but I shook him off. I backed away from the two of them and balled my hands into fists.

"You do what you want Jay," I told him. "The police are involved and obviously they haven't figured out anything. I'm not going to the police. Yet."

"They don't know about Philip. And we should tell them about what Chris said. Let's leave it to them," he pleaded with me.

I stormed to the front door of the house and yanked it open. Over my shoulder I yelled, "Go ahead. You're on your own." The door slammed behind me and I quickly realized that if I was on my own, I would be doing it by foot. My car was still parked at Sadie Weinstein's house and after the things I'd said to Vanessa, it was highly doubtful that she'd loan me her car again.

I stood there stupidly for a moment until I heard the front door open quietly and I turned around to see Jay silhouetted in the light.

"We made a promise the other day you know Kathleen," he said softly and I nodded my head mutely, knowing full well what he was referring to.

"I made a promise to stay out of it. I know that. But the moment Philip Winston waved a gun in my face and hit me on the head with it, things changed." I gave Jay a challenging look, almost daring him to back out.

He raised his hands in the air and shrugged his shoulders at the same time. "Fine. Just tell me what we're doing before we run off half-cocked."

"I want to see Oakes. Confront him."

"That could be dangerous."

"No more dangerous than things have been in the last two weeks. Only now, we can be aware of the danger. Not let it creep up on us. Okay?"

Jay nodded his agreement and dug in the pocket of his jeans for his car keys and I went back to Vee's door and knocked timidly. The door opened immediately and I knew she'd been standing on the other side.

"Sorry," was all I said.

"I know. Ev was my friend too, so do what you have to. Everything's about to crash about us, isn't it?"

"That's a fair assessment, Vee. With what's happened, I can't see that things'll stay status quo. And for that, I'm sorry too. We'll all have to get new jobs, you know. I'd already made up my mind, but I don't know what's going to happen to you, because I think Oakes has worked his last day there."

"I was working up to that anyway, knowing about the take-over. He already told me that one of the conditions from the other side is that he'll be gone within six months. He thought he was laughing all the way to the bank because of his options. I knew I'd be out of a job, with him anyway, before too long. So don't worry about me, Kate. Just let me know if there's anything I can do to help."

"You make it sound like I'm going off to war," I joked.

Her response was dead serious. "Maybe you are." We hugged each other tightly.

The only response we got from ringing the doorbell was the frantic, high-pitched barking of Baby on the other side of the door. When the dog finally quieted down, we could hear him snuffling and scratching at the bottom of the door. There was still no response from Chris so I rang the bell again. The dog started up again and Jay said, "Oakes must be passed out if he can't hear the dog going crazy."

I tentatively put my hand on the ornate brass door handle

and pushed down the latch with my thumb. The door opened and I looked up expectantly at Jay, waiting for him to say something. Instead he pushed past me into the lobby entranceway calling Chris' name. Baby leapt up at me and his claws scratched at my knee where the scrapes from the roof of Sadie Weinstein's house had only just stopped oozing. The pain of Baby re-opening the wound brought a metallic taste to my mouth and I gasped. My reaction was normal under the circumstances but when I batted him away from my legs, he yelped. He had a stupid, red bow, tied to his topknot and another one under his chin, like a bow-tie. It must be tough enough being a miniature poodle, but to add insult to injury, the male dog was decked out like a foo-foo.

"Quiet, Baby," I said as I looked around the lobby for signs of life. The house was very familiar to me and I knew the layout from memory. I had been there many times on different errands and knew exactly where we'd find Oakes.

"Downstairs," I told Jay, pointing to a Colonial style door inset in the curved walls. He looked at me with a question mark on his face.

"Television room. That's where he hides when he's drinking."

A couple of years ago TechniGroup had been about to close a debenture issue and Oakes had disappeared one afternoon. There was no response to his telephone at home, urgent voice messages were not returned, and Harold started to panic about nine o'clock that night. We were at the lawyers' offices at a pre-closing and all the documents were neatly arranged in piles around a long, rectangular boardroom table that sat thirty people. The junior lawyers from both sides were working their way methodically around the table checking the documents against the closing agenda, making sure all the i's were dotted and all the t's were crossed. The senior lawyers from both sides were huddled in the corners of the room, ironing out last minute "deal stoppers". The chairs had been removed from the table and placed against the walls where the accountants sat, biding their time and watching their fees grow. The only thing missing from all the documents prepared was Chris Oakes' signature.

There were over sixty separate documents on the closing agenda and ten original copies of each document had been prepared. Chris Oakes had to sign over six hundred documents before the deal could close as scheduled at ten the next morning. Usually in a closing such as this, all documents were signed before the pre-closing started and were held in escrow until all conditions had been met. The actual closing would then take only minutes when the lawyers from both sides would position themselves on either side of the table and with a few silent nods back and forth, it would be agreed that the deal was closed.

Didrickson cornered me where I was standing in the boardroom watching the lawyers, praying they wouldn't find any typos or other mistakes in the documents I'd prepared.

He smelled slightly sour and his breath was stale. "Where the *fuck* is Oakes?" he demanded through clenched teeth.

"I have no idea, Harold. I've put out an APB on him and I'm waiting to hear back from Vanessa." Vee was relatively new to the position of keeper of the CEO, but she was quickly catching on to his quirks. She'd assured me I'd hear from her within the half hour.

One of the legal secretaries who belonged to the law firm where we were holding the closing approached me at that point and I looked over at her. "Phone," she mouthed silently. Without a word I slid out from where Harold had practically pinned me against the wall and followed her out of the boardroom. The news hadn't been good and the plan I put forth to Harold was one of desperation.

The phone call had been from Vanessa, who'd told me in a small voice that she was at Oakes' house and he was passed out drunk. There was an empty quart bottle of Scotch on the floor beside the easy chair where she'd found him.

Harold had hit the roof when I told him but he calmed down somewhat when I told him my plan. "We'll sober him up so he can at least hold a pen and I'll get him to sign a copy of each document."

"Two of each," he'd said. "One for them, one for us." I quickly marched around the table taking two originals from each pile of documents and stuffed them in my briefcase.

Vanessa had been in the basement television room trying to force coffee down Oakes' throat when I'd arrived around ten o'clock that night. It was after two in the morning before he was in any shape to sign the documents, let alone hold a pen. He had no idea what he was signing but knew from experience that when Kate put a document in front of him to sign, he signed. No questions asked.

Harold had given the other side some bullshit story about Chris Oakes being detained at some other important meeting and the closing went off without a hitch. Until later that day at the luncheon celebrating the closing of the transaction. Everyone was being civil to each other and all of the acrimony and pettiness that had been evident over the last couple of weeks among the lawyers had evaporated. By the time everyone had eaten and the champagne had disappeared, it was well past four in the afternoon. As usual, I was the only sober one in the crowd, but we were all having a good time. Until Oakes showed up. He was drunk but in control and as usual, he was wearing his public persona and everyone loved him. He was a different man in front of people who didn't work for him and they all enjoyed his company. I remember giving Harold a knowing look and leaving the party immediately.

When Jay and I entered the basement room, it was a familiar scene to me. There was an empty bottle of scotch on the floor and Oakes was passed out in his La-Z-Boy chair, hugging a half-full bottle and clutching a small white booklet that I recognized as our internal voice mail directory in his hand. The phone on the table beside him was off the hook and a loud busy signal was coming out of the receiver.

CHAPTER
fifty-seven

"I wish I had a Polaroid," I said to no one in particular. Chris was slumped in his chair decked out in his pyjama bottoms and a dress shirt with CEO monogrammed on the breast pocket. Something wet was dribbling out of the side of his mouth and he snorted loudly as I stood over him. The sound made me jump but it also confirmed that he was still alive even though the evidence indicated he had probably ingested enough Scotch to sink the Navy.

"Well," Jay said smartly. "Go ahead. Question him. He's all yours. I'll question the dog."

"Don't get smart Jay. I'll sober him up with coffee."

"If he's had all that Scotch, I think it'll take a couple of days to sober him up."

"Maybe, maybe not. That empty on the floor could have been sitting there for a couple of days."

"No. I drankth it tonight," Oakes slurred. I jumped again and looked at him, still slumped in his chair with his eyes closed.

"Chris," I said as I edged closer to him. I put my hand out to touch him but recoiled at the thought. He didn't respond and I repeated, "Chris." This time I said it louder.

"Go 'way," he mumbled.

"I won't go away," I told him. "Until you tell me what happened to Evelyn." Another snort came from his nose and I wasn't about to allow him to pass out again so I grabbed the fabric of the sleeve of his shirt and pulled on it a couple of times to get his attention.

"Kate, it's a losing battle," Jay said. "He just keeps passing out. You'll never get any sense out of him in this condition."

"Hey, I'm used to it. This is just like communicating with him at the office. He mumbles and grunts and snorts all the time." I grabbed the bottle from Chris' clutches and poured the remains over his head. Scotch soaked into his hair and ran down his face and onto the front of his shirt.

"What the hell are you doing Kate?" Jay demanded.

Satisfied that the bottle was now empty I held on to the neck of the bottle and practiced a few swings with it.

"Emptying the bottle so I can hit him over the head with it," I told him. Jay swiftly took the bottle from my hand and laid it upright on the table beside Chris' chair.

"Have you lost it?"

"Hey, I was kidding. I poured it on him to see if I could get a reaction. Maybe I need something colder." On the back wall of the room there was a fully stocked bar and I knew from the last time I had to sober him up that the refrigerator had an automatic ice-maker that dispensed cubes out a chute in the front door. I found an ice bucket on the bar counter and filled it with ice cubes from the dispenser and then poured cold water from the tap over the ice cubes and sloshed it around a few times. The wicked grin on my face told Jay exactly what I planned to do with my ice-cold concoction.

I stood over Oakes with the bucket poised and asked Jay, "Do you think he prefers a twist of lemon with his Scotch and water?" With my index finger and thumb, I very gingerly held the collar of his shirt away from his neck to make sure some it went inside his shirt.

The reaction this time from Oakes was more to my liking and he reacted quickly, spluttering and cursing. I stood back and watched for signs of an awakening but when it was too slow coming, I filled the bucket again with ice and water and this time poured it over his head and down the front of his shirt. Oakes' arms flailed about and with his eyes open, he tried unsuccessfully to get out of his chair but I pushed him back. I yanked on the wooden handle at the side of the La-Z-Boy chair to pop up the footrest and Chris' feet flew up. It was a comical sight and a sure way to keep him prisoner in his chair.

Oakes was awake now and he looked at Jay and I through half opened eyes.

"Hooru," came out of his mouth and Jay and I looked at each other for interpretation.

"I think he said who are you," I offered. I put my hands on the arm of the chair and leaned into his face and in my best Marine drill sergeant voice, I yelled at him. "Coffee?" His head lolled to the side and rested on his shoulder. "I'll take that for a yes," I said confidently and headed for the bar. One of the lower cupboards yielded a small jar of Maxwell House Instant and I shook a generous amount in the bottom of a large beer mug. To this I added some lukewarm water from the tap and stirred it up with a pink swizzle stick with a cute flamingo on top.

"Now I need your help," I told Jay. "Just hold his head straight and I'll do the pouring."

"He could choke, Kathleen. Don't be ridiculous."

"Fine, I'll do it myself."

I grabbed Chris' chin and grimaced as I stuck my thumb in his lower lip and forced his mouth open. The lukewarm instant coffee poured out of his mouth and I wasn't sure if any was making its mark because I couldn't see his throat working. So, I pushed on the back of the La-Z-Boy to get it into a more reclined position and poured some more into his mouth. When he swallowed, I slowed down and waited for him to empty his mouth.

I looked up at Jay who was staring at me in horror. "Maybe I'd be better off just spooning the dry coffee crystals into his mouth," I suggested. "That way the caffeine would work faster."

"You're nuts."

"Maybe. But I'm not leaving here until I get some answers." I started pouring more liquid caffeine in Chris' mouth and by the time we reached the bottom of the beer mug Chris was stirring. I perched on the edge of the sofa to wait and eventually my efforts were rewarded when Chris grunted several times and wiped his hand over his face. By this time most of the various liquids that had been poured over him had dried on his face but his shirt remained soaked and stuck to his skin. His pyjama bottoms were in the same condition and the fabric covering of the La-Z-Boy chair gave off an uncomfortable squishing sound when he squirmed in the chair. Chris was probably feeling just like a newborn baby sitting in a soaked diaper.

"Come on Chris, please," I prodded him. Jay had made himself comfortable in a matching loveseat and I looked over at him. "I don't suppose you could pick him up and shake him for me?" When he gave me a blank look in return I knew I was going to get about as much response from Jay as I was getting from Oakes.

"Did you want to wait in the car while I beat him with a rubber hose?" This at least elicited a slight twitch at the corner of his mouth.

"I know you object to this. If it wasn't so serious I'd leave him here to choke on his own vomit. But I want some answers." Jay nodded wordlessly and I took this for mild acceptance of my methods.

Chris' eyes were open now and I saw a glimmer of awareness.

"Waddya want?" he asked me.

"Some answers."

"Get out," he said as he heaved himself into a more upright position. He pointed a shaking finger at me and said, "You I know." My eyes followed his hand as it slowly swung around and he pointed at Jay. "Who's that?"

"Jay Harmon," Jay told him.

A glimmer of recognition surfaced in Oakes' face and his mouth formed into a wicked sneer.

"The idiot who got himself fired. Rick's little bum-boy," Chris said.

Jay's face reacted but he didn't respond. I gave him credit for being able to hold his tongue, a trait I had yet to develop.

Now that Chris seemed somewhat sober, it was time to get this over with. "You told me on the phone that you were sorry. It was an accident. *Evelyn* was an accident. Now tell me what you meant."

"Get out of my house." He fumbled at the side of his chair for the lever and gave it a yank. The chair returned to an upright position and his feet hit the floor. His attempt to stand up was unsuccessful and he fell back into the chair.

"You're fired," he told me and I laughed.

"Really?" I asked with mock horror. "And just how long do you think the great CEO will hold on to his job? Now that we know you murdered Evelyn?"

Chris squirmed in his chair and averted his eyes.

"Answer me, dammit," I yelled at him.

He quickly looked at me and then Jay. His eyes were wide open now and he resembled a deer caught in the headlights of a car. His hand reached for the phone beside him. "I'm calling the police if you don't get out of my house."

"Please do," Jay dared him as he stood up. "Kate, come on, you're not getting anywhere here. Let's just leave."

I stood up and took Jay by the arm to the other side of the room. "Just a few more minutes. I think I can get through to him.

Go upstairs to the kitchen and make some coffee. Please. You might be intimidating him."

"Me? I may have the size but you've got the mouth. Maybe you should go make coffee."

"Go." I gave him a light push and he reluctantly walked up the stairs. Baby appeared from behind Chris' chair and followed Jay. I had completely forgotten about the dog. Chris remained in his chair looking like a deposed king. His expression was pitiful and he was a mess. I glanced at the clock on the VCR and it read one twenty-four. Almost time to call it a night but I wasn't about to give up. Yet.

"You know that it's all over," I told him, doing my best Dragnet imitation. Baby started to bark upstairs and I heard footsteps on the stairs. "You'll never work in this town again. Now tell me what happened. Please."

I was standing over Chris with my back to the stairs and Baby's persistent yelping was starting to annoy me. "Baby, shut-up," I said.

"I agree," a voice behind me said. "The dog is far too noisy." I spun around to face Philip Winston who was holding a gun in his hand. It looked like the one he had hit me with but this one had a long, tubular extension on the end of the barrel, which I surmised was a silencer. A familiar sight to any Clint Eastwood aficionado.

The dog was yipping and jumping at Philip's pant leg. He pointed the gun at Baby and pulled the trigger and the dog gave one final yelp before falling on the floor.

CHAPTER
fifty-eight

Oakes let out a bellow of rage and catapulted himself out of the chair. Philip now pointed the gun directly at me and my eyes darted to the staircase.

"I'm all alone," he said, following my eyes. Then where was Jay, I thought desperately. "The watchdog met me at the door."

Chris was sobbing and kneeling on the floor cradling the bloody dog in his arms. Philip waved the gun at me and I instinctively backed up. My gut was turning over and sweat had broken out all over my body. Philip's eyes were locked on mine and he ignored Oakes on the floor.

"You got away from me earlier, and now I'm pleasantly surprised to find you here. I'm running around the Metropolitan Toronto area looking for you and here you are." His calm voice gave me shivers and bolts of fear were shooting up my spine and through my stomach. The hand holding the gun slowly raised up and he stretched his arm outright until the gun was pointed directly at my face. My eyes closed automatically in anticipation of what was to come next. My senses were heightened and the sour smell of scotch that permeated the air wafted to my nostrils. Blood was pounding in my ears and I could hear my breath and Chris, whose sobs had now turned to a high-pitched keen.

"Your voice message, Chris," Philip was saying, "was very timely. Thank you very much. Open your eyes. Look at me." I forced my eyes open and looked at him where he was still standing in the same position, about eight feet away from me. The gun remained pointed at my face.

"Mr. Information Technology here left me a voice message. Said he'd told the girl it'd been an accident. I assumed he meant you but I couldn't be sure because he was so drunk. Now that's what I call dangerous. A drunk who spills the beans."

I glanced downwards at Oakes who was still only interested

in his damn dead dog. There was no way I was going to escape this situation and I obviously could not depend on Oakes for support. As usual.

I was praying inside that if Jay were still alive upstairs, he'd get some help but in the meantime, my only hope was to try and talk my way out of the situation.

"I agree," I told Philip. "A drunk is dangerous. But I don't drink. Guaranteed. So I'll never spill the beans, as you put it. Just let me go and that'll be the end of it."

He slowly shook his head. "Sorry. No can do. There's too much at stake. I've been working at this for most of my life and I *will not* let you, or him," he waved the gun at Oakes on the floor, "get in my way."

My hands came up, slowly, to my mouth and I pressed them over my face, trying to hold in the sobs that were building in my chest. I had stupidly got myself into this situation and my actions to this point had been impulsive. Impulsive and stupid. I tried to think clearly and logically but panic boiled around inside me.

I thought of Sadie and her deep, motherly love for her son and decided to try to appeal to his human side. "Your mother wouldn't be very proud of you right now."

"You keep my mother out of it!" he screamed at me and I backed up another step. The step backwards put the back of my knees up against the low coffee table and I felt completely trapped. "I'm doing this for my mother. She was shamed and humiliated when my father died. We were poor for so many years. I promised." He said this slowly and his voice was quieter and respectful when he talked about his mother and I wondered what the promise was all about.

"Then think about your mother," I said quietly.

The next instant happened in slow motion, and every detail remains engraved on my brain. I saw the muscles move ever so slightly in the hand that was holding the gun. Chris had put his right hand on the floor and was trying to push himself into a standing position but he fell over into Philip's leg at the same moment he pulled the trigger. Later on I would credit Chris for saving my life. The hot, searing pain I felt on my right ear automatically made me think I was dead. I fell back on the coffee table with both of my hands protecting the side of my head where the bullet had hit me. My hands filled with warm fluid that I knew was blood and in a panic now that I realized I was still alive,

I rolled off the coffee table onto the floor behind Chris's La-Z-Boy chair.

"Goddammit Chris," Philip screamed.   "You're always screwing things up."   I could hear Philip's breath coming in short gasps.   And then his voice changed again and he said calmly, as if we were standing around at a champagne reception, "If he hadn't knocked my leg, I would have had you right between the eyes. But before you die, let me tell you, you were close. Close to finding out the truth."

My eyes darted around the room from my hiding position. The clock on the VCR now read one thirty-one and I realized that it had only been a few minutes since Jay had gone up to make coffee. If he had any idea of what was going on down here, assuming he were still alive, help should be on the way soon.

"The *truth* Philip, the truth is what everyone is going to know after tonight," I said defiantly.   "You're blackmailing Chris and Chris had something to do with Evelyn's death. All of it's going to come out. You'll never survive this Philip. Your career and Oakes' is over."   I was tempted to call him some names too, but I didn't want to push my luck, whatever little I had left. He didn't respond to this so I pushed on.

"So tell me," I continued.   "What did Oakes and Everly do that made your father's company go bankrupt?"   My right hand was full of blood now from my ear and I wiped my hand on the carpet.

"They stole from him."   His voice was above me and without moving my head I raised my eyes up from the mess I was making on the carpet and looked at Philip's shoes.   My eyes continued up his pants leg and I finally had to move my head and when I did, I looked directly in his face.   The gun was held steadily in his hand and it pointed directly at me, less than a foot from my face.   "They stole his money.   And he was going to the police when they killed him.   I came home early from school.   The nurse had sent me home because I wasn't feeling well.   Mommy wasn't there so I went to look for daddy."   His voice had changed and now he sounded like a young boy.

"There were voices in daddy's den and I was never allowed to interrupt when he was having a meeting but I wasn't feeling well. So I went outside and peeked in the window to see.   They were there.   One of them was holding daddy in the chair and the other one was holding daddy's hand to his head.   And then there was a loud noise.   Mommy said daddy went to live with the angels."

The poor child had witnessed his father's murder. No wonder his mother thought she'd lost both her husband and child. The shock of seeing something like that had obvious, lasting effects.

Philip's voice changed again and this time, a man's voice spoke to me. "We suffered. Mom and me. And I promised myself that I'd make it better for us. I was probably 15 or 16 before I realized what it was I witnessed that day."

"I believe you Philip. But why did my friend Evelyn have to die?"

"It was an accident. She was only supposed to get sick. We wanted Rick Cox out of the picture but things went wrong. We needed to fire him. The woman was never supposed to die. Just get sick and be out of the picture for a couple of days. We disabled her EpiPen. Put a little peanut oil on the food. It was supposed to be no big deal. We needed access to her computer system."

I thought sadly about Evelyn and the tragic way this madman had ended her life.

"You bastards," I whispered.

Philip didn't hear me, he just continued. "Chris promised me Rick's job. He was going to pay for what he did. I wanted money. And lots of it. For my mother. Chris said if we got rid of Rick I could have his job and his stock options. He said Larry would find another company to buy TechniGroup and then we'd all make lots of money on our stock options."

Fucking stock options. The level of greed amazed me.

"Well you've succeeded. Rick's out of the way. We're about to receive a take-over bid. Your options'll make you scads of money. So just leave it at that. Let me go."

"Sorry."

I watched in horror as the shoulder muscle of his arm holding the gun twitched imperceptibly and as I waited for the shot that would kill me, my life virtually passed before my eyes. An overwhelming sense of sadness took over and I willed myself to pass out.

A groan from the other side of the room told me that Chris was still alive. And then a voice, that definitely wasn't Chris's said, "Mr. Winston. Drop the gun."

From my position on the floor, I watched Philip's eyes dart up in reaction to the voice. The voice was unfamiliar to me but I felt a surge of relief that help had arrived. Philip crouched slightly and without moving his eyes, he grabbed my arm and pulled me up. He spun me around so my back was against his chest and held me tightly with his left arm around my neck. My hands grabbed instinctively at the arm across my throat and I tore at his forearm with my fingers. My fighting made him tighten his hold. I saw one eye of a policeman's face peek around the wall at the end of the staircase. His left hand held a gun pointed directly at us.

"Just drop the gun, Mr. Winston," he was saying calmly as he looked directly at me. His eyes were telling me not to do anything stupid but I felt the situation dictated otherwise. I manoeuvred my chin under Philip's forearm and his grip tightened, which luckily forced my mouth open around his arm. So I bit down as hard as I could and stomped on the top of his foot at the same time. Philip's reaction was exactly what I expected. He yelled out and loosened his grip slightly from around my neck. I took the opportunity to pull down on his arm with my hands and then I let him have an elbow in the stomach. His arm dropped and I fell to my knees on the floor behind the chair, covering my head with my arms.

One shot rang out and the sound was deafening so I knew the police officer was the one who had fired. I heard a rush of footsteps on the staircase and voices filled the room. I remained frozen in place and listened to the sounds around me.

"He's alive," I heard someone say and then the same voice was talking to me.

"Miss. Are you all right?" An arm snaked around my shoulders, where I was huddled.

"Fine," I managed to say.

"There's an awful lot of blood, Miss. Where are you hurt?"

I put my hands on the floor and pushed myself up to a kneeling position. "My ear, I think," I said as I pointed. Adrenaline continued to rush through my body and I felt no pain from the wound. Yet. I swivelled my body around to see Philip lying behind me, face down on the floor with his hands handcuffed behind his back. I used the arm of the La-Z-Boy to pull myself to my feet and stood there on shaky knees looking down at him. He stared back at me silently with hate in his eyes.

"Can you stand him up?" I asked the police officer. "I hate to kick a man when he's lying down."

CHAPTER
fifty-nine

Chris Oakes' basement television room was full of people and because of the low ceilings, the noise level was high. I was sitting on the coffee table that had broken my fall and a paramedic was attending to my war wound. I was told I was a lucky person because the bullet from Philip's gun had only nicked the top of my ear. They were insistent though that I go to the hospital and it was there that I found out that the bullet had taken off a piece of the top of my ear that was the size of my baby fingernail.

Philip Winston was handcuffed to a stretcher with a flesh wound in his shoulder and the paramedics were taking him up the stairs to the ambulance. Oakes had already been taken out, but he had walked. Barely.

The paramedic who was working on me was packing up his large first aid kit that resembled a toolbox.

"Can you walk, or do you want a stretcher?" he grinned at me.

"I think I can walk, thank you very much."

"Well, your ambulance awaits you."

"I'll go to the hospital, but *not* in an ambulance. He'll take me." I nodded my head at Jay who was sitting across from me on the loveseat.

"I'm sorry miss. We have to insist. Your friend can follow in his car. I'll even sit in the back with you."

"Fine," I agreed rather than fight. Of course I was dizzy when I stood up but a deep breath and a conscious decision not to act weak, gave me strength.

Detective Leech appeared which didn't surprise me. In fact, I was surprised that it took him so long to get here.

"What took you so long Leech?"

He ignored my jibe. "A few questions Miss Monahan."

My paramedic saved me, for the moment. "Later Detective. This lady's on her way to the hospital. She's lost some blood and we understand she took a blow to the head earlier today. So, the questions'll have to wait." He took me by the elbow and led me away.

"For that, kind sir, I propose marriage," I whispered to him as we made our way up the stairs. "You saved me from the dragon."

He laughed. "At your service."

The street outside of Chris' house resembled a circus. Red flashing lights from all of the emergency vehicles were lighting up the street and yellow tape cordoned off the area. A television crew were set up behind the line and their bright white lights made the scene look like a large, budget film was being made.

"There she is," I heard someone yell and a surge of bodies pressed forward. My saviour paramedic hustled me up two steps into the back of a waiting ambulance and he quickly pulled both doors closed behind him.

Detective Leech finally had his way with me at the hospital. I was forthcoming with as much information as I had but he had nothing to share with me. The hospital staff kept him at bay and before he was allowed access to me, the doctors and nurses patched me up and x-rayed my head. The doctor had been concerned about the blow to the side of my head because the lump where Philip had hit me with his gun was quite large.

"It's just a mild concussion," the doctor told me. "Rest is the best cure. As for the ear, the bandages can come off in a couple of days." I was sitting up on the side of a gurney when he gave me the good news.

"A few people outside want to see you," he told me. "But protocol tells me that the Detective gets first crack at you. One person tells me his name is," he paused as he checked a name he had written on my chart, "Jay Harmon. The screaming pack of reporters are being kept outside the hospital but they all want to talk to you. I'm ready to discharge you now but if you want to hide from everyone, we can admit you for observation." I was sure he wouldn't be offering the hospital for asylum purposes if I didn't have such good medical insurance coverage, but I thanked him anyway.

"Send in the good Detective," I told him. "And thanks for the offer, but I think I'll go home tonight." I offered my hand and he returned a firm, but cool handshake. He pulled the curtain closed around my gurney when he left and I rummaged around in the small cart that held my clothes. When I had arrived, the nurses had quickly and efficiently stripped me of my clothes and I made a mental note to call my mother and thank her for always reminding me to wear clean underwear.

My clothes were covered in dried blood and I was loathe to put them back on but it was better than leaving the hospital in a gown that didn't fasten in the back and was three inches above my knees. I quickly stripped off the gown and was buttoning my blouse when a voice behind the curtain told me that Leech had arrived.

"Just a sec." I dropped my shoes on the floor and manoeuvred my feet into them without bending over. I left the gown on the gurney and pulled open the curtain to find Leech.

"Miss Monahan," he said formally. "How are you feeling?"

"Fine. Where do you want to talk?" I was anxious to get this over with and get home to bed. The large clock on the wall told me it was past three o'clock in the morning.

"Here or at the station."

"Now?"

"A few questions now, and we can finish tomorrow, if you like."

"Here then. Is there somewhere we can sit and I can have a cup of coffee while we talk?"

"I think there's a lounge on this floor. Follow me."

Jay was sitting in the waiting area and he jumped out of his chair when he saw me approaching but Leech waved him off. "Fifteen minutes, Mr. Harmon. If you'd be good enough to wait, we won't take long."

We found the lounge and Leech bought us each a coffee from a vending machine that looked like it had been installed before the Second World War. I was dying for a cigarette but there was no way I could light up in a hospital. I didn't have any smokes anyway because my purse, which I'd forgotten about, was still in either my car or Sadie Weinstein's house. I spied my reflection in a dark window. The entire right side of my head was swathed in white bandages and my blood-soaked clothes looked almost unreal. Like props in a movie.

I sat down carefully in a straight backed chair at a table covered in old magazines. Leech sat across from me and opened his ever-present notebook.

"Please fill me in on events since we spoke on Saturday night after the break-in at your apartment."

Where to start was the hardest part so I decided to take him back a few days before the Saturday night attack. And this time I tried not to leave out any details. I told him about seeing Winston and Cox at the restaurant and Jay's discovery of the link between Oakes and Everly and Weinstein Textiles. I recounted how Jay and I had met Philip's mother and discovered that he was using an assumed name. Then I told him about Philip kidnapping me in the parking garage at work and waking up in Sadie's house.

I showed him my scraped knees which the nurses had disinfected and covered with Sesame Street Band-Aids. Throughout the telling of my story I was calm and almost detached but I had to pause before continuing when I got to the part about what had happened at Chris Oakes' house. Leech smiled when I described my efforts at sobering up Chris but his expression turned deadly serious when I told him about Philip's arrival and the subsequent events.

I closed my eyes and told him about looking down the barrel of Philip's gun and how everything seemed like it was in slow motion. I felt Leech's hand cover mine and he said softly, "It's all right now." Embarrassment flushed over my face for having such a hard time getting the story out so I finished off quickly, with my eyes open, and told him about the things that Philip had said and admitted to.

"Good," he told me and he flipped his notebook shut and put it away in his jacket pocket. "Tomorrow, we'll talk some more. You go home and rest." He was sounding like a Jewish mother and I wondered why I always felt my back go up when he was around. Probably because I never told him the whole truth and nothing but the truth. I had deliberately left many things out in the past when he had questioned me and the guilty feelings had put me on the defensive.

Leech showed me the way back to the Emergency Department and I found Jay slumped in his chair, fast asleep.

"Let me warn you about the reporters outside," Leech said before he left. "They're not allowed in here, but they'll be outside, in full force. I can't tell you not to talk to them, but we'd appreciate it if you wouldn't, until our investigation is over."

I gently woke Jay when Leech finally departed and he told me that he was parked out front, away from the media. I felt like Elizabeth Taylor sneaking out of the Betty Ford Center and we laughed a little as we stayed in the shadows in the parking lot on our way to the car. It was four-thirty when we finally arrived back at my apartment and after five before we got to bed.

"When did you figure out that Philip was in the house?" I finally asked him.

"When I heard Oakes yell, I was just at the top of the stairs with the coffee. I recognized Philip's voice and froze. I didn't know what to do." He put his arm protectively around my shoulder. "I should have jumped him. You wouldn't have gotten shot."

"Maybe not, but *you* sure as hell would have. He would have shot you as soon as you started down the stairs." My hand touched the bandages on the side of my head. "Besides, this is nothing," I reassured him although my ear was throbbing. "Just an excuse not to cut my hair."

I told Jay about the things that Philip had told me. "So, you were right. He was blackmailing them all along." After a few silent moments he asked the questions that had been nagging me. "But what about all the other pieces of this puzzle? Why is Rick Cox dead? Why is Harold involved? And why did the stock price take such a dive before all of this happened?"

We didn't have to wait long to find out because by the time we arrived at the station the next day to meet with Detective Leech, he had most of the answers.

CHAPTER
sixty

The phone was ringing persistently and I struggled to pull myself out of a deep sleep. The clock radio told me it was seven thirty-five. I had been asleep for less than two hours and the painkillers they had given me at the hospital had worn off and the gentle throbbing I'd felt the night before in my ear now felt like a pounding jackhammer. Ah, the healing process, I thought. Jay slept soundly beside me and he didn't move when I ungracefully fell out of bed. My blood-soaked clothes were in a disgusting pile on the floor and I gingerly stepped over them and grabbed Jay's oversize T-shirt, taking my time, hoping the phone would stop ringing.

The ribbing on the neck of the T-shirt caught on the large bandage on the side of my head when I was pulling it on, jarring my wound and the first curse of the day escaped my lips.

I yanked the ringing receiver off the hook and automatically put it up to my right, bandaged ear.

"Yes," I yelled into the receiver as I passed it to the left side of my head. The handset felt uncomfortable against the lump over my left ear, so I held it away from my head. A hands-free set would have come in handy.

"Kathleen, is that you?"

It was my mother. Oh god. Please don't let it be some disaster, I thought in a panic. She never calls this early in the morning, and only ever calls on Sunday, when the rates are cheapest. It never occurred to me that she might be calling about *me*.

"Yes, mom. What's wrong?"

"What's wrong?" she asked indignantly. "What's wrong? You're all over the morning news and you ask me, what's wrong?"

"Calmly mother. I'm fine. Really." My interest was piqued now. "All over the news?"

"Yes, there were pictures of you getting into an ambulance. They said you'd been shot. Are you all right?"

"I'm fine. Just a small wound. On my right ear. Where are you calling from?" She was normally at work at this time of day.

"Don't end your sentences with a preposition," she lectured me and I laughed. Nothing ever changes.

"I'm at home, with your father. He came racing out of the house to get me. He'd seen you on the news."

"Well, tell him I'm fine." I briefly filled her in on the events of the previous night and promised to call later.

"And mom?"

"Yes?"

"Thanks for always telling me to wear clean underwear."

I heard her laugh as I hung up the phone and it felt good to take one thing off my list of mental notes.

My heart broke at the sight of Sadie Weinstein, sitting in the lobby of the police station. It seemed she had aged overnight, and the forlorn, lost look on her face made me wonder if she would be able to cope with what she and Philip were about to face. She didn't recognize either Jay or myself as we passed her with our escort to the second floor for our meeting with Detective Leech.

Leech's sorry excuse for an office consisted of a desk, a chair and a telephone. I was sure there wasn't room for a cockroach, let alone two guests, so we met in one of the small rooms where we were told they questioned suspects.

"Not that you're suspects," he quickly said. I gave him a smile because I believe in encouraging humour and I also believed that we were never too old to develop the skill. Besides, I was starting to like Leech. When this was all over I might speak to him about possibly changing the pronunciation of his name to Lesh or Latch or something that didn't make him sound like a Bay Street lawyer.

After we had passed the pleasantries and he had served us some coffee that tasted just the way the television cops described it, he told us that Philip was being arraigned that afternoon on attempted murder charges and that the Crown Attorney was calling on the RCMP Fraud Division for their assistance in investigating a myriad of other possible charges. Leech told us that after they had explained to Philip what 'hard-time' in a prison was all about, he had agreed to a plea bargain. Lesser charges for squealing on Chris Oakes and Larry Everly.

Chris Oakes was in a hospital lock-up under a psychiatrist's care. He had been totally incoherent when the police attempted to question him the night before.

"The only thing he said, over and over, was Baby," Leech said.

"Well, I certainly hope they have voice mail in the loony bin. He can have his sessions with his shrink over the phone." I silently chastised myself for what had just come out of my mouth and hoped that in a couple of days, or weeks, I would have more charitable feelings towards these bastards. But, Leech didn't get the joke and Jay just shot me one of those looks. The kind of look your mother used to give you when you were little. You might be at your great-aunt's house for dinner and during a pause in the conversation you make a comment about her moustache. Unable to kick you under the table, your mother shoots you that look.

"What about Larry Everly?" I asked.

"The NYPD are co-operating with us and have picked him up and they're holding him there until we can nail down all the charges. Philip Winston told us some pretty unbelievable things last night and I have no doubt that Mr. Everly will be going away for a long, long time."

"Care to share any of that with us?" I urged him.

"Winston tells us that he allegedly witnessed Everly and Oakes murder his father. Why he never came forward with that information is a question that will probably not get answered. So, he blackmailed them. He got himself well educated and worked his way around the country in various high technology companies. About a year ago he saw his opportunity. He told us he had been following Oakes' career so he was watching TechniGroup very closely. TechniGroup was acquiring a lot of companies and that was when Philip approached Oakes. He was going to make Oakes pay, and pay big time. He wanted money, and lots of it, so he came up with the plan to have Oakes buy the company he was working for and get him into a senior position at TechniGroup. He also knew that your company had been ripe for a take-over for some time and as part of his master plan, he figured Larry Everly, with his connections on Wall Street, would be more than eager to go out and find a buyer. Turns out he was right."

"Finding a buyer for a company our size, isn't that easy," Jay said.

"Easy enough when you're motivated," Leech told us. "The other side of this nasty deal was that Philip insisted on stock options. And lots of them. I'm not much of a brain when it comes to all of this high level corporation stuff, but I had a quick lesson this morning from my brother-in-law. He's an actuary," he said proudly.

Jay and I barely suppressed our laughter when the old joke came to mind. Question: Why did you become an accountant? Answer: Because I didn't have the charisma to be an actuary. Every profession has its cross to bear and because actuaries do such incredibly boring work, they are perceived to the outside world as lifeless people with no personality. I was sure this was the only joke in history that had been told about an actuary.

"He explained to me about how the price gets set and how you make money on them," he continued. "Everly and Oakes were to get the stock price down so Winston's options would be given to him at a low price. So the two of them started passing rumours around. Winston said they talked off the record to some people on the floor at the stock exchange and to industry analysts. Those are the folks that follow your specific industry and make predictions about the business," he told us needlessly. "I'm getting to like using these buzzwords. I guess the rumours were nasty enough to have the stock price go down and that's exactly what Winston wanted."

"It worked," I interjected. "He got a shit-load of options and the exercise price was pretty low. Along with the rumours that we didn't know about, there were the other things happening that the public knew about and those events themselves drove the price down even more."

"Right," he agreed. "The news that your chief accountant was resigning made the price drop." I smiled at his use of the term chief accountant. Rick would have liked that. "Oakes and Larry Everly told their sources that Rick Cox had been fired. And that made the price drop some more. But when Mr. Cox committed suicide, it got worse."

"Was it a suicide?" I asked him.

He shook his head and I watched Jay's face for a reaction but there was none. He had been sitting quietly, stone-faced through much of Leech's recital.

"We'll get to that part in a minute. The news that an employee of the company had died mysteriously and that we were investigating it as a homicide, just added fuel to the fire. So all of these events got the desired result. A low stock price, Philip Winston got his big job at TechniGroup with stock options, and there was another company, ripe to take-over TechniGroup. The plan had worked. But then you," he nodded at me, "and your partner here, got involved. The both of you were too smart for your own good."

"Not smart enough," I said ruefully, pointing to the bandage on the side of my head.

"No," he agreed. "But Mr. Winston didn't know how much you knew. When he found out that you had visited his mother, he saw all of his plans going up in smoke. He obviously got desperate."

"Obviously. It was him, you know, who broke into my apartment the other night."

"He needed to scare you off. I guess it almost worked."

"Almost," I agreed. "But then he had to double his threat and bash me over the head."

"Desperate men do desperate things," he said unnecessarily.

"I had made up my mind to let you do your job but he pushed the issue. I want to know what happened to my friend Evelyn."

"That's where it all started didn't it? So sad, that such an innocent person had to get involved. This could all have gone off without a hitch, if she hadn't died," he said sadly. "No one would have ever known."

I didn't need to hear that and once again I was overwhelmed by feelings of sadness and helplessness because I hadn't been there to help my friend. Tears welled up inside me and poured silently down my cheeks into my mouth.

CHAPTER
sixty-one

Jay and Detective Leech both offered tissues and Leech went to fetch more coffee while I composed myself, which took a while. I gave in to the tears and just sat there and let them flow and after a few minutes my tear ducts dried up. I wiped at my face with the balled-up tissue and waited for Leech's return. Jay remained silent and left me alone in my misery.

Detective Leech backed into the room carrying three Styrofoam cups of coffee.

"So where were we?" he asked needlessly.

"Evelyn," I quietly reminded him.

"Yes. Well, it seemed that Mr. Oakes and Mr. Winston put a plan together to get Mr. Cox fired. I understand that although Chris Oakes was chairman of the board and president, he didn't have all the power. He reported to the board of directors and I have been told that Mr. Rick Cox had several supporters on the board. To fire Mr. Cox outright wasn't going to work. So, the two came up with a plan, backed by Larry Everly, to discredit him. They initiated several small plans, one of which was to make it look like Mr. Cox had fixed the stock option system to benefit himself. To do that, they needed Evelyn Morris out of the way. Philip was adamant that it was an accident, that she was just supposed to be sick for a few days. It would give them the chance to do whatever they needed and when she came back to work, she would discover that something was wrong. As it turns out, Mr. Harmon here discovered it right away."

"Philip told me that last night. He said they just wanted her sick, for a few days," I said with disgust.

"They were aware of her allergy to nuts but not aware of the severity of it. They doctored the food with peanut oil and disabled her EpiPen. Philip and Chris Oakes decided to have a potluck - I think they referred to it as that. A potluck, where the employees

309

bring the food. If the caterers had been hired, Oakes and Winston wouldn't have had any access to the food."

"The greedy bastards. All of this for money. Philip Winston is more guilty because he didn't go to the police and report a murder in the first place." I felt the rage building in me and wanted to pound my fist on the table.

"Unfortunately, their plan backfired when Mrs. Morris died. And apparently Mr. Harmon, you were another victim. Mr. Cox fired you because he knew he had not caused those changes to be made, and right or wrong, he believed it had to have been you. You were supposedly the only one who knew his system password. Is that correct?"

"I agree that I knew his password. But was I the only person he told? I don't know," Jay answered.

"Everything apparently fell apart for Mr. Cox and we were led to believe he committed suicide. Philip Winston has informed us otherwise, which confirmed the Police Department's suspicions. From the evidence at the scene, it was unlikely that Mr. Cox had shot himself. That was confirmed by Philip last night under questioning."

Detective Leech sipped from his coffee and looked at Jay. "That was about the time you disappeared."

"I told you I didn't disappear," Jay retorted. "I was around all the time but our paths never crossed."

"We know that now. But you understand that we had to cover all the bases."

Jay nodded reluctantly.

"Did Philip give any explanation for why he and Rick Cox were together the night I saw them at Bigliardi's?" I asked.

"I was coming to that. Philip told us that he was worried that Rick might be on to something so he wanted to meet with him and confirm his suspicions. He got Rick Cox to meet him by telling him that he had information about Oakes that could end his job as chairman of the board. Apparently, Mr. Cox was still interested in working at TechniGroup and would have been happy to see Chris Oakes' career go up in flames." He shook his head in amazement as he told us. "The plotting and back-stabbing that went on in this company was amazing."

"What did Philip think Rick might be on to?" Jay asked.

"One of Mr. Winston's contacts in the stock market industry told him that Rick Cox had called him asking questions. Turns out this was one of the stockbrokers who had been fed all the false information by Oakes and Larry Everly. When Rick Cox called the broker, the broker took the opportunity to question Rick further on those stories. Suffice it to say that Rick Cox knew he'd been set up. Very complicated."

"So when Philip called Rick with the cock and bull story about dirty information on Chris Oakes, Rick jumped at the chance to meet him." Jay added. "Not so complicated Detective, once you'd worked there for a while."

"I'm a little confused," I piped in. "Why did Rick end up murdered?"

"Let me guess," Jay offered. "Because of the information he had. Philip wasn't about to let anyone screw up his plan so he killed Rick."

Detective Leech shook his head. "No. You've only got part of it right. The next part of the story is what will get Philip Winston his immunity from prosecution, if we can prove it. That night at Bigliardi's, Rick Cox threatened that he was going to the Ontario Securities Commission with the information that Oakes and Everly were manipulating the stock price. Winston says it was Oakes and Everly who killed Rick Cox. And once I've had a chance to question Larry Everly, I think we'll find out that they did it the same way they killed Philip's father. Philip probably thought there was some poetic justice there, forcing or blackmailing the two into killing again. The ultimate act of revenge. And that young lady and gentleman," he nodded at us, "is all of the information we've gathered so far."

I was suffering from information overload but there was one small point that needed clarifying. "How and why did Harold Didrickson get involved?"

"He's just another sad statistic," Leech said. "Philip told me that Oakes had been wanting to fire Mr. Didrickson for a long time. For what reasons, we don't know."

"He never needed a reason," I interrupted. "If the wind changed, that was reason enough. The man was a lunatic. Correct that. *Is* a lunatic."

"Well, after Rick Cox met with Philip Winston at the restaurant, he called Didrickson. They were buddies?" he asked me and I nodded my confirmation. "Didrickson panicked at the thought of Cox going to the Ontario Securities Commission because he was about to make out big on the intended take-over and he needed the money."

"Didn't we all," Jay added sarcastically.

Leech ignored his comment and continued. "I know it sounds like a plot from a dime store novel, but it seems that Mr. Didrickson and his wife have a little passion for the tables in Vegas. And the track. And the football games. They're in debt up to their proverbial eyeballs and this was going to be Harold's big payoff. Typical gambling syndrome. He knew he was going to be fired, but he managed to hang in for a long time. When the end was near and he saw all that potential cash, he couldn't allow anything, or anyone, to get in his way. Mr. Didrickson threw friendship to the wind and turned into a Benedict Arnold. He called Philip and the rest is history. He was a ready, willing and able participant in assisting Philip in luring Miss Monahan here, back into the trap."

It was all too much for me to take in and digest. All the pain and suffering that had been caused for the almighty buck. I got up from my chair and wandered over to the window where I stood facing Jay and Leech.

"I haven't read the papers or watched the news today," I said to Leech. "How soon will the whole story make the news?"

The thought of the company going down the tubes and all of the hardworking employees who had sweated blood for so many years losing their jobs was too much to fathom.

"Enough of the story is out now. I understand that trading has been halted in the shares and the Securities Commission will be involved shortly. One of the directors of the company was interviewed this morning on the news and he was adamant that they would push on."

I lit a cigarette and thought about the irony of it all. The remaining directors of the company would push on. Wonderful. A couple of the crooks had been caught and were locked up for the time being, but the rest of the morons were still on the loose with the public shareholders' money. The blind were now leading the blind.

I took a drag from my cigarette and blew the smoke out the open window. The smoke wafted through the screen and dispersed quickly in the fresh air and I thought for a moment about finding something symbolic about the smoke disappearing so quickly.

Fuck it. I wasn't into symbolism, just reality.

ROSEMARIE D'AMICO
was a law clerk/paralegal for over 20 years, working at some of Canada's largest law firms and high tech companies. O*ptions* is her first Kate Monahan novel and the second in the series is in the works. She lives in Ottawa, Ontario with her husband Darryl. Visit her website at www.rosemarie-damico.com and follow her blog at www.roses-space.blogspot.com.

ARTIFICIAL INTENTIONS

The Second Kate Monahan Mystery

Coming Fall 2010!

CHAPTER
one

The warmth of the sunlight on my closed eyelids told me it was morning but my body wasn't responding. Today I was starting a new job at the pristine and stuck-up law firm of McCallum & Watts and next to sticking needles in my eyes, my next favourite thing was starting a new job. At a stuck-up law firm.

Don't get me wrong, I was glad to have the job. I had been unemployed for six weeks and was starting to get desperate. In the past, I'd never gone more than a few days between jobs but this was 2002. Back in the nineties you could quit a job in disgust, throw everyone the finger and start a new job the next morning at nine.

My last boss, Harold Didrickson, was being investigated by the Ontario Securities Commission for manipulation of public stock prices. The company that had employed us, TechniGroup Consulting Inc. or TGC, was in the throes of being reorganized by a huge conglomerate that had purchased it for pennies a share.

My index finger gently rubbed the top of my ear where I had been shot by one of the executives of TGC in what turned out to be one of the nastiest scandals to rock the high-tech world. I'd lost the tip of my ear and my job, but six weeks later, I was relatively unscathed. Glad to be starting a new job and relieved to know I'd soon have a regular paycheck, but the job itself was a few steps back in my career. Not that I was complaining, because as I had repeatedly told myself since I'd accepted the position, one couldn't be picky.

I forced my eyes open and glanced at the clock beside my

bed and groaned. It was only six-thirty and I didn't have to be at my new desk until nine. By my standards, half the day was over by nine. At TGC I was in the office most days by seven-thirty and if I left by six, I considered it a good day. More often than not I worked weekends and in the last couple of years there, I was traveling a lot. Not a heavy workload by executive standards, but then again, I wasn't paid like an executive. I was a paralegal, with a specialization in corporate and securities law. However, compared to what paralegals made at law firms, I was well paid. *Was* being the operative word. I was taking a pay cut at McCallum & Watts but I also wasn't hired to do paralegal work. My new title was Legal Secretary.

Typing, dictaphone (yes, lawyers still dictated into those funny little machines), filing, billings, and making appointments was my new job description. And making nice-nice with the clients. Especially those who paid their bills. Definitely a step backwards for me, but a job. I was going to have to work on the nice-nice part with the clients.

I turned on my back and stretched, pointing my toes and trying to reach the end of the bed. It was a game I used to play as a child, stretching every morning when I woke up to see if I'd grown overnight. Along with the standard children's prayer every night, *"Now I lay me down to sleep..."*, I'd add under my breath, "And please God, make me grow". It hadn't worked but I still checked every morning. I was thirty-four years old and just under five feet tall. Four foot eleven, to be precise, but I considered it my prerogative to add an inch when anyone asked. I dreaded growing older because I'd heard that some elderly people shrink in height.

I gave up the game of trying to reach the foot board of the bed and kicked off the duvet. The warm morning air drifted through the open window and I could smell summer. It was the middle of June and the thought of summer gave me an excited feeling in my stomach. Baseball, sprinklers, firecrackers, hide and seek after dark, staying up late, and barbecues. I was thinking like a school kid, but whenever I smelled summer in the air, I was ten years old again. Summer meant the end of school and endless play. I quickly brought myself back to reality though and stumbled out of bed to the shower.

Two weeks later I was still telling myself that I couldn't be picky about the job. *It's a job, it's a job,* I chanted to the beat of the

316

photocopier. The repetitive sound of the automatic feeder on the monstrous photocopier was becoming hypnotic. *Che-chunk, che-chunk, che-chunk.* I'd been listening to the sound now for the last three hours as I photocopied a mountain of paper for one of the lawyers in the corporate tax section. As low man on the totem pole, I had been getting all of the dog jobs. The secretaries in our group gleefully dumped the dog jobs on me and I found myself having to practice verbal restraint on a daily basis.

I pressed my back against the counter and did a couple of deep knee-bends to get the kinks out of my lower back. Along with this job being boring and mundane, it made my body ache. The photocopy job was one that I alone was tasked with doing because the lawyer in charge told me it was too confidential to send to the main photocopy room where there were oodles of lowly paid young men who would be happy to help out. As if anyone in their right mind would find anything interesting in these mounds of paper.

The room was suddenly silent which told me that the photocopier was finally done. I pushed myself away from the counter and bent over the sorter bin on the end of the copier to retrieve the copies.

"Hey," a voice greeted me.

"Hey yourself," I said over my shoulder. "I'm almost done here, you can have the machine."

When I stood up with my arms full of paper, a very young, pimply-faced person was standing at the door to the room. This was a person I didn't recognize but that wasn't surprising because I was still seeing new faces every day at McCallum & Watts. There were reportedly three hundred and fifty people on staff, one hundred and forty-five of whom were lawyers. My sharp deductive reasoning told me that this one was definitely not a lawyer. He looked totally out of place in his dress pants, starched white shirt and thin leather tie. The fact that he wasn't wearing a suit jacket and was pushing a mail cart, told me he was one of us. Support staff.

"I don't need the machine. Are you Kate Monahan?" he asked me. I nodded.

"Ashley in Corporate asked me to tell you to get your butt back to your desk." With that he pushed off down the hall.

Ashley can go fuck herself, I thought to myself as I bundled-up three hundred pounds of paper in my arms and started the long trudge back to my workstation. Ashley had appointed herself my supervisor and if I didn't throttle her before this week was out, it would be a miracle. She had arrived at McCallum & Watts right out of legal secretarial school at the ripe age of nineteen and had been here now for three years. In our little corporate tax group she was the most senior secretary in terms of years on the premises so when I joined the group, she took it upon herself to show me the ropes. That was the first day. On the second day and each subsequent day, she had been climbing higher on her little hill, singing, I was sure, *I'm the king of the castle*.

There were five of us legal secretaries in the bullpen, as it was affectionately called by the *all-male* team of lawyers who we supported. There were eight of *them*. One partner, supervising seven junior associates. All of whom specialized in tax law. A quick shiver went up my spine and then back down again, at the thought of tax law. Dry, boring and mind-numbing was the only way to describe tax law. It was also a pretty apt description of the eight lawyers in our group.

Ashley on the other hand was cute and perky, and her voice sounded like fingernails on a chalk board. It didn't take me long to figure out that there was a high turnover in support staff in our bullpen and Ashley had assured me it was because of the boring work. Not that *she* thought it was boring. I was sure the high turnover was because of the perky Ms. Ashley. Every piece of work that came our way passed through her hands first and she doled it out. I was still getting my feet wet, she told me every day, so that was why I had to do all the photocopying and open the mail. My computer was gathering dust from lack of use and access to the files was still restricted to me, "until you understand the department," I was patronizingly told, at least two thousand times each day.

My mother would be proud of my restraint, but I had started grinding my teeth again. To keep my comments to myself I had to constantly clench my jaw and physically restrain myself. It was a job. And a paycheck.

The ton of paper I was carrying made a loud thunk when it hit my desk and I had to quickly grab it as the pile started to topple.

"Kathleen," I heard Ashley behind me. She was big on proper names and made a point of using mine.

"Yes, Ash." My voice sounded bored and I hoped she got the dig with the way I had shortened her name.

"The personnel manager wants to see you," she said excitedly. "Right away."

The little bitch, I thought. She's reported me for something and I felt like I was back in the seventh grade. I turned around and faced her.

"Is there a problem Ashley? Did I put the staples in the wrong corner on that tax return yesterday?"

Her faced flushed and she looked a little guilty.

"No." She took a deep breath and puffed out her thirty-two double A chest. "I have no idea why she wants to see you." There was defiance in her voice so I believed her. She was too young and stupid to lie well. Lying truthfully came with experience. I knew.

I made my way through the rabbit warren of workstations and waited patiently for the elevator, which, if I was in luck, would arrive before quitting time. The law offices occupied five floors and there was no way I was walking up five floors to the personnel manager's office. In the six weeks I had been off work I had started an exercise regime to get myself back in shape. Religiously every day, after dinner, I would walk briskly around my neighbourhood for an hour. I did that five nights a week and took the weekends off. I hated exercise so I refused to do any more than my nightly walk. Including walking up stairs.

I had also quit smoking which was a feat in itself. I had been a chain-smoker who would've put the Marlboro Man to shame and deep down I was quite proud of myself for successfully kicking the habit. So far. At the thought of smoking, my hands went automatically to the pockets of my skirt for a cigarette. My finger punched impatiently at the elevator button instead.

Linda Beeston was sitting primly behind her neat-as-a-pin desk when I knocked on the door frame. The lack of visible work or mounds of paper was in no way indicative of how busy I knew Linda was. She was responsible for all of the support staff in the firm and the latest numbers indicated she rode herd on over two hundred people. She herself had a staff of four just to keep track of everyone. Linda had interviewed and hired me because, being the smart lady she was, she recognized my skills and experience. However, they had no need at that time for another paralegal, so she had hired me as a secretary. I was grateful, but I was close to putting Linda on my shit list for having hooked me up with the perky Ashley.

"Come on in," she invited me. "I've been expecting you. Close the door."

She had one, uncomfortable, straight-back chair in her office. Just like the ones we've all sat on outside the principal's office. I lowered my weary butt into it and smiled at her. It was a wary smile, because I wasn't sure what was on the agenda.

"So. How's it going with the great Ashley?" Her eyes were smiling at me.

"Wonderful," I joked. "I'm thinking of naming my first born after her. She's a peerless leader."

Linda laughed. "Look, I'm sorry for having to put you in that group. We know your qualifications. The firm was thrilled to get someone of your experience and as I told you when I hired you, if something came up that was more suitable for you, we'd move you." She paid me the compliment with sincerity.

"Just don't tell me you're promoting Ashley and you want me to take over her job."

Linda shook her head. "God forbid. Ashley wouldn't move out of that group. Tax is her life. So she tells me," she said with a smirk.

"That's a very telling statement, you know Linda." We both laughed.

"McCallum & Watts has just hired a senior corporate securities lawyer from one of the rival firms and he's specifically asked for you. He's coming in as a very senior partner and when he found out you were here, he almost made it a condition of his employment. Are you interested?"

She certainly had my attention now.

"Of course. If it's corporate securities work, I'm there. And I'm flattered."

I couldn't imagine who it was but I did know most of the top guns in Toronto. I'd either worked with them, or against, them in the job I had at Scapelli, Marks & Wilson.

"Great. We consider it quite a coup that we've lured him away from Scapelli's. John Clancy, our senior corporate partner is retiring next year and between you and me, I think they might have their eye on Mr. Johnston to replace him."

When she said Mr. Johnston, my stomach sank so I waited for the sucker punch.

"Would Mr. Johnston have a first name?" I asked.

"Cleveland. Says everyone calls him Cleve."

Well, Cleve had obviously forgiven me for my past sins or this was his way of making me pay for all those nasty things I'd said to him. My mind shot back to the last time I'd seen him and how I'd been an absolute, first-class, no doubt about it, bitch.

"Monday," I heard Linda say and I jerked my attention back to her voice. "Come on and I'll introduce you to your new workstation."

I followed her meekly down the hall. Today was Friday. I had all weekend to figure out how to apologize.